DEAD PEASANTS

ALSO BY LARRY D. THOMPSON

The Trial
So Help Me God

DEAD PEASANTS

Larry D. Thompson

THOMAS DUNNE BOOKS

St. Martin's Press

New York

THOMAS DUNNE BOOKS.
An imprint of St. Martin's Press.

DEAD PEASANTS. Copyright © 2012 by Larry D. Thompson. All rights
reserved. Printed in the United States of America. For information,
address St. Martin's Press, 175 Fifth Avenue, New York, N.Y. 10010.

www.thomasdunnebooks.com
www.stmartins.com

ISBN 978-1-250-00949-4 (hardcover)
ISBN 978-1-250-01800-7 (e-book)

First Edition: October 2012

10 9 8 7 6 5 4 3 2 1

This is for Rex and Nancy Spivey,
my close friends for more years than any of us will admit.
Thanks for your friendship and your support in all of my endeavors.

Acknowledgments

———

When I was a kid, growing up in Fort Worth, it was a different era. Starting in my seventh summer, my parents let me ride the bus downtown by myself, wearing only T-shirt and shorts (barefoot), to the Fort Worth Public Library. I would return five books and spend an hour carefully picking out five more for the coming week. Those summers instilled a love of books and stories that remains with me to this day. So it is with great fondness that I say thank you to all public libraries, and express my lifelong gratitude to the Fort Worth Public Library. And, by the way, I appreciate your kindness in letting me in with no shoes.

DEAD PEASANTS

1

The tension in the Beaumont, Texas, courtroom was as real as that in the Cotton Bowl if Texas and Oklahoma were tied with one minute to go. The parties had been in trial for three weeks and two days. On one side of the aisle were the families of three refinery workers killed in an explosion that had killed or maimed dozens of others. The rest had settled with the oil company. These three families were represented by Jackson Douglas Bryant, a lawyer who in another era would have been a riverboat gambler. He convinced them to turn down million-dollar settlements before trial. The loss of their loved one was worth far more than a paltry million dollars. He even turned and walked away when the company lawyer offered five million per family at the close of evidence. He was confident that a Jefferson County jury would take care of its own.

After two days of jury deliberations, his clients had exhausted every possible topic of conversation and sat, stone-faced and nervous, on the wooden benches. Several of them wondered if they were making a mistake by rejecting enough money to provide for themselves and several generations of kids and grandkids. Still, they crossed their fingers and followed the advice of Jack Bryant.

On the other side of the rail, where the lawyers strutted their stuff as if actors on stage, the company attorneys were huddled with their client, whispering to each other about Bryant's refusal even to counter their fifteen-million-dollar offer. Bryant was standing at the bailiff's desk, resting his hands on his cane and debating whether the Houston Texans would ever make the playoffs. Bryant was a Texans fan, but the bailiff had written them off once the Saints acquired Drew Brees and won a Super Bowl. He was now officially a part of the "Who Dat?" nation. If the tension got to Bryant, he was too good a poker player to let it show. Somewhere in the neighborhood of fifty years old, he was a lean six feet with brush-cut brown hair swept back from a widow's peak, piercing blue eyes, and a chin with a Kirk Douglas dimple. He always chose an expensive Western-cut suit and Justin cowboy boots for trial. The Justin boots had been his choice since he got his first pair as a kid growing up in Fort Worth. He always carried a cane. For trial it was one with a gold knob on the top to match the gold Rolex on his wrist. Among all of his canes, he liked this one the best. It reminded him of the legendary Bat Masterson, gunfighter and poker player. The entire outfit, including the Rolex, was calculated. He had long believed that jurors would be more inclined to award big money if they saw it up close and personal.

Jack would never have admitted it, but he was getting worried. Anyone looking closely at his eyes would see they were bloodshot, a product of tossing and turning the night before as he replayed the trial in his mind and wondered what he might have done differently. They had made their final arguments two days ago and now it was approaching five o'clock. *Were they going to hang up? I damn sure don't want to have to try this son of a bitch again,* he thought.

Two loud buzzes echoed through the courtroom. One buzz was for lunch or a cigarette break. Two meant they had a verdict. The bailiff rose, and as he walked by Jack, he whispered, "Good luck, man."

Jack stepped through the swinging gate at the rail to shake hands with his male clients and hug the women. Then he returned to the counsel table as the judge came from his chambers. Judge Lucius Benton had a mane of white hair that he tied back in a ponytail. His handlebar mustache was so thick that it sounded as if his voice was muffled by a white buffalo hide. "I understand we have a verdict. Please remain standing for the jury."

The bailiff opened the jury room door, and the six men and six women filed in. Jack thought he detected one woman smiling slightly as she glanced at him before taking her seat. The bailiff handed the verdict to Judge Benton. Silence filled the room as the lawyers and litigants stared at the judge who slowly flipped through the verdict to confirm it was in order and properly signed. Finally, he turned to the jury.

"Mr. Foreman, am I correct that this is a unanimous verdict?"

"Yes, sir," a longshoreman in the first row replied.

"Then, with approval of counsel, I'll merely read the answers."

The first questions dealt with the liability of the refinery. Was the refinery negligent in its maintenance practices? The jury answered, "Yes." Did that negligence cause the deaths of the three workers? The jury answered, "Yes." Jack smiled as he looked over to the defense table and saw the dejected looks of the company representative and his cadre of defense lawyers. Now came the important part. The jury awarded each family twenty million dollars in actual damages for losing their loved one. A defense lawyer pitched his pen on the table and leaned back, disgust on his face. The company representative stared at the jury with hatred in his eyes: *maybe they would tear down their goddamn refinery in Beaumont and move it to a county where the people would appreciate the economic benefit of fifteen hundred jobs.*

Next were questions about gross negligence and punitive damages. The jury found the refinery knew its practices were dangerous and should be punished. It awarded ten million dollars in punitive damages per family. Several adult sons of the workers started whooping and hollering. The widows sobbed uncontrollably. Even Jack had tears in his eyes as he realized the total verdict was ninety million. Seeing he was rapidly losing control, the judge banged his gavel until the handle broke. The bailiff shouted for order. Worried that they might be held in contempt of court, Jack turned and motioned to his clients for silence. Slowly they returned to their seats. Some stared at the judge. Others turned to the jury and mouthed, "Thank you."

Looking around the courtroom to make sure decorum was restored, Judge Benton announced, "Counsel, I'm sending this case immediately to mediation before retired Judge Simon Jefferson. If he has an opening next week, I expect all of you to be there to see if we can get this case resolved before you spend three or four years on appeal. I commend counsel on both sides for a job well done. You are excused."

Jack took his clients out into the hallway where he huddled with them about the mediation. In Texas all big plaintiff verdicts went to mediation before appeal. The defendant had two shots at reversing the verdict, one before three justices at the court of appeals and one before nine justices at the supreme court. The bigger the verdict, the greater the likelihood of a reversal. The process would take at least four years, even if they won. He discussed the concept of a bird in the hand and reminded them that reducing the verdict a few million now would put money in their pockets immediately. A few of his clients looked puzzled. Still, they had put their trust in Jack, and he hadn't let them down yet.

2

They overflowed Judge Jefferson's conference room on the following Wednesday. In addition to Jack and his fourteen clients, there were two defense lawyers from New York and a claims representative from London who had joined the three lawyers who put up the losing defense.

They filled the chairs and stood along the walls as Judge Jefferson explained the purpose of mediation was to try to reach a settlement without taking the case through the appellate process and, perhaps, even back to another trial. He alluded to the fact that the Texas Supreme Court was all Republican: nine justices who, judging from their opinions, thought it their solemn duty to protect big business from juries in Beaumont and certain other plaintiff-leaning counties in South Texas. Jack's clients listened and were uncertain what to make of such remarks. Hadn't they just scored a giant victory last week?

When the opening session was concluded, the plaintiffs remained in the large conference room and the group of defense lawyers and representatives was led to a slightly smaller one.

After they were gone, Judge Jefferson turned to Jack. "Helluva job you did, Jack. This your biggest?"

"Biggest one in Beaumont. Had one over a hundred million in the valley a few years ago," Jack replied with a smile on his face.

"You know how this game is played," the judge said. "Give me a demand and I'll take it to them." He turned to look at the clients. "It's a little like Henry Kissinger's shuttle diplomacy from years ago. What do you say, Jack?"

"Not my move, Judge. I've got the verdict and the whip hand at this point. You're in the wrong room. You best walk down the hall. Tell them that they better get way north of that fifteen million they offered last week. Otherwise, we're walking."

Judge Jefferson nodded his understanding as he excused himself. When he returned an hour later, he again warned of the risks of an appeal in a Republican state before saying he had an offer of twenty-five million. Jack pretended to look at an imaginary hole card. "They're going the right direction, but it's going to be a long day. Tell them I'll knock two million off the verdict."

Jack was right. It was a long day. On two different occasions, once with a counteroffer of forty million dollars and once with sixty million on the table, Jack told all of his clients to get up. They were leaving. Both times Judge Jefferson convinced them to stay. At ten o'clock that night the offer was seventy-five million dollars, payable by wire transfer to Jack's trust account in thirty days. Jack got up, walked around the table to shake Judge Jefferson's hand, and told him that they had a deal. When the judge left the room to advise the other side, Jack was swarmed by his clients as they laughed, cried, and pounded Jack on the back until he begged for mercy.

Jack's fee was 40 percent. After paying expenses and a million-dollar bonus to each of his two associates, he would net close to thirty million dollars. That, he thought, is the reason that he moved to Beaumont after law school.

The next day he called his associates into his office. Still a little hungover after celebrating until the Spindletop Bar closed at one in the morning, he was unshaven and wearing jeans and a T-shirt. "Sit down, my friends. I have an announcement. I'm retiring, effective today. The office and all the cases are yours. All I ask is that you send me a third of any fees you recover on our current cases."

His associates protested, saying they needed him to head the firm. Besides, he was too young to retire. He raised his hands and asked them to stop. His mind was made up. "I'm moving back to Fort Worth, back to where I was born and raised. You guys know my son, J.D., got out of the Marines, enrolled at TCU and is trying out for the TCU football team. I'm going to buy a nice house, kick back, do a little hunting and fishing, and watch J.D. play football. I haven't been in his life to speak of in near fifteen years. It's time to change that."

3

The pool hall wasn't much, but it was the only one Breckenridge had. Breckenridge was seventy miles west of Fort Worth. A quiet West Texas town of a few thousand people, about its only claim to fame was that it turned out some of the best high school football teams in the state. If *Friday Night Lights* hadn't been written about Odessa, it could have been about Breckenridge. Most of the jobs in the area were in the oil fields or on the ranches. Men still gathered at the Dairy Queen every morning to talk about the price of beef, crops, weather and, of course, the football team's prospects.

The pool hall didn't really have a name. Instead it had a red neon sign in the window that alternately flashed BEER and POOL. It occupied a building close to the railroad tracks a few blocks from the town center. The Baptists would have preferred for it to be out on the edge of the town, or maybe down the road in Caddo or Albany. The big nights at the pool hall were weekends, excepting Sunday when it was closed in deference to the Baptists, and Monday during football season.

A man named Jim always sat at the bar where he could watch the football game as he drank Lone Star from a bottle and smoked Marlboros. If Marlboro had needed another model, he could have been their man. He wore Levi's, a blue work shirt with "Jim" on the right chest, and a Cowboys cap. He had worked as an auto mechanic for years until the recession hit and he was laid off. Fortunately, the oil and gas business still had life, so he transferred his skills to repairing oil rigs and pump jacks. Jim was quiet and never had any company. He would reply if spoken to. Otherwise he was content to watch the game, sipping his Lone Star and grunting occasionally if something dramatic occurred.

One Monday night a stranger appeared at the door of the bar. He had brown hair down to his shoulders and a neatly trimmed beard. He wore a black leather jacket over a green golf shirt. Once his eyes had become accustomed to the dim light, he took a seat at the bar next to Jim and ordered a Coors Light. He tried to strike up a conversation with Jim, who answered in monosyllables and continued to watch the game. By the end of the third quarter other customers began to drift out when Tom Brady had put his Patriots up by three touchdowns. Jim and the stranger stayed until the final whistle. That told the stranger what he wanted to know. He paid his bill and left just as Jim was putting on his coat. The stranger noted that Jim's green Chevy pickup, the only vehicle remaining, was parked along the curb directly in front of the pool hall.

Two weeks later the clock ran down on another Cowboy loss. Jim pitched a twenty on the bar and said, "That's downright embarrassing. Keep the change, Sam."

Sam nodded his thanks as Jim put on a windbreaker and walked to the door. Sam followed him, locked the door, and unplugged the sign, since the last of his other customers had given up on the Cowboys thirty minutes earlier. When Jim stepped out, he was confronted with driving rain from a storm that had blown in during the game. He pulled the jacket over his head and made a dash for his pickup. He had his keys in his hand as he rounded the rear of the truck and clicked to open the door. With the wind and the rain, he never heard a thing. And with the windbreaker pulled over his head, he never saw what hit him.

A white pickup had been waiting at the corner next to the pool hall, lights out while the driver listened to the last of the Cowboys game. When it was over, he started the engine and waited. He saw Jim's lean body leave the pool hall and run to his pickup. The driver turned the corner and floored it, accelerating alongside Jim's pickup, hitting him as he reached for the door handle. The impact knocked Jim fifty feet.

The driver started to leave Breckenridge, then had second thoughts.

He had never killed someone this way before. So he circled the block, and when he got to the corner next to the pool hall, he doused his lights again and looked both ways. The rain was now coming almost sideways from the west as a cold front blew through. Seeing no lights in either direction, he pulled in front of Jim's pickup, retrieved a small Maglite from the glove compartment and climbed out. Pushing through the wind and the rain, he got to his victim and flashed the light briefly. Blood oozed from Jim's ears, nose and mouth. His chest was crushed and both legs looked like broken pick-up sticks. The driver bent over and pressed his fingers against the victim's neck. There was no pulse.

He walked rapidly back to his truck, checked again to confirm there were no vehicles coming from either direction, and headed out of town. As he did, he retrieved his cell phone. "Boss, it's done."

4

Jack drove west on Camp Bowie Boulevard, listening to the clatter his tires made on the red brick paving laid by the Works Progress Administration during the Great Depression. Memories from thirty and forty years ago flooded back as he turned right on Hillcrest. After a block he saw Rivercrest Country Club and turned left on Crestline. He passed the clubhouse and drove slowly down Alta Drive until he spotted the house he wanted. Situated on almost two acres, with giant pecan trees shading the front, it had six bedrooms, including a large master suite overlooking a heated pool and hot tub. The driveway circled the house and led to a six-car garage. Sitting on a bluff above the Trinity River, the backyard sloped down the hill toward the river and the afternoon sun. In the distance was the old bomber plant, called various names over the years, including Convair and General Dynamics, but now closed. Jack's dad had worked there for thirty years.

Jack stopped at the curb and listened for a moment to Willie Nelson warning mamas not to let their babies grow up to be cowboys. Then he climbed from his old red pickup and reached behind the front seat for his cane. His knee felt pretty good today, and he might not have even needed it. Still, he never knew when he was going to make a wrong step and have it collapse under him. He leaned against the front fender of Lucille, the name he gave his truck when it was new, and surveyed the house. It had a front porch extending the length of the house, with a veranda of equal length above it. Both had elaborate wrought iron railing. He liked it. The realtor had told him it was unoccupied; so he walked to the house, climbed the four steps to the porch and peered in the windows. The room to the right of the front door was the living room, with a room of almost similar size to the left, this one lined with bookshelves. Behind the study was an entry into what appeared to be the dining room. He was standing at the top of the steps, leaning on his cane and surveying the golf course across the street when a green Lexus pulled up behind his pickup. *Wow,* he thought, as the realtor exited her car, *Fort Worth could get more interesting in a hurry.* The realtor's biography on her Web site put her around forty, but she looked thirty. He guessed she was about five feet four inches tall. Her short auburn hair glistened in the afternoon sun. She wore blue pants and a long-sleeved white shirt open at the collar just enough to show a hint of cleavage. As she approached, Jack saw her eyes were emerald green, his new favorite color.

Colby Stripling glanced at the red Dodge Ram pickup as she parked. When she walked toward the house, she saw a middle-aged man wearing a white T-shirt, jeans, cowboy boots, and a Texans cap. *Why am I wasting time on this guy? Maybe I can take him out west of town and sell him a tract house, something he can afford,* she thought. Still she put on her best realtor's smile and reached out her right hand. "Good afternoon. I'm Colby Stripling."

"Pleased to meet you, Colby," Jack replied. "Name's Jackson Bryant. Call me Jack. I've already taken the virtual tour of this place, and I like it. The owner willing to come off that five million he's been asking for the past eight months?"

Colby decided to cut this showing short. "Look, Mr. Bryant, It's tough to get a mortgage of any kind in this economy. Do you really think you can get one for a house this size?"

Jack grinned. "No, ma'am. I was just figuring to pay cash. Now can we have a look around?"

Still not sure if this guy was for real, Colby nodded and unlocked the front door. She stepped aside so Jack could get the full effect of the two-story entry with its crystal chandelier and curving staircase to the second floor. Jack stepped in and nodded his approval as Colby turned to show him the living room. Next they entered the study and made their way back through a dining room large enough for a table for twelve. While Jack appreciated the kitchen, he was taken with the master suite across the center hall with French doors opening onto the back patio and a bathroom with a large flat screen TV and its own hot tub for two. They stepped through the French doors to the backyard where Jack admired the immaculate landscaping surrounding the pool and another hot tub.

"I'll need that six-car garage, and the concrete pad beside it looks just about right for my RV. I've seen enough. Offer four and a half, to close in two weeks."

"Wait, wait, Jack," Colby interrupted, deciding she wanted to be on a first name basis. "Don't you want to see the upstairs?"

"No need to." Jack shook his head. "I saw the upstairs on the virtual tour. Assuming the house passes inspection, I want it." Jack glanced at her left hand and noticed there was no wedding band. "Now, how about joining me for a cup of coffee at the Starbucks over on Camp Bowie."

Colby smiled and looked into his blue eyes. "I'd be delighted. Let me call and reschedule my next appointment."

5

Jack led the way in Lucille and stood ready to open Colby's door when she parked beside him in front of Starbucks. "What'll you have?"

Colby shook her head. "No, this is my treat. After all, I'm trying to get your business."

"Don't worry," Jack said, "you've already got it, but I'll have a black coffee. I don't speak Starbucks and just always ask for something simple."

Jack stood beside Colby while she ordered his coffee and a grande skinny latte for herself. When they were seated by the window, Colby said, "I've sold a few big houses for cash, but not any lately. Mind if I ask what you do for a living?"

"Not at all," Jack replied as he took the lid off his coffee and gently blew across the top to cool it a degree or two. Then he smiled and continued, "I'm now officially retired. Before that I robbed banks. Just kidding. Until last week I was a plaintiff lawyer in Beaumont. Got my last big verdict and called it quits."

Colby thought about what Jack had said before she asked, "I think I understand what a plaintiff lawyer does. For good measure, can you explain?"

"Sure," Jack said as he tried to take a sip of his hot coffee. "I usually represent the little guy or his family if he's killed, someone who has been severely injured or killed because of the negligence of a big company. He couldn't afford to take on a Fortune 500 company if he paid by the hour, so I take those cases on a contingent fee. If we win, we both have a big payday. If we lose, I eat all my time and expenses. Fortunately, I carefully select my cases," he said. "And I usually get a big settlement or a bigger verdict if I have to try the case."

Colby absorbed all Jack said, already beginning to like the man across the table from her. "I think I follow what you're saying. Why are you here in Fort Worth?"

"I grew up in Fort Worth and wanted to move back. I still have a few classmates here and my son, J.D., is going to play football for TCU."

Understanding flashed through Colby's eyes. "Oh, yeah. He's a walk-on. The *Star Telegram* ran a feature on him. Came out of the Marines. Two tours in Iraq. Never played football in his life. Just showed up at Coach Patterson's door."

"That's my son. Pleased to know you follow TCU football. Maybe I can talk you into joining me for a game or two this fall."

Colby paused before she replied, fishing for more information. "You must have a big family. That's a giant house."

"Nope. Just me. J.D.'s mother and I divorced fifteen years ago."

Colby took a sip of her coffee. "Still, why such a big house? I'm not trying to knock myself out of a commission, but there are plenty of smaller houses with similar features."

"I'm buying it because I can afford it and I want people to know I succeeded. Look, I grew up on Byers, east of Clover Lane. I'm sure you don't show those houses. Commission wouldn't be worth your time. We had a two-bedroom frame house. Camp Bowie Boulevard was the divid-ing line. I went to South High Mount Elementary, Stripling Junior High, and Arlington Heights. The kids at Heights who lived on the north side of Camp Bowie treated the rest of us like we lived on the wrong side of the tracks. It pissed me off then and even now. Speaking of Stripling, you related to those Striplings?"

"Yes," Colby replied. "My great-grandfather started Stripling's Department Store downtown near the courthouse. He's the one W. C. Stripling Junior High is named after. My grandfather took over the family business. Unfortunately, times passed him by. Walmarts and Targets started springing up. He stuck to the old ways his father taught him and drove the business into the ground. He finally sold the store for about the value of the land. A developer tore it down and built an office building. I grew up in Monticello, not far from Rivercrest. I moved back into my family home after my parents died a few years ago."

"I know where that is. Couple of my classmates lived there. I figured they must have been rich, living in a brick house with more than one bathroom." Jack decided to be the inquisitor and asked, "Are you're married?"

Colby had removed the lid from her coffee and looked down while she stirred it. Finally, she looked up. "I, uh, I'm seeing someone." Obviously uncomfortable, Colby turned to look out the window and then changed the subject. "So you made a lot of money as a plaintiff lawyer. Why retire to Fort Worth? Why not the mountains or maybe an island in the Caribbean?"

Jack was puzzled by her change in demeanor but let it pass and answered. "Let me give you a little more background. Most of my classmates went off to college—Texas, A&M, Texas Tech, North Texas, some to the Ivy League. Quite a few stayed in town and went to TCU. My parents couldn't afford to send me anywhere to college. So, I lived at home and commuted with three other guys to Arlington State. Joined army ROTC to pay for my tuition and books. After I graduated I spent three years in the 101st Airborne, mainly jumping out of helicopters. Then I talked my way into South Texas College of Law in Houston." Jack paused as his eyes got a faraway look and he relived his growing-up years in Fort Worth. "When I graduated, I moved to Beaumont, not because it was a paradise. In fact, it's a polluted, mosquito-infested swamp with a bunch of stinking refineries and a small port." Jack smiled. "On the other hand, the United States Chamber of Commerce votes it a judicial hell hole every damn year."

"I don't understand," Colby interrupted.

"Juries in Jefferson County and a few similar counties down along the Mexican border never met a big company they liked. They're notorious for awarding giant verdicts to injured workers. I went there to get rich, and it worked." Jack thought about what he just said and added, "Well, I did get rich, but over twenty-five years, I helped out a lot of folks who couldn't afford justice if it hadn't have been for me and lawyers like me. As to Fort Worth, I always loved this town even though I don't have fond memories of a lot of my classmates, and now J.D.'s here. As to Rivercrest, a few of my classmates lived in those big houses. I just want to show them that you don't have to be a member of the lucky sperm club to buy one."

"Do you mind if I ask about your cane?"

"Not at all. I thought my military service was behind me. Then President Bush, the first one, decided he needed me in Desert Storm. I wasn't there three months before I took some shrapnel in my left knee. Gave me an early out and I returned to Beaumont. The knee works pretty well most of the time. Then for no good reason it goes out on me. That's when I need the cane. Otherwise, I'll fall on my ass."

Colby figured she had enough information. She looked at her watch. "I gotta get out of here. I'm already late for my next appointment."

Jack nodded his understanding. "And I've got to meet J.D. for dinner. I'm staying at that Residence Inn on Seventh across from the old Monkey Wards. At least that's what we called it when I was growing up. Now I see it's been turned into lofts. Anyway, I'll be there until I hear back on the offer. You've got my cell."

As they walked out into the sunlight, Colby eyed his pickup and asked, "I gather you've got other vehicles. Why do you drive that old Dodge?"

They stopped at her Lexus while Jack answered. "Good question. There's a lawyer in Palestine, Texas. Old friend of mine. Name's Johnny Bob Tisdale. I referred him a case a few years back and we both made a nice fee. Along with my cut, he gave me this pickup. I've got a bunch of other vehicles, but I'll drive this until the wheels fall off. Come around here to the back. I want to show you something."

Jack led her around to the rear of his pickup and pointed to the license plate. The frame announced MY LAWYER IS J. ROBERT TISDALE. "Next to me, he's probably the best plaintiff lawyer in the state. Hell, he may even be a little better."

Jack extended his hand and Colby shook it. Jack waited for her to back out and drive away. As he watched the Lexus disappear to the west, Jack decided he was definitely taking a renewed liking to Fort Worth.

6

Within a minute after leaving Jack, Colby was passing the old Ridglea Theater. Her mind wandered back to her encounter with her new client. It had been years since she had a romantic thought about a man. Why this one? Why now? As the thought grew, she realized why: this was a man, self-made, who had done a lot of good for needy people and made a lot of money along the way. Maybe he was a knight in shining armor, maybe not, but he was certainly different from the guys she met nearly every day. Then she shoved him out of her mind. Whatever the thought, she couldn't follow through on it.

When she got to Edgehill she moved to the left turn lane and waited for the light. She glanced in her mirror as she waited, then reached into her purse for lipstick, which she managed to apply just before the light changed. She followed Edgehill until she got to Ridglea Country Club. Ridglea was a nice neighborhood but several steps below Rivercrest. She circled around the west side of the golf course until she turned into a circular driveway with a granite monument between two giant live oaks. The monument announced RIDGLEA OAKS NURSING HOME. Colby parked in the shade of one of the oaks and took one last look in the mirror. Satisfied with her appearance, she retrieved what she called her realtor's black purse, a Dooney and Bourke with multiple pockets accessed by gold zippers. She called it her realtor's purse because it was large enough to double as a briefcase. In fact, the main pocket held, among other trash and treasures, her iPad.

Ridglea Oaks was considered among the finest nursing homes in Fort Worth. The lawn was manicured. Flowers that changed with the seasons were in beds on either side of the entrance. *There's nothing good about being confined to a nursing home,* Colby thought as she opened the door, *but if there is no other option, this is certainly better than most.*

The living room, as it was called, had a large screen HDTV on the wall to the left. Several of the guests, most of them elderly and largely abandoned by their families, watched an afternoon game show. Some understood it. Others merely stared at the screen because their chairs were facing that direction. In one corner four men were engaged in some card game. To Colby's right was the reception desk. Colby addressed the receptionist at the desk by name as she signed the register. "Afternoon, Ruth. How are things going today?"

Ruth smiled. She liked Colby and it showed. "Just fine, Ms. Stripling. You sell any houses today?"

"Actually, I'm about to land a big one." She leaned over and whispered. "In Rivercrest."

"Wow. Good luck," Ruth replied.

Colby walked toward a hallway and paused when she saw a shriveled-up old lady in a yellow dress, sitting in a wheelchair by herself. Colby kneeled beside the wheelchair so Ms. Newman could see her face. "My, you're looking pretty in that yellow outfit. Even have a yellow rose in your hair. I bet you've got some family coming for a visit today." It took a moment for the words to sink in. Then Ms. Newman slowly nodded her head.

"Well, you tell your daughter I said hello. I haven't seen her in ages."

Colby rose and walked down the pale blue hallway, her heels tapping on the tile floor as her eyes wandered over pictures of landscapes, gardens, and mountain scenes. *They certainly tried to make a dreary place cheerful, anyway,* she thought. She nodded at the nurse at the nurses' station. When she got to the fourth door on the right, she drew in a breath and entered without knocking. The single occupant of the room was a man, lying still on the bed in the center, his eyes open but seeing nothing. He was fed by a tube in his stomach. A sudden ruptured aneurysm in his brain had put him in that condition. The neurosurgeon did everything he could, but he could not change the inevitable. The doctor had said he might live five years. That had been ten years ago.

Colby walked over to the head of the bed and kissed the man on the cheek. "Hi, Rob. It's me. Let me pull up a chair and I'll tell you my good news."

Colby placed a straight-back chair facing the bed and took the occupant's hand in hers. "I've got a lead on a sale in Rivercrest. Four and a half million, can you believe that? Of course, I'll have to share the commission with the listing broker, but my share will be around a hundred thousand. That means I can catch up on my payments to the nursing home and use the rest to pay down my 401(k) loan."

Rob said nothing, which is what Colby expected. She knew he neither saw nor heard her. Still, when she visited she felt a moral obligation to treat him like a human being who had thoughts and feelings.

Colby stayed half an hour, then kissed Rob on the cheek again before she left the room. In the hallway she found an attendant pushing Ms. Newman toward her room.

"You have a good visit with your family, Ms. Newman?"

The attendant shook her head. "Nobody came. So, I'm taking her back to her room for dinner."

Colby shook her head in disgust as she walked away, wondering how people could just abandon family members like they were animals in a shelter.

7

Don Allison sensed desperation in his brother's voice when Dwayne asked him to drop by the office. Don spent twelve years in the navy after high school and then became his brother's insurance manager, overseeing the insurance products sold in his brother's dealerships for the last twenty years. Don drove to his brother's office that afternoon, waved at the secretary and opened the door to find Dwayne on the phone. The office was at the front of Dwayne's ranch, built to look like a large bunkhouse until a visitor got through the front door. The front office belonged to Ann, Dwayne's secretary for twenty-five years. A door to the side led to a bull pen, full of cubicles for bookkeepers, clerks, and staff. Dwayne's office was massive, with leather furniture and nearly every space on the walls filled with the head of some trophy animal he had killed in hunting trips throughout the world. Behind his desk were plaques recognizing his service to multiple civic organizations and photos of Dwayne with politicians, mostly Republican. Dwayne was ten years older and starting to get a little beefy, with jowls and dark circles under his eyes. A few prominent veins on his nose acknowledged his love of good whiskey. What little hair he had left was now mostly gray. Don walked to the bar by the window and poured two fingers of Tito's vodka over ice and returned to sit in front of the desk until the conversation ended.

His brother slammed down the phone. "Damn bankers! They're nothing but a bunch of leeches, out to drain the last bit of blood from my body. Fuck 'em. Fuck 'em all!"

Don didn't say a word as he sipped his vodka. He knew Dwayne's rages were like a summer thunderstorm, loud and raucous but passing quickly. His brother suddenly leaped from his seat, circled the desk to the bar, and filled a large glass full of ice and scotch. He downed half of it and returned to his desk. "Look, Don, I've spent thirty-five years building this business. At one time I had a hundred and twenty-five dealerships in three states. Along the way I've been a good citizen. Hell, I've been chairman of the board at Methodist Hospital and potentate of the Shriners. This year I'm president of the stock show and rodeo. Everyone in Fort Worth knows my name. I'm even being asked to run for mayor. I built my business on borrowed money and always paid it back on time, every damn time. Then the 'Great Recession' hit." Sarcasm dripped from his words as he discussed the recession. "All of a sudden the bottom dropped out. The goddamn bank won't renew my loans. Quillen acts like I just rode into town on the back of a turnip truck. On top of that my customers can't borrow money to buy a fucking used pickup. Shit, I haven't changed the business practices that made me a success. It's the politicians, mortgage lenders and Wall Street that created the problem."

Don rose to refill his drink and said, "I've heard that speech at least a dozen times. I can't do a damn thing about it."

Dwayne walked to the window and gazed off in the distance at some of his prize quarter horses that were running in circles around their pasture. He smiled at the sight and then turned back to Don.

"I've been here sweating every phone call, thinking it will be from Quillen, ready to foreclose on a dealership. I'm barely able to make payroll, much less pay interest on any goddam notes. Then it hit me. I've got thousands of assets I haven't tapped. I must have life insurance policies on over five thousand current and former employees."

"Actually it's closer to seven thousand," Don replied.

"I've kept up the premiums on all of the former employees, some even before you started here. Been a good tax write-off and we occasionally have a payday when one of them kicks the bucket, only those paydays are now too few and far between. People must be living longer. I was figuring those policies would make for a nice retirement Now times have changed. Let's cancel every damn one of these policies. The cash surrender value ought to be enough to get me out of this hole I'm in."

Don shook his head as he downed the last of his vodka. "Sorry, bro. You're wrong. We took out term policies on all of those employees. If you quit paying premiums, you get nothing."

'What the hell?" Dwayne exploded. "You're telling me I've been paying premiums on policies that aren't worth anything? How could we be so stupid?"

"That was your call early on. They're worth something only when the employee dies."

8

Jack had time to check into the Residence Inn, clean up a little, and pick up J.D. at his apartment, not far from TCU. After being greeted by a young man wearing a TCU golf shirt, Jack pulled his bag to the elevator, leaning on his cane as he rode to the third floor. When he got to his room, he pulled his T-shirt off and put on his own "Horned Frogs" golf shirt. Satisfied he was suitably dressed for dinner, he returned to his pickup and drove south on University. Two blocks from the campus he turned onto J.D.'s street and spotted him tossing a football with another guy about his size, obviously another football player. When J.D. spotted him, he tossed the football to his friend and loped to his dad's truck. Jack had gotten out on the driver's side and walked around to the curb. "Junior, boy, I'm glad to see you."

J.D. bear-hugged his dad until Jack broke away. "Easy, Junior. I'm in good shape except for a bum knee, but I'm fifty now. So go easy on your old man."

"Sorry, Dad, and remember I'm not Junior any more. I've got your name, but I've been called J.D. since I entered the Marines."

Jack nodded his understanding as he appraised his son. *I damn sure couldn't have done much better,* he thought. *Six feet four inches of muscle, and he looks like me, even down to that Bryant dimple in his chin.* J.D. had had a bumpy road, but now he was on the right track. His mother had jerked him out of Jack's life when he was eight, saying Jack was married to his law practice. *Truth be told she was right,* Jack thought. She had hauled him off to Los Angeles where they lived off her half of the community estate, which was pretty damn good, even then. Jack knew that his son had made it through the two tours in Iraq without a physical injury, but he still worried about the mental toll of war. *Was he a victim of post-traumatic stress disorder? It might take years to know for sure.* For now Jack just had to be the father he could not be for all those years.

Jack had seen J.D. for thirty days every summer until his son was fourteen. By then he was six feet four inches and weighed two hundred pounds. Unfortunately, he started running with a bad crowd and had no interest in visiting Beaumont. J.D.'s mother told Jack he was getting in trouble, petty stuff, at least when he got caught. And his grades were so bad he couldn't even try out for football. In the spring of his senior year J.D. got in a fight with three guys in the parking lot of a bar, leaving all three unconscious. One nearly died and J.D. was charged with felony assault.

Jack flew to Los Angeles and cut a deal with a young assistant district attorney. If the charges were reduced to a misdemeanor, J.D. would plead no contest and promptly enroll in the Marines upon graduation, never to set foot in Los Angeles again. The ADA agreed. The problem was the Marines. At first they looked at J.D.'s grades and his brushes with the law and were about to reject him. They changed their minds only when they gave J.D. a battery of tests that told them that J.D. had a potential for leadership and a little-used IQ of 140. The Marines took him and did as their ads promised. Four years later Lance Corporal Bryant completed a second tour of duty in Iraq and was honorably discharged.

J.D. showed up at his dad's office in May and announced that he was going to enroll for the summer session at TCU. He had always liked Fort Worth when he visited his grandparents. Now he wanted to major in computer science and walk on to the TCU football team that he knew was becoming a national power. Jack gave him his blessing and promised to fund his tuition and expenses, provided he made respectable grades.

After J.D. enrolled, he found his way to the athletic department and asked to see the head football coach. Coach Patterson invited him into his office, which was rapidly filling with trophies and plaques as TCU ascended in the ranks of major college teams, and invited him to take a seat. Patterson obviously liked J.D.'s size. If there was an ounce of fat on him, Patterson couldn't see it.

"Tell me about yourself, son," Patterson said.

J.D. unloaded it all, including his misspent youth, his lousy high school grades, his trouble with the law and finally got to the four years in the Marines.

The coach steepled his hands under his chin as he listened. When J.D. was finished, he said, "We've got a damn strong program here. I pretty much built it myself. These days we compete with Texas, A&M, and Oklahoma for some of the best athletes around. You'll have a big learning curve since you never played organized ball. Still, I'll give anyone a chance. Go down to the basement of this building. Ask Smitty to give you a shirt, shorts, shoes and a jock. I'll meet you on the field in thirty minutes."

J.D. did as he was told and was stretching and jogging around the field when Patterson joined him. *Wow, what a specimen,* Patterson thought. *Too damn bad he never played before.* "J.D., come over here," he hollered. J.D. joined him at the goal line. "You warm?"

"Yes, sir."

"Okay, I've got a stopwatch. Go out to the forty and sprint this way when I drop my hand."

Not sure what to do, J.D. dropped into a four-point stance and waited. Patterson dropped his hand and hollered, "Go."

J.D. strained as he drove his legs into the ground and up-righted himself in five yards. He remembered Olympic athletes flattening their hands to cut down wind resistance. In ten yards he was in an all out sprint. When he breezed by the goal line, he trotted to a stop and circled back around to the coach who was staring at his watch.

"Must be something wrong with this damn thing. Should have made sure I had one with a new battery before I came out."

"I don't understand, sir."

"This damn watch clocked you in a 4.45. Nobody your size has ever done that in my twenty-five years of coaching."

'Sir, I'm pretty fast. I always led the sprints in the Marines."

"Well, son, go back there and let's see if you can do it again."

J.D. did 4.48. Patterson shook his head in amazement.

"If you can catch a football, you're gonna be a tight end. Hell, with your size and speed, I may try you at linebacker, too. Go tell Smitty to give you a locker and some practice gear."

"Yes, sir. Thank you, sir," J.D. said as he started to trot off. After two steps he turned and asked, "Can you tell me about the construction, sir?"

Patterson gazed up to where the western stands had been imploded in December 2010. "Sure. Our goal is to remain a national power and bring TCU and Fort Worth a national championship pretty damn soon. We got more fans than we do seats. So, we're starting there. Construction will be complete in time for opening day. Adding ten thousand seats and some luxury boxes and suites. Hopefully, it won't be long until we expand again."

J.D. turned and resumed his trot from the field. Coach Patterson smiled as he thought, *Hell, this kid is big and fast and was a combat marine. If I can't make him a football player, I better just turn in my whistle.*

9

Fort Worth had several nicknames and was proud of most of them. The original fort was built on a bluff overlooking the Trinity River, a suitable location for spotting marauding Indians. Then someone said Fort Worth was "Where the West Begins," a shot at the neighboring city of Dallas, whose inhabitants people in Fort Worth thought belonged back east, maybe somewhere in the vicinity of Philadelphia or New York City. Dallasites retorted that Fort Worth was so dead that a panther could sleep in the middle of Main Street. In return the people in Fort Worth adopted the panther as the official mascot for their first high school.

Then the cattle drives started in the late 1800s. One of the two main trails to Abilene passed through Fort Worth where the drovers would make one last stop to spend their wages on whiskey, women, and gambling before heading into the Indian territory. Butch Cassidy and the Sundance Kid spent time there as did Bonnie and Clyde years later. The area of downtown where they congregated was known as "Hell's Half Acre" and the drovers began calling Fort Worth "Cowtown," a moniker that folks in Fort Worth wear with honor to this day, more than a hundred years after the drovers quit coming and fifty years after Swift and Armour closed their plants and stockyards on the North Side.

Dwayne Allison was born and raised in Fort Worth. He went to TCU for two years before he dropped out to sell cars. Over the years he had sold cars and trucks to half the people in Tarrant County. At least that was his claim. He started doing his own television commercials at a time when he couldn't afford an actor or announcer. Back then a much thinner and very handsome Allison would be featured, dressed in a coat and tie with one foot on a truck bumper, his Nocona boots glistening in the morning sun. He always ended his commercials with the tag line, "Where deals are done."

He had started his empire when he learned that a small Chevrolet dealership was in trouble and for sale in Euless, a small town northeast of Fort Worth. He marched into a bank down the street from the dealership that Beauregard Quillen had inherited from his father. Quillen reluctantly agreed to loan him the ten thousand dollars he needed for a down payment.

It turned out that Allison had a knack for selling cars. He was front and center on the sales floor every morning and stayed there until the store closed. If a pretty woman came in, he would look at her and tell her he had just the right blue to match her gorgeous eyes. If a farmer came in, Allison could take one look at him and know what size pickup he wanted. Usually, he managed to up-sell the farmer. Soon he was buying more dealerships. Beau Quillen started opening more banks, primarily to service the business brought to him by Allison's success.

Along the way Allison married. He and his wife had two sons, each of whom now ran a dealership, one in Oklahoma and one in Louisiana. He'd lost his wife to breast cancer several years before. In hindsight he was glad she did not have to witness the downfall of Allison Southwest.

By the time Allison had 125 stores, Quillen had fifteen banks and had proudly changed the name to Quillen Bank and Trust. They both moved to mansions in Shady Oaks, a newer golf course community for the ultrarich just a stone's throw from Rivercrest. They often golfed on weekends and toasted each other's success in the Shady Oaks men's grill.

Then came the great recession. Overnight, people quit buying cars. Many were no longer working. Others found no bank would loan them money. Car dealers around the country shuttered their doors and passersby discovered weed-filled, empty lots that were once overflowing with shiny new vehicles. Allison had no choice but to consolidate some of his dealerships. Now he was down to sixty-five, and that number was getting smaller by the month.

10

Allison gave his Cadillac to the valet and walked into the Fort Worth Club to meet with Quillen. He knew what Quillen wanted. The son of a bitch wanted money that he didn't have. He took the elevator to the sixth-floor dining room. As he stepped from the elevator, he threw his shoulders back, ready to do battle with the person who had become his worst enemy: his banker. He spotted Quillen at a corner table. Quillen rose as Allison approached. Quillen was taller than Allison, with short gray hair and prominent gray eyes. His mustache managed to offset a slightly prominent nose. Unlike Allison's, his waistline was still trim. His personality could dominate any boardroom. Even on Saturday he was dressed in a dark custom-tailored suit with a red tie.

"Thanks for coming, Dwayne," Quillen said as they shook hands. "I figured a Saturday meeting away from either of our offices would be best. Have a seat."

Allison sized up Quillen's demeanor and didn't like what he saw. Still he joined in small talk until the waiter took their orders. When the waiter returned with their lunch, they ate in uncomfortable silence. After he had cleared the table and brought coffee, Quillen spoke.

"It's down to this, Dwayne. I've got customers at every one of my banks who are behind on their notes. I've got people just walking away from mortgages. I've had to put repo men on as full-time employees to repossess cars when people just quit paying. But, by far my biggest problem is you, and that's because you're my biggest customer. The interest on your notes alone is near twenty million, all of it overdue. Any day the bank examiners may show up at one of my banks, and it'll be shut down within twenty-four hours. What the hell are you going to do about it?"

Allison's face reddened as he fought to control his temper. "Don't push me, Quillen. You think I don't know I'm behind on my notes? Shit, I'm doing good just to make payroll. Half my dealerships are gone. You want a lot to put those repossessed cars on? I got a bunch of them. I'm not doing a goddamn thing different than I've done for thirty-five years."

"Dammit, Dwayne, you didn't answer my question. What are you going to do about it? I could shut every one of your dealerships down tomorrow. Hell, I'll even own all of those quarter horses out on your ranch."

Allison pushed back and tossed his napkin on the table. His voice rose. "You do that, Quillen, and you'll regret it. I'm the only one that can pull Allison Southwest out of this mess and eventually pay my debts. You shut me down, and all you'll have are dealerships full of cars and trucks. Good luck selling them. I'm out of here."

Others in the club were now staring at the two businessmen whose raised voices were disturbing their lunch. Quillen lowered his voice. "Look, Dwayne, I didn't mean to piss you off. You're right. I need you. Sit down, please."

Allison hesitated before returning to his chair. Finally, he reached into his shirt pocket and pitched a folded check over to Quillen. Quillen unfolded it and saw it was for four hundred thousand dollars and made out to his bank. "That'll put a small dent in the back interest. Can I expect more where this came from?"

Allison looked around the room to make sure no one could overhear him. "One of my former employees died a few weeks ago. He never even knew I had a policy on his life. I had kept up the premiums after he quit. The company's the beneficiary."

"Ah, yes," Quillen said, his mind searching back several years. "I remember. You've been taking out policies on your employees for years.

You used to give me a spreadsheet of the employees and insurance amounts once a year. I haven't seen a spreadsheet in a while."

Dwayne stared into his cup as he absentmindedly stirred the coffee. "Yeah, when I started buying dealerships, I was still a young man. Most of the employees were fifteen, twenty years older. At one time I figured that those policies would put my retirement on easy street. Looks like that dream is over. Hell, I'll never be able to afford to retire. I'll be selling cars until they put me six feet under. In fact," he managed to smile, "I told one of my managers the other day my exit strategy is feet first."

Quillen considered his options before replying. "Look, Dwayne, I'm sorry I said I'd close you down. We've got to work together. I will require a current list of every one of your assets, down to the last screw in every one of your parts departments. That way if the examiners call, I can show them that there are assets to back up your loans. And I want a current list of every one of those life insurance policies, including names, Social Security numbers, amount of coverage and last known address. I'll be monitoring the Social Security Web site. If I find one of them dies, I'll expect to have a check in my hands a few weeks later. Understood?"

Allison nodded his agreement. "Understood. You're just doing what you have to do. You didn't create this goddamn mess either. I'll even get you a financial statement on Allison Southwest monthly instead of quarterly."

11

The house closed for $4,600,000 and Jack had a problem. He had given his house in Beaumont to his longtime legal assistant, complete with furnishings. By doing so, he knew he would have to hire an interior decorator in Fort Worth and start from scratch. The only thing he didn't anticipate was that his interior decorator would be Colby. He called her for a recommendation and she invited him to her house for a drink. When he walked through the front door, he understood why. From the entry chandelier to the stairway to the dining room, the living room and kitchen, everything blended perfectly. Jack couldn't describe the style, but he loved it. Hell, for that matter, since it wasn't Western, he wouldn't even know what to call it.

Colby led him to the kitchen and asked his drink preference. "Tito's vodka on the rocks," he replied.

She smiled and poured two before escorting him out to a patio facing a small back yard, complete with waterfall and babbling brook.

As they settled down beside the waterfall, they toasted. Colby asked, "What's your preference in design?"

Jack hesitated. "Damned if I know. I've only ever had Western. I'm willing to try something different, but it's got to be masculine."

Colby sipped her drink and thought. "How about Mediterranean?"

Jack stared back with a blank look.

Colby smiled and went into the house, returning with a couple of magazines. "Here, let me show you."

She flipped pages slowly and Jack nodded with each page. When she completed the two magazines, Jack said, "That's for me. Who do you recommend?"

Colby smiled coyly. "Why, me, of course."

"Price?"

"I'll make my money from the retailers. I'll make fifteen percent off the retail price and it doesn't come out of your pocket. To do the house right, you're looking at a quarter million. I'll be well paid. If you like the finished product, I'll accept dinner on the patio as a tip."

Jack nodded his agreement and Colby got to work. She furnished the kitchen and master bedroom first so Jack would have a place to live.

Colby made Jack sleep upstairs in a room fitted only with a bed and a chair until she completed the master bedroom. She also made him promise that she could lock the master bedroom door and that only she would have a key until it was done. Jack grumbled but agreed. Two weeks later she was ready for the showing.

"Shouldn't we have a band playing or something?" Jack asked as Colby unlocked the door.

"Jack, behave yourself," Colby replied. "I've spent a lot of time to make sure it perfectly fits your personality."

Colby opened the double doors to reveal a twenty-by-twenty master bedroom. A king-size four-poster bed occupied one wall and extended out into the rest of the room. A plush green spread covered the bed. A sitting area included a leather couch and two leather chairs. Canister lights filled the room. A thick brown carpet consumed all but the loudest sounds. Green drapes covered the windows, easily opened with the push of a button. The remote on the nightstand controlled a sixty-inch HDTV that dropped from the ceiling.

Jack nodded his appreciation. "It's beautiful. Thanks." He grinned. "Now I just need to find someone to share it with."

Colby was tempted, but demurred. "Remember that I'm just the interior decorator."

The next day Jack came back home in the middle of the afternoon to find a moving truck backed up to his front steps. Colby was supervising the unloading of the dining room table and chairs. Wearing jeans, a white T-shirt and a bandanna around her head, sweat glistened on her face and arms.

Jack parked in the driveway at the front of the house and walked toward the porch with a grocery sack. "Looks like you could use a break," he said.

Colby wiped her face on her sleeve. "You got that right. Just let me make sure they get this table through the doors without scratching it, and I'll join you."

Jack observed for a couple of minutes while Colby barked orders to the furniture crew, then went to the kitchen where he placed his package in the freezer and sat at the kitchen table. When Colby came from the dining room and collapsed on a kitchen chair, he went to the refrigerator.

"Here, I figure you could use this." He retrieved two cartons of ice cream. "Chocolate chip is my favorite, but I kinda figured you for a cherry vanilla kind of girl."

"You must have been peeking in my fridge." Colby smiled. "Three scoops for me."

Jack filled two bowls and set one in front of Colby as he pulled his chair back to the table.

"Delicious. Couldn't have come at a better time. You do this for all your decorators?"

"Yep. Of course, you're my first."

Then came the rest of the house. After six weeks it was done, subject to a couple of pieces on back order. At about the same time, Jack had his other vehicles hauled from Beaumont. In addition to his pickup, he had a blue Bentley, a red Ferrari, a black Harley, and a dark green Hummer. Counting the pickup, that left one garage for storage, a riding lawn mower, and garden tools. The last to arrive was his luxury RV that he bought several years before to use as an office and residence in a marathon case in the Rio Grande Valley. Jack had the driver back it onto the concrete pad next to the garage, and looked past the garage, over the Trinity to the old bomber plant. *You'd be proud of me, Dad,* he thought. *I made it from Byers to Alta Drive. I'm just sorry you're not here to share the moment with me.*

12

Two months earlier, four men finished their regular Saturday morning golf game at Shady Oaks and made their way to the men's grill. Dwayne Allison and Beau Quillen were still on reasonably good terms at the time. They were joined by Buddy Johnson, a real estate developer, and Ralph Warren, an independent oil operator.

"That was a helluva chip for a birdie on number seventeen, Beau. Tiger Woods would have been proud of that one."

"Everyone gets lucky once in a while. Any predictions on how the Cowboys will do this year?"

"Hell, if they finish eight and eight, it would be a miracle," Buddy snorted. "Jerry Jones built that Taj Mahal for a football stadium. Hundred thousand seats and half of them may be empty in December."

"Hell," Allison added as he sipped his beer, "the Cowboys may be America's team, but Houston is about to become Texas's team. Looks like they may finally have their act together this season."

After ordering lunch, the talk turned to politics and the recession. "Hell, Ralph," Buddy said. "You're about the only one around who's in a recession-proof business. Oil prices may go up and down, but somebody's still going to buy your product."

Ralph was distracted, watching the news on the big-screen television mounted on the wall. The sound was off, but with closed-caption capability, the newscaster's words were at the bottom of the screen. Suddenly, Ralph burst out laughing. "Can you believe that? Some son of a bitch wanted his wife killed and paid five grand to a hit man, only it was an undercover cop."

"Reminds me of T. Cullen Davis twenty years ago," Allison said. "He used to be one of my best customers at the Cadillac store."

"All right, here's a question," Ralph said. "Suppose you wanted to have someone bumped off, how would you find a real hit man?"

"Beats me," Allison said.

"I wouldn't have a clue," Quillen added. "Although there have been a couple of times in my career that I might have considered using one."

"I know what I would do," Buddy said. "I'd go see Nico."

"Nico?" Beau asked, a puzzled look on his face.

"You all know Nico," Ralph said. "He's that Italian that has the breakfast and lunch place on Vickery down by the railroad yard."

"Yeah, everybody knows him," Dwayne said. "Started that place to cater to the railroad workers, but now everybody in town gets by there once in a while. Best breakfast in town."

"Well, if you'd been going there for years like I have," Buddy said, "you'd know that he's been closed down a couple of times, once for six months and once for about a year. After the second closing, I asked him about it. He just matter of factly said he'd been in the joint for selling heroin. I'll bet he'd know someone from his prison days, and he'd keep his mouth shut for a couple of grand."

13

The customer parked in front of Nico's Diner around three in the afternoon, just about closing time. He noted that the parking lot was deserted. When he entered the empty diner, Nico was at the cash register, counting the day's receipts.

"Hey, Boss. Good to see you." Nico called every male customer "Boss," even the little kids, who got a big kick out of it. "We're about to close. You want some coffee?"

"That would be great, Nico. I know where it is. I'll help myself. When you get finished, I have something I want to talk with you about."

Nico nodded as the customer poured black coffee and took a seat at a corner table by the window. When Nico finished, he made his way to the table, stuffing his pants pocket with a roll of money. "Good thing about being the owner is Uncle Sam doesn't know what goes into my pocket every afternoon, and I damn sure ain't going to tell him." Nico took a seat across from his customer. "Now, Boss, what can I do for you?"

The customer hesitated and then plunged ahead. "Nico, what I'm about to say has got to remain between you and me. If you can't help me, just say so and forget I ever asked."

"Don't worry, my friend," Nico replied. "I've got a very convenient memory, and I can forget a lot of stuff."

"I'm in over my head with a loan shark. He's threatening me and my family. I'm looking for someone that can get him off my back. I figured you might know someone from your days in Huntsville."

Nico nodded and thought about the proposition. He also weighed how much his customer would pay for his services. "I think I know just the man. Him and me shared a cell for a while. He's out now and also living in Fort Worth. My finder's fee's gonna be ten grand. That too steep for you?"

"I can handle it."

Nico pulled a piece of paper from his pocket. "Here's my bank account and routing number. You get that to my account first thing in the morning. Once I know it's there, I'll call my friend. Plan to meet him at Sly's Place out on the Jacksboro Highway tomorrow night about nine. Give me your cell number. I'll call you if there's a problem."

The next night, the customer pulled into a gravel parking lot in front of a dimly lit bar. SLY'S PLACE was hand painted on a small sign. When he got out of his pickup, he decided he would tell the man to call him Boss and thanked Nico for the idea. He entered the bar. Three men were playing pool. He walked up to the bartender. "Give me a Bud."

The bartender put a bottle on the bar and took a five dollar bill in exchange. Boss moved to an empty table at the back and took a seat. He was half an hour early. He ignored the beer and counted the minutes. About ten after nine the door opened, and a man approached his table. The man had hair down to his shoulders, a neatly trimmed beard, and wore horn-rimmed glasses. A baseball cap covered his eyes. A gunfighter from a Western movie came to mind.

"Name's Hawk. I hear you're looking for some help."

Boss nodded. "Call me Boss. What do you do for a living, Hawk?"

Hawk lowered his voice as he glanced around the bar. "In the daytime I saddle my horse and ride around the stockyards amusement area. Kids like to pose for pictures with me. Otherwise, I take on an occasional job if it strikes me as the right thing to do and the money's good. I presume you're not wanting me to pose for pictures."

"You ever killed anyone, Hawk?"

"That's really none of your business, Mr. Bossman." Hawk scratched his beard before he continued. "I can tell you that I'm not opposed to the concept."

"I want someone eliminated. I should have the information you'll need on him in another day or so."

Hawk nodded his head. "What's in it for me?"

Boss rubbed his hands on his thighs and finally said, "Forty thousand on this one, wired to your bank account once I have confirmed the death."

Hawk raised his eyebrows slightly at the amount. "That'll be quite satisfactory; only on this job, since I don't know you, I'll need twenty thousand wired in advance with the balance when the job is done. You said 'this one.' Should I be expecting more jobs in the future?"

Boss shook his head. "Let's not get ahead of ourselves. I agree with the split payment. I'll evaluate your performance at a later date." Boss reached into his pocket and retrieved a cell phone. "Keep this with you twenty-four hours a day. I'll contact you on it. Use it only for calls from me. After I call you the first time, you'll have the cell number I'll be using."

Hawk smiled as he took the cell phone and put it in his shirt pocket. "As far as I'm concerned we have a deal. My only other requirement is that we only discuss a meeting place on the phone. The details of the assignment will be worked out in person. I'll pick the place for the meeting."

Boss reached over to shake Hawk's hand.

"There's one more thing," Hawk said. "I know who you are. At least I know your face. I read the *Star Telegram* every morning, and I've seen your picture from time to time. Don't worry, though. I don't rat out a business partner."

Boss gulped, but then realized that he had jumped into the deep end and couldn't crawl out now. He nodded to Hawk, pitched a ten on the table and left the bar. When he got to his car, he drove to the edge of the highway where he stopped and stared at the cars speeding by. He pounded the steering wheel, thinking that he had been a business-man his entire life and expected to drive hard bargains, but this was the first time he had ever stepped all the way over the line.

14

Boss turned into the parking lot in front of the Forest Park duck pond at dusk. Hawk had insisted their meeting would be there. Boss got out of his car and watched a young mother and father with two children feeding the ducks. The boy and girl, who looked about five and six, would retrieve pieces of bread from a sack held by their dad and rush down to the water's edge to toss the bread as far as they could, usually a few feet. The ducks would converge on the place where the bread landed, and one would emerge victorious, gulping down the bread before the others could take it away. Then they would turn back to the kids and the game would start again.

Boss envied the carefree family and wished for those bygone days. Life had dealt him straights and flushes for thirty-plus years. Now the good cards were gone, and he was lucky to draw a pair of deuces. He sighed as the father called his brood together and told them that it was getting too dark to stay in the park. The family walked to their car with the kids begging to come back the next day. Once the kids were buckled into the back seat, the parents climbed into the front. When they drove away, Boss noticed that the emblem on the trunk was from an Allison Southwest dealership.

It was ten minutes before he heard the creaking of boards on the bridge over the pond and saw the glowing end of a cigarette. Hawk appeared. "I've been parked on the other side. I wanted to make sure no one else would interrupt us. Nice family," Hawk said.

When Hawk got close, Boss asked, "Why this place and why now?"

Hawk smiled as he lit another cigarette. "The duck pond is usually busy up until about sunset. Then in another hour or two it'll become a lover's lane. We should have it to ourselves now. You got something for me?"

Boss started to reply, then stopped. He hesitated for long enough that Hawk was becoming suspicious, then erupted with a sneeze. "Sorry, must be something around here I'm allergic to. There's a man in Breckenridge. Name's Jim Morris. Used to be an auto mechanic. Now he works in the oil fields. He's your first target. I want it done in the next two weeks." Boss handed Hawk a piece of paper. "Here's what I've got on him. Gotta look like an accident. Clear?"

"You got it, Boss," Hawk replied as he ground his cigarette under his boot. "I assume you'll wire twenty thousand dollars to my bank account tomorrow. I'll let you know when the job's done." Hawk turned. Again Boss heard the creaking of boards on the bridge as Hawk disappeared into the darkness.

15

Once the house was complete, Jack invited Colby over for a housewarming dinner. She did as Jack directed. She punched in the code at the driveway gate and drove around to the back where she found Jack dressed in shorts, flip-flops, and a blue T-shirt. When he saw her Lexus appear in the driveway, he hustled to help her out. Colby was wearing her own T-shirt, green shorts, and sandals. Her shirt had a slogan emblazoned on the front, WHERE THE BEST BEGINS. Jack hoped that was prophetic as his gaze took in green eyes accentuated by laugh lines showing through her sun-browned face; sensuous red lips that broke into a smile, revealing near-perfect teeth; a figure that had to see the gym three or four days a week; and deeply tanned legs. *Damn,* he thought. *She's not wearing makeup. Better yet, she doesn't need any.* And the hint of perfume coming from behind her ears reminded him of a vineyard at harvesttime. She'd said she had a boyfriend, but at least he could give it his best shot.

Her eyes sparkled when she said, "I presume this is not a formal occasion."

"Formality is in the eyes of the beholder," Jack replied. "And my eyes tell me you are perfectly dressed for this occasion. What can I get you to drink?"

"My usual, of course," Colby said as she walked over to check out the barbecue pit. "I don't think I ever noticed this until now."

The pit was made of brick to match the house. It had a gas grill for most cooking but had a smoker on one end. Jack had filled the smoker with mesquite earlier in the day and had been carefully tending ribs and reading Steve Berry's latest novel as the sun moved across the horizon and was now creating a rainbow-hued sunset.

"Oh," Colby said, as she inhaled the smell of sizzling pork being cooked over mesquite. "Are you cooking ribs? I hope not. I'm a vegetarian."

Jack stepped back from the outdoor bar where he was mixing two Tito's martinis on the rocks and turned, about to apologize, when he saw her face break into a laugh.

"Just kidding. You're not allowed to live in Cowtown if you're a vegetarian. I just hope you cooked enough ribs."

Jack noticed she wrinkled her nose when she laughed as he handed her a drink and threw open the pit to reveal what appeared to be ribs from half a pig. "That enough?"

"That's about right for me. What are you having?"

Jack shrugged his shoulders and said, "Suppose I'll just have to eat your leftovers. Here, come sit in one of these recliners and we can watch the sun finish painting the clouds." They each took a seat and watched the sun dance from cloud to cloud, each of them content to sip their drinks and watch the Great Artist at work. Jack broke the quietness of the evening.

"I've been sitting out here a lot in the past couple of weeks. I look at the old bomber plant off in the distance beyond the Trinity and think back to when I was a kid. Once a year they had a family day, complete with a picnic and games. They'd haul a few planes out from the hangars, and we kids got to climb around on them. I even got to sit in the cockpit of an old B-36, the one with the propellers facing the rear. I know it's closed, but I still see fighters taking off, particularly on weekends."

"That's the Air National Guard," Colby interrupted. "Ever since the plant and Carswell Air Force Base closed, they fly out of there."

"Most folks would say I've come a long way from Byers Street to here. I certainly accomplished my goal of making money. Now, I suppose I'm looking for a little more happiness," Jack mused.

"Weren't you happy in Beaumont?"

"Sure, by almost any way you would measure happiness the answer would be yes. And it's a little strange to talk about it. My dad and mother probably never even contemplated the word. My dad just worked across the river over there and brought home a weekly paycheck. My mother took care of the house and me. That's what people did back in those days."

"Don't kid yourself. That's how most people live today, at least once you get out of Rivercrest and Shady Oaks."

Jack nodded his agreement as the day whispered into evening. Lights on the patio began to glow as the sun faded. Jack checked the ribs once more and went to the house to retrieve potato salad, baked beans, and freshly baked bread. He insisted that Colby keep her seat as he prepared the table. When it was ready, he took a giant platter from under the barbecue pit and loaded it with ribs. He invited Colby to the table while he made one last run to the kitchen, returning with a basket of napkins and a bottle of red wine.

"I think we're ready. There are five napkins for each of us. Hope that's enough."

Colby replied by picking up a rib and gnawing the meat from it before she even reached for anything else. "Wow. Absolutely fantastic. You use a special sauce?"

"Yep," Jack replied. "Family secret, handed down from my granddad to my dad and then to me. I spent most of yesterday making it, and, while you're a friend, you're not special enough for me to divulge the recipe, not yet anyway."

"I understand about Texas men and their recipes. I dated a man once that had a chili recipe he wouldn't reveal to anyone. He even won the chili cook-off at Terlingua one year."

Jack turned to Colby. "Now, that's really impressive. People come from all over the world every year for that cook-off. I might be willing to trade him my barbecue recipe for his chili."

"No chance of that. He's long gone. Moved to Arizona, I hear. On the other hand, I've got my own chili recipe that might be worth a trade."

They ate and made small talk. Jack wanted to talk about J.D. When they finished, Colby insisted on clearing the table and suggested that Jack take a seat on the next level down by the pool. When she came out, Jack rose from his seat and said, "Let's try out the hot tub."

Colby turned to face Jack, their faces no more than a few inches from each other. Jack could smell her perfume again. "Look, Jack. I like you, and I'm really attracted to you. Only, I told you that I'm seeing someone. I won't have a relationship with anyone else. I'm good for lunch and

Starbucks and maybe an occasional dinner, but we're just going to be friends." She stood on her tiptoes and kissed his cheek. "Is that okay?"

Jack stepped back and shook his head. "I guess I don't have any choice; so, yeah, it's okay, but don't expect me to give up. What does this guy do, anyway?"

Colby turned away. "Let's don't talk about him. I'm going to be one of your best friends. Talking about him won't accomplish anything."

Jack nodded his understanding as he concealed his frustration.

16

Jacob Yates had risen to sales manager of a Buick dealership in Oklahoma City. He had taken an early retirement some twenty years ago when his wife developed ovarian cancer. Like most women with ovarian cancer at that time, she fought and lost. Yates had few ties left to Oklahoma City, so he moved to Muskogee to be near his daughter, her husband, and grandkids. He was a great babysitter, sang baritone in the church choir, and volunteered at the community hospital. He lived in an older brick house on a tree-lined street where he managed to win "Yard of the Month" at least every year or two. He was so comfortable with the quiet life of Muskogee that he rarely locked his doors at night.

Hawk checked into a Ramada Inn. He spent a week following Yates to learn his routine. He parked down the street from Yates's house early in the morning and watched him tend his flowers before it got too hot. He followed Yates to the hospital three afternoons and parked in the front while Yates manned the volunteer desk just inside the entrance. He attended the First Baptist Church on Sunday. Even sitting in the back row he could see the joy in Yates's face as he sang "What a

Friend We Have in Jesus." He watched as Yates took his grandkids to the park and felt a pang of regret that they soon would no longer have their grandfather.

Yates returned from babysitting, warmed up some pot roast for a sandwich, and popped open a Coke while he watched the ten o'clock news. He had no way of knowing that Hawk was watching from behind his garage.

Hawk waited thirty minutes after the last light was out and approached the back door. As expected, he found it unlocked. He blew out the pilot on the gas stove and turned the four burners to high. Next he walked around the stove to a closet that housed the gas water heater. After confirming that the pilot light was on, he left the closet door open and crept out the way he came, silently closing the door behind him. Hawk circled the garage and walked three blocks up the street to his pickup. He lighted a cigarette, lowered a window and waited. Before he finished his cigarette, he saw and heard the explosion as the house erupted in flames. Satisfied that no one could live through that inferno, he started his pickup and slowly drove away. As he did so he said a silent prayer for Yates's family.

17

Colby greeted Ruth at the reception desk and hurried back to the room. She had an appointment to show a house in an hour but had not stopped by the nursing home in a week. When she entered the room, she found the same sterile, antiseptic environment. The smell told her that someone had scrubbed down the room that morning, something that was very important to prevent infections from attacking Rob's weakened immune system. As usual, she kissed Rob on the cheek and received no response.

"Hi, Rob. It's me. You doing okay?" She didn't expect a response but continued to try to treat him as a human being. "You know that big house I sold in Rivercrest? I got hired by the new owner to decorate it. He's a nice guy. Maybe one of these days you can meet him. I'm occasionally seeing him for coffee or lunch or something like that. Nothing serious you understand, but I don't have a lot of friends these days. I can't stay long. Let me check you over before I go. It's been a couple of weeks, and I want to make sure they are doing their job."

Colby pulled back the cover and evaluated his body. Next, she unfastened his diaper. "Okay, I'm going to turn you over on your side just to check your buttocks. The last thing we want is another ulcer forming on your butt."

Colby gently turned Rob to his right. When she looked at his buttock, she gasped in horror. A decubitus ulcer was forming, at least a stage two. She mentally kicked herself since she hadn't checked in a couple of weeks. *Dammit,* she thought, *I got too comfortable with this facility.* She stormed out of the room to the nurses' station.

"Dammit all, Irene," she yelled. "Rob's got an ulcer forming on his butt. You guys haven't been doing your job."

Irene was taken aback, but quickly recovered. "Ms. Stripling, you know that we turn him every two hours. Sometimes these things can't be avoided. Please try to calm down."

"I'm not about to calm down. Let me see his chart."

Irene reluctantly turned to retrieve Rob's chart and handed it to an irate Colby. Colby flipped through the pages until she found the page she was looking for. The staff was required to turn Rob every two hours and document that it had been done. If they didn't do their job, ulcers could form and mushroom into ugly open sores that were breeding grounds for multiple infections, including MRSA, one that was immune to nearly every known antibiotic.

"Shit," Colby said. "He's only been turned three times in the past forty-eight hours."

"Ms. Stripling, please calm down," Irene said. "I'm sure that he was turned and someone just forgot to chart it. We've got a lot of patients and care is more important than charting." Irene failed to add that all too often charting was done at the end of a shift even when patient care had been ignored.

Colby pitched the chart on the desk. "You know that's bullshit! You've been here since seven, and you've done so little for Rob that I had to be the one to find the ulcer. And I bet you pulled a twelve-hour shift yesterday and never spotted it then. I've been dealing with Rob's care for ten years. This is the fourth nursing home I've moved him to. I thought you guys were the best. If this is all I can expect, he's better off dead. Now, you get his doctor over here this afternoon. I want cultures done and I want Dr. Winston to figure out what kinds of antibiotics we need to fight this. Mark my words, if this happens again, I know a damn good lawyer."

Colby stormed from the nurse's station, not even going back to Rob's room. Irene watched her go. *This woman is going to be trouble,* she thought. *Damned if I'll get fired because of some pissed-off relative.*

When Colby got to her car, she remembered that she had not told Rob good-bye. She started to go back in and then thought better. Telling him good-bye was for her benefit, not his. She started her car and drove slowly away, trying to get her temper under control before her appointment.

18

Jack joined Rivercrest and found golf with old men boring, even though he always won a couple of hundred bucks. Poker in the men's grill was the same. He got no kick out of taking five hundred or a thousand dollars from the same old men. His life as a trial lawyer had been a high-stakes poker game. Winning in the men's grill didn't compare with winning in front of a jury. And the first home game was still two weeks away.

He called on Colby to fill the void. Having established that their relationship was nothing more than platonic, Colby accepted his invitation to be his tour guide of the new Fort Worth.

Colby called him early one morning. "Jack, you awake? Here's what I propose. You and I are going to the museums today. When I'm not working, we're going to start visiting all the tourist attractions in this town: museums, zoo, stockyards, botanical gardens, nature trails. There's a lot to see. In case you didn't know it, Fort Worth has some of the most famous art in the world. The Kimbell Art Museum and Amon Carter Museum are world class. There's a ton of money among the rich in Fort Worth, and they constantly try to one-up each other as civic benefactors."

One of the great things about Fort Worth was that nearly everything was within a fifteen-minute drive. He walked out to the garage and started the Bentley, Colby's choice. He drove the five minutes to Colby's house, and ten minutes later they were parked across the street from the Kimbell. Jack was not about to tell Colby that he'd rather take a swim in the Arctic Ocean than pretend to be interested in the works of the old masters. On this day he got lucky. The museum had a traveling exhibition of Mayan art, something that Jack found fascinating. He explained to Colby that he had visited Mayan ruins several times over the years. If he had another life to live, it would be as Indiana Jones.

After lunch at a small café in the museum district, they drove a few blocks to the Amon Carter Museum, formerly known as the Amon Carter Museum of Western Art, but changed a couple of years ago when they expanded the museum and chose not to be limited to Western paintings and statuary. Still, the museum was filled with original Remington and Russell paintings, and statues of cowboys, Indians, Western landscapes and buffalo herds. Colby noticed the smile on Jack's face as they walked slowly through the halls, stopping to admire nearly every work of art. When they got to the museum store, Jack filled a large bag with books about the displays.

Over the next two weeks Colby took Jack to every place of interest in the Fort Worth area and even to a couple in Dallas. Still, even after her working hard to play local docent, Jack was bored. Fortunately, the first home game was in three days.

19

Boss stopped at the entrance to the Fort Worth Zoo at ten o'clock in the morning. The attendant was just opening up when Boss paid his admission and entered. He stopped and studied a sign before turning to his right in the direction of the tiger exhibit. As he approached the tigers, he saw a lone man on a bench, feeding peanuts to pigeons. It was Hawk.

Hawk didn't look up as Boss took a seat on the bench beside him.

"You ever spent much time here at the zoo, Boss? It's one of my favorite places. I don't like seeing animals behind fences, but if that's how it's gonna be, this is one of the best. They take really good care of their animals. Look at those tigers. See that male, walking up and down along the back fence. Magnificent specimen. He's waiting for his keeper and breakfast. If I didn't like the kids in the stockyards so well, I might get a day job out here. And, by the way, thanks for that last wire transfer."

Boss interrupted. "Look, I'm pleased that you like our zoo. I've even contributed to it myself. Only, that's not why we're here. I've got another job for you."

Boss looked around to make sure that no one was in sight as he reached into his pocket and handed Hawk a folded piece of paper. The target this time was in Brownwood, a hundred miles or so southwest of Fort Worth.

"I know the area. Used to go to church camp on Lake Brownwood when I was a kid. What's my bonus on this one?"

"Sixty thousand."

Hawk stood to face Boss. "Let me understand something here. My fee varies from victim to victim. What's the deal?"

Boss stood to face Hawk, not wanting to give up the position of control and dominance. He had a good four inches on Hawk and wanted to take advantage of it. "Let's just say I have a financial interest in each of our projects. I made the very generous decision to reward you with ten percent of what I recover. In hindsight, I probably should have made it a flat fee, but I figure I'll keep your attention with that ten percent."

"I get it," Hawk said. "There's some life insurance involved somehow, right?"

"I've said enough. I want this one done in ten days. Once you've accomplished your mission, it's still about four to six weeks before I get the money." Boss lowered his voice. "I may appear to be successful, but the swamp is rising and I've got alligators snapping at my ass."

"Understood. Okay, you just get up and mosey on out of here. I'm going to wander around among the animals for a while. Morning's the best time to see them frisky and acting up."

Boss nodded and walked back toward the gate. Hawk resumed feeding the pigeons until he saw the tiger handler starting to toss meat over the back fence. He laughed as one tiger ripped into the beef, tearing off large chunks and then having to fight off the other tigers as he devoured his breakfast. *Damn tough world,* he thought, *whether you're behind bars or not. The fittest survive to eat another day.*

20

Jack had the Bentley washed and polished the day before the game and arrived at Colby's door at five o'clock for the seven o'clock kickoff. The time was dictated by the start of the season in late August when temperatures were still regularly hitting a hundred and five. Jack walked up the sidewalk to Colby's door, rang the bell, and stepped inside to get out of the heat. He was wearing black slacks with a purple jacket over a white shirt. He waited in the entryway and hollered, "I'm here."

"I know." Colby's voice came from the back. "I'll be right out."

Colby stepped into the foyer, wearing her own purple and white— purple slacks and a white short-sleeved shirt.

"Perfect," Jack said as he kissed her on the cheek, noting that she did not push away. Jack opened the door and gestured for Colby to go first. Colby saw the Bentley and asked, "Why the Bentley? Is Lucille sick?"

Jack hesitated. "Well, I've heard that a lot of these TCU alums have money. We're parking in the reserved lot. I didn't want anyone to think that J.D. came from the wrong side of the tracks."

Colby paused when she heard Jack's comment and turned to face him. "Jack, you've got a chip on your shoulder, and you need to get rid of it. You resent the fact that you were born poor and some of your classmates were rich. So what? Now you've made it. We've got a lot of poor folks in this town. Are you going to treat them as second-class citizens?"

Jack shrugged his shoulders. "No. Of course, not. But I hear what you're saying." Jack paused. "And you're right."

They parked in the place reserved for Jackson Bryant and made their way to the Frog Club, now big, modern and newly remodeled, with giant windows looking down from the south end zone. Expecting to go up and down steps, Jack carried his cane, this one with an antler for a handle. They found a place to have coffee as the club filled with alums as excited as if it were Christmas day and they were six years old. A few of the alums greeted Colby and commented that it had been years since they saw her at a game. One of them stopped to visit.

"How's Rob faring these days?"

Colby glanced at Jack to see if he had heard the question. He had.

"Rob's fine. Thanks for asking. Now if you'll excuse us, I see one of my former clients on the other side of the room." She took Jack's arm and led him through the crowd until they were at the windows overlooking the field.

"Wow, look at that, Jack. We could watch the game from here."

Jack nodded. "Now, where's that client?"

Colby looked around the crowd. "Must have lost her. I'll catch her another time."

She breathed an inward sigh of relief when the crowd started applauding. Albertson Reed was making his entrance. He was the oldest living letterman, having played on Sammy Baugh's team back in the thirties. When Jack saw someone talking to Reed and nodding in his direction, Reed made his way over. Jack shook his hand. "Jackson Bryant."

Reed was stooped in the shoulders but still had a firm handshake and piercing blue eyes. "You're J.D.'s dad?"

"Yes, sir."

"I've watched some of the practices. Mark my words. It may take a while, but he has a chance to be something special."

Jack beamed as he thanked the old man and then noted that people were starting to leave the club. He and Colby followed, making their way to padded seats on the forty yard line, twenty rows up. The TCU players drifted onto the field, wearing purple jerseys and white pants. Jack spotted J.D. wearing number 81. The Baylor Bears came from the other end.

After warm-ups, the teams retired to their locker rooms, and the TCU chancellor introduced various dignitaries, thanking them, the fans, and the city of Fort Worth for making the new stadium possible. Then the players returned to the field as the TCU band played "The Star-Spangled Banner" and four fighters from the Air National Guard flew over in formation. After a prayer and school songs, it was time for kick-off.

The score at halftime was Horned Frogs 24, Bears 17, a little closer than the Frog fans wanted. The second half was better with the final score Horned Frogs 57, Bears 38. J.D. rode the end of the bench even when the game was in the bag.

Jack and Colby followed the crowd to the parking lot. As they approached the Bentley, he put his arm on her shoulders. Pleased that she didn't pull away, he asked, "The night's still young. You want to recommend a place for a nightcap?"

Colby stopped and turned to look at Jack. "You understand we're not dating, right?"

Jack nodded.

"Then my favorite place for a drink is the Library Bar on Houston Street downtown. They've got a piano bar and the best martinis in town."

Downtown was full of revelers, most of them celebrating the Horned Frog victory. Jack had to pass by the Library Bar to find a parking place two blocks away. Just like the streets, the bar was packed. Jack slipped the girl at the front a twenty to get the last two-person table in the place. The piano player/singer played a medley of Frank Sinatra, Tony Bennett, Dean Martin, and Sammy Davis, Jr., hits. Jack thought for a minute that he was swept back to Las Vegas thirty years ago as he ordered two double Tito's martinis on the rocks with olives, just a little dirty. Colby smiled her agreement.

They listened to the singer until the waitress brought their drinks. Jack lifted his for a toast. "Here's to what I learned tonight."

A puzzled look crossed Colby's face. "I don't understand."

"I learned your boyfriend is named Rob."

Colby took a large sip of her martini before speaking. "Yeah, I was worried that might happen."

Jack sat his drink down and leaned over the table. "I don't understand. I'm okay with you having a boyfriend. You've established the boundaries and I've accepted them. Only, why aren't you ever out with Rob? Believe me, I'd rather have you out with me, but I'm confused."

Colby took the olive spear from her drink and plucked one off, chewing it slowly before she spoke. "He's a driller. Works in Alaska up on the North Slope. He's usually there two months and back here for two weeks, sometimes less."

"And you're okay with that kind of long-distance relationship?"

Colby refused to meet Jack's eyes. "Yeah, for now anyway. They're opening up more rigs out in the Gulf. He hopes to land one of those this next year. We see each other on Skype two or three nights a week. That'll have to do for now."

Jack finished his drink and ordered a second. He knew that he was not getting the real story from Colby, but decided not to push. It would come out sooner or later.

21

Monday was a cloudy, dreary day with rain in the forecast. Jack awoke and watched the news while he ate a bowl of Cheerios. He wandered around the house and had second thoughts about buying one so big that he never even went to the second floor. Finding his way to the backyard, he picked up a pool skimmer and removed a few pecan leaves from the water. When he glanced up at the trees, he could tell that the pecans were getting ripe. Next, he opened all of the garage doors and started the engine on each of his vehicles, including the RV. After letting them run for five minutes, he went back in the house and found Lisa. His thrice-weekly maid had come. *She's got to be the envy of her friends,* he thought. *I use what amounts to a one-bedroom apartment and she gets paid to clean the whole house.* Still, she was punctual and pleasant and filled her hours by washing all the downstairs windows once a week and sweeping the sidewalks. After a shower and shave, he put on his usual casual attire of jeans, boots, and a T-shirt, telling Lisa that he was going for a drive. At the back door, he paused to look over his collection of canes and chose one he had found in an old shop in Hamburg on a European trip. It had a carved boar's head for a handle.

He started for Lucille, then stopped. Today he would drive the Ferrari, maybe open her up if he found the right stretch of road. He returned to the house, replaced the pickup keys on the board by the kitchen door and grabbed the ones to the Ferrari. Jack stopped once more at the pickup to take his Texas map from the passenger door side pocket. He spread it on the hood of Lucille and chose a route of back roads leading at least to Mineral Wells.

Jack strapped himself into the Ferrari and started the engine, pausing to listen to its low roar. The Ferrari had paddle shifting, which Jack loved. No more four-on-the-floor. Now with his hands at the three o'clock and nine o'clock positions, he could shift up through six gears by flicking the right paddle and back down with the one on the left. No clutch, and he didn't even have to take his foot from the gas pedal. It was a marvel of Italian automotive engineering. Jack put the car in first gear and eased down the driveway. He passed the Rivercrest clubhouse, waving to a couple of the gardeners whom he had befriended and turned right on Camp Bowie and went to second gear. Doing so, he made sure his fuzzbuster was working. It was a Valentine One, capable of spotting both radar and laser beams coming from police vehicles. Soon he was driving through the western outskirts of Fort Worth, headed toward Weatherford. He took a right after a few miles and wandered the back roads. When he found one straight and empty, he went to fourth and fifth gears, hitting a hundred and fifty at one point. On curves that were rated for 35 miles per hour, he dropped to second and took them at eighty, always with a grin on his face. *Maybe,* he thought, *he should do like Paul Newman did and take up road racing in middle age.* He slowed as he passed through Weatherford and soon found himself in Mineral Wells, where he turned and took the freeway back to Fort Worth. Driving down Camp Bowie, he spotted Colby's Lexus in front of her office. He went in and found Colby was on the phone. She motioned at him to have a seat. He was flipping through a local realtor's magazine when she ended her call and circled around the desk to give Jack a brief hug before breaking away with an embarrassed look. "Hi, there." She smiled. "What brings you here? Can I sell you another house?"

Colby sat in the chair beside Jack and waited for him to speak. Finally, he relayed his day's activities. "I think I'm bored. You've done a great job of keeping me entertained, but I don't want to visit the museums again."

Colby frowned.

"What the hell am I supposed to do with the rest of my life? I don't want to go back to being a trial lawyer. Sixty- and eighty-hour weeks are behind me."

Colby pondered his situation before speaking. "Why don't you volunteer to do some pro bono work? Times are tough. I'll bet there are tens of thousands of people in this area who could use some free legal advice. You could set your own hours, go and come as you please, and do some good for folks who can't afford a lawyer."

Jack nodded his head. "Actually that thought had drifted through my mind lately. I just might give it a try. Got nothing to lose but a little time, and I've damn sure got plenty of that."

22

The next morning Jack put on a white dress shirt, slacks, and boots. He located the Fort Worth Volunteer Lawyers Association on the Internet and drove two blocks past the courthouse complex on Weatherford to a small two-story building with the association name above the door. He parked Lucille at a meter and dug four quarters from the center console of the truck. After feeding the meter, he entered the building to face a receptionist.

"Can I help you?"

"Name's Jack Bryant. I'm a retired lawyer and would like to volunteer."

"Have a seat, sir, and I'll be with you in a few minutes."

Jack cooled his heels for fifteen minutes before the receptionist reached into the bottom drawer of her desk and retrieved a multipage form and a clipboard. "Mr. Bryant, if you'll step over here to get this form and complete it, I'll have our director talk to you when he's free."

Jack stared at the woman and wondered why she couldn't get off her butt and walk to him. After all, he was the volunteer. Still, he rose and walked back to the reception desk. When he looked at the form, it was ten pages. He filled in his name, address, bar number and prior employment in Beaumont before returning to the desk.

"Here. This ought to be plenty. Your director can read about me on the state bar Web site. As you can see, I'm not a baby lawyer and don't need to give you my life history."

"Well, Mr. Bryant," the receptionist huffed, "these questions are important and necessary."

Jack bent over her desk, his face about six inches from hers. "Why don't you give this to your director and see what he says?"

The receptionist took the clipboard and motioned him to return to his seat as she went through the door behind her desk. Thirty minutes later a small man, wearing a bow tie, opened the door. "Mr. Jackson Bryant, please come in."

The director didn't offer his hand as Jack approached and passed through the door. They rode the elevator in silence to the second floor and walked to a corner office with GRAHAM HILL, JD on the door. Jack thought back through his career and could not recall any lawyer who put his academic degree after his name.

Hill went around his desk to his swivel chair. "Have a seat, Mr. Bryant. I've looked over the very brief information you provided about your career."

Jack leaned forward. "Look, Mr. Hill, I don't need to prove that I've earned my spurs. Did you check me out on the bar's Web site or on Google?"

"I certainly did, sir," Graham said as he tented his hands under his chin. "We can certainly use you. Since you obviously know your way around the courtroom, we can use you handling divorces. You'll have to commit to certain hours. We want the same six hours every day. And, your outfit will have to be modified. We want our attorneys to be dressed for success even in the office. That means wearing a suit and tie at all times. We need to be respected by our clients, don't you agree?"

"No, sir, I don't agree. I don't need a goddamn tie to get respect. Forget it. I'm out of here." Jack stormed out of Hill's office, slamming the door behind him.

23

That night Jack thought about the wasted meeting with Hill. To hell with him. He still had too much free time and could do some good for people that couldn't afford lawyers. He'd start his own clinic without the red tape. The next morning he left the house and started driving, this time east on Camp Bowie, past the museum district until it became Seventh Street. After he passed Monkey Wards, he got to the bridge over the Trinity River. He found it interesting how memories of growing up in Fort Worth popped to the front of his brain. Now he remembered "the tamale man," a short Hispanic immigrant who had a tamale cart that he parked on the grass on the side of the road just before the bridge. His wife made tamales and he stood there beside his cart every day, rain or shine, selling those tamales. Somehow he and his wife managed to eke out a living, at least enough to feed themselves and two kids. Jack did a double take when he saw the tamale man still at his post. Jack changed lanes and came to a stop. The man's face was now wrinkled, but he still smiled as Jack lowered his window.

"Good morning, sir. How many today?"

Jack didn't really want the tamales, but ordered a dozen and tipped the man well before he drove away. Approaching downtown, he marveled at how much it had changed. The so-called skyscrapers of his youth were twelve-story brick buildings. Now those old buildings were dwarfed by forty-story glass towers, mainly built by the Bass brothers, multibillionaires who'd inherited a few hundred million dollars from their bachelor uncle, Sid Richardson, and then made enough shrewd investments that each of them became billionaires. Jack slowly circled around downtown as an idea formed and took shape.

When he turned onto Main, he saw the old red courthouse, now surrounded by other buildings in the courthouse complex, but still standing out with its red granite exterior, massive columns at the top of the steps and domed roof, complete with a clock. *That's what a courthouse should look like,* he mused. *People should feel a certain sense of awe as they climbed the twenty steps to seek justice.*

Jack drove around the courthouse and crossed another bridge over the Trinity as he descended from the courthouse bluff to the river bottom below. The area on both sides was run down. About the only businesses were a couple of bars, a topless club, and some bail bondsmen. That changed as he approached the stockyards. Although the area had been abandoned and in disarray for many years, some farsighted citizen had seen the potential for a tourist attraction among the ruins. In a matter of years, the covered pens became shops. A tourist train weaved through the area. Steak houses and Mexican restaurants sprang up. Billy Bob's Texas billed itself as the world's largest honky-tonk, attracting some of the best singers that Nashville had to offer. Cowboys were hired to stall their horses there and ride them among the tourists, pausing to pose for photos and accept a tip for their efforts. Every afternoon the cowboys drove a small herd of longhorn cattle through the area, emulating the cattle drives of another era. The folks in Fort Worth liked the stockyards because they served to remind visitors that Cowtown really did have its roots in the Old West.

Beyond the stockyards there was little more to see. A couple of car dealerships had been abandoned, brought down by the great recession. When Jack got to Meacham Field, once Fort Worth's commercial airport but now used only by private-aircraft owners, he turned and headed back south. Once past the stockyards, he noted a cop shop, the Stock-yards Police Station, on the right. A few blocks later he spotted an old-fashioned icehouse at the corner of Refinery and North Main. Beside it was a vacant lot where he parked and walked the property, using his cane to pick his way among rocks and debris. *Big enough,* he thought. He looked up to see that the lot was served by electricity. When he got to the back, he looked over the fence to see a neighborhood with homes barely fit for habitation. The roofs on most were patched. Old cars appeared abandoned in front yards. The streets were filled with potholes. *These people could use a good lawyer,* Jack mused.

Jack walked to the front and studied the icehouse. It, too, was a throwback to days gone by. With rusted metal walls, it had two garage doors in the front that were opened on warm days. A couple of old wooden tables, each with two chairs, were on the concrete apron in front. With no air conditioning, ceiling fans stirred a decent breeze. Jack stepped across the threshold. To his right were four old men drinking beer and loudly slamming dominoes on a table. A worn and scarred bar ran across the back. Three barstools had seen better days, maybe twenty years ago. Jack limped a little, having twisted his knee in the vacant lot, as he took a seat on one of the stools. The bartender had a fringe of gray hair and a black handlebar mustache.

"What can I get for you?" he asked.

"Lone Star. Coldest one you got."

"They're all cold, my friend. I still ice them down every morning. No refrigerated coolers in this place."

Jack nodded his appreciation as he downed half the beer and wiped his mouth with the back of his hand. "Wow, that's good. Can I ask you a question?"

"Fire away."

"Who owns that lot next door?" Jack nodded in the direction of his pickup.

"Was owned by an investor who thought that the stockyards tourist area would eventually move this way, but I hear that the bank just foreclosed. You got any interest in it?"

"I might." Jack finished his beer and put three dollars on the counter. As he rose, he stuck out his hand. "Name's Jack Bryant."

The bartender shook it and said, "Moe."

Jack nodded, paused to watch the domino game and then went to his pickup. Now he had a plan.

24

A week later a small sign appeared on the vacant lot. SOLD it announced. The following week Jack arrived at his new property early, armed with a large Starbucks, the *Fort Worth Star Telegram,* and the *Wall Street Journal.* He parked in Moe's lot and waited until a contractor arrived. First his crew leveled the lot, and then started placing two-by-fours and laying rebar. By afternoon an electrician had arrived. He ran 110-and 220-voltage lines from the main utility pole through metal tubing along the rebar to a place Jack designated for electrical boxes. The next day Jack watched as trucks lined up on North Main, awaiting their turn to pour concrete onto the lot. As they poured a section, finishers smoothed the concrete under the watchful eye of the contractor. At the end of the day the contractor walked around the lot and satisfied himself that the pitch was just enough to allow rainwater to flow to the street. Next he walked to Moe's parking lot where Jack was leaning up against Lucille, confirmed that Jack was satisfied, and climbed into his own pickup. About that time Moe walked out of his icehouse.

"Jack, my new neighbor, what the hell are you doing? You going into the used car business?"

Jack grinned. "You'll know in a few days, Moe."

Once the concrete was dry, the electrician returned to install flood lights around the perimeter on twenty-foot poles. He was followed by a team from an alarm company. When Jack was satisfied that everything was done to his satisfaction, it was time for the RV. By then he and Santos, his handyman, had stripped the back of its bed, dresser and nightstands. They were replaced with a moderate-sized brown desk, executive chair and two guest chairs. There was just enough room along one wall for a small sofa. Now, Jack had an office.

The next morning he walked out the back door of his mansion, breathed in the morning air and greeted Santos. "Santos, I'll drive the RV. You follow in Lucille."

Jack pushed a button on the RV key ring to unlock it and climbed into the driver's seat. After fastening his seat belt, he turned the key, and the big diesel engine rumbled to life. With one last look at his mirrors, he slowly circled the house and headed downtown and out to his vacant lot. Once there, Santos stopped traffic momentarily for Jack to back the RV into the property. It took three tries before Jack was able to position the RV beside the electrical outlets with the front facing the street. Jack climbed from the RV, looked around and nodded his head in satisfaction. He and Santos were hooking up the electricity when the alarm company arrived to finish their job. Once they were gone, Jack took a piece of a cardboard box and, using a black marker, wrote LAWYER, NO FEE! He placed the sign on the dashboard facing the windshield and told Santos, "Now, I'm open for business."

The next day he arrived around ten, expecting to see clients lined up around the block. Finding no one, he started the engine to activate the air conditioning, made coffee, and turned Bloomberg on the fifty-inch flat-screen TV. Figuring that he had not gotten the message out, he ripped another side from the cardboard box and wrote OPEN on one side and CLOSED on the other.

Several hours later the door opened, and he expected to see his first client, only it was Colby.

"Jack! What the hell are you doing?"

Jack rose to greet her. "Just what you said. I'm offering my services for free. How'd you know where to find me?"

Colby plopped down on the couch. "I called the house, and Lisa said just to go out North Main until I spotted your RV. Jack, this is not what I meant. I assumed you'd go to the Tarrant County Bar and volunteer."

"I did. Let's just say that the director and I had a little disagreement on the first day."

"But, but, don't you know this part of town is dangerous?"

"Damn sure do. That's why I've got this. He reached into a drawer and brought out a Magnum. You forget that I was Airborne? And I still go hunting four or five times a year." He aimed the pistol out the front window. "I could put out a man's eye at twenty-five yards with this peashooter."

"Wait a minute," Colby stuttered. 'You can't leave this RV here. It'll be gone in a week."

Jack motioned Colby to follow him as he stepped outside. He handed her his keys and said, "Push that button there on the right."

Colby did so and watched in amazement as the RV was transformed. Quarter-inch steel shutters silently slid down to cover every window as the flood lights came on.

"Now, step up and jiggle the door handle."

When Colby did, a piercing, high-decibel alarm erupted, forcing Colby to cover her ears until Jack grabbed the keys and pushed the button again.

"What if someone unplugs this thing?"

"Got battery backup for eight hours. I doubt if any bad guys can get away with it without the cops showing up in that length of time. Besides, the cops have a station just down the street. I aim to befriend them in the next day or so."

Colby offered her last lame argument. "They could steal your tires and mirrors."

Jack smiled. "If they can find a jack big enough to lift this monster, they can have the tires. Besides, I had Santos buy a set of old used tires. The good ones are back at the house. I'm going to take the mirrors off this afternoon. Come back in. Coffee's made."

Colby sat on the couch while Jack poured her a cup of coffee. "When did you do all of this stuff to the RV?"

"I had a case down in the valley a few years ago. It was gonna last for a couple of months. I bought this as my office and home. Those counties along the Rio Grande are among the most lawless in the country these days. So I had all the armor and alarms installed for that trial. Worked out well. I didn't have to rent an office or a motel room and got a verdict north of a hundred million. Let me show you around."

Jack pointed out the features of the RV. It was the biggest and most luxurious available. It came with a full kitchen, dining room, sitting room, one and a half baths, and a bedroom in the back.

"This was the bedroom. I stripped it, and now it's my office. I can have clients wait out here in the front if I'm busy in the office."

Colby sighed. "Well, it looks like you're sure about this. I just hope you don't have to use that peashooter, as you call it."

"Rob in town?" Jack changed the subject.

"He just left. Had a few unexpected days off. That's the reason you haven't heard from me," Colby responded.

Jack ignored what was surely a lie. Something was keeping Colby from opening up to him. He figured his best plan was just to wait until she was ready to talk about it. In the meantime he would just enjoy her company. "Now, let me take you next door to meet Moe and some of my friends. I spent my life around refinery workers and longshoremen. I'm a whole lot more comfortable with these guys than the Rivercrest crowd. They're even teaching me how to play dominoes. One of these days I'm going to win a game."

25

Johnny looked at the big wall clock advertising Purina and noted the time was 8:00 a.m. Where was Victor? His starting time at the feed store in Brownwood was always seven thirty. Victor was never late. When it got to be eight thirty, he hollered at Don that he was going to drive out to check on Victor.

Don walked in from the loading dock, wiping his face with a bandanna. "You think there's a problem?"

"Don't know. Maybe he's sick. He lives alone and doesn't have a phone, not even a cell. He's a good hand. Just checking. That's all. I'll be back in an hour."

Johnny got in his blue Ford pickup and turned onto the highway. He turned toward Lake Brownwood and crossed over a bridge spanning a finger of the lake. Two hundred yards past the bridge he turned onto a dirt driveway and parked in front of the small frame house that Victor rented. Victor's Harley was parked in the driveway beside the house. Johnny climbed out of his truck and knocked on the front door. No answer. He walked around to the back where he knew Victor always left the door open. Victor's garden tools were neatly arranged, leaning up against the porch rail.

Johnny knocked and got no answer. As he opened the door, he hollered, "Victor, you home?" Silence.

He walked into the kitchen. Johnny knew Victor was obsessively neat. The kitchen table and counter were as clean as an operating room in a hospital. Johnny looked into the bedroom. The bed was made, which wouldn't be a surprise except that Victor's Harley was parked at the house.

Johnny went out the back door and walked around the house before he called the sheriff's office to report that Victor was missing. Then he drove back to the feed store to report what he found to Don.

Three hours later a sheriff's car parked in front of the store. Johnny and Don met Luke Simpson, a friend and regular customer, as he exited the vehicle.

"Well, we found him. He's dead. Body was under the bridge."

"He drown?" Don asked.

"Doesn't look like it. We found bruises on his neck. He have any enemies?"

Johnny shook his head. "Not that we know of. Showed up about three years ago. Said he had been a counterman at a Ford dealer that closed in Abilene. He was a loner. Did his job and kept to himself. Did go to the Baptist church down the road here. If he was under the bridge, why was his Harley parked back at the house?"

Simpson took off his cap and scratched his head. "Damned if I know. Key was in it. I started it and it ran just fine. We may never solve this one."

26

It had been a week, and Jack still was awaiting his first client. A few cars had driven slowly by the RV. A couple had parked in the lot while the occupants talked before driving off. Each afternoon at about four Jack would lock the RV and go next door. He took his own bourbon and just ordered a glass of ice, which he filled to the brim with Wild Turkey, his favorite whiskey since college days. Of course, he always left Moe a tip as if he had drunk at least a six-pack of beer. And he enjoyed playing dominoes. The domino table could hold eight comfortably and was ethnically mixed among Hispanics, African Americans and Anglos. For each game the players would ante a quarter apiece, winner take all.

One morning Jack had just unlocked the RV and put on coffee when he heard a loud knocking. He opened the door to find a black woman, large and of indeterminate age, dressed in a pink muumuu, with a purple scarf around her head and carrying a large beige imitation leather purse. She stood at the bottom of the steps.

"What kinda scam you running? You trying to take advantage of us poor folks?"

"No ma'am." He grinned at the apparition in front of him. "I'm a retired lawyer and just want to help out folks who can't afford one."

"You sure you're not gonna scam me?"

"Cross my heart and hope to die, if I do."

The woman sized him up one more time. "All right. Help me up these steps."

Jack did and invited her to take a seat on the bench at the dining room table.

The woman looked around the interior and settled on the flat-screen TV. "You be careful with that. Somebody steals it, they can sell it for five hundred or so."

"Can I ask your name?"

"Mona. Mona Thomas Lee."

"Pleased to meet you. I'm Jackson Bryant. How can I help you?"

Mona rummaged through her purse and pulled out a citation. "This damn credit card company is trying to bankrupt me. I fell for their gimmick. Signed up for a credit card with a five-hundred-dollar limit. Times are tough, you know? Got a little behind on my payments. Next thing I know they've upped the interest to thirty-five percent and now they're penalizing me every month. On top of that they're calling me at all hours of the day and night. Can you believe that?"

Jack nodded solemnly. "Yes ma'am. I can. The government lets credit card companies get away with murder. How much do you owe now?"

Mona pitched the court papers on the table. "They say I owe twenty-nine hundred dollars and they want another thousand in attorney's fees. What's going wrong with this country? Can you do anything about it?"

Jack looked over the documents. "Yes, ma'am. While I can't do much about the country, I believe I can help you with the credit card company. I may even file a counterclaim and get you a few bucks."

Mona looked at Jack, suspicion in her eyes. "How much you gonna charge?"

"Not a thing, Mona. Didn't you see that sign in my window? My services are free." Jack pulled a document from a drawer and scribbled in a few blanks. "I'll need you to sign this to make it official."

Mona looked over the contract and back at Jack. "You sure, now?"

"Yes, ma'am. I'm sure. Now, tell me a little more about these calls, particularly the ones late at night."

27

Jack appeared in the county court at law, accompanied by his client, Mona Thomas Lee. Jack chose not to dress as a rich lawyer, not for this case. He found an old pair of brown trousers and an equally old brown tweed jacket. He carried a plain wooden cane. He talked Mona into wearing her Sunday-go-to-meeting clothes: a black dress that was a little too tight around the middle and black pumps. She took Jack's arm as they entered the courtroom. Among her kind nothing good ever came out of setting foot in court.

County courts in Texas rarely handled big litigation. Their bread and butter was an assortment of fender benders, foreclosures, homeowner disputes about loud neighbors and barking dogs, and these days credit card litigation where the bank usually just went through the motions to get a default judgment and then accelerated its harassment of the card-holder. The courtroom itself had seen better days. The walls were scratched. Before the days of metal detectors, some enterprising young men had carved initials and occasional profanity on the benches while they waited. Clifford Smith, the judge, had been on the bench for thirty years, not because he deserved it, but because no other lawyer in the county wanted the job.

The courtroom was packed as the judge monotoned his way through the docket, accepting agreements and entering default judgments. When he got to *Cowtown Financial Corporation v. Lee,* he called for announcements. A young lawyer from one of the major law firms rose and said he represented the plaintiff. They were ready for trial. Jack pushed himself up with his cane like he was a cripple and made the same announcement.

"What?" the judge asked. "You're going to try this case? Mr. Bryant,

I don't believe I've seen you in my court before. You've asked for a jury trial. You really believe there's a fact issue?"

"Yes, Your Honor. We believe as a matter of law that the bank's claim is frivolous and should be dismissed. However, we have a counterclaim that we believe a jury will find most interesting."

"Very well. You two lawyers go into the jury room and discuss this. Maybe you can find some middle ground, and we can avoid having to waste the time of six jurors for the afternoon."

Jack told Mona to remain where she was and limped toward the jury room with the young lawyer for the plaintiff not far behind. When the door was closed, Jack eased into a chair and laid his cane on the table. "Sorry, my lumbago is acting up. I didn't get your name."

The young lawyer sized up his opponent and figured that he occasionally found his way out of a bottle long enough to make a court appearance. "Name's Alfred, Alfred P. Goldenberg."

"Well, Alfred, what do you propose we do? I'm ready to go to trial."

"So am I, Mr. Bryant," Goldenberg said with a solemn face as if he tried cases every day instead of being sent to the courthouse to take defaults or cut the best deal he could. "I could waive my attorney's fees if we could work out a deal, maybe even a payment plan."

"Not interested," Jack said as he took his cane from the table and rose to his feet. "I've got a counterclaim that's pretty near a sure thing. Your bill collectors knew it was wrong to harass my client in the middle of the night. That's a violation of federal law."

Goldenberg's shoulders slumped slightly, but Jack noticed. "Come on, Mr. Bryant. Even if you get a verdict, you'll never make that stand up on appeal. My client says it didn't happen. You've sued for ten thousand dollars. I don't think you can prove Ms. Lee is out of pocket one red cent."

"As to the ten thousand dollars, you know I've also pled mental anguish and treble damages. That means that the jury can award my client the ten thousand, treble it, and then listen to what your client has put her through and treble those anguish damages. Fortunately for you, I can't get more than a hundred thousand in county court."

Alfred gulped. "So what do you want, Mr. Bryant?"

"Drop your case and pay my client twenty-five thousand, and I'll waive *my* attorney's fees."

Never faced with this kind of decision, Goldenberg excused himself to the hallway and called his boss. "Mary, is Herman around?"

Alfred explained the situation when Herman got on the phone.

"Horseshit," he said when Alfred finished. "Go try the case. By the way, who's defense counsel?"

"I know he's Jack Bryant. Hold on, sir. Let me look at the pleadings. Name's Jackson Douglas Bryant."

There was silence on the phone. Goldenberg asked, "Are you still there, sir?"

"What the fuck is Bryant doing in Fort Worth, and why's he defending some old black woman against our bank? Is he carrying a cane?"

"Yes, sir."

"It's him. That changes everything. I don't want you facing Bryant in your first case. You've got authority to meet his demand. Try to save a little off that twenty-five thousand."

Goldenberg clicked his cell phone off and returned to the jury room. "Look, Jack, I just talked to my boss. I can meet your demand, but I've got a personal favor to request."

Jack nodded.

"I'm already looking bad back at the firm. Could you consider just taking twenty thousand?"

Jack smiled. "I understand your predicament. Tell you what, I'll take twenty-two thousand five hundred. You can tell the client that you negotiated hard." Jack put his cane over his shoulder and walked to the door. "Let's go tell the judge we've got a deal."

Jack turned to leave the courtroom when he spotted Colby, seated in the back row. He motioned her to follow him into the hallway. "What are you doing here?"

"I just wanted to get an idea of how this pro bono stuff actually worked. Did you really get that woman twenty-two thousand five hundred dollars?"

Jack leaned on his cane. "Yep. Sure did and got the company to waive its claim on her credit card."

"And how much of that do you take?" Colby asked skeptically.

Jack looked a little offended. "Maybe you don't understand the meaning of pro bono. I helped her for free. I get nada, nothing. Didn't ask for anything and won't take anything from people like her."

Colby's skepticism turned to admiration. "Well, then," she said as she took his arm, "If you can direct me to a good shop around here, coffee's on me."

While they waited for the elevator, Colby thought, *Maybe this guy really is someone special.*

28

Colby signed in and walked down the hallway to the nursing station where she found a new nurse. "I'm Colby Stripling. Where's Irene? I thought she usually worked this shift?"

"Pleased to meet you, Ms. Stripling. I'm Jackie. Irene no longer works here."

"Had to do with patient care, didn't it? Decubitus ulcers, among other things, right?"

"I'm not allowed to discuss it." She pointed to Room 4. "Dr. Winston is in there right now."

Colby nodded and walked to the door, knocking quietly before she opened it.

Dr. Winston had the covers off the patient and was carefully evaluating him. "Ah, Colby, I'm glad you're here."

Colby nodded and walked over to stand beside the doctor.

"Look here, the ulcer is improving. I'm glad you caught it at stage two. These bastards can be damn near impossible to cure once they get to three or four."

Colby looked at the buttock. "It's certainly looking better. But, I'm still pissed off at this facility. I've made a lot of sacrifices and paid a lot of money to put him here. I told that attendant the day I discovered it that he'd be better off dead if this is the kind of care he is going to receive. She didn't seem to give a damn."

"Believe me, Colby, I'm extremely sorry about the problem. Once I looked into the situation, I made sure that Irene was terminated immediately. To say the least, she wasn't happy. Said she wouldn't be able to find another job," Dr. Winston added. "I'm afraid I must bear some of the responsibility. I can't tell you the number of meetings I've had with the staff about taking care of patients like this who can't care for themselves. I'm afraid it's the caliber of people they hire."

"I picked this place because it was supposedly the best in the area," Colby said as she sat down and buried her head in her hands. "I don't know what more I can do. Keeping him here is costing me five thousand dollars a month. I'm not sure how much longer I can afford it."

"I'm sorry, Colby," Dr. Winston said. He hesitated and then continued. "Maybe you just ought to let nature take its course. He's never going to get any better."

"You mean let him starve to death like Terri Schiavo? No," Colby sobbed. "I married him until death do us part. I'm still his wife, and I'm going to be faithful to him and care for him the best I can until God calls."

29

Boss didn't like it. Here he was at seven o'clock in the morning, parked in Billy Bob's parking lot at the stockyards. The lot was littered with trash and empty beer cans. A couple of pickups were parked across the way. Either their drivers were arrested or some friend had convinced them to leave the driving to someone else. *Shit,* he thought. *How the hell did I get myself into this mess? I've always been a law-abiding citizen, at least until now.* He kept his eyes rotating from the front to the side mirrors and the rear mirror, ready to leave if he saw anything even remotely suspicious. He even had a story for the cops, should one circle through the lot. He had just dropped off a friend who was too drunk to drive last night. The friend left just as he had to take a cell phone call. After fifteen minutes Boss was about ready to leave when he saw a horse and rider approaching from the south edge of the parking lot. As the rider got closer he recognized Hawk.

He waited until Hawk was at the driver's door before he lowered his window.

"Morning, Boss. Beautiful day, isn't it?"

"I don't really want to make small talk," Boss groused. "Why'd you pick this place anyway?"

Hawk grinned as he made a sweeping motion with his arm. "Why, this is my stomping ground, my home territory. I know everyone who works around here. Even the stockyard cops are my buddies. If they see us here, the cops will just wave at me and be on their way. By the way, your plan seems to be working pretty damn well. I haven't seen reports of any of our jobs in the *Star Telegram*. Nobody's connecting the dots. What do you have for me?"

"This one ought to be easy. Old man lives north of Denton. Likes to go fishing at a creek about a mile from his house most mornings when the weather's good. I figure that if he fell and hit his head on a rock, that would do him in."

"Look here, Bossman, I don't tell you how to do your job, and I don't need any advice from you about how to do mine. Understood?"

Boss nodded as he handed Hawk a piece of paper. "Here's what I know about him. Oh, and your fee is forty grand. Should be easy money."

Hawk tipped his hat as Boss drove away.

30

The old black man used a cane pole and worms to fish. He had grown up fishing that way. Caught a lot of fish over the years and never saw a reason to try a rod and reel. He left his house just before dawn on his fishing days, usually four or five of them a week. He always quietly shut the door so as not to awaken his wife. He put his pole, a bucket full of dirt and worms and a small tackle box containing hooks, line and a few bobbers in the back of a pickup that was so old that it had fenders. She might be old, he told his friends, but she still runs good. All he had to do was change the oil and replace the sparks plugs every so often. He figured that she would last at least as long as he did, maybe longer.

He and his wife lived on a county dirt road in the same house where they had raised three kids. He had a few acres that he farmed every spring. The beans, potatoes, corn, and other vegetables helped stretch the Social Security check that they lived on. Other than grandkids, fishing, and church he had no other hobbies or interests. Well, he did drive into Fort Worth a couple of days a week to have a beer and play dominoes with some of his old cronies.

The old man turned onto the dirt road and drove five miles. He passed a couple of other pickups and waved at neighbors who were accustomed to seeing him at this time of morning. When he got to an old wooden bridge, he pulled off the road. He took his pole and the small tackle box with his right hand and grabbed the worm bucket with his left. He carefully stepped down an incline and crossed the bar ditch to a path that ran along the creek. His favorite spot was about a hundred yards away. The water there formed a small rapid as it flowed over rocks and then pooled. It was in the pool where he usually caught some very fine bass.

When he got to the pool, he had to step over the rocks to get to the other side where he sat his tackle box and bucket on a flat rock and unwound the line from around his pole. Setting down his pole, he opened the bucket and fished around in the dirt with his hand until he found a worm that tried to wriggle away as he pulled it from the bucket. *Nice, big fat one,* he thought. *Oughta catch me a big fat bass.* He baited the hook and measured the distance to the bobber. Five feet. Just right. With that he pitched the worm and bobber out into the water. Once he was satisfied that the location was a good one, he sat down on the flat rock in the shade of a live oak and stared at the bobber as he enjoyed the sounds of two mockingbirds talking with one another.

He was startled by the crack of a branch behind him. He looked around and saw nothing, deciding that it must have been a branch falling from a tree.

Fifteen minutes later Hawk walked up behind his target, making no sound. He had a big rock, weighing about ten pounds, which he held in both hands and slowly raised. Then he crashed it down onto his victim's head. The old man dropped his pole and fell to his side, blood oozing from his scalp, ears, nose and mouth. Hawk waited for a minute and then felt for a pulse. Nothing.

Hawk picked the old man up and tossed him into the water. Then he carefully scooped up all of the dirt and blood from where his head had lain moments before. That went into the water too. Satisfying himself that it would appear that the old man had slipped on a rock, Hawk backtracked, taking pains to brush his footsteps with a pine bough. As he got to his pickup he thought, *Boss actually had a pretty good idea.*

31

Dwayne Allison had spreadsheets scattered about his desk and a table in his office. Once again he was facing a decision to close more dealerships, hopefully no more than three this time. And he hoped they would be the last. He despised having to put more people out of work, but he had to reduce overhead. After anguishing over the decision all morning, he picked two small-town Chrysler stores and one Chevrolet dealership on the east side of Dallas.

"Mr. Allison," his secretary called through the intercom, "Mr. Quillen is calling. Can you talk to him?"

Allison had actually avoided talking to Quillen for several weeks. Now he figured the son of a bitch was calling about wanting more payments on his loans. He sighed as he leaned back in his chair. "Put him through."

"Dwayne, Beau Quillen here. How are those quarter horses of yours doing?"

"Fine, Beau. Your wife and grandkids doing well?"

"Glad you asked," Quillen said. "Just got another one. That makes six. Dwayne, this is not about business. Shady Oaks has a members-only best ball tournament this Saturday. I figure that two old farts with high handicaps like us might have a shot. You want to be my partner?"

Allison considered the options. He was pissed at Quillen. Still, it was best to stay on good terms with your banker. "You're on. I hope your putter's hot."

The tournament was a shotgun start at 9:00 a.m. Allison caught up with Quillen on the driving range. "Morning, Beau."

"Dwayne, good to see you," Beau said as he extended his hand. "We're paired with a couple of new flat-bellied members. Take a few swings, but don't use up all of your good shots on the range."

Allison nodded as he went through his stretching routine and then selected a seven iron. After a couple of slices he settled down and started hitting them down the middle about 165 yards. "That's enough. I see we're starting on number ten."

The men went to their cart, drove to the tenth tee, and introduced themselves to their playing partners.

After the two young guys had powered their drives 265 yards, Allison stepped to the tee and drove one about 210 yards right down the middle. Quillen put his ten yards farther out. After seven holes the two older men were playing close to their handicaps and were hoping for at least a small trophy. On the par-five seventeenth hole Allison and Quillen hit their second shots and then drove down the cart path while the two other men stood on the fairway, sizing up the water on the right and sand traps on the left.

Out of earshot from the others, Quillen said, "Dwayne, I want to tell you I really appreciate what you've done over the last several months to catch up some of that back interest. Makes me breathe a lot easier if I can show the examiners you're making progress."

Allison offered Quillen a cigar and lighted both. They puffed their cigars to make sure they were sufficiently lit. Allison lowered his voice. "Beau, I don't know what's going on. All of a sudden a bunch of my former employees have kicked the bucket. I suppose they're just getting old, but I'm damn sure glad I kept paying those life insurance premiums."

Quillen nodded his agreement as he exhaled cigar smoke. "If they're going to die, let's just hope the deaths are accidental and not a damn heart attack or stroke. That double indemnity is good for both of us."

32

Jack put on a dark suit and tie. On the way out he told Lisa that he'd be gone most of the day. When he stepped out the back door he saw thunderclouds forming overhead and felt a slight chill in the air. *Fitting day for a funeral,* he thought. He punched in the code for the Hummer, and the garage door opened. He circled around Rivercrest and soon was headed downtown and out North Main to the icehouse.

Jack glanced over to his RV to determine that it was secure as he turned into the icehouse parking lot where several of the regulars were milling around, awaiting his arrival. Moe was in the process of taping a sign to the front. CLOSED FOR FUNERAL.

Jack greeted his friends, some dressed in suits, others in clean jeans and white shirts. Moe got in the passenger seat and the others piled in the backseats. It was a solemn occasion and little was said on the drive to north Denton County. Jack commented on the thunderstorms as they made their way over to I-35. Silence. Moe mentioned that the Cowboys were probably going to lose again on Sunday. More silence, punctuated only by the GPS voice giving them directions to the Greater Mt. Zion Baptist Church. The men were lost in thought about Willie Davis and his sudden death. He had been in the icehouse playing dominoes only three days before. Now he was gone. The GPS directed them north on I-35 to Denton where they went west on a two-lane road. They wound farther back into the hills and were on a gravel road when Moe spotted the church up ahead on the right.

It was a small white frame structure in need of paint, with a gravel parking lot in front and a small cemetery in back. Jack noticed dirt piled at the edge of the cemetery, almost surely dug to make the final resting place of Willie Davis. There were a few cars and pickups parked in front but no people. Jack glanced at the dashboard clock and realized they were late. He parked the Hummer and checked the clouds as they exited, hoping that the rain would hold off for another hour.

When they entered, the preacher was standing at the pulpit, saying the opening prayer. The men waited with bowed heads until he was finished and then took seats in the back two rows. The small church was about half-filled. Other than his group he saw only one other white person. It was a woman, seated in the second row behind the family. Jack studied her for a moment before realizing that it was Colby. *What's she doing here? Did she somehow know Willie, too?*

His thoughts were interrupted by a woman at the piano who started singing a solo, "The Lord's Prayer."

When she was finished, the preacher returned to the podium. "Thank you, Sister Mary, for that fine solo." He looked at a black woman, who had to be Willie's widow, seated with family members on the front row. He nodded to her. "Ladies and gentlemen, June, we come here today not to mourn the loss of Willie Davis, but to celebrate his life . . ."

He was interrupted by a wail from the front row. June Davis couldn't hold it back. She and Willie had been married for over fifty years. In her mind, there was nothing to celebrate. It was her loss. Her two daughters joined in the wailing. Her son, a large man in a pressed blue shirt and black slacks, put his arm around his mother and tried to console her. Colby reached over the pew and patted her back. The preacher waited until her wailing became a whimper.

The preacher talked about what a fine man Willie had been, how he had been a devoted husband and with June had raised three fine children, also members of the church. They gave Willie and June six grandchildren who were seated in the second row beside Colby. June's crying grew louder as she again realized that her grandchildren would never see Willie again. The preacher tried to speak over her. Finally, he decided to move on. "Now, Willie, Jr., would like to say a few words about his dad."

The big man rose and lumbered to the pulpit. His head was down and he spoke staring at the floor. His voice was soft. "He, he was my dad. He taught me to play baseball. We hunted and fished together. He spanked my butt when I stepped out of line." The audience was glad to have a moment of levity and laughed politely. "That's about all I've got to say. He was my dad and I'll miss him." Then Willie, Jr. lost it, and he burst into tears as he returned to his seat.

The preacher announced they would all sing "Amazing Grace" and he would say a final prayer before going out to the cemetery for the burial. Sister Mary returned to the piano and everyone rose to sing. As they finished, there was lightning followed by a clap of thunder. The preacher hurried through the final prayer and six pallbearers rose as one to carry the casket through the front door and out to the cemetery. Jack stood on the aisle as they passed, followed by the family and the rest of the congregation. When Colby saw him, she whispered, "What are you doing here?"

With thunder rolling in the west, the mourners gathered around the burial plot. The preacher told the pallbearers just to hold the casket while he said another few words, ending by saying that Willie was now in a better place. June burst out in wailing again as the pallbearers lowered the casket. The preacher said one more prayer and the congregation dispersed, leaving two of the pallbearers to take shovels and cover the casket with dirt.

Jack caught up to Colby. "Willie was a friend of mine. We played dominoes at the icehouse. Follow us over there. We're having a small wake in Willie's memory."

Colby nodded her agreement as the rain began to fall. Jack escorted her to her Lexus and joined his friends at the Hummer, getting in just as the deluge came.

33

The clouds were covering all of North Texas. If anything, it was raining harder at Moe's. Jack dropped his passengers at the icehouse and parked beside his RV where he went inside to find an umbrella. Then he joined the other men as Moe opened the garage doors. When Colby pulled into Moe's parking lot, Jack rushed to her car with the umbrella, shielding her from the rain as they hurried inside. He saw that she too had been crying and hugged her. When she said she was okay, they joined the men at the domino table.

Moe had purchased bottles of Wild Turkey, Johnny Walker and Tito's for the occasion. He set them on the bar with glasses and ice, inviting his guests to help themselves. One by one the men walked to the bar, most of them opting for their usual beer. Jack poured two Tito's over rocks and handed one to Colby. Colby took a large swallow and let out a sigh.

"I must say I was surprised to find you in a little country church for a funeral today. I started to call you this morning and decided just to leave you to your business until I got back," Jack said. "How did you know Willie?"

Colby took another sip of her vodka. "When I graduated from TCU, my first job was with Allison Southwest, the big mega car dealer in this part of the country. It's owned by Dwayne Allison. He's a pretty big cheese around here. You've probably seen him in the *Star Telegram* or on the news at some civic event."

Jack nodded.

"Within a couple of years I was finance manager of the biggest Cadillac dealership in the metroplex. Three years later I was managing the finance department for five dealerships with a staff of fifty working under me."

"But, what does that have to do with Willie?"

"Willie worked for the dealership, too. Can you refill my glass?"

Jack returned to the bar, freshened both their drinks and handed Colby's to her.

"Willie was a porter at the Cadillac store. Whatever broke he fixed. He treated me like his daughter. Several times a day, he would appear in front of my desk, a big smile on his face, just checking to see if I needed anything. He retired about fifteen years ago. June cleaned houses. She started taking care of mine right after I went to work. She came once a week for ten years or so. They're good people. I know all the kids and grandkids, too. I was one of the few white faces at their weddings in that little church." Colby teared up. "I'm sorry. I'll miss Willie, and I'm worried about June." Composing herself, she asked, "So, did Willie beat you at dominoes?"

"Are you kidding?" Jack grinned. "When I walked in here and saw Willie playing, I knew I was going to lose a couple of bucks."

Moe pulled a chair up to the table. "I don't know how it could have happened."

"What's that, Moe?" Jack asked.

"How Willie could have slipped and hit his head on a rock bad enough that he died, and no one found him until almost sundown. Willie had been fishing that creek since he was a kid. He may have been getting on in years, but he was alert and agile. Just don't make no sense."

"Miss Colby?" Colby looked across the table to Jefferson Compton, a small, wizened black man who was quietly drinking a beer.

"Sorry, Jefferson. I didn't mean to ignore you."

"That's all right, ma'am. I just want to say this. Your Jack is a blessing. All of us folks have got financial woes these days. He's helped me and practically everyone I know."

"Thank you, Jefferson. He's not my Jack, but I'm learning that he's really a good man." Colby looked at Jack and squeezed his hand. Her gaze led to the Lone Star Beer clock on the wall. "Oh my God, I'm late. I've got to get out of here."

"Colby, it's still raining cats and dogs. Nobody's going to be looking at houses in this storm."

Colby shook her head. "Sorry. I've got to go." Colby pushed back her chair and was out the door before Jack could even hand her his umbrella.

Enough of this strange behavior, Jack thought. *Colby won't like it if she catches me following her.* At least he was in his Hummer, which didn't stand out quite as much as Lucille.

34

Jack dropped three twenties on the table and said he had to be going, too. He ran to his Hummer and pitched the umbrella in the backseat. Pulling out of the parking lot, he had to turn on his lights. He could barely make out what he thought were the taillights of Colby's Lexus heading south on Main and going up the bridge over the Trinity. Jack accelerated until he closed the gap to two blocks. He was thankful for the storm since there was no way Colby could spot anything but headlights in her rearview mirror. He prayed the storm would continue until she got to wherever she was going.

Soon she was going through town and out Seventh Street; then she continued on Camp Bowie when the streets intersected at the Museum District. She passed the Starbucks where they first had coffee, and Jack concluded that she must have an appointment at her office. Then she passed it by. In Ridglea she pulled into a left-turn lane at a light. Jack looked for somewhere to hide and drove into a shopping center parking lot a block behind her. When the light turned to green, Colby turned and Jack left the parking lot, trying to make the turn before the light changed. He was too late.

Jack was trapped at the light with cars already moving east. "Shit!," he said, pounding the steering wheel. All he could do was wait. When the signal turned green again, Colby had disappeared. He passed the shopping center and wound through an upscale neighborhood until he came to a golf course. With Colby's Lexus nowhere in sight, he mentally flipped a coin and turned right, looking through the storm for Colby's car and hoping she wouldn't spot him.

There it was. The Lexus was in an almost deserted parking lot in front of the Ridglea Oaks Nursing Home. Jack drove slowly by. *What the hell is going on? Colby's never talked about having a relative in a nursing home. She told me that both of her parents died several years ago. Is this a friend?* Jack thought through all of the options and struck out. He drove slowly up the street until he thought it was safe to park and watched his rearview mirror. Half an hour later Colby left the nursing home and turned back in the direction of Camp Bowie.

Now what do I do? Jack thought. The only idea that came to mind was flowers. He drove a block to the next intersection and made a U-turn. Back on Camp Bowie he searched until he spotted a flower shop. Flowers were not something that often entered Jack's life. In fact, his best recollection was that he had ordered some for his mother's birthday before she died, probably fifteen years ago. Otherwise, he always had a secretary to handle such chores. Still he popped the umbrella and entered the shop.

"I'd like to buy a dozen roses in a vase."

"What color, sir?" The girl at the counter asked.

Jack looked in the refrigerated case. "Red will do just fine."

Five minutes later Jack was back in his Hummer. He parked in the nursing home lot and was about to get out when he realized he was still wearing a coat and tie. *That won't do,* he thought. He stripped them off and stepped into what was now a slow drizzle. He opened the door to the nursing home and walked to the reception desk.

"Evening, ma'am. I've got this delivery for . . ." Jack looked among the roses. "Darn it. Looks like they forgot to put the card with the flowers back at the shop. Can I put these down here on your desk?"

The receptionist nodded. "You'll need to sign the visitor log. You must be new to this job."

"Yes, ma'am. Third day." Jack signed the log and fumbled in his pockets until he pulled out the receipt he had received when he bought the flowers. "Here, maybe this will help. These were ordered by someone named Stripling in Toledo, Ohio. You have someone by that name here?"

"No, sir. We don't. Now, Ms. Colby Stripling comes here once or twice a week to see her husband; only, he's got a different name."

Jack was stunned and could only stare at the woman behind the desk. *Colby's married and hasn't told me. What the hell?*

"Sir," the receptionist said, drawing Jack's attention.

"That must be him," Jack finally said. "Can I take these to his room?"

"Won't do him any good."

"I don't understand."

"He's been in a coma for ten years or so. He won't even know they're in his room."

Jack stumbled for words. "Well, then, why don't I just leave them on your desk for you and the other guests to enjoy?"

The receptionist nodded her agreement. Jack turned and rushed out the door. When he got to the Hummer, he sat quietly for about fifteen minutes, pondering what he had learned and what to do about it. Now he had some answers about Colby, but he also had just as many new questions. Finally he concluded that confronting her would be the worst possible move. He would keep what he knew to himself and be attentive to Colby. He would continue to be her best friend. Eventually, she would tell him about her husband.

35

TCU ended up losing one game that season and was selected to play Florida State in the Sugar Bowl. It wasn't for the national championship, but it was an acceptable consolation prize. J.D. became a starter in the third game and was the first freshman all-conference tight end in decades. Sportswriters were already touting him as an all-American next season.

Jack got on the phone as soon as the announcement was made. The first call was to a ticket scalper who charged him five thousand dollars for two seats on the fifty-yard line. His next call was to a plaintiff lawyer friend in the Big Easy who wrangled a suite at the Royal Sonesta Hotel in the French Quarter, three-night minimum, of course. He managed to get reservations at Emeril's New Orleans the night before the game and Brennan's after the game. The Brennan's reservation was for six since he hoped that J.D., Samuel—TCU's quarterback and J.D.'s best friend—and their dates would join them. The last series of calls were to limo services until he found a company that still had one available.

On the day before the game Jack picked Colby up at her house at noon for a two o'clock flight. They turned their bags over to a skycap and then found a parking place close to the terminal. With first-class tickets they took the shorter line through security. Once in the air, Jack ordered black coffee and sipped it while Colby snuggled against his shoulder and dropped off to sleep. When they got to the baggage area, they saw several limo drivers holding signs. One said JACKSON BRYANT.

"You didn't tell me we were going by limo." Colby grinned.

"I've got him for the whole trip. We won't need him much, but I didn't want to fight the Sugar Bowl traffic."

Jack walked up to the uniformed black man holding the sign and stuck out his hand. "Jack Bryant."

The chauffeur took his hand. "Johnson Bowles. Pleased to meet you. Is this Mrs. Bryant?"

Colby also stuck out her hand. "Colby Stripling. I'm not his missus, just a friend."

Jack pointed out their bags as they appeared. Johnson grabbed the bags and escorted them to his Lincoln limousine, parked at the curb.

Thirty minutes later they stopped in front of the Royal Sonesta. The doorman assisted Colby out. Jack waved him off as Johnson retrieved their bags from the trunk.

"Welcome to the Royal Sonesta. You folks here for the Sugar Bowl?"

"You bet," Jack replied. "Horned Frogs are gonna send the Gators back to the swamp."

After checking in, the bellman led them to the elevator and punched the button for the third floor. They went to the end of the hall where he opened the door and stepped back to allow the couple to enter.

"As requested," Jack said. "A suite with separate bedrooms. We'll meet only in the living room. And for good measure, your room has a lock on the door."

Colby kissed Jack on the cheek. "Jack, you're sweet, but I'm sure that won't be necessary."

The living room had a chandelier that looked like it belonged in the entry hall of a plantation. The center of the white marble floor was covered by an oriental rug. The French doors to the balcony were framed in drapes of green and rose. Colby threw open one of the doors while the bellman brought their bags.

"Jack, this is a corner room." They stepped out onto the balcony. "Look, there's Bourbon Street. We can sit up here and watch all the action tonight. You think someone will ask me to show them my boobs?"

"Damn right they will. One look at you peering over the balcony will draw a crowd."

"Can I do it?"

"Depends, I guess, on how many beads they'll throw up here."

"I'm just teasing. Go tip our bellman."

"Now, I do have a very special set of beads, purchased just for this occasion." Jack opened his bag and handed Colby a small black velvet box with a white ribbon. Colby's eyes sparkled like a kid at Christmas as she carefully removed the bow and opened the box.

"Mikimoto pearls. Jack you shouldn't have." Colby's demeanor changed. "Maybe I shouldn't accept these. Look, Jack, you know how fond I am of you, but I don't want you to think this is a date that will lead to something else."

Jack folded his arms. "Colby, I've told you I understand the boundaries of our relationship. I'm not trying to change them. Just do me a favor and take the pearls."

Colby smiled as she walked to the mirror and clasped the pearls around her neck. Turning to Jack, she said, "Maybe one of these days our relationship will change, just not now."

Jack looked at his watch. "We've got time for a nap before dinner, in our separate bedrooms, of course." Jack took Colby's bag to her room. "Sleep tight," he said as he closed her door and walked across the living room to his bedroom.

Colby unpacked her bag and hung her clothes in the closet. She stripped down to her panties and bra and studied herself in the mirror. Then the bra and panties were on the floor and she was looking at her nude body, adorned only with Mikimoto pearls. She rubbed her hands down her body to her hips and next caressed her breast until the nipples rose. *Maybe it's time,* she thought. *It's been ten years since I've been with a man.* She turned and slowly walked to the door, put her hand on the knob, and hesitated. She opened it just a crack when a blank look came over her face. Colby quietly closed the door and crawled into bed, her mind overflowing with confusing thoughts.

Jack put on white pants, a white shirt and a new purple blazer with the Sugar Bowl insignia on the breast pocket, bought just for the occasion. No one would mistake him for a Gator fan. He crossed the living room and knocked quietly on Colby's door. "Time to wake up. There'll be a martini on the bar for you. I'll be out on the balcony."

Colby murmured she would join him in a few minutes. He stepped out onto the balcony into a crisp evening and pulled two wrought iron chairs to the rail to watch the partyers already filling the street below.

Fifteen minutes later Colby joined him on the balcony, martini in hand. She was wearing a purple cocktail dress with the front cut low enough to reveal cleavage below the pearls. "Like my new dress?"

"Sweetie, with that dress and your figure, you're either gonna stop traffic or cause accidents when the male drivers can't take their eyes off of you. Have a seat. We've got a few minutes. By the way, we're hoofing it to Emeril's. It's only a few blocks. In fact, I told Johnson that we wouldn't need him until the game tomorrow night."

After they finished their drinks, Colby draped a white shawl around her shoulders to ward off the night air, and they took the elevator down to the first floor. When they stepped out, there was a white horse-drawn carriage, pulled by a giant white Percheron at the curb. The driver was dressed in a white tuxedo and matching top hat.

"Oh, Jack, isn't that beautiful. Can we ride in one of those before we leave?"

"How about right now?" Jack walked up to the driver and shook his hand. "Evening. I'm Jack Bryant."

"Good evening, Mr. Bryant. We've been waiting for you."

Colby looked at Jack with amazement in her eyes. "Now I understand what you meant about hoofing it. You're just full of surprises, aren't you, Jackson Douglas?"

Jack only smiled as the driver assisted Colby into the carriage.

36

The next day Jack and Colby played tourist. They started with breakfast at Brennan's even though they had reservations there that night. They walked the French Quarter, stopping in antique shops and art galleries. Colby insisted on going into a voodoo shop where she bought a doll, wrote "Gators" on it and, with a gleam in her eye, drove a hat pin through the belly. At five o'clock that evening, Johnson was waiting at the hotel with the back door of the limousine open. In honor of his guests he was wearing a purple TCU baseball cap. When they arrived at the Superdome, Johnson dropped them in a passenger zone, and said he was going to drive a few blocks away to watch the game on the television in the backseat. He would return toward the end of the fourth quarter.

TCU fans had gathered at the side of the stadium, using the back of a pickup for a podium. When Jack and Colby got close, they could hear someone introduce Bob Lilly, the TCU all-American from the fifties and later all-pro lineman for the Dallas Cowboys. He talked about the history of Frog football, starting with the golden years of Sammy Baugh and later Davey O'Brien. He played in the era of the Southwest Conference when Coach Abe Martin usually won the conference and a Cotton Bowl berth about every four years. Then came the dry years and the

Frogs wandered through the backwaters of major college football until Gary Patterson became head coach. He got a commitment from the school administration to turn TCU into a major power and rewarded their decision with a dozen years of steady progress toward the top of Division I. The pep rally ended with the TCU fight song.

After pregame festivities, the game started promptly at six o'clock, the time dictated by the network. It was a high-scoring, offensive battle. Fortunately, on this night Samuel had a hot hand. In the second quarter, TCU was on its forty. In the huddle J.D. said, "Samuel, they're laying back on me. I'm going to drop back like I'm going to block for you. Then, I'll drift over to the right flat. If I'm right, there won't be any defender within twenty yards."

Samuel nodded and broke the huddle. When he took the snap, he dropped back two steps and intentionally looked to his left. Just as a defender was about to hit him, he turned to his right and tossed the ball to J.D. Samuel sidestepped the tackler and did the unexpected. As J.D. caught the ball, Samuel ran into the defense and led J.D. up the field. When he laid the safety on his ass, the purple crowd cheered as J.D. flew down the sideline to the goal. At halftime Coach Patterson chewed out his quarterback.

"Dammit, Samuel. You scared the piss out of me. I have ten guys that can block, but only one that can throw."

Samuel nodded solemnly and broke into a grin as he walked to the bench where J.D. was sitting and high-fived him. He threw five touchdown passes, one more to J.D. in the second half. The game ended with a Horned Frogs victory, 48–38. Jack and Colby were so hoarse afterwards that they could barely speak. They found Johnson in the passenger loading zone and told him to wait while they made their way through the crowd to the TCU dressing room.

A throng of people was waiting for the players to exit. Other fans shook Jack's hand and patted him on the back. He declined an interview by a reporter, saying that he was only J.D.'s father. Jack spotted

Tanya, J.D.'s girlfriend. Tanya was a sophomore computer major, five feet ten inches tall with flowing blond hair and the figure of the varsity volleyball player that she was. She was with Samuel's girlfriend, Trish, an equally beautiful African American woman. Jack waved them over and hugs were exchanged.

After an hour the players started filtering out, greeted by cheers from their fans. The biggest cheers came as J.D. and Samuel appeared together. The media surrounded them, insisting on comments. J.D. had learned how to play this media game. He sung the praises of the offensive line and his quarterback. He touted Samuel for all-American next year, saying that his job was pretty easy. He just had to run the route and he knew the ball was going to be there. Finally, they motioned with their hands that interviews were over and made their way to Jack and the others. Jack gave his son a hug and congratulations. J.D. kissed Tanya and hugged Colby. Samuel accepted congratulations, and they walked to the limo. When they got there, they introduced Johnson, who insisted that both players sign his hat.

J.D. took in the interior of the limo and said, "Nice ride, Dad. After this season if I pull a four point next spring, can I have one of these? We'll just move Johnson to Fort Worth."

"Nice try, kid. Your pickup ought to last another three years and then I suspect you can afford to buy about any ride you choose."

"Excuse me, Mr. Bryant, is it okay if I call my parents while we're driving?" Samuel asked. Samuel's parents lived in the northeast and couldn't make it down for the game. They actually couldn't afford the airfare and jacked-up hotel prices, but Samuel told everyone that they didn't want to fight the crowds.

"Sure, Samuel. Tell them we're proud of you."

After dinner, Jack told Johnson to take his guests back to their hotels while he and Colby walked Bourbon Street back to the Royal Sonesta. Jack gave his son one more hug and waved as the limo pulled into the traffic.

Jack and Colby flowed with the crowd. Of course, they didn't have any choice as Bourbon Street was wall to wall with revelers, most of them drunk or close to it.

"Wow," Colby said, "you'd think this was Mardi Gras."

"New Orleans doesn't need much of an excuse for a party. The Sugar Bowl is second only to Mardi Gras, except for the year the Saints won the Super Bowl."

They paused at a balcony where a crowd had assembled. The men were shouting, "Show us your titties," and tossing beads up to two coeds leaning over the balcony. Finally, the two girls looked at each other and pulled their sweaters up. The crowd cheered like TCU had just scored a touchdown.

As they neared the hotel, Jack noticed Colby was glancing over her shoulder. "What are you looking at?"

"There's a man who has been about ten feet behind us ever since we left the restaurant. When we stop, he stops."

Jack turned and looked, spotting a large man with long brown hair and a beard. He was wearing glasses. When he saw Jack, he turned to look in the door of a topless bar. "It's just a coincidence," Jack said.

"Still, he gives me the creeps. Let's get to the hotel."

They picked up their pace, dodging revelers until they reached the Royal Sonesta. Colby breathed a sigh of relief as the doorman greeted them with a smile and opened the hotel door.

37

They ordered room service for breakfast the next day and discussed what to do before they caught the late afternoon flight back to Fort Worth.

"I know," Colby said. "Let's take a ride on the Natchez."

The Natchez was the steam-powered paddleboat that docked at Jackson Square. It went out several times a day to take tourists along the Mississippi River to the south and back up the river for a two-hour ride. Jack nodded his agreement and called the concierge to reserve two tickets for the eleven o'clock departure.

When they arrived at Jackson Square, they found a crowd along with street vendors and performers. They paused to watch a mime go through his routine, bringing laughter to adults and children alike. Jack glanced at his watch and motioned toward the Natchez. They joined a large group walking on the levy along the Mississippi until Colby walked to the edge where there was no barricade to block her view and marveled at the vastness of the river as the crowd passed behind them.

Jack pointed down. "Look at how swift the current is. It must pick up speed as it approaches the Gulf."

They heard a noise behind them and someone saying, "Watch it, buddy." Then Colby felt a shove in the back, and she went flying over the levy down to the river thirty feet below. "Oh my God!" someone screamed.

Jack saw Colby hit the water head first and instantly knew that the force of the impact may have knocked her out. He kicked off his shoes and jumped in after her, waving his arms and trying to maintain his balance to hit the water feet first. Even feet first, the fall took his breath away as he descended somewhere between ten and fifteen feet. He looked through the murky water for Colby, not even noticing how cold it was. When he thought his lungs were going to rupture, he had no choice but to rise to the surface where he gulped a breath and looked around to see if Colby had surfaced. She hadn't.

He took another breath and dived under again, this time swimming with the current. He saw an object in the distance and swam as fast as he could toward it. When he got close, he recognized it was Colby, face down and obviously unconscious. He swam to her, put his arm around her chest and kicked for the surface. *Come on, baby. Hang in there.* He broke the surface and gulped air again. The crowd on the levy cheered. Jack looked at Colby. She didn't appear to be breathing. The current had carried them toward the Natchez, and Jack kicked his legs, using his left arm to sidestroke toward it. When they got close, one crew member tossed Jack a buoy while another lowered a rope ladder. Jack grabbed the buoy and the crew member quickly pulled them to the side of the boat. The other had stepped down the ladder and extended his hand.

"Give her to me."

Jack pushed Colby to him. He grabbed Colby around the chest and pulled while Jack pushed on her butt. As soon as she cleared the edge of the boat Jack clambered up the ladder. The crew members were putting her on her stomach until Jack interrupted.

"No. Do it this way." He flipped her to her back and alternated between mouth-to-mouth and chest compressions. "Come on, Colby, breathe. Breathe, dammit!"

It seemed like minutes went by but it was only seconds before Colby coughed. Jack turned her head to the side and she vomited, then coughed again.

"Go ahead. Get it all out."

Colby blinked open her eyes and looked at Jack. She managed a smile. Between coughs she asked, "Were you the one who pulled me out of the river?"

"At your service, ma'am."

A crowd had gathered as the boat was filling with tourists. Naturally, they all wanted to see what had happened to the woman who fell in the river. The crew kept them back a safe distance until an older man broke to the front.

"Stop, sir."

He was waving Jack's shoes and cane.

"Let him through," Jack said.

The man was breathing hard and red-faced. Jack wondered if he was about to have a heart attack. He handed Jack his shoes and cane and bent over at the knees. When he straightened up, he was breathing more slowly. "I saw what happened. I saw him."

"Go on," Jack said.

"This guy was stumbling around and bumping through the crowd carrying a half-full Hurricane glass, acting like he was drunk. When he saw your wife, he moved toward her and pretended to lurch against her." The man's eyes narrowed. "He was just faking everything. That wasn't no accident. As soon as she went over the edge, he turned and hurried back through the crowd, only this time he didn't appear to be drunk. I think he did it on purpose."

Jack had raised Colby to a sitting position and was supporting her back. She asked, "You get a look at him?"

"Yes, ma'am. Big guy, long brown hair, beard, wearing glasses, jeans, and a Saints T-shirt. Looked like he might be a bodybuilder."

Two EMTs broke through the crowd. "Ma'am, my name's Andrew. First here's a blanket for each of you." He wrapped a silver thermal blanket around Colby and handed one to Jack. "I need to check you over."

Colby nodded as he kneeled beside her and pressed his stethoscope on the front of her chest and then the back. Then he took her pulse while he checked his watch. He flashed a light into her eyes and ears. "Can you understand what I'm saying?"

"It would be better if you spoke English instead of Chinese," Colby said. "I'm just kidding."

"How many fingers am I holding up?"

"Three, and I don't see a wedding ring on that left ring finger. Why's a cute guy like you wandering around New Orleans still single?"

Andrew looked at Jack. "I heard what you did. That was both brave and foolish. We could just have easily been dredging the river, looking for both your bodies. There are some undertows out there that can suck you clean to the bottom and not spit you out until the river hits the Gulf."

"Sometimes you just do what you gotta do." Jack shrugged.

"We're going to take her to the hospital. She should be fine, but we need to keep her overnight just for observation."

"I'm not spending the night in any damn hospital," Colby said as firmly as she could.

Jack looked at the determination in her eyes. "Tell you what. You guys take us in your ambulance back to the Royal Sonesta. We were going back to Fort Worth today, but we'll stay the night. I'll be with her the whole time. I had a little medical training in the army. If I see any problem, I'll call the emergency room."

Colby nodded her agreement.

Andrew shook his head. "That's not our protocol, but I can't make anyone go to the hospital."

Jack was already helping Colby to her feet. The crowd started applauding and then erupted into cheers as they passed. Andrew helped Colby into the back of the ambulance where she insisted on sitting rather than lying on the gurney. Jack sat beside her with Andrew facing them. Two minutes later they stopped in front of the hotel. Jack thanked the two EMTs. Andrew gave him a card and asked Jack to call if he could do anything.

As Jack turned away, Andrew called, "Oh, Mr. Bryant, after what that tourist said, I'm reporting this to the police. I've got the guy's cell number. You'll get a call this afternoon. I'll ask them to wait a few hours to give you two a chance to rest. That guy is long gone by now anyway."

Jack nodded. The doorman took one look at the ambulance and the condition of his two guests and called for a wheelchair. When a bellman pushed it out the door, Colby shook her head. "I think I can stand in the elevator just fine, thank you very much."

Colby took Jack's hand and they walked through the lobby. The concierge nodded to a bellman who called housekeeping to mop up behind them. When they got to their suite, Colby collapsed on her bed.

"Not so fast," Jack said. "We have to get you out of those wet clothes. When you wake up, maybe you'll feel like a shower."

Jack allowed Colby to sit on the edge of the bed while he took off her shoes, pants, and blouse. "When nothing remained but her bra and panties, he pulled her to her feet and dried her with a towel. Jack was contemplating what to do next when Colby smiled and said, "Turn around and don't peek."

Colby stripped off her bra and panties and crawled under the covers. Instantly, she was asleep. Jack pulled a chair up beside the bed so he could watch her. He didn't read. He didn't turn on the television. He didn't move except to strip off his own wet clothing and put on a hotel robe. Three hours later Colby stirred, then opened her eyes. "Hi, handsome. How's my hero?"

"The question is how are you?"

"Considering all I've been through, I'd say I'm doing pretty damn good."

Colby started to push herself to a sitting position. Jack grabbed several pillows to place behind her back.

"Tell me what happened," Colby said.

Jack explained the events of the morning, including the tourist's description of the man who bumped into her. Colby's eyes got big.

"Jack, that's the man I saw last night, the one I said was following us." She paused and stared at the opposite wall. "He was trying to kill me." Colby's voice quivered as she finished. "Why? Why would anyone want me dead?"

"Let's don't jump to conclusions."

"I'm not jumping to any conclusions. That's the only one we can draw. The question is why?"

Jack shook his head. "I'm still not sure. The police are supposed to be calling any time now. I'll report what happened, but don't expect a miracle." Jack handed Colby a robe and helped her to the shower, returning to the bedroom as the phone rang. Colby completed her shower and came out with a towel around her head. "Okay, I'm going to live. Amazing what a hot shower can do."

"Officer Edwards with the New Orleans police called. He's downstairs. I wanted to wait until you got out of the shower before I went down to meet him."

Jack went to his room, slipped out of his robe and put on shorts, a T-shirt and sandals. When he started to leave, Colby said, "When you get back, I think it's time for us to have a talk."

An hour later Jack returned to the room and found Colby still in her bathrobe, sitting on the couch and staring at the wall. "Is he going to be any help?" she asked.

"I doubt it. He'll file a report. He's already talked to that tourist and is going to have him meet with a sketch artist. It'll stop there."

"Jack, I'm scared. I've been racking my brain. I've never harmed anyone."

"Maybe it was a case of mistaken identity. Maybe the guy was after his ex-wife and mistook you for her."

"I suppose that's possible, only it doesn't give me much comfort. I know I've got to stay here and not fly until tomorrow, but I'm not setting foot out of this room until Johnson has the limo at the front door." Colby patted the sofa beside her. "Sit here. There is something about me you don't know. You just saved my life. It's time you heard my whole story."

Jack sat beside her. Colby took his hand.

"This is going to be difficult. I haven't talked about it in years. When I get through, if you decide we won't be seeing each other anymore, I'll understand."

Jack shifted around on the couch so he could face her. "Go on."

"I'm married." She sighed. "There, I've said it."

Jack's faced changed, but he tried not to let on what he already knew.

"Please don't say anything. Let me keep going. My husband, Rob is his name, was the general manager of Allison Southwest's largest Ford dealership. We got married when I was twenty-five. Life was really good. We both had good jobs. We traveled a lot, took vacations in exotic places. On top of that we really were in love. I was getting close to thirty, and we decided it was time to start a family. I, I came home after work one day and found him lying on the floor in the living room." Colby's voice choked as she relived the memory.

Jack went to the bathroom and came back with a box of tissues. "You want to stop, maybe continue this conversation after we order room service?"

Colby shook her head. "No, I want to get it all out now. I called 911 and they rushed him to the hospital. Jack, he never woke up, not to this day."

Jack pulled her close and hugged her while she composed herself.

"An aneurysm had ruptured in his brain. By the time they got him to surgery, it was too late. I had to put him in a nursing home, well, several over the years. He's still in one today, out in Ridglea. I see him about twice a week. He doesn't even know I'm there, but I talk to him, tell him what's going on in my life. It's probably more for my benefit than his."

Jack stood and walked around the room, obviously thinking. "You still love him?"

Colby rose to face Jack. "I do. I took a vow to be with him until death do us part. I won't break that vow."

Jack still kept what he had learned about Rob to himself. This was neither the time nor the place to reveal that he had followed her. "I understand all you're saying. Can I ask a question?"

Colby nodded.

"Why don't you talk about him? You could have told me this right from the start. It wouldn't have changed anything."

"I was under the care of a psychiatrist for depression for two years after this happened. He encouraged me to talk about Rob as a part of my healing process. I couldn't take it. Every time someone asked about him, I was in agony. Finally I quit my job to get away from a place where everyone knew about Rob and me, and I became a realtor. Since then I've put on a happy face and gone to work every day. Then, I go home at night and read or watch television. My old friends finally quit calling. Hardly anyone even asks me about Rob anymore, and that's what I want. It may sound strange, but that's how I've chosen to deal with it."

"You could have told me," Jack said.

Colby shook her head. "With you it was different. You and I have a special bond. I, I'm not ready to call it love. I wanted to tell just you, but I was worried that if I did, you'd be out of my life." Colby tried to remain calm as she said, "Now you know the whole story. If you choose, we can fly back to Fort Worth and go our separate ways. I'll understand."

Jack drew Colby to him and hugged her. "I'm not going anywhere. You need a friend, and that's me. I can't promise I'll be there for you forever. Then again, I might. We'll just see what tomorrow brings."

38

Two days later Jack met one of his pro bono clients outside county court in the Tim Curry Justice Center. Raúl Rodriquez was a young man who drove a cab to support a wife and two children. Empire Texas Mortgage was trying to evict him from his home. He had been sweet-talked by a realtor and mortgage broker into buying a house that he couldn't have afforded if he had driven his cab 24/7. He hadn't read the fine print. All he knew was that he was making a payment of $850 a month and had been able to do that for several years until the mortgage ballooned. He was given the option of paying off the entire mortgage or refinancing with payments of $2,200 a month, about what he took home. When he explained his predicament, Jack had him bring all of the papers to his RV. He spent the better part of a day going over them before he found a way to get Rodriquez off the hook.

Jack and Raúl entered the courtroom and took a seat in the back row, waiting for the case to be called. Jack had chosen his Bat Masterson cane for this appearance.

"*Empire Texas Mortgage, Inc. v. Raúl Rodriquez,*" Judge George Miller called. Truth be told, Judge Miller was sick of the foreclosure docket. They were all the same. Some lawyer called a witness from the mortgage company who proved up the documents and that no payment had been made for six or ten or twelve months. Usually, no one showed up for the homeowner. He signed the papers handed to him by the mortgage company lawyer and moved on to the next.

"Robert Graves for Empire Texas, Your Honor. We're ready to proceed."

The judge was about to motion him up when Jack said, "Jackson Bryant for the defendant, Your Honor. I'm ready, too."

The judge looked up with surprise as Jack and his client walked down the middle aisle, stepped through the swinging gate and stood at the counsel table.

"Well, well, this is interesting. Mr. Bryant, I've looked over these papers. Looks like your client hasn't made a payment in nine months. Do you really think you have a defense."

"Yes, sir. I do. I think you'll agree with me when I put on my case."

Judge Miller nodded and turned to Graves. "Call your witness, Mr. Graves."

Graves called a minor official from Empire Texas who officed in Dallas. He proved up all the necessary documents, marked them as exhibits, and passed the witness. He had what was known among lawyers as a prima facie case.

"Mr. Bryant, you may cross-examine."

"No questions, Your Honor."

"Empire Texas rests, Judge," Graves said.

"Your turn, Mr. Bryant."

"We call Sara Hilliard."

A frail, middle-aged woman dressed in a white shirt and gray pants approached. After she was sworn, Jack established that she worked for Quillen Bank and Trust. He noticed Graves whispering to his client, who motioned with his hands that he didn't know Sara Hilliard.

"Ms. Hilliard, you're a mortgage clerk in the Fort Worth office of Quillen, who I subpoenaed to be here today."

Sara Hilliard's eyes darted around the room before she said, "Yes, sir."

"Let me hand you these exhibits that Mr. Graves introduced. Did you notarize the signatures of Howard Jefferies, a loan officer at Quillen when this mortgage was bundled with a bunch of others and sold to Empire Texas? Take your time and look at all of the documents."

Hilliard looked at them one by one and turned them over on the rail of the witness stand as she did so. "I did, Mr. Bryant."

"Do you note something strange about the multiple signatures of Mr. Jefferies?"

Sara Hilliard paused and flipped back through the documents.

"Let me help you, Ms. Hilliard," Jack said. "They are all exactly the same, aren't they? Eight signatures among these papers—all exactly alike."

Hilliard nodded.

Jack rose and walked to the witness stand where he leaned on his cane. "In fact, those were all done by a machine, weren't they?"

"I suppose so, Mr. Bryant. I didn't mean to do anything wrong. It was just my job."

Robert Graves had stopped taking notes and stared at the witness as reality sank in. His client was about to be screwed, big time, and not just in this case.

"You notarized that signature, swearing as a notary that Mr. Jefferies signed those documents and that you, as a notary, witnessed him signing, when some machine in the back office was programmed with his signature, true, Ms. Hilliard? Or, maybe you were back there, witnessing a machine and notarizing its signature?"

The witness seemed to shrink down into her chair. "We were very busy then. We had to process hundreds of mortgages a day sometimes. I'm sure that if Mr. Jefferies would have had the time, he would have signed for the company."

Judge Miller had enough. "Stop. I've heard enough. I'm declaring this mortgage null and void. Mr. Bryant, I presume you'll have the appropriate order to me by the end of the week."

"Your Honor," Graves said as he rose, his voice reflecting concern, "my client knew nothing about these machine signatures."

"Judge, I'll have an order for you," Jack said. "As to Mr. Graves's comments, I suspect his beef is with Quillen Bank and Trust. His client has been taking money from a lot of folks on mortgages they didn't even legally own."

The judge turned to Graves and stroked his chin. "Mr. Graves, it looks like we've got one helluva mess on our hands. I want you to start by going back through the files on all of the mortgages you've brought me in the past two years. I want an accounting of the cases where this conduct has gone on, starting with Quillen, and then we may expand the investigation. I also want you to come up with a plan to unwind all of these foreclosures."

"And, Judge," Jack said, "I'm putting on the record here in open court that I'll be bringing a lawsuit against Empire Texas for all of the payments my client has made and will be seeking punitive damages for fraud."

Jack excused himself and walked with his client into the hallway where Rodriquez shook his hand, then hugged him. At the elevators, Rodriquez went down to ground level while Jack waited for an elevator to take him to the eighth floor. When he exited, he saw a sign pointing to the office of the district attorney. Jack approached double doors and pulled one open. A pleasant lady sat behind a counter and smiled as he entered.

"Can I help you?"

"Yes, ma'am. I'm Jackson Bryant. If Joe Sherrod is in, I'd like to visit with him. I don't have an appointment, but he and I were in law school together."

"Just a minute. I'll call his secretary." The receptionist made the call and replaced the phone. "He'll be right out."

Almost before the words were out of her mouth, the interior door opened and Joe Sherrod burst through. "Jack, man, it's been a long time."

Joe Sherrod was a few years older than Jack with white hair, wire rim glasses, and a politician's exuberant personality that served him well as district attorney. Jack also knew that he had the reputation of being a fine trial lawyer and, unlike so many of his peers who became administrators when they rose to his level, he still liked the courtroom and would personally try one or two capital cases a year.

"Has been, Joe. Actually, I think you and I last visited over a drink on the river walk at the state bar annual meeting in San Antonio about ten years ago."

"Come on back." Joe motioned him through the door to his corner office. Besides the usual large desk, credenza, guest chairs and a seating area in front of a fake fireplace, the most notable part of the office was a wall filled with newspaper clippings of trials where Joe had sent the defendants to death row.

Jack admired the clippings. "Very impressive."

"Won them all but for that damn T. Cullen Davis. I'll go to my grave believing that son of a bitch was guilty as hell, but Racehorse Haynes kicked my butt, and he walked away a free man." Joe motioned Jack to have a seat and buzzed his secretary to bring coffee. "What are you doing in town?"

"I live here now. I retired last summer and moved back to Fort Worth. Bought a house in Rivercrest just because I could afford it, maybe just a little bit to thumb my nose at some of our classmates. Spent the fall going to TCU games and just got back from the Sugar Bowl."

A light came on over Joe's head. "J. D. Bryant. That's your son. Boy, are we glad he showed up in Fort Worth. My youngest son is playing football for Arlington Heights. You think we can get you and J.D. out to the house for dinner?"

"You name the date and we'll be there. Let me tell you why I'm here. It's about a woman named Colby Stripling."

Jack took the New Orleans police report and sketch from his briefcase and handed it to Joe. The district attorney took his time absorbing the event and studying the sketch. "Damn, Jack, lucky you were there. What do you want me to do?"

Joe's secretary brought in two TCU Horned Frogs mugs with steaming coffee and placed them on the table. Jack declined cream or sugar, thanked her and took a sip. "I'm not sure. She's scared. If that tourist is right, it was intentional. We can't figure out who would want her dead."

"Doesn't she live in Monticello? Seems like I've seen real estate signs around there with her name on them."

"She does. Lives in the house where she was raised. After her parents died, she moved back. Lives by herself."

"She's got an alarm system, right?"

Jack nodded.

"Here's the good news. I live in that same neighborhood." He smiled at Jack. "We public servants can't afford to live in Rivercrest or Shady Oaks. Our homeowners' association pays off-duty cops to patrol the area every night from 7:00 p.m. to 7:00 a.m. We have two officers in two patrol cars circling around. They know most of the cars that belong in the neighborhood. Folks tell them when they're going to be out of town." Joe picked up the New Orleans police report. "I'll have this on our computer system so every cop in Fort Worth and surrounding towns will have a copy of it. Then, I'll personally deliver it to our neighborhood cops and tell them to pay special attention to Colby's house. That's the best we can do." Joe paused. "Maybe it'll be enough. If not, Colby could be in real trouble."

39

Jack's conversation with Joe Sherrod somewhat reassured Colby. She returned to her work, and as weeks went by with no other incident, she began to relax. Oh, she still kept a close watch on her rearview mirror and jumped at the slightest noise. She acquired a full-grown German shepherd from a place that trained them as attack dogs. She named the dog Killer and soon had him sleeping at the foot of her bed. Jack bought her a Ruger LCP with a laser sight and went with her to a course to get her concealed handgun license. Thereafter, he took her to the gun range nearly every Sunday afternoon.

One evening Jack and Colby were sitting on Jack's back patio, watching the sun go down. Killer lay quietly at Colby's feet until he would spot a squirrel sneaking down from a tree, intent on retrieving a couple of pecans. Killer would focus on the squirrel without moving a muscle until he thought the squirrel was far enough away from the tree. Then, he would spring to his feet and charge the squirrel, causing it to beat a fast retreat back to the tree where it would taunt Killer with chatter. Killer would circle the tree several times before going back to his position at Colby's feet.

"Look, Colby," Jack said, as he turned to face her. "I know you've done everything you can to protect yourself. You've even got Killer here going with you to the office and staying in the car when you have an appointment to show a house. There's one more thing you might consider. Why don't you move in with me? I have five bedrooms just gathering dust. The upstairs would be yours." Jack raised his hand in a Boy Scout salute. "I pledge not to set foot on the second floor."

Colby smiled while she gazed off toward the setting sun and thought. Then, she took Jack's hand. "I appreciate the offer. I really do. Still, you know I can't make a commitment. Until something changes in my life, I prefer to have my own house and my own space. Does that make sense?"

Jack sighed. "I suppose. I just don't want anything to happen to you."

"I'll be okay. Hey, did I tell you I started tae kwon do this week? Private lessons three times a week. I didn't want to be in a group. I figured I need to learn fast."

"I know something about the martial arts from my military days.

I'll be your sparring partner whenever you're ready. And my other offer remains open indefinitely. I'd really prefer to have you as my house-guest. It would be a lot safer."

"I know, Jack, but my mind is made up."

40

The next day Jack was about ready to lock up the RV when he heard a car door slam in the parking lot. When the stranger knocked, he hollered, "Come on in. You just barely made it. I was about ready to shut down for the day."

The door opened and a slender white man in his midthirties climbed the steps. He was dressed in slacks and a white shirt with a blue checked tie at half mast around his neck. He carried a steno pad in his left hand. As he walked back to the office, he stuck out his hand. "Hartley Hampton. I'm a reporter for the *Star Telegram*. I cover the courthouse beat."

Jack rose to take his hand and motioned him to have a seat. "I didn't figure you to be one of my clients. Most of them don't even own a tie. What can I do for you?"

"Mr. Bryant . . ."

"Call me Jack."

"Jack, the bailiff in Judge Miller's court told me about your win against Empire Texas. I gotta say that was most impressive and about damn time that someone took on these lousy mortgage companies."

Jack took a sip from his water bottle. "Thanks, but I'm not looking for any publicity. I loved it when I was a plaintiff lawyer in Beaumont, but those days are behind me."

Hampton raised his hand. "It's not a question of publicity. It's both a human interest story about you and a news story about what Quillen has done to thousands of people. I've checked you out. I know your background and what you've done for the people out here on the North Side. Sorry, Jack. You may not want it, but you're newsworthy, and I'm grabbing on to the story before some of my competition does."

Jack gazed out the window and finally turned back to Hampton. "Okay. I can see you've got the bit in your teeth, so I might as well co-operate. You interested in a beer? I was just about to head next door to Moe's."

Hampton smiled as he realized he had at least gotten his foot in the door. "Sure. Maybe I can get Moe to tell a few tales behind your back."

The two men walked out into the parking lot where Jack started to show Hampton how he secured his RV.

"Wait, wait a minute. Let me get a camera." Hampton opened his Toyota Camry and retrieved a Canon digital to take a picture of the RV before Jack implemented the security. "Okay, show me what happens."

Jack pushed the button on his key chain, and the metal shutters covered the windows. "Wow, that's cool shit," Hampton exclaimed as he took more photos of the RV. "Hell, I may hit the front page with this one."

They walked over to Moe's where everyone greeted Jack before he and Hampton took two seats at the bar.

"Moe, this is Hartley Hampton. He's a reporter. Wants to do a story on me and the mortgage industry. Give us a couple of Shiners."

"Uh, make mine a Miller Lite," Hampton said.

When Moe handed them their beers, Hampton insisted on clinking his bottle with Jack. "Here's to a great story."

As they sipped their beers Hampton told Jack what he had learned about him. Hampton had done his homework and needed no notes to walk Jack through his life from Byers Street to Beaumont to Iraq, back to Beaumont and eventually to Rivercrest. Jack nodded as he realized Hampton was a very thorough reporter. No point in pussyfooting around with him.

"So, I get moving back to Fort Worth, and you can damn sure afford to live in Rivercrest, but why do pro bono work and hang out here at Moe's instead of at Rivercrest?"

"Call the pro bono payback or whatever you choose. I find I like helping these people. The world's a mess these days and the poor are suffering the most. I don't need the money, so why not?" Jack waved his arm around the bar. "As to these people, I'm really one of them. I don't choose to run with that Rivercrest crowd."

Hampton started to ask another question, but Jack interrupted. "And one more thing. Helping people who can't help themselves gives me a rush I never anticipated. To see the look of gratitude in their eyes is beyond explanation."

"Tell me about the *Empire v. Rodriquez* lawsuit. How'd you figure out what was going on?"

Jack ordered another beer for each of them before he replied. "Not rocket science by any means. Contrary to what some of the talking-head lawyers on television say, most lawyering isn't. It's hours and hours of poring over medical records in a malpractice case, looking for that one error that caused a patient's death. Or maybe it's spending days in a conference room of some silk-stocking law firm that's defending a products case, looking for that one memo, like in the Pinto cases where Ford was caught red-handed years ago with a memo saying that it would be cheaper to defend wrongful death cases arising out of a defective gas tank than to issue a recall."

"I've heard that. You're telling me it's really true?"

"Damn right. Some people at Ford decided their bottom line was more important than saving lives. As to the Rodriquez case, I spent a day reading documents, and it hit me. It didn't even take a document examiner to see what had happened. Empire tried to foreclose on paper it didn't even own. Pisses me off every time I think about it."

Hampton sipped his beer and then banged it down on the bar, causing the domino players to look up to see who was causing the ruckus. "Hell, this is going to be a series, maybe three parts. I'll start with you, then the Empire case, and follow it with the repercussions to mortgage companies around here. Jack, I suspect you and I are going to be friends for a long time. I could hang around your RV and come up with a story a day."

Jack shook his head. "I can't say I like it, but it's a story that needs to be told. Just try to downplay anything about me."

Hampton rose to shake his hand. "No promises, Jack, but you'll like my series."

41

The series started the following Sunday with a story on Jack Bryant and his pro bono work out of his RV. The story about the Rodriquez victory followed on Monday. The Tuesday story was almost an afterthought. By then Jack was confronted with a parking lot full of people with mortgage problems. After he complained to Colby that evening that his parking lot was overrun, Colby drove out North Main the next morning and parked across the street from the RV. She watched as the parking lot filled. About every half hour Jack would escort someone from his RV and beckon to the next one in line who would follow him in the door. Colby watched for three hours, leaving only once for coffee. Driving back to her office, she realized that there wasn't a phony bone in Jack's body. *I could easily fall in love with a guy like this,* she thought. Only her next thought was about her husband, lying in the nursing home, and she shoved her feelings for Jack to the back of her mind. *Maybe one of these days, but certainly not now.*

Jack tried to handle the cases at first, but soon realized that he would be back in the full-time practice of law, something he neither needed nor wanted. After a couple of weeks he worked out a referral arrangement with a few good plaintiff lawyers. He put another sign in his window: IF YOU'RE HERE ABOUT A FORECLOSURE PROBLEM, PLEASE CALL JACOB VAN BUREN.

The knock at the door of the RV was so soft that at first Jack thought it must have been the wind. It came again. He rose from his chair and opened the door. An elderly black lady whom he recognized as June Davis stood at the bottom of the steps.

"Mrs. Davis, I'm sorry. I didn't hear you at first. Please come in. It's chilly out there for early May." Jack went down a step and extended his hand to assist his visitor, then offered her something to drink.

Mrs. Davis perched on the edge of the cushioned bench that circled the table. "Water would be nice," she said in a soft voice.

Jack went to the refrigerator and returned with a bottle. He twisted the cap a half a turn and handed it to her. She twisted the cap the rest of the way, took a small sip, replaced the cap, and set it on the table.

"How are you doing, Mrs. Davis? I mean since your husband died have you been managing okay?"

"I'm fine, Mr. Bryant. My house is paid for and I get a little Social Security check. Besides, my kids look after me." She reached into her purse and retrieved an envelope which she slid across the table to Jack. "This came in the mail, addressed to me. I, I wasn't sure what to do with it, so I called Miss Colby. She said I should take it to you."

Jack picked up the envelope. The return address was the United States Postal Service. He opened it and found another envelope, this one torn and mangled with the addressee illegible. The letter from the postal service read,

Dear Mrs. Davis:

One of our sorting machines jammed and mangled this letter. We apologize for the problem. Your name was the only one we could make out on the letter, and we were able to get your address. Please handle as you see fit. Very truly yours.

Jack looked at the mangled letter. It was from Euro Life Insurance Company, based in Gibraltar. It stated that Euro had determined that one William Davis was married to June Davis. Under the terms of the policy, since it paid double indemnity in the event of an accidental death, the benefit was four hundred thousand dollars, payable to Allison Southwest. Jack looked through the documents a second time before he looked up.

"Did you know that they had insured Willie for four hundred thousand dollars?"

"Lawdy, no, Mr. Bryant. Willie only made twenty thousand a year. Why would anyone insure him for that kind of money? Besides, he retired from Allison fifteen years ago."

"Good question. Let me keep these papers and the check. I'll get back to you in a couple of days."

That evening Jack had Colby, J.D. and Tanya over for dinner. This time he fixed spaghetti with his own special sauce. As he served it, he said, "And Colby, this is also a secret family recipe, which I will not disclose to you . . . yet."

Colby turned down her lower lip in a pout before she grinned. "I just may get J.D. to tell me all the family secrets. With me and Tanya working him over, I bet he'd spill them without even the need for a waterboard."

Tanya gave her a thumbs up before everyone dove into the spaghetti.

While they were eating, Jack described his meeting with June Davis and the puzzle about the big life insurance policy on a porter.

J.D. got so excited that he started talking with a mouth full of spaghetti. "Dad, I know . . ." J.D. swallowed and took a sip of water. "Sorry, I know about those. They're called 'dead peasant' policies. We studied them in my business ethics class this semester."

"Go on."

"Walmart got in a shitload of trouble with them a while back. They were taking out life insurance policies on all kinds of employees— cashiers, greeters, stockers, you name it. Not just key man policies on executives. They never told the employees and would keep paying the premiums even after the employee left Walmart. At one time, according to the media, they had over three hundred thousand of these damn policies. Helluva deal for them. They got a tax write-off for the premiums and collected a lot of money when one of their ex-employees died. You know how old some of their employees are. They paid enough in premiums that there were no physicals, no underwriting requirements, no nothing. If Walmart wanted a policy, it got one."

"That sounds a little ghoulish, particularly on employees they might not have seen for fifteen or twenty years," Colby said.

"You got that right," J.D. said. "When word about the dead peasant policies leaked out, Walmart got such bad publicity that they finally just canceled all of them."

"Hell," Jack said as he poured more wine, "I'm not sure they're even legal once the employee leaves the company. After that, the company has no more insurable interest in an employee's life."

"Exactly," J.D. said. "In fact, the Texas legislature and most other states passed laws to put a stop to them. Still, according to my professor, they exist. A corporation can send an officer to one of the few states where they're legal and fill out the applications. Some even go to islands in the Caribbean."

"There's really no way to know about them," Tanya added. "The

employees are never told. The only ones that know are a few high-up
corporate executives, and they aren't about to spill the beans. Our professor says that the premiums are buried in their financial reports with
some accounting mumbo jumbo that nobody can figure out."

Silence filled the table until Jack spoke. "Well, I suppose I better pay
a call on Dwayne Allison. He's not going to like what I'm going to tell
him."

"Dad, I have a request. I aced all of my courses and don't have to
take finals. I want to work for you this summer and learn something
about being a lawyer. Maybe I'll get a law degree and become a sports
agent."

"Okay, you're hired on one condition. Move here for the summer,
until two-a-days start. That way we can spend more time together, and
we can talk law until we're blue in the face."

"Deal, Dad."

"Your first job as my legal assistant will be to be my chauffeur. When
I get an appointment with Mr. Allison, I want to arrive in the Bentley,
complete with driver."

42

Jack called Allison Southwest's corporate office the next morning.
Dwayne Allison's secretary was reluctant to make an appointment for
Allison with a stranger, but she finally relented when Jack said he was an
attorney and was bringing a substantial check. Ann put Jack on hold and
checked the state bar Web site to determine that he really was a lawyer
and officed out on North Main. When she got back on the line, she said,

"Mr. Allison is a very busy man, but if you can be here promptly at ten in the morning, I'll fit you into his schedule."

Allison was standing beside his secretary's desk when he heard a vehicle drive up. He glanced out the window to see a blue Bentley. A big man in dark blue pants and matching shirt buttoned to the top was opening the door. *Interesting,* Allison thought. *How does a lawyer who offices on North Main afford a chauffeured Bentley? Did he rent it for the day to impress me?* A man Allison realized must be Jackson Bryant stepped out of the car, stretched out his left leg, and walked with a cane up the front steps. The chauffeur leaned against the car, arms folded.

"Keep him out here for thirty minutes," Allison said to his secretary. "Tell him I'm on a conference call. He's going to waste my time anyway."

Jack spent the time studying the trophy heads on the wall. Each one was accompanied by a picture of Allison, gun in hand, with a smug look on his face, and by a gold plaque, providing the date and location of the kill.

"Mr. Bryant, you can go in now," the secretary said.

Jack opened the door to the right of the secretary and stepped through into another larger room, also full of trophy heads. Allison stood behind his desk and waited for Jack to approach and extend his hand.

"Mr. Allison, I'm Jackson Bryant."

After a perfunctory handshake Allison motioned for Jack to take a seat.

"I won't take up much of your time, Mr. Allison. I suspect you're a busy man." Jack reached into his inside coat pocket and pulled out a check. He handed it to Allison. "I believe this is yours."

Allison studied the check for four hundred thousand dollars payable to his company. His demeanor immediately warmed. "Why, thank you, Mr. Bryant." His face hardened. "How did you get your hands on this check?"

Jack smiled. "I represent June Davis, Willie's widow. The post office screwed up somehow and she got the check. She brought it to me, and I told her that we needed to return it to the rightful owner. That would be you, well, actually your company."

Allison relaxed once more. "That's very kind of you, Mr. Bryant. You could have saved yourself a trip. If you had called, I could have sent a messenger to pick up the check."

Jack shifted in the chair, placed his cane between his legs and leaned on it as he spoke. "There's one more thing. That's a dead peasant policy on Willie. Those have been outlawed in Texas for years. You haven't had an insurable interest in Willie's life in about fifteen years. The rightful beneficiary of that money is June Davis."

"You're wrong." Allison's voice changed to a sputter when it suddenly dawned on him why Jack had personally delivered the check. "Willie Davis would have signed an employment agreement authorizing us to insure his life for at least ten thousand dollars, which would go to his beneficiary. That same agreement gave us the option of placing more coverage on him, with Allison Southwest choosing the beneficiary. If Mrs. Davis didn't get the ten thousand, I'll certainly look into it and make sure she gets her share of the benefit."

Jack crossed his legs and leaned back, purposely creating a picture of a man in control. "She hasn't received any ten thousand dollars and wouldn't accept it if you offered. She's entitled to the full four hundred. Look, I'll make you a deal. You calculate the premiums you paid on his life over the years, and you can have that amount back with June getting the rest. That way you're not out anything."

Allison walked around the desk to stand over Bryant. "Absolutely not. I won't be blackmailed by some two-bit lawyer practicing out on North Main. Listen, I know every good lawyer in Fort Worth, and you're not one of them."

Jack got up to face Allison. "Fair enough, Mr. Allison. If that's your attitude, you can expect a lawsuit for fraud and unjust enrichment. And I've checked around. I know you own the insurance agency that placed the coverage. You have an insurance office in every one of your dealerships. I'll prove that you've violated the Texas Insurance Code and the Texas Deceptive Trade Practices Act. That trebles the amount on the policy and gets me attorney's fees. Hire yourself one of those good lawyers, Mr. Allison. This ought to be interesting."

Jack turned to walk away, but stopped. "By the way, you might want that good lawyer of yours to check me out. My full name is Jackson Douglas Bryant, formerly a plaintiff lawyer in Beaumont. You have a good day."

43

Why the fuck am I sitting on a bench in front of a bunch of yellow roses in the botanical garden at dusk with an umbrella over my head? The gates to this place close in twenty minutes. You'd think I was in the middle of one of those Jason Bourne movies. Next time I'll be looking for a chalk mark on the north side of some abandoned building.

Hawk came out of the mist, wearing a hooded sweatshirt and sat down beside Boss. "Evening. Thought this would be a pleasant place to meet. Most people are gone by this time. Beautiful roses behind us. I grow some in my backyard. Love the smell. I've even won some local competitions with my roses."

"I'm not really interested in your horticultural endeavors. Here's your next assignment." Boss handed him a folded piece of paper.

Hawk unfolded it and read about the next victim. It described a sixty-year-old woman who lived by herself on Caddo Lake close to the Louisiana border.

"I know that area pretty well. I like to go fishing on Caddo. That's a swampy old lake, but it has some of the best largemouth bass in this part of the country. You got to know the channels through those big old cypress trees. Otherwise, you'll get lost and never find your way out. Did you know that the Texas Bigfoot Research Conservancy is located there? I've been to their annual conference a couple of times myself. Never sighted old Bigfoot, but I'll swear I've smelled him a couple of times."

"Stop. That's enough. Do the job and you'll have thirty thousand in your account."

"I understand. By the way, I'm sorry about that Colby Stripling lady. I thought I had her in New Orleans. Nobody should have survived that fall into the Mississippi. I just didn't figure on her crazy boyfriend jumping in after her. Shit, he must have been out of his mind."

Boss sighed. "Okay, one more question, and then we need to leave. Why haven't you gotten her yet?"

Hawk shook his head. "Sorry, Boss, I know she's a big trophy for you, but she's gotten extremely cautious. I've followed her. Now she never goes out at night unless it's with that guy. She's packing and goes to the range every Sunday. I've watched her two or three times. She's damn good. On top of that she's got about as big a German shepherd as I've seen, riding shotgun everywhere she goes. I could take a shot at her, but it's too risky in the middle of the day. I'll think of something. Just give me a little time. Meanwhile, I'll take my fishing gear and head on over to Caddo."

The next morning Hawk left early and drove east on I-20. He stopped for breakfast in Longview and got to the lake around noon. He wasn't in any hurry, so he drove around the lake, admiring the cypress trees and marveling at the mysterious aura of the lake. He stopped by the Bigfoot Center to check on sightings this year and was disappointed to

find there had been none; still, he snagged a brochure on the next conference. He rented a cabin on the edge of the lake and thought that after
Brownwood, this was becoming Hawk's tour of Texas lakes. He found a
convenience store and bait shop a few miles away where he purchased
coffee, cereal, milk, snacks, and a six-pack of Bud. After he stowed his
supplies, he set out to find Cassie Villanueva. He had an address on a
rural road, but nothing more.

The house number was written on a board that was nailed to a tree.
A dirt path barely wide enough for a pickup led through the forest. He
drove down the highway two hundred yards until he found a wide place
on the shoulder where he parked and walked back to the path to Cassie's
house. It was still light, and he had no trouble finding his way, although
his senses were on alert for the slightest sound or movement. Hawk
didn't get along with alligators and snakes, both of which were prevalent
in the area. He stopped when he heard something off to the left, but
smiled when he saw he had disturbed a heron that was fishing in a small
pond close to the road. He rounded a bend and saw a small house on
stilts. The wood siding was old and gray, with a couple of boards missing. The most astonishing feature was a full-size hot tub on the front
porch with a telescope pointed to the sky beside it. *So, maybe Cassie is an
astronomer,* he thought. His eyes then focused on something in the yard.
It was a pit bull, sleeping in the sun and chained to a tree. *That would be
a problem,* he thought. He saw nothing wrong with killing a person, but
an animal was different. He would have to deal with the dog without
harming him. Hawk crept away so as not to disturb the dog and returned to his pickup.

That evening after the sun was gone and the moon was beginning to
rise, casting a shimmering glow across the lake, he parked in the same
location. After checking the direction of the wind, he crept through the
swamp downwind from the house and dog, praying that he didn't step
on an alligator. When he had a view of the house, he used night-vision
binoculars to observe a large woman with gray hair, wearing a black

swimsuit, sitting in the hot tub, alternately sipping from a glass of red wine and gazing into the telescope. As he watched, he saw her begin to yawn and lie back in the hot tub. The rumbling sound of an alligator startled him until he realized that it was Cassie snoring. Now he had a plan.

The next day Hawk bought two pounds of hamburger meat, hoping that would be enough to keep the dog quiet for a few minutes. He returned to the house at the same time that evening and again circled around to have the wind in his face. He watched through the binoculars, and, sure enough, she was again in the hot tub, sipping wine and watching the stars. When he heard her begin to snore, he crept toward the dog and pitched half a pound of meat at him. The dog looked puzzled, but dived in. When it was gone, Hawk pitched the remainder at him and, making sure to stay outside the perimeter of the dog's chain, he walked to the house and up the steps. When a loud creak came from a step, he stopped until he heard the snoring again. He walked across the porch to find Cassie passed out in the hot tub. Hawk reached into his pocket and retrieved latex gloves before walking around behind Cassie. He placed his hands on her shoulders and pushed her head under water. She thrashed and fought for maybe thirty seconds and then was quiet. He held her under for another minute before placing his fingers on her carotid artery. Nothing. When someone found her, it would be assumed that she had passed out and drowned. For good measure, he took the wine bottle and poured the remainder of her wine over the rail to the ground below.

He walked down the steps. This time the dog barked until he recognized this was the man who had just fed him. His bark turned to a whine for more as Hawk walked up the dirt road. When he got to the highway, he retrieved his pickup and headed back to Fort Worth to report another successful mission.

44

The deputy parked in front of Allison's headquarters and knocked on the door. Ann opened it. "Afternoon, Deputy. No one ever knocks on this door. Come on in."

"Thank you, ma'am. I'm here to serve some papers on Mr. Allison. Is he here?"

"Nope. Out to a meeting at one of the dealerships. Should be back in an hour or so. You want to wait for him?"

The deputy nodded. "If it's all right, I'll just sit on one of the rockers on the porch."

"Suit yourself."

The deputy took off his hat and folded himself into one of the rockers. He was just settling in when the door opened and Ann handed him a bottle of water.

"Many thanks. Mr. Allison own all of these quarter horses?"

"They're his pets. The ones over there to the left are his racing stock. See that Palomino?" She pointed over to a muscular blond horse standing under the shade of a tree. "He's got a long name. Mr. Allison just calls him Diablo. He's worth half a million at least. Make yourself at home. Mr. Allison just called and is on his way back. I told him you were here. That didn't make him very happy."

"When I pay someone a call, I'm usually not bearing good news."

The secretary went back inside, and the deputy dozed off in the rocking chair until he heard the sound of a vehicle. He opened his eyes to see a Lincoln Navigator with dealer plates parking beside his vehicle. A heavyset man he took to be Dwayne Allison got out of the car.

As the owner of multiple car dealerships, Allison was accustomed to getting sued. Just part of the cost of doing business. He knew the deputy was just doing his job.

"Afternoon, Deputy. I'm Dwayne Allison. I hear you've got some papers for me."

The deputy reached for his hat before rising from the chair. "Yes, sir. Some lady named June Davis is suing your corporation and the insurance agency. Sorry to have to serve these on you, sir. I'm chairman of the sheep and goat committee of the livestock show and appreciate all of your efforts for the folks in Fort Worth, particularly those kids who get scholarships from the livestock show."

"Thank you, Deputy. I appreciate your service, too. We've all got to give back to our community. Would you like to come in?"

"No, thanks. I've done my job. I have three other stops to make this afternoon."

Allison went to his office and glanced at his watch. Four o'clock. That was close enough to cocktail hour as far as he was concerned. He walked to the bar and poured bourbon over ice and returned to his desk to flip through the petition. It was routine, similar to many that he had to deal with every year. The only part that got his attention was the dollar amount: $1,600,000, plus a claim for punitive damages and attorney's fees. He gulped half of his bourbon and picked up the phone to call Phillip "Ace" Leyton, his attorney, who agreed to meet him the next morning at the ranch. *Doing business is getting a whole lot more complicated,* he mused. *Maybe I just ought to shut all the stores down and raise quarter horses.* Then he remembered that he had personally guaranteed the floor plans on all of his dealerships with Quillen Bank and Trust. "Damn Quillen," he yelled. "Why can't we go back to the old days when I sold and serviced cars, made most customers happy and had money in the bank?" Then his voice dropped and he said to himself, "Shit, those days are gone forever."

45

A dusty black Toyota Tundra pickup turned into the ranch and parked. A tall, lean man dressed in a white shirt and dark tie stepped from the vehicle. He had hooded eyes and a flat nose above a turkey gobbler neck. The lawyers that frequented the Tarrant County Courthouse called him "Lizard," but not to his face. Leyton was the senior Fort Worth partner of a national law firm. He took one last drag on a Camel and crushed it under his boot, then entered the front door without knocking.

"Morning, Ann," he said.

"Mr. Allison is waiting for you. Go right on in. I'll bring your coffee with cream and sugar in just a minute."

"Thanks, darlin'. If you ever get tired of working for old man Allison, you give me a call, you hear?"

He opened the door to find Dwayne looking out a picture window at his quarter horses. "I heard that, you son of a bitch. Don't you go trying to steal my secretary."

Allison smiled as he turned to shake Leyton's hand. "Take a look at Diablo out there. That one's going to win me the All American Futurity at Ruidoso Downs this year. Purse is supposed to push two million. I guess the economy doesn't have everybody scared. Have a seat."

Ann brought Leyton his coffee. After he had a chance to sip it, Allison pitched the petition at him. "Take a look at this pile of horseshit."

Leyton slowly drank his coffee and flipped the pages of the petition. When he got to the end, he asked, "How many of these dead peasant policies do you have?"

"Dammit, Ace, don't call them that. Makes me sound like some feudal lord preying on my serfs. To answer your question, somewhere around seven thousand."

Leyton let out a low whistle. "My friend, you could have a big problem. Texas outlawed these about ten years ago. Unless you've got an executive where you can justify key man insurance, say a store manager, you shouldn't have been taking out these policies. Now, I don't think it's anything more than a misdemeanor if you get caught, but your insurance agency could lose its license."

"Ace, I took care of that years ago. In fact I think one of your partners told me how to do it. All my employees sign an employment agreement. In fine print buried in the middle of the last page is a clause that authorizes Allison Southwest to provide ten thousand dollars in life insurance coverage to employees and further permits additional insurance in an amount to be decided by the company with Allison Southwest as beneficiary. Additionally, the applications are signed in Jamaica, where the coverage is not prohibited."

Leyton took out a Camel, lit it and inhaled deeply. Allison pushed an ashtray his direction. "Still, I think this is a case of first impression in Texas courts and the question of insurable interest looms like a thundercloud overhead. Mrs. Davis get her ten thousand?"

Allison paced the floor behind his desk. "Damned if I know. If she didn't, I'll write her a check. I don't understand what the big deal is about insurable interest. I had a right to insure them when they worked for me."

"That's the whole deal with insurable interest. If an employer doesn't have any more insurable interest because an employee doesn't work for him, who's to say that he might not just hire someone to bump off that employee. Not likely to happen, but the department of insurance wants to eliminate the temptation.

"And what about you running for mayor of Fort Worth?" Leyton asked. "I know you've been considering it, and, from what I hear, you have a pretty good chance. If this hits the media, your previously good reputation as a civic leader is going to become tarnished, to say the least."

Allison ignored his lawyer's admonition. "You know this Bryant? I figure him for nothing more than an ambulance chaser."

Leyton flipped to the signature at the back of the petition. "If it's who I think, yeah, I do know of him. I thought he practiced in Beaumont, but this address is out on North Main. He's one of the state's better plaintiff lawyers. Damn sure not an ambulance chaser. You thought about settling this?"

"That son of a bitch wants the entire policy except the premiums. I'm not about to give up what I bargained for. Besides, I've already spent the four hundred thousand. Go fight him. I'll deal with the media if the problem comes up."

46

New cases filed in Tarrant County were randomly assigned to one of several civil district judges. *June Davis v. Allison Southwest* landed in Judge Bruce McDowell's court. Leyton could not have been more pleased. McDowell had been a solo practitioner, working out of a storefront office on Henderson Street, a few blocks from the courthouse. He made a modest living handling divorces, traffic tickets, drawing up the occasional will and praying for the day when someone would be wheeled through the door, having been in a wreck with an eighteen wheeler. He also was active in politics, working as a foot soldier for the party in power. When he first graduated from law school Texas was a Democratic state, and he dutifully worked the polls for Democrats. Once he sniffed the wind and realized that the scent of the elephant was in the air, he jumped to the Republican party. Someday he thought he might land a bench and maybe be set for life and a sweet retirement.

Judges in Texas didn't make much money, compared to the rest of the profession. For that reason, most judges came from one of two backgrounds. Some were young lawyers, wet behind the ears with no idea what went on in a courtroom until they were appointed or elected. They usually used the judicial appointment as a stepping stone to a job with a big firm at double the salary. Then there were the ones like McDowell who sought the position because the one hundred twenty-five thousand dollars it paid would be a giant pay raise.

When McDowell's predecessor died of a heart attack midway through his four-year term, McDowell hightailed it to Ace Leyton's office. As senior partner of the largest law firm in town, Leyton had the governor's ear when it came to judicial appointments. Of course it didn't hurt that the firm was a significant contributor to the governor's campaign. In fact, the firm contributed to any campaign where the elected official would have an impact on Fort Worth and Tarrant County. The political party was irrelevant. The firm backed winners and had been known to contribute to both candidates in the same race if it was too close to call.

When McDowell had shown up in his office, pitching his loyalty to the Republican party, Leyton had listened with feigned interest and said he would be back in touch. After interviewing several other candidates, he concluded that McDowell was no worse than the rest and would certainly be beholden to his firm and the clients it represented if he got the bench. With a phone call to the governor's appointments secretary, it was done. Bruce McDowell became Judge McDowell.

Jack Bryant was familiar with how judges got their jobs in Texas. It was the same throughout the state. Still, he was new to Fort Worth and didn't really know the political lay of the land. When he saw Ace Leyton's name on the answer to his lawsuit, he knew the firm and could only assume that members of that firm carried a big stick around the Tarrant County Courthouse. Nonetheless, he decided to fire his opening salvo with a motion for summary judgment, alleging that Allison Southwest had long ago lost any insurable interest in the life of William Davis.

McDowell's court was in the old red courthouse. Sitting at the top of Main Street overlooking the Trinity River, it had been refurbished but not changed. From the outside, anyone would know it was a courthouse. It took twenty steps to get to the entrance that was guarded by four granite columns. The interior had marble floors with a rotunda in the center of each level. Judge McDowell's courtroom was on the second floor. A twenty-foot ceiling was awe-inspiring for most visitors. The bench was elevated four feet above the rest of the courtroom. Behind the bench was an ornate wooden facade, flanked with the United States and Texas flags.

Jack climbed the steps to the entrance, once having to use his cane for balance. J.D. was with him. At the metal detector, Jack explained his knee and received a cursory wanding before taking the elevator to the second floor. When they entered the courtroom, they found nearly every seat taken, not a surprise since Judge McDowell had that day reserved for his motion docket.

Judge McDowell entered from the door to the left of the bench. He was sixty, completely bald and overweight by fifty pounds. He breathed heavily as he mounted the stairs to his bench and sat with a grunt. "You folks be seated," he said. "Let's sound this docket."

As he called the cases, various lawyers announced their appearances. Jack was disappointed to find that they were next to last. Then Judge McDowell said, "Let's hear the *Davis v. Allison Southwest* case first. Mr. Leyton, would you please come forward?"

Jack noted that he was not also invited to the front even though it was his motion. He rose, carrying his file, and followed Ace Leyton to the bench, where he said, "Good Morning, Judge McDowell, I'm Jackson

Bryant. This is the first time I've had the pleasure of being in your court." Professionalism would carry the day even though the deck might be stacked against him.

"Welcome, Mr. Bryant. I see you've got a cane. Would you feel more comfortable arguing your motion seated at counsel table?"

"No, Judge. I usually do just fine. I would like to introduce myself to Mr. Leyton."

Jack turned and stuck out his hand. Leyton took it and nodded without a greeting before turning back to the bench.

"You may proceed, Mr. Bryant. Please note that I have read your motion and Mr. Leyton's reply."

"Thank you, Judge. The motion is not complicated. My client's husband died a few months ago. By happenstance she learned that Allison Southwest had taken out a very large life insurance policy on her husband back when he worked as a porter for one of the defendant's dealerships. He was never told Allison had taken out a policy or that Allison kept paying premiums all these years. It's what is known as a 'dead peasant' policy, Your Honor."

"Your Honor, I object," Leyton interrupted. "It accomplishes nothing to characterize the policy in that way. It's a term life insurance policy, plain and simple."

"Sustained. Mr. Bryant, please refer to it as the life insurance policy or the policy."

Jack nodded. "In any case, Judge, there's no doubt that the defendant took out a two-hundred-thousand-dollar policy on the life of a porter who never made more than twenty thousand dollars a year. It paid double in the event of accidental death. The law in this state is quite clear that a company or person must have an insurable interest in the life of another before placing a policy on that person. That insurable interest must continue throughout the life of the policy. I've cited the cases in my motion."

McDowell turned to Leyton. "Your response, Mr. Leyton."

"Judge, Mr. Davis signed an employment agreement permitting exactly what occurred here. He gave Allison Southwest the right and my client exercised it. The benefits under the policy belong to Allison."

Jack was about to respond but Judge McDowell raised his hand. "I've heard enough. The plaintiff's motion is denied."

Jack stared at the judge for a moment before turning on his heel and walking through the swinging door, motioning J.D. to follow.

Once they were in the car Jack said, "Well, we know what we are up against. Looks like it's two against one. My biggest concern is that now that Leyton knows which way the judge is going on this issue, he'll be filing his own summary judgment, claiming that Willie approved it. That could be a major problem."

Leyton waited a week so it would not appear too obvious that he was paying for favorable rulings. It was late in the afternoon when Judge McDowell's direct line rang.

"Judge, Ace Leyton here."

"Nice to hear from you, Ace. I was just thinking about calling you to go to lunch. Election season is rolling around and I've already drawn an opponent."

"Great minds think alike, Judge. I was just calling to offer my help. I'll start by telling you that I'll make sure that every person in our Fort Worth office contributes the two-thousand-dollar maximum to your campaign."

Both the judge and Leyton knew that was a not too subtle way to get around campaign contribution laws. Two thousand dollars was the maximum, and certainly file clerks and secretaries didn't have $2,000 to throw at a campaign. However, in their next paycheck there would be a bonus of $2,000 plus enough to cover the taxes on that amount with a suggestion that the firm was supporting Judge McDowell. The employees were well trained and knew what to do.

After Leyton ended the conversation with the judge, McDowell thought for a minute and estimated that with lawyers and staff, Leyton's firm probably had a hundred and fifty employees. *Three hundred thousand dollars,* McDowell thought. *Now that's the way to kick off a campaign.*

47

Colby was driving on Camp Bowie toward a downtown mortgage company to help a client with closing on a small house on the Southside. It was the first she had sold since Jack's. Like nearly everyone else, she had been impacted by the economy. This was turning out to be her slowest year since she became a realtor, and she was getting worried. She made a good commission on Jack's purchase, but the five thousand dollars a month she paid to the nursing home was a constant drain on her bank account. She briefly considered asking Jack for a loan and then rejected the idea. It was her problem, and she had to deal with it. She still had several listings. Maybe one or two of them would turn into sales sometime soon. She lowered the passenger window so that Killer could stick his head out and feel the breeze riffling his fur.

Colby was approaching the Seventh Street Bridge over the Trinity and started to wave at the tamale man when a pickup pulled beside her. She never noticed the pickup until it swerved into her left front. She lost control but managed to slam on her brakes as the car bumped the curb. The tamale man saw what was happening and abandoned his cart. Colby hit the brake and lowered her speed, but not enough to avoid the bridge abutment which she hit at about fifteen miles an hour. Killer yelped as it happened and then whined when the air bags deployed and engulfed Colby and Killer. Colby deflated her bag and then Killer's. Her door was jammed, so she climbed to the passenger seat and opened that one. Killer leaped from the car. Colby wondered if she would ever be able to get him in a car again. Other cars stopped, but Colby ignored them. She wanted to make sure that the tamale man was okay.

He was. He timidly stepped from behind the bridge abutment and burst into tears when he saw the wreckage of what had once been his cart. Colby spoke to him in Spanish. "You're okay?"

"*Sí*, but look at my cart."

"Don't worry. I'll get you a new one."

The police and EMTs arrived. Colby waved off the ambulance and was talking to a police officer, explaining that she couldn't identify anything except that the other vehicle was a pickup. As she was talking she glanced at her watch. "Excuse me. I'm late for an appointment."

She called the mortgage company and apologized, telling them to go on with the closing. Then she called Jack. Within fifteen minutes Jack and J.D., driving separate vehicles, were at the scene.

When the officer released her, Colby said, "Jack, I need you to run me downtown. J.D., would you take José home and then drop Killer by my house? I've told the wrecker driver to take my car to the Lexus dealer. Oh, and J.D., give José my phone numbers. I promised to get him a new cart."

48

Boss was sitting in the shade beside his dollar-sign-shaped backyard pool. The lines through the dollar signs were designed to permit twenty-five meter laps. He was drinking his morning coffee and reading the *Star Telegram*. He got to the back page and nearly choked on his coffee when he read a two-inch story about Colby Stripling, local realtor, being run off the road and almost killing the tamale man. "Son of a bitch," he said as he slammed the paper down and picked up his cell phone.

When Hawk answered, Boss said, "We have to meet this morning."

"Boss, I'm just saddling my horse. The kids will be waiting for me."

Boss paced around the pool. "I don't give a good goddamn about those kids. I want to see you face-to-face in an hour."

"Look," Hawk said, "I know you're upset and I know why. Let's meet in the parking lot up by the old packing plants. That way I won't miss many of my rounds through the stockyards."

"Hell, no. I pick the place this time. There's a Starbucks on Camp Bowie about ten minutes from my house. It has outdoor seating. If we can't be alone, we'll sit in my car. Be there in an hour." Boss clicked off his phone and went into the house to shower.

When he got to the Starbucks, he saw Hawk seated at an outdoor table on the side patio with empty tables around him. Boss forgot about getting coffee and took a seat opposite him. "Goddamn it. I'm really pissed. You tried for Colby Stripling again and screwed up again."

Hawk raised his hands, palms up. "What am I supposed to do? I told you that it was going to be tough. I had to try something, and it had to be in the daytime." Hawk pulled a Marlboro out and lit it.

Boss stuck out his hand. "Give me one."

"I didn't know you smoked."

"I don't. At least not in the past twenty years."

Hawk lit both cigarettes. Boss took a deep drag and immediately started coughing.

"You want some water?"

"I'll be okay. Just give me a minute."

Hawk drank his coffee until Boss spoke again. "I'm okay now. Let's put Colby Stripling on the back burner for a while."

Hawk shook his head. "Wait a minute. That one would net me a cool half a million bonus. I don't want to forget her."

Boss leaned over the table and replied, "You'll damn sure do what I tell you. Otherwise, you can walk away, and I'll find someone else. And I didn't say forget her. Let's give her a little time to feel comfortable again. If you come up with a plan for her, I want to approve it first. Understood?"

Hawk considered his options as he took a drag on his Marlboro. He blew out smoke and replied, "Okay. You're the boss. Only, let's not wait too long."

49

Jack and Colby parked Lucille in the garage and walked in the back door. The sounds of a football game came from the man cave. Jack walked through the kitchen and dining room to find J.D. watching film of TCU football games from the past season. Killer was snoring quietly in a recliner beside him.

When Colby saw Killer, J.D. said, "I took him to your house, but he refused to get out of my truck. When we got here, he saw me getting out and pawed the door until I opened it. After today I think he didn't want to be left alone."

Killer saw Colby and yawned as he stood in the chair and stretched.

"Killer, are you all right, baby? Mommy's sorry for what happened today. That airbag hitting you in the nose must have hurt." She sat on the edge of Killer's chair and scratched him behind the ears.

"Colby and I are going to go out on the patio and discuss the day's events. Join us if you like."

"Be there in a few minutes. I just want to watch a few more plays."

Jack and Colby returned to the kitchen. "Name your poison," Jack said.

"After what I've been through, I'll take a double Tito's on the rocks. Maybe a couple of shots of vodka will calm my nerves."

Jack poured two drinks and led the way out to the patio. They sipped their drinks until Jack said, "I know this is tough on you. Are you holding up okay?"

"Hell no, I'm not! We don't know who or why, but someone is trying to kill me. Is that offer to move in here still open?"

Jack was about to respond when J.D. joined them, Shiner Bock in hand. "I can answer that. We still have four bedrooms open. You can have one and Killer can have his own private suite." Killer had joined them and his ears perked at the sound of his name.

"I'll take the one next to yours, facing the river and the setting sun."

"Colby, you can pick any one of my other vehicles to drive till your car is fixed or you get a new one, but not Lucille."

"Then, I'll take the Bentley."

Jack turned to his son. "J.D., have a seat. We've got to solve two attempted murders on Colby and we have no idea where to start."

Jack drummed his fingers on the side table beside his glass, waiting for one of the others to speak. Suddenly, he rose and threw his glass against the barbecue pit where it shattered into a hundred pieces. "Boy, aren't we great detectives. Nobody even has an idea."

"Look, Jack, I'm the one in danger here, and I'm trying to remain calm. You can damn sure do the same."

"She's right, Dad," J.D. said. "What the hell brought that on?"

Jack took in a slow breath and returned to his seat. "Sorry. I'm used to controlling what goes on in my life. Now it looks like I can't even protect Colby."

"That's the problem, Jack. We're not detectives. We're not even sure the incident in New Orleans is related to what happened yesterday."

"Sorry, Colby. I have never believed in coincidences. They're related somehow."

Silence filled the evening as each of them was lost in his own thoughts, searching for a connection.

"What about that old man that died while he was out fishing up in Denton? You went to his funeral," J.D. said.

"Willie Davis, that's an interesting thought. He and Colby once worked together. Still, that was ruled an accidental death. June told me that the detective with the sheriff's department up there was a friend of the family and did a thorough investigation. Following up on his death would be a waste of time."

J.D. had moved from his chair and was doing sit-ups. He stopped and said, "I have an idea. Don't you know the DA here? Let's have him pull us a computer run on all the violent deaths in the area for the past year."

Jack tapped his cane on the patio in front of his chair as he thought. "What's the purpose?"

"Fishing, Dad, fishing for some more coincidences that might lead to a motive for trying to kill Colby. Maybe it's a shot in the dark, but we've got to start somewhere."

Jack thought a minute and nodded his head, "Not a bad idea, but your search field is too big. Let's narrow it."

"How about violent deaths within a hundred and fifty miles of Fort Worth?" Colby suggested.

"Geographically, that's okay but otherwise still too broad. That would include domestic murders, barroom brawls, you name it."

"Then," J.D. said, "how about unsolved violent deaths within that distance, and eliminate the common forms of one-on-one murder: guns, knives, that kind of thing?"

"No," Jack said. "That might eliminate too many. Let's get any violent deaths, only the unsolved ones, and see how big our search is. We'll leave out domestic disputes."

"Going how far back, Dad?"

Jack thought a moment and said, "We'll try for a year, and we may have to cut it off at six months, depending on what we find. Let's see if Joe is still in the office."

Jack retrieved his cell from his pocket and scrolled to Joe's private number.

Joe picked it up on the second ring. "I presume you're just checking to see if your vastly underpaid civil servant is still at the office at six thirty in the evening. What's up, Jack?"

"Glad to see you're still on the job. I'll sleep much better tonight. I need a favor."

"Name it."

"Can you get me a list of unsolved violent deaths other than domestic quarrels within a hundred and fifty miles of Fort Worth in the past six months?"

"Wow, you're asking for a ton of information. What's this for?"

"Colby was run off the road yesterday, and we think that may be the second attempt on her life. I'm not looking for murders with guns, knives, that kind of thing. I'm looking for unusual, unexplained deaths with no suspects."

"Yeah, I read that little article. Meant to call you. Sorry."

"No problem, Joe. Can you do it?"

Joe hesitated before he answered. "I can do it. May take a little while, though. We can go to the Web sites we have access to, but there are a lot of small counties in that radius that haven't discovered the Internet. I'll just have to put a clerk to work, calling the sheriffs in those counties and asking them to search their file cabinets. It'll take longer than you'd like, but I've got a good summer clerk from Texas Wesleyan here, and I can put her on it. Figure it'll take a few weeks at least. Anything else I can do?"

"I think that'll do it. Oh, and tell your neighborhood patrols that Colby is moving in with me for a while. They still ought to keep an eye on the house, but there shouldn't be any activity other than Colby or someone checking her mail. Wait, now that I think about it, there's one more thing. I want to be sworn in as a reserve deputy sheriff. Can I drop by tomorrow and get you to do it?"

"Why do you want to be a deputy?"

"Once we get the information, J.D. and I may do a little investigating ourselves. I figure that if I'm a Tarrant County deputy, the cops in some of these counties may be a little more candid."

"That's a little tougher. Our reserve deputies have to go through a training program and pass a test."

"Tell the sheriff that I was in the 101st and was in combat in Iraq. That ought to count for something. I can qualify on the range with any weapon he chooses. Then, I'll study the Texas Criminal Code and take the test."

There was silence on the phone while Joe thought about it. "Okay, I'll call in a couple of favors with the sheriff. Understand, Jack, I'm putting my ass out there for you. You create any problem and it'll be your ass."

50

———————

Jack knew the motion was coming. The postman delivered the certified envelope while Jack was sitting at his desk in the RV, reviewing documents brought to him by a Hispanic man seated across the table from him. Frank mowed yards for a living and was in danger of having his pickup repossessed by an Allison Southwest dealership. When there was a knock on the door, Jack opened it to greet the postman.

"Morning, Dave. What do you have for me?"

"Looks like the usual, a couple of letters from lawyers, some junk mail and one certified that I need you to sign for."

Dave handed the mail to Jack who signed the green card and handed it back to the postman.

"You need a bottle of water? It's already pretty hot out there."

"I'd appreciate that, Jack."

Jack went to the refrigerator and returned with the water. After the postman left, Jack said, "Here's what we're going to do, Frank. I'll file an injunction to delay them from going through with the repossession. That'll buy us a little time. Maybe I can talk them into refinancing with a lower monthly payment."

Frank nodded his head. "Thank you, Mr. Bryant. "I'll keep looking for some more jobs. I never had any problem with making the payments until this past year. Now a lot of my old customers are mowing their own yards."

After Frank shook Jack's hand and left the RV, Jack turned to J.D., who had been sitting quietly in the driver's seat. "J.D., get on the computer and find a form we can use for an injunction. This certified letter is from Ace Leyton. I suspect I know what it is."

While J.D. moved to the computer, Jack poured himself another cup of coffee, settled into a seat in the living area, and tore open the envelope. The document was Leyton's motion for summary judgment, asking the court to find as a matter of law that Allison Southwest was entitled to the proceeds of the life insurance policy on William Davis. The motion relied on an employment agreement attached as an exhibit where the fine print permitted Allison Southwest to take out a policy on Willie's life in any amount as long as at least ten thousand dollars went to Willie's heirs. Further, the document stated that Allison Southwest could keep the life insurance in force even after termination or retirement.

Jack flipped to the back page and saw Willie Davis's signature and the date of March 31, 1980. Below Willie's signature was the signature of Henry Simon, apparently a manager of some kind at the Cadillac store. Jack took a sip of coffee and went back to the first page of the document and read each of the paragraphs slowly until he was back to the signatures. He knew that June never got the ten thousand dollars but also knew that could be solved by Leyton if he raised it. Leyton would have a check in hand at the next appearance before the judge. Jack presumed McDowell would accept an apology and tender of the check. He wasn't in this fight for ten thousand dollars. Still, when he finished reading the document a second time, he smiled.

"J.D., when you get to a stopping point, let me have the computer. Leyton's filed a motion for summary judgment, but I think I've figured out a way to beat it. And remind me that we need a second computer in here. When we go out for lunch, we'll buy one."

Four weeks later they were back in Judge McDowell's court. Once again McDowell moved them to the head of the docket.

"Morning, Judge," Jack said as he approached. He had a pretty good idea that McDowell was in Leyton's back pocket, but he had an ace up his sleeve.

"Morning, Mr. Bryant. Mr. Leyton, you may proceed on your motion."

"Your Honor, this is a very simple motion that should end this lawsuit. Attached as an exhibit is the original of the employment agreement between one William Davis and Allison Southwest. It's pretty old and my client had to dig it out of storage, but the document speaks for itself. William Davis clearly consented to everything that has transpired with this life insurance policy. There's no fact issue and my client is entitled to a summary judgment."

Judge McDowell turned to Jack. "Seems pretty clear-cut to me. Do you see a fact issue anywhere, Mr. Bryant?"

Jack couldn't resist taking a shot at the judge. "I presume, Your Honor, that you didn't have time to read my response. If you had, you would not be taking that position."

McDowell narrowed his eyes at Jack as he spoke. "Mr. Bryant, you're suggesting that I don't do my job?" The judge flipped through the file until he picked up a document. "Here it is. Must have gotten buried under something else. Proceed, Mr. Bryant."

"Judge, there's definitely a fact issue that will require you to deny Mr. Leyton's motion. Someone has written William Davis's name on a line on the last page. However, the signature is not notarized, and there has been no proof that William Davis actually signed this document. It could have been done after Willie died for all we know."

The judge leaned over his bench and used his most intimidating judicial stare as he spoke. "Mr. Bryant, are you suggesting that Mr. Leyton, a longtime distinguished member of the bar in this county, is attempting to perpetrate a fraud on this court?"

Jack had been before too many judges to ever be intimidated. "Nothing of the kind, Your Honor. He has a duty to somehow authenticate this signature, and he has failed to do so. If you grant his motion, I'm giving notice that the next stop with this case will be at the court of appeals."

The judge put down Jack's reply and picked up Leyton's motion. He looked at the signature page, then put the motion down and folded his hands. He stared at his bench for nearly a minute before he looked up. "Mr. Leyton, he may have a point here. Understand I could grant your motion, but I don't like getting reversed."

"Your Honor . . ."

"Wait, Mr. Leyton. I'm not through. There's another signature on this document. Henry Simon signed it for Allison Southwest. Can't you get an affidavit from him, confirming that he was there and saw Mr. Davis sign the document?"

Leyton shook his head. "Judge, I've already checked into that. Mr. Simon died five years ago."

McDowell pursed his lips and then ruled. "I'm sorry, Mr. Leyton, but I have to deny your motion."

Leyton nodded at the judge and walked out of the courtroom. When he got to his pickup, his cell buzzed. It was Dwayne Allison.

"I suppose you won our motion. Get me a certified copy of the judgment and I'll fire it off to Euro Life. My insurance department had to notify them of this case, and they're worried that they may have to pay for this death twice. I need to let them know we have it under control."

"Hold on, Dwayne. Judge McDowell denied our motion."

"What? That son of a bitch. I just had twenty of my employees contribute to his campaign. And, and you told me this was a sure thing," Allison fumed. "What the hell kind of lawyer are you? I don't pay you four hundred and fifty dollars an hour to lose. Maybe it's time for me to find a lawyer who can win."

"Dwayne, calm down. First I didn't say this was a sure thing. I said the odds were in our favor that we could win this motion. Bryant pointed out that no one had authenticated Davis's signature and the judge bought into it."

"Dammit. You should have seen that coming."

"You're right. I can only apologize, but I have a plan. I'm going to subpoena June Davis and get her to confirm that was her husband's signature. Then, we'll ask for a rehearing."

"You do whatever you think is necessary," Allison yelled. "I've already deposited that check."

51

June was seated at the end of the table in the RV, dressed in her Sunday best. Jack was sitting at the other end, with J.D. in what used to be the driver's chair. Now, both it and the passenger seat were always swiveled around to face the back.

"June, Mr. Leyton and the court reporter are going to be here in about half an hour. The court reporter will give you an oath to tell the truth. Mr. Leyton will take over and start asking you questions. He wants to try to prove that the signature on this employment agreement is that of your late husband."

June nodded her understanding.

"Now I want you to tell the truth, but if you say it's Willie's signature, we're going to lose the case. If there's any doubt in your mind, it would be best for you to say you can't identify it."

"I understand, Mr. Bryant," June said with a slight twinkle in her eye. "I think I can handle Mr. Leyton."

Leyton and the court reporter arrived at the designated hour.

"Jack, it would have been a lot more comfortable to have done this in one of our conference rooms."

"Maybe for you, but your fancy offices and big conference rooms might have intimidated my client. Ms. Court Reporter, if you'll slide around the table to the middle, we'll let Ace sit at the end. Ace, this is Mrs. Davis."

Ace nodded at the witness.

"Pleased to make your acquaintance, Mr. Leyton," June said. "Mr. Bryant has told me what a fine lawyer you are."

She's certainly not intimidated here, Leyton thought as he took his seat. Jack took the passenger seat while Leyton put his briefcase on the table, opened it and retrieved the employment agreement.

"If you would, please swear the witness."

The court reporter turned to June and asked her to raise her right hand. "Do you swear that you will tell the truth, the whole truth, and nothing but the truth, so help you God?"

"I do."

"Mrs. Davis, I intend to make this very short. First, let me extend my condolences for the loss of your husband."

"Thank you, Mr. Leyton. My family and I miss him. He was a fine, Christian man." A tear rolled down her cheek, and Jack gave her a tissue to brush it away.

"I'm handing you a document that I've had the court reporter mark as Exhibit A. It's an employment agreement between your husband and Allison Southwest. Have you seen it before?"

June straightened her shoulders and spoke in a strong, clear voice. "Mr. Bryant showed me a copy of it this morning. That's the first time that I ever laid eyes on it. I can't agree with your statement that it is an agreement between my Willie and Allison Southwest."

Leyton realized that while June Davis looked as if she could be blown over in a modest wind, she was not going to be an easy witness. He fumbled for his next question. "Maybe you didn't have a good copy. Would you please take a look at the exhibit?"

He handed the original to June who started reading at the top of the first page. It took her ten minutes to get to the second, and Leyton was becoming frustrated. "Mrs. Davis, perhaps if you just went to the last page, we could speed this up."

June looked up from the document. "Mr. Leyton, you asked me about this document and I understand this is important. So, if you please, just be quiet until I've read it all."

Leyton stared at the witness as she went back to her reading. "I'm going out for a smoke."

Jack chuckled as he watched Leyton leave the RV and light a cigarette in the parking lot. He paced until, at last, he threw the cigarette on the ground, stomped it out, and climbed into the RV where he found June reading the last page line by line, moving her index finger along as she said the words to herself. When she got to the signature line, she studied it and then turned the page upside down to look again. Last, she turned it sideways before putting it back on the table.

"I have read the document, Mr. Leyton."

"Then, can you identify the signature on that document as that of your late husband, William Davis?"

June looked at Jack and back to Leyton. "No, sir. I cannot."

What the hell? Leyton thought. "Mrs. Davis, would you explain why you cannot identify this as your husband's signature?"

"Glad to." June smiled. "Of course, you didn't know my Willie. He wasn't much for reading and writing. He only went to the fourth grade. When he wasn't working at the Cadillac place, he was tinkering with his car, fishing or playing dominoes with his sons or his friends at Moe's icehouse. I took care of the family finances and paid the bills. I expect that if you looked at our checking account going back twenty years, you wouldn't find one check with his signature on it. On top of that, this agreement is thirty years old. No way I would remember what his signature looked like that long ago. So, Mr. Leyton, I don't know who signed 'William Davis' to that agreement."

Leyton was fumbling again and already thinking of his call to

Dwayne Allison after the deposition. "But, but, you would agree that it is possible this signature is Willie's?"

"I suppose anything is possible, Mr. Leyton."

Leyton announced that he had no more questions, grabbed his briefcase, and left the RV. Jack watched with a smile as Leyton kicked the tire of his truck before getting in. After the court reporter left, he told June that she had done a great job. He was certain that Leyton would not even reurge his motion. Now they would be getting ready for trial.

52

The financial pressure had begun to encroach on Leyton and his law firm. He was sitting at his desk one afternoon two weeks after June Davis's deposition, talking to an associate about a case in which their client was a trucking company. The company's eighteen-wheeler had run over and killed a man and his two young children in a Toyota Prius, leaving his wife surviving with no family. They were discussing strategy to defend damages, and the associate was reporting on the results of an investigator who had spent two weeks tailing the widow when Leyton's intercom buzzed.

"Yes," Leyton said as he blew out smoke and answered the phone. "Give me fifteen seconds and put him through." He turned to the associate and asked him to come back later. When the associate shut the office door behind him, Leyton picked up the phone on the first ring. "Afternoon, Stephen. How are things in Manhattan?"

Stephen was Stephen Morganson, the managing partner of the

nationwide law firm. "Hot and humid, Ace. I just keep hoping those green sprouts the economists talk about would start growing. Meantime, I spend most of my time on the phone, chasing after a bunch of clients that seem to be getting further and further behind."

"I know what you're calling about. It's Allison Southwest, right?"

"You got it. They used to be our best client in the Fort Worth office. Now it seems like we only get a payment every once in a while. What are you going to do about it? Do we need to just terminate them as a client and sue for our past-due bills?"

Leyton took another deep drag on his cigarette before he spoke, knowing that Allison was his biggest client at one time and the primary reason he had become senior partner in Fort Worth. As he exhaled the smoke he said, "No, we're not there, yet. I'd say we should stick with them another few months. Allison may be turning the corner here before long."

Silence on the other end of the line. "You have four months. If there's no improvement, we'll be talking about Allison's status and your status with the firm along with it." Morganson clicked off the phone without another word.

Leyton stared at the phone and then punched in the number to Allison's private line. When Allison answered, he said, "Dwayne, Ace here. Just got off the phone with our managing partner in New York. He wants your bill brought current."

"Screw him and the horse he rode up on," Allison replied. "I have bigger worries than paying lawyer bills."

"Dwayne, shut up and listen. I'm trying to do you a favor here. I have four months to get your legal affairs in order unless you start paying our bills. You've only got a few active lawsuits that aren't covered by your liability insurance. One of them is June Davis. I'm going to ask Bruce to push it up toward the top of the docket. If the boys in New York fire you as a client in a few months, at least that one ought to be behind you. You okay with that?"

"Sure," Allison replied. "Just be one less thing to worry about."

That afternoon Leyton had an associate draft a motion for an expedited trial setting. Knowing the local rules required him to confer with Jack Bryant, he called his opposing lawyer. "Jack, I want to move this case along. You okay with a trial setting in about ninety days?"

"Damn, Ace, you didn't even have to waste a call. Of course I'm agreeable. And I've already figured out that you get almost anything you want in McDowell's court. Like old Brer Rabbit said, 'Please don't throw me in that briar patch.' Hell, make it a joint motion. I'm not even going to bother to show up for the hearing. Just tell McDowell, I'll be ready to go. Let me know the trial date after the hearing."

53

It took a few weeks, but Joe Sherrod kept his word. His summer intern sent a list of violent deaths in twenty-five surrounding counties and parts of two states in the past six months. No guns, no knives, just violent deaths with little rhyme or reason and, more importantly, no suspects. J.D. printed off three copies. They locked the RV, watched as the metal shades slid into place, and clicked on the alarms, knowing the lights would come on at sunset. Jack called Colby and asked her to meet them at his house to evaluate the information. Colby, who had driven Jack's Bentley, was already at the kitchen table with a glass of iced tea in her hand when they parked in the garage and entered through the back door. Colby gave both of them a hug, saying, "Damn, J.D., hugging you is like hugging a block of granite. Your body fat must be about three percent."

J.D. nodded. "You're pretty close. Any more and my forty time might be 4.7. Here's your copy."

Jack grabbed bottles of water and handed one to J.D. "We asked and we received; only, I didn't anticipate how violent our world is these days. There must be two hundred unresolved violent deaths, and that's just in the last six months."

J.D. flipped to the last page. "Two hundred and fourteen, to be exact. What do you suggest?"

"Let's divide them up. I'll take the first seventy-five. J.D., you get the next seventy-five. Colby, the rest are yours. We can make duplicate copies; so highlight and mark anything you find interesting. Put an *X* by any that you think couldn't possibly have any connection to the attempts on Colby's life."

The three assembled around the table and worked in silence, occasionally taking a sip of their drinks.

"Here's a ten-year-old boy that was hit on his bicycle. Closed head injury," Colby said.

Jack looked up. "I think for our purposes we can eliminate any kid under the age of, say, fifteen."

"How about bar fights?" J.D. asked. "I see several on my list, usually in the parking lot with the assailant getting away."

"They stay," Jack said.

"Drownings?" Colby asked.

"For certain," Jack replied.

"Here's a hit and run outside a pool hall in Breckenridge," J.D. said.

"Remember, Colby was close to a hit and run fatality," Jack replied.

"Here's Willie Davis. Sure appears to be accidental," Colby said.

"Keep him on the list," Jack instructed.

After two hours, Jack rose to stretch his legs. "I'm about through with my list. How're you coming?"

"Done," Colby said.

"On my last," J.D. added.

Jack walked over to the old wooden barrel that contained his favorite canes. He picked out a shillelagh he had purchased several years before in Ireland. "This is made of blackthorn wood." He turned it over in his hands. "I guarantee you I could put a knot in someone's head with this."

"That's interesting, Dad. In one of these parking lot fights, the cause of death was a blunt object, like a baseball bat. Maybe it was a shillelagh."

Jack nodded as he replaced the cane. "Give me a count."

"I have eighteen on my list that I think deserve further investigation," Colby said.

"Twenty-two here," J.D. said.

"And I have twenty. That's sixty total, and we're not even sure where we're going with this. J.D., I think you and I'll start in the morning."

"Okay with me, Dad, but where do we begin?"

"Let's start with Willie. He's the only one with a known connection to Colby and since I represent his wife, that'll make it easy."

"But, Jack, aren't you just wasting your time," Colby said. "Everyone agrees that he fell crossing the creek and hit his head."

"Maybe, maybe not, but we're starting in Denton in the morning."

54

Jack was up early. He entered the kitchen, opened the back door and whistled for Killer. Killer's job was to roam the fenced yard at night, growling a warning at any unusual sound. Once his nighttime chore was over, he was allowed the run of the house. Jack scratched his ears and thanked him for a good night's service before refilling his bowl. After Killer had his breakfast, he knew Killer would find one of several comfortable places to sleep until Colby was ready to go to work. When

Colby left for work, he would lie on the carpeted floor of her office until it was time for her to keep an appointment. Trained as an attack dog, he knew his friends and understood the commands that would turn him into a vicious protector of his master.

Jack put on the coffee and went to the front driveway to retrieve the *Star Telegram*. Never a breakfast eater, he settled down with the paper and coffee, starting with the sports section since he knew that J.D. would want it when he showed up. Five minutes later he heard J.D. coming down the stairs.

"Morning, Dad. How you doing there, Killer? You keep us safe?" he said as he petted the dog.

"Morning, son. Grab your cereal, and let's get on the road in about fifteen minutes," Jack said, as he slid the sports section across the table.

J.D. poured a large bowl of Cheerios and doused the cereal with sugar and milk.

"Paper says you guys are starting volunteer workouts."

"Yeah, we start this evening. We've encouraged all of the players to make the workouts. Most of them have stayed around Fort Worth for the summer. No coaches allowed, but Samuel knows every play on offense, and one of our linebackers will handle the defense." J.D. put the bowl to his mouth and gulped down the last of his cereal. Both men grabbed go-cups, filled them with coffee, and were soon in Lucille on the way to Denton.

Denton was thirty-five miles from downtown Fort Worth, straight up I-35W. Originally a sleepy college town, it was now just one more part of the Dallas-Fort Worth metroplex that still tried to maintain its separate identity as home to the University of North Texas and Texas Women's University. The courthouse and the sheriff's office were in the middle of town. Jack parked Lucille in a space reserved for officers and placed a cardboard card announcing it was the vehicle of a Tarrant County reserve deputy.

They entered the building and were met by an attractive receptionist with a professional smile. "Good morning, gentlemen. What can I do for you?"

"Morning, ma'am," Jack said. "I'm Deputy Jack Bryant with Tarrant County. This is J.D. We're here to do some follow-up on an unexplained death a few months ago. The deceased was William Davis, lived up in the north part of the county."

Jack took out his billfold and showed her his Tarrant County creds.

The receptionist glanced at them and turned to her computer. "Sergeant Reeves was the investigating officer. We don't have any suggestion that there was any foul play."

"Understood, ma'am. You think Sergeant Reeves could spare a few minutes with us?"

Five minutes later they were escorted into a small, featureless conference room, furnished with a table and four chairs. Jack and J.D. spent the next half hour talking football and staring at pale white walls. The door opened and a large black man dressed in jeans, boots, and a white shirt entered. "Deputy Bryant, I'm Sergeant Reeves. How can I help you on this Willie Davis death?"

Reeves took a seat and put a small manila folder in front of him.

"First of all, I don't want to be here under false pretenses. I am a reserve deputy, but I'm also an attorney and represent June Davis in some litigation that arises out of Willie's death."

Reeves remained silent.

"And there's one more thing you should know. A friend has had two attempts on her life. Both remain open. There's a connection to Mr. Davis in that they used to work at the same Cadillac dealer a number of years ago."

Reeves opened the file. "I don't think I can be of much help. I actually knew Mr. Davis. I played Little League with his son. Fine, gentle old man. I studied the scene myself. All I could determine was that it was accidental. Take a look."

Reeves turned the file around so Jack and J.D. could see the photos of the body at the scene. One of them showed him head down in the creek with the back of his skull caved in.

"The back of his skull was crushed," Jack said. "You figure that much damage could have been done just by a small man falling back on a rock? And how did he end up face down if he fell backwards? Did you consider that someone could have crushed his skull with one of those big rocks around the creek?"

A scowl crossed the sergeant's face. "Look, Mr. Bryant, I don't appreciate your questioning my investigation. I told you that I knew him personally. Yes, it was a lot of damage from slipping in the creek. I looked but found nothing to suggest anything other than an accident. Besides, there's hardly any motive to kill an old man like that. Let's see, he had eight sixty-seven on him, a pocketknife, and a little fishing gear. It was still at the scene. If you can prove it was a murder, more power to you, only we don't have any evidence. Now, if you'll excuse me, I have some real felonies I need to be solving."

Reeves pushed his chair back, banging it against the wall, and left the room, taking his file with him.

J.D. looked at his dad. "I think that's our signal to leave too."

"Yeah," Jack said. "I wanted to tell him about the life insurance, but he didn't give me a chance."

That evening after football practice, Jack and J.D. drove to a bar north of the stockyards. Off the beaten path, it was definitely not on any tourist map. They parked in front and were met by the sound of mariachi music as they pushed their way through multicolored beads hanging from the door. The smell of stale tamales mixed with that of beer. The music was loud and the patrons, all Hispanic men, raised their voices louder to be heard. They approached the bartender.

"Two Coronas, please," Jack said.

The bartender turned to the cooler and handed them the beers. "That'll be six bucks," he said. Jack handed him a ten and told him to keep the change.

J.D. took a sip of his beer and surveyed the room. At one table four men were talking loudly and pointing toward them. "Dad, I get the feeling that we aren't welcome here."

Jack nodded and turned to the bartender. "I need some information." He dropped a fifty on the bar. "Two months ago a man was killed in your parking lot. Looked like he was clobbered with a baseball bat. You got any idea about who did it?"

"No, señor. The guy that killed him wasn't one of our regulars. At least, that's what one of the witnesses said."

About that time the four men rose from the table J.D. had been watching. J.D. said, "Dad, we're about to have a little trouble."

Jack dropped another fifty on the bar. "Look, we may be in a little hurry here. How about a description?"

"It was dark. Someone said he was an Anglo, had long hair and a beard. That's about all. There hadn't been any ruckus in here. So I don't know what caused it."

The first man approached and stood in front of J.D. "We don't like your kind in here. You see any other gringos?" The other three men pushed him almost into J.D.'s face.

J.D. decided that the best defense would be a good offense. He drove a shoulder into the chest of the first man, shoving him and the one behind him across the room and over a table. Before the one to his left could react, J.D. had kneed him in the balls. When he folded over, J.D. put him out with a right uppercut. The one to the right, a few feet in front of Jack, flicked open a switchblade and started toward J.D.

Jack raised his cane and pushed a button on the handle. A ten-inch blade sprang from the end and into the man's neck. "Drop your pig sticker, hombre, if you don't want this one to slice open your neck."

The Mexican may not have understood English, but he certainly understood the blade pressed against his neck. He dropped his knife as the room fell silent. J.D. picked up the knife and stuck it in his pocket.

"Gentlemen," Jack said. "We'll be on our way. We seem to have over-stayed our welcome."

Jack flicked the button again, and the blade retracted into the cane. He nodded to J.D. and they pushed their way through the beads out into the night air. "Hell, J.D., I wasn't in the mood for Mexican food anyway. By the way, don't be carrying that switchblade around. They're illegal in Texas."

J.D. nodded his understanding, then said, "Dad, where'd you get that cane?"

"Bought it at a gun show a few years back. Hell, it's illegal, too, but I never thought I'd use it. I have a few others with tricks in my collection. Remind me to show them to you sometime."

When they drove away, J.D. asked, "Did we do any good, Dad?"

"Yep, son, at least a little. We have the beginnings of a description of a killer, kind of matches that New Orleans police sketch. Not much, but it's a start. And I don't believe that Willie's death was an accident. Now let's go home. We have fifty-eight more deaths to go."

55

It was late in the afternoon, way past time to head over to Moe's for a couple of drinks and a game or two of dominoes. Jack had counseled a continuing stream of pro bono clients on the usual credit card, mortgage and car payment problems. J.D. manned the computer, taking notes as each client came through the RV. About midafternoon J.D went to the house to change for afternoon practice. Finally, the line outside grew short and Jack was able to put a sign on the window, CLOSED. PLEASE COME BACK TOMORROW.

What have I gotten myself into? Jack thought. *I was okay until I won that mortgage case and made the* Star Telegram. *Since then I've been inundated with potential clients. Still, on balance, I enjoy helping those who can't help themselves.*

Jack was at the computer, checking the closing prices of his stocks, when the door opened. Without looking back, he said, "Sorry, I'm closed for the day. You're welcome to return in the morning." When the door closed, Jack realized that the stranger was standing at the top of the steps. He turned to see a tall, lean, gray-haired man wearing a three-piece suit in spite of the hundred-degree weather.

"Well, you don't look like my usual clients," Jack said as he rose to face the stranger. "What can I do for you?"

"Mr. Bryant, my name is Beauregard Quillen. I believe you've heard of me."

A look of understanding crossed his face as he noticed that Quillen was not sticking out his hand. "Certainly have, Mr. Quillen. In fact, I believe I exposed some irregularities in your bank mortgage practices, and an associate of mine is building up quite a clientele who are suing your banks for a bunch of wrongdoing." It was then that Jack noticed that Quillen had turned to grab the windshield sign, directing persons with mortgage problems to Jacob Van Buren.

"Mr. Bryant," Quillen said between clinched teeth, "My banks are being served with five to ten lawsuits a week. Mr. Van Buren is suing Empire and some other financial institutions that I sold packaged loans to, along with my banks. His name is on the pleadings, but I know they're coming from this RV and this goddamn sign." His voice trembled and his hands shook as he ripped the sign in half and dropped it on the floor.

Jack picked up his cane and rose, holding it in front of him as he sensed he was facing a man out of control. "Mr. Quillen, I don't know what your purpose is in coming here, but I suggest you leave right now."

Quillen's face reddened. "Not before I give you this warning, you two-bit shyster. My banks could go under because of your goddamn lawsuits. If they go down, I go down. You quit referring clients to Van Buren, and we'll go our separate ways. But, hear me good, you keep fucking with me and you do so at your peril. I will not go down without a fight, and it won't be in a courthouse, Mr. Bryant!"

Quillen turned and stepped out the door. As he left the RV, Jack called Van Buren. "Jacob, we've got one pissed off banker."

"Which one?" Van Buren asked.

"Quillen. He just left here after threatening my life if we keep up these lawsuits."

"What do you want me to do, Jack? We're going make a good-sized fortune on these before it's all over and done."

"We're going to keep doing exactly what we have. I don't need another fortune, but I'll be damned if we'll abandon our clients who were screwed by Quillen and his buddies. Not the first time in my life I've been threatened, and it won't be the last."

Jack clicked off and rummaged in a drawer until he found some Scotch tape. He taped the sign back together and put it back on the windshield.

56

Jack turned into the driveway and circled around to the back where he parked Lucille in her garage. He clicked the garage door shut and started toward the house. After a few steps, he realized his knee was aching, and he used his cane to traverse the driveway and climb the steps. Colby met him at the door.

"Gee, you look like you've been rode hard and put up wet. I've just finished peeling three pounds of shrimp. That'll be a half a pound for you and me and two pounds for J.D. If I fix you a drink, you up to grilling when J.D. gets home?"

After Colby made two drinks and poured peanuts into a bowl, they adjourned to the patio above the pool. Killer joined them and settled down at Colby's feet.

Colby reached over to squeeze Jack's hand. "Okay, spill it. I've never seen anything other than the upbeat, exuberant Jackson Douglas Bryant."

Jack took a swig of his drink before he started. "I had a visit from Beau Quillen about an hour ago."

Jack described the confrontation while Colby listened. When he finished, Colby said, "I've known Beau Quillen since I was a kid. He's never been a violent man. He works behind the scenes for charities, gets in the paper and the media occasionally, but doesn't seek attention for what he does."

Jack excused himself to fix another drink. A slight buzz was over-taking his thinking, but he really didn't care. He was home and figured he could navigate his way to bed without a DUI. When he returned, he faced away from Colby toward the setting sun.

"Times are changing. Businessmen saw the money being made by their contemporaries and saw that the government didn't really give a damn what they did as long as they didn't rob a bank with a gun. They seized the opportunity to rape and pillage the people of this country and the economy," he continued as he returned to his chair.

"Quillen is pretty small potatoes compared to robber barons on Wall Street, but he was loaning money for a house to anyone who could fog a mirror, usually with interest only for five years and a balloon. Then, he'd package his bank's mortgages and sell them to the big boys. Until 2008 he was worth several hundred million on paper. Then the wall came tumbling down and he went the way of Humpty Dumpty. I suspect that he still puts on a good facade, but he's barely keeping his head above water."

While they were talking, J.D. drove down the driveway and parked his pickup in the RV spot. He took a seat beside his dad and listened.

"Dad, you need to do something. You can't have Quillen threatening you and ignore it."

"If I were to file a complaint with the police, it would go into a computer as nothing more than a verbal dispute between two businessmen. Cops have better stuff to do."

"Well, at least you could call Joe Sherrod and have him make a note of it."

Jack turned to face his son. "Look, J.D., I'm not concerned and I don't think you should be either. This so-called Great Recession is wreaking havoc with nearly everyone. You see the lines outside our RV every day. Businesses are suffering, too. Maybe the Wall Street banks are too big to fail, but not local ones."

"Look at Allison Southwest," Colby said. "No one can check Allison's books since it's a private company, but just drive around this part of the state and you'll see weed-filled parking lots where Allison dealerships once thrived."

Jack sipped his drink and chewed a mouthful of peanuts as he rose to face J.D. "Quillen saw what the other bankers were doing and went for the easy money. Before you got here, Colby was saying that he's not a violent man. I believe her, and I'll continue to believe he's just making verbal threats until something happens that convinces me otherwise. Still, just to make you happy, tomorrow I'll start packing my gun." He smiled at Colby. "However, I'm not quite ready to get myself a guard dog to ride shotgun. Now, son, what's your schedule tomorrow?"

"Samuel's giving us a day off. You want to do some more police work?"

"Yep, I'll pick out three or four tonight and we'll get an early start."

"I want to go too," Colby said. "Talking about the economy, my business has gone colder than a brass cup in the Yukon. I'm not even getting any showings, much less sales."

57

Their plans were interrupted by a 3:00 a.m. call on Colby's cell. She groped around the nightstand until she found it and put it to her ear. "Yes," she said in a groggy voice. Then her voice changed. "Oh my God! We'll be right over."

She threw on a robe and ran down the stairs, throwing open the door to Jack's room.

"My house is on fire! I'm going back upstairs to put on some jeans."

Jack jumped out of bed in his boxers. "Wake J.D. too."

Colby raced up the stairs and beat on J.D.'s door, yelling about the fire. Then she returned to her room where she put on jeans and a T-shirt. She dashed from her room and ran into J.D, wearing shorts, T-shirt and flip-flops. They met Jack at the bottom of the stairs.

"What happened, Dad?"

"Don't know, but we're about to find out."

Killer barked as they left the house, surprised to see all three of his humans rushing out at that hour of the morning.

"Killer, you stay," Colby commanded.

Five minutes later they were in Monticello and could see flames and smoke coming from Colby's house. The fire department had established a perimeter as flames appeared to engulf the entire house. They parked and rushed to the fire line and were pushing under it when a firefighter stopped them. "Sorry. You can't go past here."

"That's my house!" Colby screamed.

"Ma'am, I'm sorry, but there's nothing you can do now. Is anyone living there?"

"Thank God, no."

Jack felt someone touching his shoulder and turned to find Joe Sherrod in shorts and an undershirt. "Joe, what are you doing here?"

"You forgot I live two streets over. Our patrol called me. Give them a few minutes to get it under control and make sure it's not going to spread to the neighbors' houses. Then, I'll get the captain over here."

If ever there was a helpless feeling, it had to be watching your own house burn to the ground. Colby started crying quietly and soon was sobbing as Jack pulled her to his chest. "It'll be okay. Houses can be rebuilt."

"But I was born there. All my family heirlooms are gone, my photos, my albums."

They watched in silence for another half hour when Joe motioned to the captain to join them. "Captain, I'm Joe Sherrod, Tarrant County district attorney."

The captain took off his helmet and unbuttoned his coat. "I know who you are, Mr. Sherrod."

"This is Colby Stripling. That was her house. I know it's too early to know much, but what happened?"

Colby wiped her eyes with her T-shirt and listened.

"Our fire station is over on White Settlement, no more than three minutes from here. The patrol called it in and we were here in less than five minutes. By then the house was totally engulfed. We were forced to do damage control. I'm sorry, Ms. Stripling."

"Are you suspecting arson?" Joe asked.

The captain hesitated before he spoke. "Yes, sir. That'll be at the top of the list. Houses in this neighborhood don't go up like a stack of kindling from the usual fire sources. Also, there appear to be two ignition points, and that smells like arson. I have an arson team on the way. They'll start their investigation as soon as it's safe."

Joe turned to Jack and Colby. "I'll open an arson file and put one of our team on it too. Sorry, Colby, but that's all we can do for now."

"Thanks, Joe," Jack said. "Come on Colby. Let's go back to the house. We can return as soon as it's light." Jack wrapped an arm around Colby and gently led her away.

Back at the house J.D. made coffee and they sat in silence around the kitchen table. Colby teared up again and cried softly.

Finally Jack broke the silence. "Look, Colby, at least you weren't living there and weren't hurt."

"Dammit, Jack, that's not any consolation. That makes three attempts on my life, and now my house is gone." Colby lowered her voice. "I'm sorry. It's not your fault."

Jack nodded his acceptance of her apology. "I see a little light in the east. Do you want to go back or get a little rest first?"

"Let's go back. I want to see it now, not later."

Boss was watching the news while he had breakfast when he saw the report of a house destroyed by fire in Monticello. Hearing it belonged to Colby Stripling, who, fortunately, was not home, he picked up his cell phone and walked to the backyard. When Hawk answered, he said, "Meet me at that abandoned Chevy dealership on North Main. Right now." Not waiting for a reply, he clicked off the connection.

Thirty minutes later he pulled into the parking lot and saw Hawk's pickup parked beside the building. When he stopped next to the pickup, he lowered the passenger window and commanded, "Get in."

Hawk left his vehicle and took the passenger seat.

"You dumb son of a bitch. What the hell did you think you were doing?"

Rarely intimidated, Hawk knew he had screwed up. "Look, Boss, you told me that you were getting short. I thought that the quickest way to make both of us whole was to take down that Stripling woman. It was a perfect plan. I pitched two Molotov cocktails through her front windows, and the house erupted. I executed it perfectly too; only, I didn't know that she wasn't living there."

"Goddamn it. I don't pay you to think. Some hired killer you're turning out to be. One more strike and you're out. I still want Stripling, but I'll tell you when. For now, she's going to put up even more defenses. Go back to your horse and kids."

"Just a damn minute, Boss. Let's get one thing straight here. There are two killers in this pickup, not one. And we're both in it for the money. The day you forget that is a day you'll regret."

58

After Jack, Colby, and J.D. took another look at the remains of Colby's house, they returned to Jack's. Colby took two sleeping pills and slept until late afternoon. While she slept, Jack called her office to learn the name of her insurance carrier, called in the loss, and arranged to meet the claims adjuster the next morning. Not wanting to leave Colby, he called Moe and asked him to make a sign that said the office was closed until further notice.

Colby woke about five that afternoon and immediately poured a large glass of vodka. She took it into the man cave, flipped on the television, and drank until she was close to passing out. When Jack saw she was dropping off, he carried her back to bed and turned out the light.

The next morning he made sure that J.D. was staying home, and then drove to Monticello to meet the adjuster. It was a short meeting. She surveyed the charred remains from the street, made a few notes, and then picked her way down the driveway to the back. When she returned, she said, "No reason to look any further. It's a total. We've just got to figure out the value of the house and contents. When Ms. Stripling feels like talking, ask her to call me. I understand how devastating this is. Here's my card."

After she was gone, Jack walked to the place where the front door had been. Once he determined it was safe, he avoided what appeared to be a couple of hot spots, and used a charred stick to pick through the rubble. The first thing he found was a leather-bound family album. The leather was scarred from the fire, as were some of the pages, but at least half the photos were in good condition, including one with Colby as a young girl with buck teeth standing between her parents. Next he found a locket. When he managed to open it, he saw a photo of Colby's mother. While he studied it, a police car stopped at the curb and a young officer exited. "Sorry, sir, but this is still a crime scene until we take this tape down. You'll need to step over here to the curb."

Jack did as he was told. "Sorry, Officer. The owner is a friend of mine." He showed the officer the album and locket. Okay if I take these to her?"

The officer glanced at what he held. "Sure. I suspect the arson guys will be finished today. If the tape's gone this evening, you're welcome to come back."

Driving back to his house, Jack's cell rang. He glanced at the caller ID to see that it was Joe Sherrod. "What have you got for me, Joe?"

"It was definitely arson, Jack. Looks like two fire sources. Someone tossed two Molotov cocktails through the front windows. The arson guys found pieces of two bottles."

"Any suspects?"

"Not a damn one right now. Unless some neighbor saw an out-of-place vehicle that night, the evidence is destroyed. My guys are canvassing the neighborhood. I'll let you know if we turn up anything."

Joe was about to hang up when Jack said, "One more thing, Joe. May not be important." Jack described his run-in with Beau Quillen.

"You want me to do anything?" Joe asked.

"Nah, I think that he's got some money problems. He blames me for a big chunk of them. As long as it's verbal, I don't want to do anything. I just wanted you to know about it."

Jack drove home to find Colby still asleep and J.D. watching game

film. He put the album and locket on the kitchen table. He poured a
glass of water, picked up the latest *Sports Illustrated,* and found a shady
spot on the patio where he studied the top twenty-five college teams in
the country. TCU was ranked number eight in the preseason poll. He
heard the back door open and close. Before he could turn around,
Colby's arms slid down his chest and her cheek nuzzled his.

"Thanks for finding the album and locket. Let me go get the album
and a glass of tea, and I'll tell you about those photos."

59

Over the next couple of weeks things slowly returned to normal. Colby
made one last search of her property and arranged to have it razed. She
sat on a neighbor's lawn across the street with her arms wrapped around
her knees and Killer beside her, watching the bulldozer work. When the
last of the dump trucks drove away, she teared up but promised herself it
would be the last time. Jack convinced Colby that she didn't need to be
running all over town alone, so Colby cleared it with her boss to work
part-time out of the house and have other realtors show houses if necessary.

One morning Jack turned on the computer in the RV to find a request
for production of documents from Ace Leyton. Leyton wanted every
document in June Davis's possession that might have Willie's writing on
it. That included checks, income tax returns, savings-account records,
scraps of paper where he might have written down measurements in the
garage, wall calendars, applications for Social Security, anything that
they might use to establish that Willie's signature on the employment
agreement was really his. Jack leaned back and thought. *Well, well, Ace is*

worried about that insurable interest issue at the time of Willie's death. He must figure that even if he prevails with McDowell, the appellate courts might reverse him. This could be interesting since June said Willie rarely signed anything. Might as well see what June has.

Jack reached for his cell phone and pulled up June Davis's number. When she answered, he said, "Morning, Mrs. Davis. This is Jackson Bryant. How are things with you today?"

"Just fine, Mr. Bryant. The kids have been working in the vegetable patch since their dad's not around anymore. I expect I'll have you a basketful the next time we meet."

"I'd appreciate that. I'm calling about your lawsuit. As you know, it's going to trial in a couple of months. Allison's lawyer is worried about this employment agreement and trying to prove Willie's signature. He just sent me a formal request for any checkbooks, tax returns, applications of any kind, wall calendars where he might have written a note, anything that bears his writing. Off the top of your head, what do you think you might have?"

"Maybe this is not a good thing, Mr. Bryant, but I'm a pack rat. I don't ever throw anything away. I have canceled checks going back twenty-five or thirty years. We haven't made enough money to file tax returns since Willie retired, but before that we paid a little income tax and Willie would have to sign the returns. I put up a new wall calendar every January and keep track of kids' and grandkids' birthdays, weddings, funerals, that kind of thing. It's possible Willie put something on it occasionally. I always roll up the old one and stick it in a box with the others. Willie was on Social Security, and I remember helping him fill out the form. I'll have to look to see if a copy's around here."

Jack shook his head as she rattled off the possible places for signatures. When she paused, he asked, "Can you gather all of that stuff up and get Willie, Jr., to bring it to my RV, say, day after tomorrow?"

June thought a minute. "Yes, sir. I should be able to get most of it together. If I turn up anything else, I'll have Willie, Jr. make a second trip."

Jack clicked off the phone with a sigh.

J.D. turned from the computer where he was drafting a petition, alleging fraud against a credit card company. "We have a problem on the Davis case?"

Jack rose to pour himself a cup of coffee. "I hope not. She apparently has a lot of places where we might find Willie's signature." Then he smiled. "Fortunately, I've been down this road before. If we turn up a signature or two, Ace will hire a questioned documents examiner to evaluate the writing."

"I don't understand, Dad."

"That's someone who is basically a handwriting expert. If you were to decide to become a trial lawyer, you'd learn that for almost any issue in a case, there are people whose opinions are for hire. Doctors in every specialty, accountants, engineers, accident reconstruction experts, you name it. This case could boil down to whether Willie actually consented to Allison Southwest taking out a big policy on his life, even though he couldn't read that four pages of fine print and just signed where someone told him." Jack said. "Most of us don't read legal documents. Put yourself in Willie's place. He was uneducated and needed a job. He was going to sign whatever they put in front of him."

"But, Dad, isn't that a defense? I mean if he didn't know what he was signing, why should he be responsible?"

"Nope. Rule is that if you sign it, short of proving duress—like maybe someone had a gun to your head—or incompetence, you're bound by what is in the document. Actually, that's the way it should be. Otherwise, when one person tried to enforce a contract, the other guy could just say, 'Poor me. I didn't know what I was doing.' Fortunately, I know an old boy over in East Texas who's a first-class document examiner. He talks country but no lawyer wants to have to cross-examine him. And, like most of these experts, he'll claim to call them as he sees them, but he knows where the butter is on his bread and he'll tailor his opinion accordingly. Hell, I might as well call him now and get him hired before Leyton does."

Jack scrolled through his contacts until he found Jeremiah Buchanan and placed the call. Buchanan lived in a small house down a dirt road outside of Palestine in East Texas. Johnny Bob Tisdale had recommended him many years before. He was a short dumpy man who lived with two dogs he had found roaming the highway near his house. His frowzy white hair and mustache gave him the appearance of Albert Einstein, which he used to his advantage in front of a jury. He worked in a spare bedroom with large picture windows he had installed to bring the sun into his work area. To complement the sunlight, he had the ceiling filled with fluorescent lights. His desk faced one of the windows. To his right was a large bookcase, filled with a variety of magnifying glasses and microscopes. A laboratory table stood against the far wall. He worked there when it was necessary to establish the age of a document or ink. When his phone rang, he put down a magnifying glass.

"Buchanan, here."

"Jerry, this is Jack Bryant. How are things in East Texas today? You seen my friend, Johnny Bob, lately?"

"Jackson Bryant," Buchanan said. "I heard you retired. In fact I think it was Johnny Bob who told me."

"I'm trying, Jerry. Moved to Fort Worth and started doing a little pro bono work just to pass the time. Wasn't long before I was swamped. Look, I'm representing a widow lady named June Davis. We're suing a company called Allison Southwest about some life insurance proceeds. Allison is represented by Ace Leyton. Has he contacted you on this case?"

"Nope. Sure hasn't."

"Then I want to retain you. I should have some documents in the next few days."

"Tell me a little more, Jack."

"They say my client's husband signed an employment agreement about thirty years ago and buried in it was some language authorizing Allison to take out life insurance coverage on him and keep it on him even after he left the company. It's a long story that's not pertinent to you, but after her husband died, she learned that Allison had a two-hundred-thousand-dollar policy that paid double for accidental death and that they'd kept paying the premiums even after he retired. They claim he agreed to it. Ms. Davis says she can't confirm it was his signature. I'll send you the agreement and whatever exemplars of his writing my widow can find by next week. Obviously, I'm hoping there is no comparison between the signatures."

"You didn't have to add that last comment." Buchanan laughed. "I knew which side of the case you were on. Get the stuff on down here and I'll have a look."

"You got it, Jerry. And, this case is set in two months. Shouldn't take you long to come up with an opinion. I just ask that you don't let it sit on the back shelf too long. And, of course, I'll send your usual five thousand-dollar retainer."

"Gone up, Jack."

"Pardon?"

"Retainer's now seventy-five hundred. I'm swamped with all these damn mortgage lawsuits. Figured I might as well go up on my fees. Everyone else is making money on this mortgage crisis. I might as well take a little bigger piece of the pie."

Jack put down the phone and gazed out the window.

"What are you thinking about, Dad?"

"Just going over the *Davis v. Allison* facts in my mind, trying to figure out if we need any discovery ourselves. Right now I don't think so. We have June, and I figure that Buchanan will come through for us. Whoops, almost forgot to get an insurance expert. I can take care of that with a phone call. They'll call Allison and maybe another employee or two and find their own document examiner to swear that the signatures match and, of course, a defense insurance expert. There's always the possibility that we may have to subpoena someone on short notice, but that's okay. I think we'll be good to go. Willie, Jr., is coming in on Wednesday. Let's you and I do a little more gumshoe work tomorrow."

60

Jack turned Lucille across the highway and parked in front of the small police department in Breckenridge. They entered the front door into a room maybe twenty by twenty. One wall was filled with wanted posters. A back door led to the jail. Three desks filled the small space. Two faced each other along one wall and one in the middle had a nameplate with SHERIFF LUTTRELL on it. The man at the desk wore a tan uniform with an open shirt. His sidearm rested in its holster on the desk while he worked on a computer.

As they approached, he turned. "What can I do for you?"

"Sheriff, I'm Jackson Bryant. I'm a lawyer and a reserve deputy over in Tarrant County. This is my son, J.D."

Luttrell rose to shake their hands. "J.D. Bryant. Well, I don't cotton to lawyers much, but I know who your son is; so you're welcome. Have a seat."

"Sheriff, we're here trying to find out why someone has made three attempts on the life of a friend of ours. We're checking into unsolved violent deaths in Fort Worth and surrounding counties, looking for a connection. It's admittedly a shot in the dark."

The sheriff folded his hands on his desk and said, "Go on."

"Back in November there was a man named Jim Morris who was run over and killed in front of the pool hall here. Just wondering if you turned up any leads."

"Hell, I remember it. Happened in a driving rainstorm and late at night. He got hit and the driver never stopped. May be that the driver never even saw him."

"Can I ask a question?" J.D. said.

"Fire away."

"Can you tell us anything about the victim?"

The sheriff rose to go to a cabinet where he pulled open a drawer and flipped through a few files. "Here it is," he said as he returned to his desk. "I ran across Morris a time or two at the Dairy Queen or at Nellie's Diner. Quiet type. Let's see. Now I remember. He was an auto mechanic for the Dodge dealer we used to have in town. They sold mostly Dodge Ram pickups. Old Man Bridgers owned it; sold out to some mega dealer a few years back, but it was still known as Bridgers Dodge. Wasn't but a couple of years later that the economy collapsed and the dealership closed. Bridgers died of a heart attack last year. As to Jim, he got a job with an oil field service company. Nice guy. Too bad what happened to him."

"Thank you, Sheriff," Jack said. "Here's my card. Let me know if you remember anything else."

"Sure thing, and, J.D., we want us a national championship this year, you hear?"

J.D. just nodded and smiled as he turned to leave.

After they buckled up, J.D. asked, "Where to now?"

"Brownwood is just a little piece down the road south of here. That's where they found a man drowned below a bridge, but his Harley was back at the house. He worked at a feed store on the edge of town. That's our next stop."

The forty-five-minute drive between the two towns was hardly a scenic route, particularly in the middle of the summer. Other than a couple of rolling hills, the land was flat. A summer drought had left the landscape barren, save for a few mesquite trees and a good smattering of cactus. The water tanks were down by three feet and what few cows there were in the pastures huddled under the scant shade thrown off by the mesquites.

"Thank God for air-conditioning," J.D. muttered as he looked out the window.

Brownwood was announced by a few billboards advertising motels, service stations, a McDonalds, and a couple of churches.

As they approached the town, J.D. said, "There it is." He pointed to a feed store to the right of the highway. Jack parked, and they got out of the pickup. "Must be a hundred and ten in the shade."

J.D. pointed to a thermometer on the building as they climbed the steps. "You should have been a weatherman. The thermometer registers one hundred and nine."

The sign over the door read JOHNNY AND DON'S. Little more than an oversized shack, the store smelled of hay and horse feed, the two main products sold by Johnny and Don. The walls were covered with saddles, bridles, reins, cowboy hats, and an assortment of gimme caps. What little light that filtered in came from the front door and a back bay where customers could load their pickups.

A man, wearing overalls with no shirt, came from a side room, pushing a dolly loaded with dog food. "Just a minute, gentlemen. I'll be right with you."

He pushed the dolly over to a wall where there was other dog and cat food and left it. He pulled a bandanna from his pocket and wiped the sweat from his brow. "I'm Johnny. Now, what can I do for you?"

"Name's Jackson Bryant. This is my son, J.D. We're from Fort Worth and are following up on a series of violent deaths in connection with some attempted murders in Fort Worth. Victor Henry worked here a while back, didn't he?"

"Yep, he sure did. Was a good hand. Me and Don hated to lose him.

Hold on a minute. I need to grab a bottle of cold water. You two want one, just fifty cents apiece?"

Jack nodded his agreement. Johnny stepped to a refrigerator behind the counter and withdrew three bottles, handing one each to Jack and J.D. Jack handed him a dollar.

"Boy, I tell you what," Johnny continued. "This here is about the hottest summer I've ever been through. What do you want to know about Victor?"

"Start from the beginning," Jack said.

"Well, he showed up here one day on his Harley. Said he had been a counterman at a Ford dealership in Abilene. He got to work one day and found it was closed. He'd been riding all over this part of the country looking for work. I can tell you gentlemen that jobs are hard to find these days. We'd just put up a sign looking for a hand. Only paid minimum wage, but he took it."

"What can you tell us about his death?"

"Not much more than what was in the paper. Well, one of our deputies is a customer of mine so he filled in a few details. See, Victor was a churchgoing man. He went to Wednesday night prayer meeting at the Baptist church just down the road here. He usually stopped for a bite at the Dairy Queen before church and then he'd ride home afterward. One Thursday morning he didn't show up for work. Not like Victor. I drove out to his house. He didn't have a phone. His Harley was parked in the driveway. I went in the back door. He always left it open, you see. He was a neat man, always washed his dishes and made his bed before he went to work. His garden tools were lined up just so on the back porch. I looked around. No sign of him. I called the sheriff and went back to work. Two, three hours later they found his body in the shallow end of the lake, almost under the bridge."

Jack took a long sip from his water and the other two men did the same. "Any guesses as to what happened?"

"Oh, yeah. My friend told me that he had marks on his neck like someone strangled him. They never caught nobody, though."

"Anyone ever figure out why his Harley was back at his house?"

"Nope. That's part of the puzzle."

"You know the name of the Ford dealer where he worked before?"

"Hang on a minute." Johnny walked to a table behind the counter. "I'm not much on filing," he said as he rummaged through some piles of paper on the table. "There it is." He held up a manila folder with two sheets of paper in it. "His file folder says he was last employed with Cowhand Ford in Abilene. I got a note here saying I tried to call to get a reference, but the message said they were closed. Now unless you gentlemen want to buy a few bales of hay, I best get back to work."

Jack thanked him for his time and they headed back to Fort Worth.

"What do you make of the fact that two of the victims were former employees of car dealerships?"

Jack shrugged his shoulders. "Actually, you can add Willie and Colby to those two. They worked for a car dealership too."

61

J.D. got up in response to a knock at the RV door. He found Willie, Jr., at the bottom of the steps, a basket full of beans, peas, potatoes, onions, corn, squash, and okra at his feet. "Morning, Mr. J.D."

"Wait, wait, Willie. I'm younger than you. If you want to call my dad 'Mr. Jack,' that's between you and him. You call me J.D. and I'll call you Willie, okay?"

Willie looked down at the ground and kind of shuffled one foot around. "I was brought up to treat white folks with respect, that's all."

"Willie, times have changed. This isn't the Old South. You're my equal, understand?"

Willie nodded. "I brought you that stuff from my mom. It's in the truck. And these vegetables are for your dad."

J.D. stepped down to pick up the basket. "You tell your mama we appreciate her kindness. Now, go get that box and then come in for a cup of coffee or some water."

J.D. sat the vegetables on the kitchen counter.

"Looks like we'll have some good eating for a few days," Jack said. "Bet you could shuck that corn and it would be so sweet you could eat it raw."

Willie returned to the top of the steps with a box of papers and documents. "Mama says this is the stuff you were asking about."

Jack got up to face Willie. "Thanks, now how about joining us for a cup of coffee?"

Willie looked down at the floor. "Mighty kind of you, sir, but I can't stay. Got work to do." He turned and left the trailer.

"He didn't really have that much work, did he, Dad? He just wouldn't have felt comfortable making small talk with us."

"You're right, son. Old habits die hard. Now, let's see what's in this box."

Jack started picking things out, then decided just to dump the contents on the table. "That's more than I expected. We're going to have to go through every piece of paper, looking for anything that might look like Willie's writing. We have plenty of examples of June's, so we should be able to eliminate hers pretty easily. Might as well get started."

Father and son sat at the table and started what Jack called a once-over-lightly, just to get an idea about the scope of the documents. After half an hour, Jack paused. "Son, you start two-a-days next week, don't you?"

"Yes, sir. I'm raring to go."

"I've been thinking. Let's shut down the RV and head for the house. I have an idea that will get Colby involved on these documents. I want to put you on a different project that maybe you can finish before summer camp starts."

J.D. looked puzzled. "You care to enlighten me?"

"Save it for the house," Jack said. "That way I won't have to say it twice."

62

Colby was sitting in the backyard, clad in white shorts and a yellow halter top, when the two men came around the corner and parked Lucille. A pitcher of ice tea was on the table beside her cell phone. She got up to greet them. "I'm giving you fair warning. I'm liking being a kept woman. This lifestyle can be addictive. My cell hasn't rung once this morning. I did go over to the nursing home to check on Rob. The ulcer is nearly gone, thank God. I think my tantrum got their attention."

J.D. opened the back door of the quad cab, hauled out the box, and set it on the patio table.

"See that," Jack said. "We're about to put you to work."

"Well, before I decide if I'm going to accept whatever this project is, let me go inside and get two more tea glasses."

When they were settled around the table, Jack said, "Here's the deal. I told you last night that Leyton had subpoenaed any document that might have Willie's signature on it. Willie, Jr., dropped this box by the RV. Supposedly it has at least twenty-five years of canceled checks, maybe some tax returns, and a bunch of wall calendars. We're going to have to produce all of this stuff, but I want to know what the problem documents are before we do so. I've got an expert waiting to examine anything that appears to be Willie's writing. I want to send him the originals first, and once we get the lay of the land, we'll make copies and send them to Leyton."

Colby took a sip of her tea. "And what is it you want me to do?"

"I'm going to leave the bank records with you. Then after lunch, I'll take the rest of the stuff back down to the RV. I'll review my part there. I've got a little bit of a guilty conscience since I haven't been around enough lately for my pro bono clients."

Colby nodded her agreement. "Got it. Only what does that leave for our big, smart football player to do?"

"I was just about to get to that. As you know, J.D. and I have been on road trips, looking for connections to some violent deaths and the attempts on your life. We could get on the phone, but I figured that we're going to get more information with boots on the ground than we would by talking to someone on the phone. People, particularly law enforcement officers, are more likely to open up if they are face to face with us. Problem is that we still have fifty-five to go and they're scattered over North Texas, Oklahoma, and Louisiana. It could take us two months to hit all of those towns. I've come up with a better idea."

"Go on," Colby said. "I'm all ears."

"J.D.'s a computer major. He's told me that except for his combat tours, he had a lot of free time and used it to learn as much about computers as he could. Now he's added a year of computer science to what he already knew. I want him to hole up in his room this week and start using the Internet to look for any connections that might give us a clue about these murders."

"That means I've got about five days before I report," J.D. said. "I better get upstairs and get to work. Where do you want me to start?"

"We've got names, Social Security numbers and driver's license numbers on these other victims. You can take that information and dive into their backgrounds, spouses, kids, addresses, employers. I'll bet on most of them you can create a biography that takes them back to the womb. Once you put it all together, we can look for connections or patterns. Hell, we might be dealing with a really smart serial killer who is randomly selecting his victims."

"Wait a minute," Colby interrupted. "I've read some about serial killers. Don't they usually choose similar victims, usually in the same geographic area, and kill the same way with each victim? You know, like on *Criminal Minds*, where the killer chooses young blondes and hangs them in his basement?"

"That's why I said a really smart serial killer, one who knows he has to vary his victims and how they die. Maybe even spread them out over three states, and in small towns to boot. We may be barking up the wrong tree, but we won't know until J.D. finishes the project."

"Here's a thumb drive with all we know about the victims, son. Colby and I will work on document production . . . right after Colby fixes us some sandwiches, right, Colby?"

"Just a woman for all seasons. Give me ten minutes in the kitchen."

That evening Jack returned home and, after pouring a drink, sat across from Colby at the kitchen table to compare notes.

"My job was pretty easy. She did have about twenty-five years of bank records, but they only wrote a few checks a month—utilities, twice a month trips to the grocery, and the occasional check to cash at the bank to get some pocket money. Oh, and, once a month, a check for their tithe to the church."

"And I know that they never wrote one to the IRS. When Willie was working, they always got a couple of hundred bucks refund. What about signatures besides June's?"

"I found three checks that were signed by someone besides June." Colby passed the three checks across the table. "As you can see from the dates, these are in the last few years. The signatures are really nothing more than a scrawl. By the way, I didn't have a copy of that agreement to compare them to."

Jack shook his head as he reached for his briefcase. "I must be getting senile. I meant to leave this with you." He extracted a copy of the agreement along with a magnifying glass. They studied the three checks and compared the signature with the one on the agreement.

"I don't think we have anything to worry about here," Colby said as she put down the magnifying glass. "I know from personal experience with my dad before he died that his signature as an old man was nothing similar to what it was when he was younger. You find anything?"

"Yeah, we may have a problem with a couple of the tax returns. Take a look."

Jack showed her the signatures. Colby studied them and compared them to the agreement, then picked up the magnifying glass.

"I can see a few differences, but it's a close call."

Jack nodded. "That's what I have my man in Palestine for. I think he'll come through for us, and remember when the case is a widow against a big company, the tie goes to the widow. You heard anything from J.D.?"

"I went up to his room about an hour ago and found him hunched over his computer. He said he's making slow progress. He asked for two club sandwiches and two Cokes. I took them to him and he started munching on one before I left, never taking his eyes off the screen."

"Then I'll leave him alone. Would you accept an invitation to dinner with a hungry man?"

"Give me two minutes to check my makeup and grab my purse."

On the way to the RV the next morning Jack dropped a package off at a FedEx office for overnight delivery to Jerry Buchanan. The rest of his day was spent with pro bono clients. He followed the same routine for the next two days. When he was driving to the RV on the third day, he got a call.

"Jackson Douglas Bryant?"

"Jerry, what do you have for me?"

"I can tell you that you don't have any problem with those checks. Signature could have been made by a monkey. The tax returns are problematical. I'll support your position, but you must know that if the other side had hired me, I could make an equally compelling argument that the signature on the agreement is that of William Davis."

"That's kinda what I figured," Jack said as he stopped beside a police car at a red light. Jack glanced over to see the police officer watching him talk on the phone. Fortunately, "driving and talking" was not against the law yet in Texas, except in school zones. So, Jack merely smiled and waved to the officer as the light changed.

"Jerry, FedEx that stuff back to me. As you know, those are the originals, and I want to lock them up for safekeeping."

63

J.D. bounded down the stairs with four days growth of beard, still wearing the same clothes he'd had on when Jack last saw him. "Dad, Dad, where are you?" he yelled.

"Colby and I are in the cave, just finished watching *Red* with Bruce Willis and a bunch of other great actors."

J.D. burst through the door with a stack of papers. "I think I'm on to something. We need a table to work on. Let's go into the dining room."

There was just enough daylight coming through the windows that Jack could make out J.D. spreading his bounty on the table. Jack paused to flick on the chandelier.

"You two take a seat and I'll walk you through this," J.D. said, excitement erupting in his voice. "I have a bunch of Excel spreadsheets for each of you. I've also got the backup in this stack and on my computer. Skip all the stuff about where these people were born, where they lived, that kind of stuff. Go to the last column on the right where I've listed all of their employers from their first job up until the time they died."

"I'm there," Jack said.

"Go to the second page and look at the yellow highlights on the jobs on victim number three. See, he worked for a car dealer. Then look at the following numbers."

Jack and Colby studied the spreadsheets page by page until they got to the end.

"Okay," Jack said. "We have more dead people who worked for car dealers. This is starting to get interesting."

"Seventeen, to be exact," J.D. replied. "Here's the important part. Every one of those people worked for a dealership owned by Allison Southwest. When you add in Colby and Willie, that makes nineteen."

"Wait a minute," Colby objected. "I don't like being lumped in with a bunch of dead people." She pinched herself. "Yep, I'm still alive."

"I get it, J.D. Fantastic job," Jack said.

"Sorry, but I'm a little slow here," Colby replied.

"It's not complicated, Colby, now that J.D. has figured it out. Dwayne Allison puts on a good public facade, but like most car dealers, he must have been struggling financially. We know he had a dead peasant policy on Willie. I'll bet he's got them on a bunch of employees and former employees, including you. He's managing to stay afloat by collecting on some of those policies, using the proceeds to keep some of his creditors away from the door, like my good friend, Beauregard Quillen."

"Wait just a damn minute," Colby almost shouted. "Are you saying that Dwayne Allison has been trying to have me killed? I don't believe that for one minute. I worked for him for eight years. He couldn't have been a better boss. He promoted me every year. I was making a damn good living and so was my husband. Dwayne Allison is liked by practically everybody in this town. He's even being talked about for mayor. Hell, every time I run across him, he tries to talk me into coming back to work. No way are you going to convince me he's a killer."

Jack rose from the table and paced behind the chairs. "Wait, Colby. I'm not accusing anyone of anything, yet. I'm just saying it could be Allison. Every one of these deaths is in a different town, not even in Fort Worth or Tarrant County. And if they are murders, the killer is smart enough to make them all different. Not likely that anyone would have ever connected the dots if we hadn't done so."

Colby rose and pointed her finger at Jack. "All you've got is a theory. I'll admit that Allison is smart enough to have planned it—if there was planning involved, I might add. I'm not a judge or a jury, but show me some evidence."

"She's right, Dad," J.D. said, coming down on Colby's side.

Jack returned to his chair, rubbing his face and eyes with both hands before he spoke. "Okay, here's what we're going to do. I'm going to file a motion to require Allison Southwest to produce all of the life insurance policies they have on employees or former employees. Well, on second thought, let's make it on former employees, since these deaths all involve former workers. That will cut down the numbers and make it a little more palatable to Judge McDowell. We won't get a hearing on the motion until a couple of weeks before trial, but that's the best we can do."

"Where does that get us in either solving the attempts on my life or in helping June's case?" Colby asked.

"If we could find that Allison Southwest had a dead peasant policy on your life, we'd have motive. I would take the evidence to Joe and let him take it from there. Problem is we just can't ask for any policies on your life. You're not a party to the lawsuit. Also, I don't want to ask for policies on just the other Allison employees we know met violent deaths. I'm not willing to show all of my cards yet. So, we've got to argue in our motion that the policy on Willie's life is part of a deceptive practice that potentially includes hundreds or thousands of former employees whose lives were wrongfully insured by Allison."

"Are you suggesting that not only is Dwayne Allison trying to kill me but also he's had eighteen former employees killed to collect life insurance proceeds? I don't believe that for a moment. He's been impacted by the economy, but he's still doing well."

Jack pondered her comment before replying. "Well, let's just see about his financial condition. It just happens that I'm the biggest customer of my banker in Beaumont. I've got his cell phone number and his permission to call him any time, day or night."

Jack retrieved his cell from his pocket and tapped on a name. The phone rang twice and Charlie Wilson answered.

"Jackson, my good friend and client, how goes it in Cowtown?"

"Doing well. How are the wife and kids?"

"Hell, Jack, you lost track. I've got a grandchild now."

"Time flies." Jack smiled. "Listen, I need a favor. By the way, I've got J.D. and my friend Colby Stripling on the speaker."

"J.D., I was never a TCU fan until you went there. Now, I've even got a purple shirt. Nice to meet you Colby. Now, Jack, tell me what I can do for you."

"Get on your computer and check into a Fort Worth company called Allison Southwest and its owner, Dwayne Allison."

"Hold on a minute, Jack. Let me get to the right screen. Here it is. Mega car dealer until the economy collapsed." There was silence while Wilson studied the screen. "Boy, he's in deep shit. Pardon my expression, Colby. He's down below seventy dealerships from a high of a hundred and twenty-five. He's behind on principal and interest on every one of his floor plans. Been that way for nearly three years."

"I take it he's not a very good credit risk," Jack said.

"Let's see . . . the only unencumbered property he appears to have is a small herd of quarter horses. Put it this way, if he walked into my bank,

I wouldn't even approve him for a new credit card. Not to say he can't pull out of it, but it's going to be a long haul. Looks like he was highly successful until the economy collapsed. Five years ago I would have loaned him ten million in a minute. He knew how to sell cars back then, probably still does."

Colby and Jack each fixed a double martini while J.D. went to the refrigerator to pour himself water from the dispenser. When they adjourned to the patio overlooking the pool, three very talkative people said nothing as they sipped their drinks and pondered what to do next. Finally, Colby spoke.

"Okay, I admit it's a possibility, but I'm not going to accept that Dwayne Allison is trying to kill me just because he's financially strapped."

Jack nodded his understanding. "Let's go back to Plan A. I'll file the motion. If McDowell buys into it, we'll know for sure if there is a connection between these deaths and dead peasant policies. We'll also know if there's a policy on you. I'm not sure how I can get whatever we find into evidence, but we'll worry about that when the time comes. One thing for sure, if we're right and the judge lets it into evidence, we'll damn sure be able to get the jury pissed off at Allison and his company. That potentially will make for some big damages for June Davis, and if this all comes out in the open, it should end the killings."

Colby sipped her drink. "Wouldn't it also put an end to Allison Southwest?"

"Colby, if we're right, it may put an end to Allison Southwest and send Dwayne Allison to death row."

64

Colby poured her coffee and joined Jack at the breakfast table.

"I already miss J.D." she said.

"Yeah, me too," Jack replied as he glanced up from the newspaper. "That's okay. He's living his dream and, besides, I don't have to fight with him over the sports section."

Colby took a sip of her coffee. "Can I have the women's section. Well, it's not called that anymore, but that section that you never read."

Jack smiled and pushed it toward her. Colby was thumbing through it when she stopped. "Jack, we almost missed this."

"Missed what?"

"The annual Fort Worth Zoo Beastro is tonight."

"So?"

"I volunteered for it for years. We've got to go. The whole zoo is open. The best restaurants in the area will be there serving appetizers, entrees and desserts. It's only a hundred dollars apiece, and every dollar goes to maintain the best zoo in the state."

Jack put down the sports section. "You sure you're up to leaving the house?"

Colby thought for a few seconds. "Yeah, I'll be okay. It'll be packed with people. And you'll get to see the new Texas section of the zoo. It's so good, Disney himself could have designed it."

The Beastro started early enough to still see some of the animals before they settled down for the night. Colby had gone online and purchased two tickets. She talked Jack into driving the Bentley. The event was cowboy casual. Jack wore freshly pressed jeans, a blue long-sleeved shirt with white stars and a pair of his Justin boots. To top it off he pulled a white Stetson out of the closet. Colby wore a cowboy-cut green pants suit, her own Justin boots and, of course, her Mikimoto pearls.

Among the first to arrive, they handed their tickets to a volunteer and were served champagne in return. Colby grabbed Jack's hand and led him to the left of the entrance to the Texas exhibit. They wandered through an old town, straight from a John Wayne movie set, seeing bobcats, mountain lions from West Texas, longhorns, sheep, goats, feral hogs, and guinea hens. As they made their way around the area, more attendees filled the zoo. Jack was delighted to find a display of horned frogs with a purple sign above them proclaiming NATIONAL CHAMPIONS, 2012.

When they exited the bat cave exhibit, they met face to face with Dwayne Allison. Allison seized the moment.

"Colby, how nice to see you. Glad to see you are out and about. So sorry about your house."

Colby grabbed for Jack's hand before speaking. "Thank you, Mr. Allison."

Before she could say anything more, Allison interrupted. "Of course, I must say that I disapprove of your escort for the evening. Still, Mr. Bryant has come back to his roots. I suppose we should just accept him in spite of the fact he's suing my company for a couple of million dollars."

At that, Jack smiled. "Mr. Allison, you have nothing to worry about if your business practices are on the up and up. If not, we'll just have to see what a jury does."

Allison frowned as he stepped away. "I see my banker over there by the lion compound. Please excuse me. Got to be on good terms with my banker."

Allison walked up to Quillen and pulled him over to a corner behind some decorative hay bales. "Damn it all. I come out here for a pleasant evening, and I'm confronted by that damned Jack Bryant. You know him?"

"Unfortunately, I do. He's responsible for daily lawsuits being filed against my banks. His name's not on the pleadings, but I know he's behind them. Fort Worth would be a helluva lot better off without him around. You're still my biggest problem, but he's running a close second."

"That bastard is suing me for four hundred thousand dollars plus treble damages, punitive damages, and a bunch of other horseshit. He claims I took the money from June Davis, the widow of one of my old porters, Willie Davis. Bunch of crap, I tell you."

"Yeah," Quillen replied. "I remember. He's the one who fell in the creek up in Denton and hit his head."

Allison stared at Quillen. "How'd you know that? It wasn't in the papers."

"No, it wasn't." Quillen smiled. "Still, when you send me a check like that, I have one of my staff check out the circumstances. Just doing my due diligence, Dwayne."

Allison stared at Quillen, not believing all he was hearing, but then looked around to make sure no one was watching as he pulled a check out of his coat pocket. "Here's five hundred thousand toward what I owe you. Seems like a lot of my old employees are kicking the bucket. Just glad I kept up those policies. That brings me back to that damn lawyer. If he had his way, all of these policies would be canceled, and then there would be no way for either of us to survive this recession. I need to win this lawsuit. Then we'll both breathe a little easier."

"How soon is it going to trial?" Quillen asked.

"About six weeks. Hopefully, I've got this Bryant jackal out-lawyered with Ace Leyton and his team."

65

Boss parked in front of Polytechnic High School on the east side of Fort Worth. Hawk was standing beside a small granite monument in front of the high school, as usual, smoking a Marlboro. Boss walked up to him. "Why meet here, on the east side? Run-down neighborhood, bad high school from what I hear."

"You're right, Boss," Hawk replied. "Not much these days. Only when I went here it was different. See this monument to C. A. Thompson. He was the principal when I was in school. Bunch of us graduates donated to put this here." Hawk pointed at the inscription. "He drilled this motto on the monument into us: REMEMBER WHO YOU ARE AND WHERE YOU'RE FROM. We wanted him to be remembered."

"I'm impressed, but look how you turned out. You think your principal would be proud of you?"

"Just depends on how you look at things. I've never been charged with a crime in my life. The rumor among my classmates is that I inherited some money and just do what I damn well please."

"Look, I don't have time to talk. Here's your next assignment. Fifty thousand if you get it done in a week."

Hawk rented a nondescript Taurus and parked for three days in front of the nursing home, watching the comings and goings of the staff and visitors. When darkness came, he crept up to peer into the windows to observe the living room and dining room. Dinner was usually over by six. Some of the more mobile patients made their way to the living room to watch television. Others went back to their rooms to read. The older ones in wheelchairs were taken, one by one, back down hallways to their rooms. It appeared the entire staff was engaged at this time of the evening. By eight thirty there was a second group in the dining room. Once the patients were down for the night, the staff had dinner together. Slowly, an idea formed. The way to gain entrance would be through the kitchen where the kitchen help came and went twenty-four hours a day. The staff all wore white uniform shirts, white pants, white tennis shoes, and a blue name tag over the right shirt pocket. *This ought to be easy,* Hawk thought.

The next day he found a uniform shop on Henderson close to the medical center. He described what he wanted, and in thirty minutes he was walking out with a suitable uniform, including a blue name tag with MIKE on it. That afternoon he parked the Taurus in the lot and again watched the comings and goings. As evening approached he was surprised to see a Bentley pull into the lot and Colby Stripling get out, leaving that damn dog in the front seat. He wondered who she was seeing here and considered changing his target, but then remembered the Boss's warning to forget about her for a while. So, he smoked a cigarette and waited. Thirty minutes later she came out the front door, started the Bentley, and left. Checking his watch, he saw that the dinner hour would be over and the kitchen staff would be removing dinner trays from the rooms.

He walked from the Taurus to the side of the building. He wasn't surprised to find that the kitchen door was locked but figured it would only be a short time before someone came out, having finished a shift or hauling something to the Dumpster. He lit another cigarette and waited. It wasn't long. Before he had finished his smoke, a male employee came through the door with a cart loaded with garbage. Hawk held the door open for him.

"Thanks, man," he said as he pushed the cart to the edge of the parking lot. Once he was past, Hawk went through the door and surveyed the kitchen until he spotted a serving cart. He pushed it through the kitchen to the interior door and found himself in the dining area. No one paid him any attention. As he knew from experience, if you acted like you knew what you were doing, people generally left you alone.

The entire staff seemed to be coming and going from the dining room, taking patients back to their rooms and getting them ready for bed. Hawk started cleaning the dining tables, placing the trays, plates, and silverware on his cart. When it was full, he pushed it back to the kitchen where he spotted the black man who had been taking out the trash.

"Hey, man. This is my first day. Where am I supposed to put this stuff?"

"On that counter. I'll load it into the dishwasher."

Hawk went back for two more loads until the tables were clear. When he spotted a utility closet in the kitchen area, he retrieved a dry mop and started mopping, first the dining room and then the hallways. When he saw the staff making their way to the dining room, he entered the hallway he knew led to Rob's room. As expected, the nurses station was empty. He knew the fourth room on the right would be the one. Still, he checked the nameplate beside the door: ROBERT W. JONES. Hawk pushed open the door and quietly closed it behind him. A thin man with black hair lay still under a sheet and light blanket. His eyes were open but not seeing.

"Rob, you've been here long enough. You're going to a better place," Hawk whispered.

He placed a finger and thumb over Rob's eyes and gently closed his lids. Next he pulled one of the pillows from under Rob and placed it over his face. He pushed hard for two minutes, getting no resistance or response. When he removed the pillow, he felt for a pulse and found none. Hawk replaced the pillow under Rob's head and moved quietly to the door. Cracking it, he found the nurses' station still empty. He stepped into the hall and walked to the end where he could see the entrance. This late at night the receptionist was no longer at her desk. He quickly walked past the dining room to the front and out the door. Then he was in the Taurus and gone.

66

Patients like Robert Jones were supposed to be checked every two hours. Blood pressure and pulse were to be documented, and a pillow was changed from his right hip to his left, or vice versa. After Irene was fired, the night attendants were careful to document patient checks when they went off shift, even when they weren't done. After all, they said to each other, why disturb a soundly sleeping patient? Sadly, if a doctor were to check the chart, two-hour checks were always documented even though the attendant never left the nursing station.

Shift change was at seven in the morning. Nurse Bertha Higgenbottom, an LVN, took over. A stickler for protocol, she checked each of the patients on what she called her hall as soon as she got reports from the staff going off duty. When she got to Robert Jones's room she entered with a smile on her face and said, "Good morning, Rob," as if she thought he would respond. He looked no different from any other day until she noticed his chest was not moving. She checked his pulse and found none. She calmly left the room, thinking it was probably for the best, and went to the nurses' station where she placed a call to Dr. Winston's answering service. Dr. Winston returned the call in fifteen minutes.

"This is Dr. Winston. I'm returning a call to my answering service."

"Dr. Winston, Robert Jones in Room 4 died during the night."

The doctor looked at his watch. Knowing there was no sense of urgency, he said, "I'll be by there within an hour. I'll call Colby Stripling after I check him."

When Dr. Winston got to the bedside, he studied the body for a moment, then pulled back the covers, not really looking for anything in particular, but thinking that Rob's time had come. He opened Rob's eyelids and bent over to within a couple of inches of his face. He looked from one eye to the other; then he called Nurse Higgenbottom over to confirm what he saw.

"Both eyes have petechiae, nurse. This is not a natural death. This patient was suffocated. We'll need to call the police after I call Colby."

Jack and Colby parked, and Colby leaped from the truck. She scribbled her name on the visitor log and rushed into the room with Jack trailing behind her. Dr. Winston came from another room to join them. "Colby, I'm sorry."

Colby was sad, but not tearful. "Thank you, Dr. Winston. Oh, this is Jack Bryant, a friend of mine. I knew this was going to happen sooner or later. I suppose I've been preparing myself for it ever since the day of his aneurysm."

Dr. Winston took Colby's hands in his. "Colby, this was not a natural death. I believe someone suffocated your husband."

Colby's hand went to her mouth. Jack put his arm around her shoulders.

"Oh, no," Colby gasped. She turned to Jack. "It's another one. Rob used to work for Allison Southwest."

Jack's eyes got hard. "I know. You told me when we were in New Orleans."

There was a knock on the door and two policemen pushed through the door. "Dr. Winston?"

"I'm Dr. Winston. This is Colby Stripling, Rob's wife, and her friend, Jack Bryant."

The first policeman nodded. "I'm Officer Blaise and this is Officer Gomez."

Dr. Winston explained what he suspected and showed them Rob's eyes. Then he outlined Rob's condition for the past ten years.

"Ms. Stripling, we will need to do an autopsy. Can we get your permission?"

Colby nodded. "Certainly."

"While we're here, do you mind if we ask you a few questions?" Blaise asked.

"Of course not," Colby replied.

"Officers, if you don't mind, I'm going to excuse myself," Dr. Winston said. "Here's my business card. I've written my cell number on the back."

When the doctor was gone, Officer Blaise asked, "When did you last see your husband?"

"Last night, probably around five or so. The time will be in the visitor log at the front desk. There's not anything I can do, but I get by here a couple of times a week, mainly just to make sure he's well cared for."

Gomez had taken a small pad from his pocket and was making notes as Blaise talked.

"And can I get your address?"

"I live in Monticello. No, I'm sorry. Right now, I'm staying with Jack. My home in Monticello was destroyed in a fire a few weeks ago. Jack's address is 34 Alta Drive."

"Can you tell me where you went after you left here yesterday evening?"

"Back to Jack's house."

The officer turned to Jack. "Can you confirm that, Mr. Bryant?"

"Absolutely," Jack said. "Well, I should clarify. My son plays football for TCU. I took him shopping at one of those stores on University across from the campus, and then we went to eat. I got home about nine thirty. Colby greeted me at the back door after I parked in the garage."

"Okay, that'll be all for now. Again, I'm sorry for your loss. I may have more questions after the autopsy is completed."

The officers started for the door. Officer Blaise turned back. "Just one more question. Did you have any life insurance on Mr. Jones?"

Colby hesitated before she replied. "Yes, I pay twenty-five dollars a month on a term life policy. Rob and I took out policies on each other, really for our future kids' protection, shortly after we got married. I'm not even sure now of the amount, but I think it's two hundred fifty thousand dollars."

After the medical examiners released Rob's body, it was buried in Greenwood Cemetery next to Rob's parents. There was nothing in the *Star Telegram* about his death. Colby didn't even want a minister. She, Jack, and J.D. stood beside the casket. Colby shed a few tears and said good-bye to Rob. In her mind, he had been dead for ten years. Afterward they turned and walked away.

67

The door to the grand jury room opened, and Irene, the nurse that was fired from Ridglea Oaks, walked out. When she saw Colby, she walked over to stand in front of her. "Don't worry, Ms. Stripling. I just told them the truth about what you said that day." Before Colby could reply, Irene turned and walked to the elevator.

The door opened again and the bailiff stepped into the hallway. "Ms. Colby Stripling," the bailiff said.

Colby, dressed in a plain black suit and black pumps, rose with Jack. She turned to hug him and followed the bailiff. As the door closed, Jack thought he had never felt more helpless. Joe Sherrod had called him a few days before to advise that the grand jury had taken up the death of Robert Jones and wanted to interview Colby. It was rare for Jack to lose control, but on this occasion he yelled. "Dammit, Joe. What the hell are you trying to do? After all that Colby's been through, now are you threatening to indict her?"

"Jack, calm down. I'm staying out of this. I have a young prosecutor

working with the grand jury. Both Dr. Winston and the medical examiner agree Jones was murdered. The grand jury is mandated to get to
the bottom of what happened."

"Shit, Joe," Jack exploded. 'You know as well as I do that if your
prosecutor wants an indictment, he'll just have to ask the right questions. A grand jury would indict a ham sandwich if the prosecutor led
them into it. And the worst thing is that I can't be in there with her."

Joe blew out a breath. "I know, Jack. Believe me, I know. She could
take the Fifth Amendment; only then they wouldn't hear her side of
what happened and that would almost surely lead to an indictment.
I've been doing this as long as you. Colby's smart. She should be able
to handle herself."

Jack slammed down the phone and cussed the system. He rubbed
his eyes and stared at the phone. Deep down he was worried, worried
sick that Colby was caught up in a system that was likely to lead to
only one result.

When Colby walked into the grand jury room, she was confronted
with twenty men and women, supposedly a cross section of the county,
along with the young prosecutor that Joe had mentioned to Jack. To say
she was intimidated would have been an understatement. She looked
around, not sure what to do until a gray-haired gentleman, dressed in a
conservative suit and tie, beckoned her to come forward.

"Step up, please, Ms. Stripling." He smiled. "I'm William Simmons,
a retired school principal and the foreman of this grand jury. We'll try
to make this as painless as possible. If you'll raise your right hand to be
sworn, we'll get started."

Colby did as she was directed and took the witness seat where
she looked around to see who might be asking questions. Jack had
warned her that not only the prosecutor but any one of the grand jurors
could pepper her with questions.

"Ms. Stripling, I'm Sam Elliott, an assistant district attorney assigned to this grand jury." His demeanor was pleasant and professional, but Jack had warned her to be on her guard. "I understand that you were born and raised in Fort Worth and have lived here your whole life. Could you summarize where you went to school and your various jobs?"

Not sure where to look as she responded, she chose the foreman as she described her growing up in Monticello, her high school years, the years at TCU and her employment with Allison Southwest, followed by her decision to become a realtor.

"You met your husband, Robert Jones, during your employment at Allison, is that correct?" Elliott asked.

"Yes, sir."

"And eventually you were married?"

"Well, not eventually, as you put it. We fell in love and were married three months later."

"Ms. Stripling," Elliott interrupted. "Let's move this along. After several years of marriage, your husband suffered an aneurysm and was in a coma for ten years."

Colby dabbed her left eye with a tissue. "Yes, sir."

"Instead of trying to arrange for Medicaid, you chose to pay for his care?"

Colby straightened her back and glared at the prosecutor. "I certainly did, Mr. Elliott. The amount that Medicaid would allow for his care was ridiculous. The facilities that took those patients were so bad you wouldn't kennel your dog in them."

"I understand, Ms. Stripling, you were paying about five thousand dollars a month for a better facility. We have your bank records and know that was a constant drain on your finances. Isn't it true that at the time of his death you were four months behind on your payments to Ridglea Oaks?"

Colby looked around the room for help and found none. Instead, she saw a number of the grand jurors staring at her with skepticism on their faces. "That's true, Mr. Elliott, but I had gotten behind before and always caught up."

"Exactly, Ms. Stripling." Elliott drove in his point. "It was a constant struggle to provide care to your husband."

"It was a struggle, Mr. Elliott." Colby raised her voice. "But I did it, and I expected to continue to do it as long as he lived."

Two of the women grand jurors nodded their understanding of what Colby had gone through and how she had handled such a devastating problem thrust on a young woman.

"And a half a million dollars would have solved a bunch of financial issues with you, right, Ms. Stripling?" Elliott asked. "You had only sold two houses in the past two years, one in Rivercrest and one tract home where you made a three-thousand-dollar commission."

Colby saw where Elliott was headed and didn't like it. *Why couldn't Jack be here,* she thought. "Mr. Elliott, I resent your insinuation. You know my husband and I had taken out mutual life insurance polices on each other shortly after we got married. The premiums were only twenty-five dollars a month. You're suggesting I wanted him dead. I had spent ten years keeping him alive."

Elliott was not bothered by her outburst. In fact he expected it. "Now, Ms. Stripling, the medical examiner has determined that Mr. Jones died somewhere between eight and nine on the night in question. Can you account for your whereabouts during that time?"

Colby tried to control her anger. "I saw my husband earlier that evening and was back at the house by about seven."

"But, between eight and nine was anyone there with you?"

"No, Mr. Elliott, not until about nine thirty when Jack got home."

Hard looks greeted her from several of the grand jurors. They clearly weren't buying her story.

"Home is actually the Rivercrest home of Jackson Bryant?" Foreman Simmons interjected.

"It is, Mr. Simmons. Jack Bryant is a friend of mine. The records before you should reflect that I've had several attempts to kill me, including one where my house was destroyed."

"But, Ms. Stripling, you moved into Mr. Bryant's house before your house was burned, and haven't you been seen about town and at TCU football games with Mr. Bryant? You even shared a suite with him in New Orleans at the Sugar Bowl," Elliott added. "Seems from all outward appearances that you were more concerned with your relationship with him than with your husband."

Colby lost it. "Mr. Elliott, you're a heartless bastard! It's clear you've already decided to charge me with a crime I didn't do. It doesn't matter what the truth is about my very platonic relationship with Jack Bryant. Do whatever you damn well please. I'll deal with it. Now, can I be excused?"

68

A few days later Jack received a call from Joe Sherrod. "Jack, Joe here. We need to talk. Can I drop by in about fifteen minutes?"

"Sure. It's one of the few times that the RV's empty." Putting down the phone, he suspected he knew why Joe was coming. If the grand jury had no-billed Colby, a phone call would have sufficed. Ten minutes later Jack heard a car door slam and Joe entered the RV.

"Come on in. I just made a fresh pot of coffee." Jack poured two cups and beckoned Joe to sit at the table.

Joe sipped his coffee and set it down. "I don't like to be doing this. I better just lay it all out on the table."

"Shoot," Jack said, now worried about what was coming.

"The grand jury is going to indict Colby."

"What charge?"

"First-degree murder."

"First degree? Joe, are you out of your goddamn mind?"

"Calm down, will you? I wasn't involved in any of it, and I'll have nothing to do with the prosecution. Here's what the cops say they have." Joe laid out the grand jury findings.

"No, Joe," Jack yelled. "Have you forgotten that Rob once worked for Allison Southwest? We're going to trial in a few weeks, and I think I'll prove that Allison had about eighteen of his former employees killed to collect on insurance policies. Rob has to be his latest. Your damn cops ought to be looking at him."

"Jack, calm down. Don't kill the messenger. Cops here are like cops everywhere. They pick a likely suspect. Rule of thumb is start with the spouse. They built a damn good circumstantial evidence case and are not about to dismantle it by looking elsewhere. I'm sorry, Jack."

Jack's shoulders slumped and his hand trembled as he brought his coffee cup to his lips. Resigned to the inevitable, he asked, "Okay, what do you want me to do?"

"First, Jack, you better win that case and prove just what you've said. You do that, and I'll see that the charges are dropped. Meantime, I need you to bring Colby in. I'll talk to my assistant who will be handling her case. We'll make the bond as low as we can without getting criticism from the media. I'll even call the judge as soon as I get back to the office. With a little luck, she'll only be in a holding cell for a few hours."

Jack drove home and found Colby on her computer at the kitchen table. Colby smiled as Jack entered and got up to greet him.

"Colby, you better sit down. Another shoe has just dropped."

Jack told her about his conversation with Joe. When he finished, Colby buried her head in her hands and cried quietly. Jack walked around the table and put his hand on her shoulder. When she composed herself, she looked up. "Jack, I'm not sure how much more I can take. First someone has been trying to kill me. Then my house is torched. Now I'm getting indicted for murder. What am I going to do?"

Jack gently pulled Colby to her feet and put his arms around her. "You're going to be okay. I told Joe I'd take you down to the police station. I'll get you out on bond as soon as it's set. Then, we're going to win June's lawsuit. Once I prove Allison is the one behind these murders, Joe said he would drop the charges. You have my word that we're going to win." As Jack made the promise, he realized it was one that he might not be able to keep.

69

Joe had already called the booking desk and alerted them that Colby was coming in. After being fingerprinted and photographed, Colby was escorted to a holding cell adjoining Judge Butler's courtroom. Jack made his way to the courtroom and waited until Judge Butler called Colby's name. When she was led from the holding cell to the bench, Jack joined her. A young prosecutor approached and stood on the other side of Colby.

"Your Honor, I'm Jackson Bryant, Ms. Stripling's lawyer."

Judge Butler nodded. "Ms. Stripling, the state is charging you with murder in the first degree. Are you prepared to enter a plea at this time, or would you prefer to defer?"

"We can enter a plea right now, Judge," Jack said. "The plea is not guilty."

"I need to hear that from your client, Mr. Bryant."

"Not guilty, Your Honor," Colby said in a quiet monotone.

"Very well." The judge turned to the prosecutor. "I understand the prosecution has a recommendation as to bail."

"Yes, Your Honor. We recommend bail be set at two hundred fifty thousand dollars."

"That's acceptable to the defendant, Judge. I'll be putting up a cash bond by wire transfer. I believe I can have it in the district clerk's bank account in no more than two hours."

"If you're going to post bond that fast, I'll permit Ms. Stripling just to wait in my holding cell rather than be returned to the general population. You're excused, Mr. Bryant, to go to the district clerk's office and complete the necessary paperwork. I'll have the clerk call me when the bail money is transferred."

When they got home that evening, Colby collapsed on a chair in the living room.

"Now what?" she asked.

"I've called Jacob Van Buren. He's going to appear as cocounsel and will handle anything that comes up until we get through with June's trial. I don't want you thinking that I'm abandoning you to take care of June. You understand how important it is that we win her trial, don't you?"

"Of course I do. If she wins, I win too. Don't worry about me. Your plate is full for the next several weeks. I'll help anyway I can."

The next day a headline appeared in the city section of the *Star Telegram*. SOCIALITE INDICTED IN MURDER OF HUSBAND. The story described the indictment and facts that led to it. Jack read it and concluded that the details had been leaked by one of the detectives or a prosecutor. Jack considered calling Hampton to put their version in front of the public but reconsidered, thinking that it would accomplish very little. Far better just let it fade from public attention as most murder cases did until trial approached. That would be six months to a year away. By then he planned to have the charges dropped.

The problem was Colby. She withdrew to her bedroom, coming

out only to try to be a member of the team when Jack and J.D. were talking about June's case. On one occasion Jack suggested getting professional counseling. Colby shook her head and quietly went back to her room.

On the Monday morning two weeks before trial, Jack arrived at an almost deserted parking lot at seven forty-five. For some reason the judge had scheduled the hearing at eight, and there were very few cars in the lot with even fewer people on the street. That, of course, would change in an hour. Jack parked Lucille and grabbed his briefcase and cane. He had decided that it was time to impress the judge with his attire; so he was dressed in the suit he wore when he got his last big verdict in Beaumont and carried his Bat Masterson cane. The light at the corner turned red as he reached the street, and he was thinking about his argument while he waited for it to change.

"Mr. Bryant . . ."

Jack had tried not to show it, but his nerves had been on edge even before Colby's murder charge. Now they were taut like the strings on a banjo. He swirled, ready to drop his briefcase and launch an attack with his cane. The man behind him had no visible weapon.

"Cool it, Mr. Bryant, I'm unarmed. I'm here to tell you that you are not welcome to practice law in Fort Worth anymore. If you want to stay here, you'll be better off just watching your son play football. Otherwise, you may regret it."

Jack turned full face to the man who had long brown hair, a beard, and glasses. Clearly not a lawyer, he was dressed in black jeans and a blue Western shirt with snaps for buttons.

"Look, you son of a bitch, I don't know who the fuck you are and don't care. Whoever told you to deliver your message, you tell him that I'll practice wherever I damn well please. If he doesn't like it, shove it. That clear?"

Hawk smiled. "Just delivering the message, Mr. Bryant. You have a good day."

Jack turned to walk across the street just as the light changed to yellow. *Shit, the stakes can't get much higher. I'm on my way to try to convince the judge we need the other dead peasant policies, evidence that may get the charges against Colby dismissed and win June's case. I'm confronted with the guy that matches the sketch done by the New Orleans police department. It can't be a coincidence. Someone wants me to drop this case and this motion. That narrows it down to one man.* When he got to McDowell's courtroom, he saw Leyton and beckoned him out into the hall.

"What the fuck are you and Allison trying to do?"

Leyton looked at him with blank eyes. "I don't have a clue what you are talking about."

Jack relayed what had just occurred, sparks flying from his eyes.

"Look, I didn't have anything to do with it, and I can guarantee you that my client didn't either." Leyton stared at Jack like he had lost his mind and returned to the courtroom.

Jack entered the courtroom and realized that there were no lawyers present on other matters. For whatever reason, his motion was the only one set. He walked through the gate to the counsel table opposite Leyton and laid his cane on the table. Then he opened his briefcase and took out his motion. When he took his seat, he could feel his heart pounding in his chest, requiring him to take a few slow, deep breaths before the thumping disappeared. The judge came out of his chambers without an announcement by the bailiff. Both lawyers rose as McDowell climbed to his bench.

"Mr. Leyton and Mr. Bryant, you may come forward."

When they approached the bench, Judge McDowell asked, "Mr. Bryant, are you feeling all right? You're sweating and your face is flushed. Should we wait a few minutes before we hear your matter?"

"No, Judge," Jack said. "I'm fine. May I proceed?"

McDowell nodded his head.

"Judge, we have filed a motion for production of any dead peasant policies . . . I apologize, Your Honor . . . I meant life policies on former employees of Allison Southwest. It's a simple motion. In fact, I'll settle for a computer run of the names of the persons insured, the amounts, when the policies were taken out and current status. Should be able to be produced with a few computer strokes."

"Mr. Leyton?" Judge McDowell said as he turned to face the other lawyer.

"Judge, there are a multitude of problems with this request. First, there are privacy issues with the persons insured and their beneficiaries. Next, what possible relevance could there be about other policies on other Allison Southwest employees? We're dealing here with who is entitled to the benefits of one policy on William Davis."

"Judge, if I can explain," Jack said, his voice rising. "Discovery is permissible in this state if the results of the discovery may potentially lead to relevant evidence. We have pled under the insurance code and the Deceptive Trade Practices Act that Allison Southwest has engaged in a pattern and practice that is illegal and can lead to punitive damages. The only way we can prove it is to know the names of other employees who Allison has insured and then discover whether they or their loved ones knew if the policies existed. As to the beneficiaries, we believe that the only beneficiary on all of the policies will be Allison Southwest. We can also determine whether the other employees actually signed these so-called employment agreements as Allison claims that Willie Davis did. And, of course, we will agree to a confidentiality order, restricting my team from disclosing the names of the employees and any personal information about them until the court approves such disclosure."

"Mr. Bryant," the judge said, making no effort to control the volume of his voice. "It looks to me like this is nothing more than a fishing expedition with no hope of ever landing anything other than a couple of minnows. Besides, I promised Mr. Leyton that we would be going to trial in two weeks. If I grant this motion, all it will lead to will be more discovery and a delay in the trial. That's not going to happen. Your motion is overruled. Good day, Counsel."

Jack knew when he was beat. It suddenly hit him that Leyton had set up this early morning hearing with the judge to avoid other lawyers and litigants from hearing the discussion about the dead peasant policies. Was it also set up at this time so that he could be threatened on the street without anyone overhearing? He turned on his cane, went to counsel table where he loaded his briefcase, and banged the railing gate as he left the courtroom.

70

Jack called Colby as soon as he got out of court and told her about the threat. She promised to lock herself in the house with the alarms on. Next he called Joe to report the incident and told him just to take a look at the New Orleans sketch to identify the man. Jack was steaming when he got back to the RV and breathed a sigh of relief when he saw that there were no pro bono clients lined up in the parking lot. He needed to focus on the Davis case and the threat made on him in the street. After unlocking the door, he tossed his briefcase on the passenger seat and sat at the table, pondering what to do. How could he deal with the threat from some unknown person? It almost surely came from Allison, but he couldn't be certain. He considered Quillen and the other dozen or so financial institutions he and Van Buren had sued. Obviously they were suspects, but his mind kept coming back to Allison and Leyton. Somehow he had to address the threat. Finally, he concluded that he could only leave it in Joe's hands. For him it would be like finding the proverbial needle in a haystack.

Then his mind drifted to McDowell's ruling an hour ago. There had to be a way to put pressure on McDowell so Leyton didn't win every battle. If these rulings continued throughout trial, he knew he was going to lose, leaving appeal as his only hope. Even if he got Mc-Dowell reversed on appeal, it would be too late for Colby.

At last he had an idea that he thought might potentially solve both problems. He picked up his cell phone and called Hartley Hampton.

"*Star Telegram,* Hampton here. How you doing, Jack?" Hampton said as he glanced at his caller ID.

"Could be doing better. Can you drop by my RV sometime this afternoon? I may have a story for you."

"Hell, Jack, after the props I got on that last series I did on you, I'm not waiting until afternoon. I'll see you in about thirty minutes."

Twenty minutes later a car pulled into the parking lot, the door opened and Hampton climbed the RV's steps. Hampton stuck out his hand. "Ace reporter at your service. What do you have for me?"

Jack invited Hampton to take a seat at the table and retrieved a bottle of water for him from the refrigerator.

"To start, let's keep this on background at first. When I get through talking, we'll decide what you can use."

Both men understood that background meant the information was confidential until Jack said otherwise. Jack walked Hampton through the lawsuit from the very beginning when June knocked on his door with the envelope and check from the postal department, his unsuccessful meeting with Allison, the filing of the lawsuit, and the morning's hearing.

"Of course nearly all of that is public information, except my confrontation with Allison, which I don't want you to use. For some reason you guys in the media haven't picked up on this story."

Hampton nodded. "Up until this very moment it was just one more civil lawsuit. We media types usually aren't much interested in civil litigation unless there's a bigger story surrounding it."

"I tried to get a computer run on Allison's dead peasant policies this morning, and Judge McDowell denied my motion almost before I could finish talking. You can have a copy of the motion."

"Wait a minute," Hampton interrupted. "Isn't there something about an insurable interest? Where is that when one of Allison's employees quits or gets fired?"

"Leyton found an old employment agreement from thirty years ago that he says gave Allison the right to continue coverage on Willie Davis even after he retired. I suppose they will claim the same thing on all of the dead peasant policies."

Hampton was scribbling as fast as he could on his steno pad. "Anything else?"

"Oh, we're not through. I'm getting fucked by McDowell every time I go in his courtroom. I've been around courtrooms long enough to know when the judge is intentionally favoring one side. Best guess is he's gotten a lot of money from Leyton's firm, maybe Allison, too. I figure that Leyton and Allison have decided to pull out all stops to win this one to discourage other such lawsuits. It's common practice with big corporations. If they think there's potential for a bunch of lawsuits, they'll throw the kitchen sink at the first one. Whatever it takes to win, they'll do it."

Hampton raised his hand. "Only we have contribution limits. No one can give more than two thousand dollars to the judge's campaign in one election. That's not enough money to buy off a judge."

Jack shook his head. "I'll bet if you go to the public records, you'll find that a lot of money has been flowing into McDowell's campaign, most of it from people associated with Allison or Leyton."

Hampton was already reaching into his briefcase to retrieve his computer. "You're wireless here?"

Jack nodded.

Hampton fired up his computer and clicked a few keys. When he got to the screen he was looking for, he scrolled down as his eyes grew big. "Shit, McDowell already has about two hundred contributors, all for the max. That raises a bunch of red flags right there. It's really early in this election cycle to have those kinds of contributions in a local judicial race. Of course, they give only home addresses, not employment."

"I'll bet you've got search capability that can identify their employers. Care to place a small wager that most of them are working for Allison or Leyton's law firm?"

Hampton closed his computer as he thought. "Wow, this could be big, maybe bigger than that last story I did on you. I knew I should have just camped out in your parking lot and waited for the stories to roll in. Anything else?"

Jack put his elbows on the table and rested his chin on his hands as he debated the last two issues. Then he spoke. "This is definitely background. We think that Allison may have caused the deaths of twenty of his former employees and had dead peasant policies on all of them. One of them was Robert Jones. He was suffocated in a nursing home just two weeks ago. Colby Stripling is a friend of mine and was his wife. You know she's been charged with the murder. She didn't do it. Allison did. Of course, the charge against her is public, but I'd appreciate it if you would leave her out of your story for now. That case hit the headlines and then disappeared. Colby can't handle any more publicity."

"I'll make you a deal," Hampton said. "We'll leave her out of the story provided I get an exclusive when you're ready to talk."

"Done."

"Okay, I'll ask one more time. Anything else?"

Jack nodded. "One more thing. I had parked my car in that lot across the street from the courthouse this morning and was waiting at the light. McDowell scheduled us for eight o'clock. No one else was around until I heard this guy behind me saying in a low voice that I better quit practicing law in Fort Worth. He threatened me. I told him to go fuck himself, but it shook me up. Someone tried to kill Colby while we were in New

Orleans for the Sugar Bowl. An eyewitness gave the New Orleans police enough of a description that they did a sketch. It looks like the same guy threatened me this morning."

"You think he was working for Allison?"

"Don't know and you can't suggest that. Besides the case with Allison, I'm involved in close to five hundred lawsuits involving multiple banks and mortgage companies. Seems I've managed to make a lot of enemies in a very short time in Fort Worth."

"Can I just say that your life has been threatened?"

"That's okay. In fact, I want you to do it. Maybe the publicity will back them off for a while. But, you also have to understand I called you because I'm trying to level the playing field with Judge McDowell."

"I get it. When does your trial start?"

"Two weeks."

"You can bet my story is going to get McDowell's attention as well as that of Allison and Leyton."

"I appreciate it, Hartley. At this point, I don't care if I bring them all down." Jack paused. "They have it coming."

71

Jack got home that evening and was surprised to find J.D.'s pickup beside the garage. He found his son in the man cave, leaning back in a recliner with crutches next to him.

"J.D., what the hell happened?"

"I pulled a goddamn hamstring in my left leg at practice this afternoon. Hell, I'm in better shape than anyone out there. You know I worked my butt off all summer. Nobody stretches more than me. Then this happens a week and a half before our opening game."

"Could have been worse. How long are you on crutches?"

"Trainer says about a week. I go in for therapy every day during the next week. Then I may be able to do it on my own. I may be back for the third game of the season. Shit! Why couldn't this have happened six weeks ago?"

Colby had come downstairs to fix a sandwich. "I told him that all major sports athletes sustained injuries. J.D., you might as well calm down and accept it. A few weeks isn't your entire career."

J.D. relaxed. "Both of you are right. Let's change the subject. What's going on with the charges against Colby and June's lawsuit?"

Jack shook his head. He recounted the events of the day, including the threat on his life, as he paced in front of the blank television. He finished with his interview with Hampton.

"Damn, Dad, you're pulling out the heavy artillery. You really think McDowell will change his attitude?"

"Put it this way, he couldn't be any worse."

Colby had remained silent until Jack finished. "Look guys, I'm not worried about some damn motion, even if you do say it's important. You received a threat on your life this morning. Someone's trying to kill me. On top of that I'm charged with murder. None of us is safe. Is this ever going to stop? I feel like I'm confined to a bunker as it is. I had a peaceful, pleasant existence until you set foot in my life, Jackson Douglas. Now my life's hell and you don't seem to give a damn." Colby bolted from the room and up the stairs.

"She's right, of course," Jack said in a low voice. "I really have screwed up her life, ours, too, to some extent. I could use a little help, though. Since you're out of football for a few weeks, you want to be my trial paralegal?"

J.D. pulled his dad into a bear hug. "Damn right I do. You think one of us ought to tie one arm behind his back to make it a fair fight?"

Jack broke into a laugh. "That's the Bryant spirit. Now I need to go make amends with Colby. Maybe I can talk her into getting out of her bedroom a little more."

Jack climbed the stairs and tapped on Colby's bedroom door. Ten minutes later J.D. heard his footsteps and Jack joined him in the man cave.

"Colby okay?"

Jack shook his head. "About as well as can be expected. She's calmed down for now, but the pressure is really getting to her. The sooner we get to the bottom of this, the better."

72

Jack crawled out of bed and found a T-shirt and some cutoff jeans. He shut the bedroom door behind him and found Killer sleeping in the kitchen. With the events of the night before, no one let him out, so Jack hooked a leash to his collar to take him for a morning walk before he retrieved the newspaper from the driveway. When they approached the front door, Killer stopped and growled, baring his teeth at something on the other side. Jack opened the door to find a handful of reporters on the lawn. Killer started barking and straining at his leash. There were strangers on his lawn, and he would vanquish them.

Jack knew what was happening even before he got his paper. Hampton had put a rush on his story. He wanted it on the front page.

Before he could retrieve the paper, he had to come to an understanding with the reporters. "Heel, Killer."

Killer stopped his barking and stood alongside Jack. "Morning, ladies and gentlemen."

"Mr. Bryant, what can you tell us about Allison's dead peasant policies?" one asked.

"Is it true your life was threatened yesterday?" a woman chimed in.

"Did you know that Judge McDowell had taken nearly four hundred thousand dollars in contributions from Allison and his law firm?"

Jack put up his hands. "Truce, guys. Let me grab my newspaper so I'll know what the hell you're talking about. Then I'll take a quick shower and put Killer out in the backyard so he can take a leak. I'll be back here in thirty minutes."

Jack returned to the kitchen where he let Killer out the back door, knowing he would immediately make a beeline for the driveway's wrought iron gate where he would warn the strangers to keep their distance. He poured a cup of coffee from the automatic brewer and sat down to read the *Star Telegram*. It was the lead story.

JUDGE ACCEPTS $400,000 FROM LITIGANT AND LAW FIRM

JUDGE REFUSES TO RELEASE DEAD PEASANT POLICIES

LAWYER'S LIFE THREATENED

My God, Jack thought, *seeing it in bold print and all caps makes it sound even worse.*

Judge Bruce McDowell, a longtime Tarrant County District Judge, has received $400,000 from two hundred contributors in a campaign for reelection that has only just begun. The *Star Telegram* has traced the contributors to employees of Allison Southwest and its national law firm. Phillip Leyton is head of the firm's Fort Worth office. Allison Southwest is embroiled in litigation in McDowell's court with June Davis, a widow whose husband was once a porter for Allison. The lawsuit stems from a life insurance policy on William Davis. In court papers Ms. Davis said neither she nor her husband ever knew about the policy until a postal error delivered a $400,000 check to her. The check was payable to Allison Southwest.

In the insurance industry, such policies have gained the name of "dead peasant policies" because they are usually placed on low-level workers and the premiums are paid even after the employee leaves the company. The policy is routinely kept secret from the employee and his family. According to a spokesman for the department of insurance, such policies were banned in Texas a number of years ago but are still available in some states.

June Davis is represented by Jackson Bryant, formerly a prominent plaintiff attorney in Beaumont who recently moved to Fort Worth. Bryant reports that he was going to the courthouse yesterday for a hearing about production of a spreadsheet of all of Allison Southwest policies on former employees when he was accosted in front of the courthouse. His life was threatened if he continued to practice law in Tarrant County.

"At the hearing I asked Judge McDowell to require production of the other dead peasant policies still being carried by Allison Southwest. Clearly, it's deceptive for Allison to place these polices on employees in secret, knowing it will ultimately reap the benefit of such ghoulish practices. I fully expected him to rule that they were discoverable, but he summarily rejected my motion. So, as of right now, only Allison Southwest and its lawyers know the scope of the deception."

Jack chuckled as he put down the paper. He'd read enough. Now he would make short order of the mob outside. After a shower and shave, he dressed in brown slacks, a white shirt, and loafers. He knew what he was going to say and also knew it would not make the reporters happy. Before going to the front door, he whistled to Killer from the back. Killer rounded the corner and stopped at his feet. "Good dog, Killer. You protected us once again. Now come on in the house."

Jack told Killer to stay in the kitchen and walked to the front door where he motioned for silence. "Sorry to keep you folks waiting. I've now read the *Star Telegram* story and really can't add anything more to it."

"Are you going to ask that Judge McDowell recuse himself?" a voice yelled.

"That's really trial strategy that I prefer not to discuss. However, let's see how events unfold over the next couple of days. I wish I could tell you more, but Mr. Hampton certainly has done his homework. I have no reason to disagree with what he has reported. You all have a good morning."

Judge McDowell stepped out to pick up his paper and was also confronted by reporters. "What the hell? What in tarnation are you doing on my lawn? You're trespassing and I demand that you get off my property."

He grabbed his paper and hurried back to the sanctity of his house. As he read the paper a scowl settled on his face. How the hell did this happen? All he did was take campaign contributions. And what business is it of some damn reporter that he ruled the dead peasant policies weren't discoverable? After refilling his coffee, he reached for his cell phone and called Ace Leyton. When Leyton answered, the judge spewed out a string of expletives. As he paused to get a breath, Leyton jumped in.

"Judge I've got a couple of reporters on my lawn too. Calm down."

"Calm down? You son of a bitch, you may have just cost me my election and just when my pension was about to vest. How the hell could this happen?"

"Judge, it's just business as usual. Our employees contribute to campaigns all over the state. They list their home addresses, and no one ever looks beyond that. Someone talked this Hampton guy into digging. My guess is it's Bryant. Unfortunately, it's all out there on the Internet. We're going to have to come up with another plan to support our fine judicial candidates like you."

"Hell, the horse is out of the barn. Some other future plan doesn't do me any good."

Leyton paused while he thought. "I have an idea. Suppose you call a press conference this afternoon and say you just learned of the contributions coming from my firm and Allison when you read the story. You're an honest judge and you're sending refund checks to everyone remotely connected with the lawsuit."

At four that afternoon the bailiff stuck his head in the judge's door. "It's time, Judge. You've got a whole courtroom full of reporters. Lights are everywhere and cameras are rolling."

McDowell wiped the sweat from his brow and, pushing his shoulders back, he walked into the courtroom and made the effort to climb to his bench as if he were thirty years younger and fifty pounds lighter. He poured himself a glass of water.

"Be seated ladies and gentlemen. Thank you for coming. I'm pleased to clear up some misconceptions that have surfaced today."

Two reporters in the front row looked at each other and shook their heads.

Another reporter asked, "What misconceptions, Judge? You received four hundred thousand dollars in campaign contributions from lawyers and litigants on one side of a case I understand is going to trial in two weeks."

McDowell was not accustomed to having questions thrown at him in his own courtroom. "Sir, if you'll give me a moment, I'll explain. All we have on our computer and all that's reported to the election commission are names and home addresses. We have no idea where these people work. Now that this has come to light, I've instructed my campaign staff to return every one of the questionable contributions. That task will be completed in a week."

A television reporter in the front row blurted out, "What about Leyton's firm? They had to know what they were doing."

McDowell wiped the sweat from his face again. "That's up to Mr. Leyton. I think that he and his firm have abided by the letter of the law. You may want to check other sitting judges' reports. Maybe they've done this for a number of judges they consider well qualified." McDowell tried to smile.

Hartley Hampton rose from the back row. "Judge McDowell, are you going to recuse yourself from the Davis case?"

McDowell had enough. He rose from his chair and pointed his finger at Hampton. "Absolutely not. I'm one of the most senior judges in this county. My reputation for impartiality is beyond reproach. Anyone and everyone who sets foot in my court will be treated equally. Good day."

Another call took place that day. Dwayne Allison called Leyton. His voice was surprisingly calm. "Ace, you've created a helluva mess, haven't you?"

"I'm doing my best to unwind it. I never figured all of this would come out in the open. It never has up until now, and our firm does it in at least twenty states where judges are elected, maybe more. Dwayne, do you want me to resign so you can get other counsel?"

There was silence on the phone before Allison spoke. "No, not at this late date, but if you don't win, let your partners know I'll be suing your firm for malpractice. If I lose, the amount of the loss will come to rest at your feet. Understood?"

"Understood, Dwayne."

That evening Jack convinced Colby to join him and J.D. in the man cave. J.D. flipped local channels to catch coverage of the story. When it got to be seven o'clock, Jack clicked off the TV.

"You going to try to have him recuse himself?" Colby asked.

"Hell, no," Jack replied. "Before today I would have done about anything to have gotten rid of him. Now he'll be watched like a hawk by the media. He'll call them straight for damn sure. By the way," Jack grinned. "Remind me to send Hampton a case of scotch at Christmas."

73

Jack went into his pretrial mode. Every waking minute was spent at one end of the dining room table: outlining the examination of each witness, thinking through the order of exhibits, and carefully preparing for the voir dire examination of the jury panel and the opening statement. After five days Jack shut down the computer, satisfied he was basically ready, and headed for the kitchen. J.D. was coming through the back door.

"Afternoon, son. What happened to your crutches?"

"Trainer said I'm through with them," J.D. replied as he turned to rummage through Jack's canes. "He suggested I use a cane for a few more days. I told him I knew just where I could get one." J.D. picked out a solid oak cane with an eagle for the handle. "Okay if I use this one?"

"Be my guest. You want a glass of water?"

J.D. thought a minute. "Well, since I'm not actually in training right now, I suppose an occasional beer wouldn't hurt."

Jack nodded and opened the refrigerator, pulling out two Bud Lights. As he handed the beer to his son, Colby appeared in the kitchen, sleep still in her eyes from an afternoon nap. Jack smiled as he realized she was making the effort to crawl out of her shell.

"So, if everyone's having a drink, where's mine? Chardonnay, if you please, bartender. Then I suggest we all adjourn to the patio. I think we may be in for a first-class sunset."

After they had settled into chairs on the patio and Killer had made the rounds to be petted and have his ears scratched, J.D. asked, "So, how's the trial prep coming, Dad?"

Jack sipped his beer as he thought through what he had done over the past several days. "I'm basically done. I'm sure I'll come up with some more questions and thoughts for opening statement over the next week. That's the beauty of the computer age. When I was a baby lawyer, we'd fill yellow pads with all of this stuff and then had to make notes in the margins when something else popped up. Now, I can go into whatever document I need and insert a question in its rightful place.

"The only pieces missing from the puzzle are those other dead peasant policies the judge blocked me from getting."

"Just how important are those policies?" Colby asked.

"In reality, we should win the case without them. Still, I don't know what impact they might have since we haven't seen them. Like I said before, if we had them and could get them in evidence, the jury might be so pissed off that they would award several million in punitive damages for June. More importantly, they could also get you off the hook on the murder charge, particularly if we're right and Allison had policies on those other employees who met with violent deaths. I'd at least like to have a look at them before trial and then try to figure out a way to get them in evidence." Jack sighed. "Only, I gave it my best shot and struck out."

Jack thought for a minute, then turned to J.D. "Son, you're supposed to be the computer whiz. You think you could hack into Allison Southwest's computer system and get the information on the policies we've been looking for?"

J.D. nodded. "I think I can probably do it, but if the state bar finds out you're using evidence that we got from hacking into Allison's system, won't you get in trouble?"

Jack walked over to stand behind Colby and put his hands on her shoulders. "Son, Allison raised the stakes when he killed Rob and got Colby charged with murder. Her life is on the line. If what we're doing helps get her off, I'll deal with the state bar later. I wouldn't give a damn if I had to trade my license for her life."

74

The next morning Jack was awakened by a pounding on his door. "Wake up, Dad. Get your ass out of bed. I've got everything."

Jack put on shorts and a T-shirt and met J.D. at the kitchen table. After pouring a cup of coffee, he took a seat beside his son.

"It took me all night, but here's what you want—copies of all of the applications and policies and a spreadsheet that lists the employees and former employees who have insurance coverage, their Social Security numbers, the amount of the coverage and amount of the premiums, along with their last known addresses. The beneficiary on every one is Allison Southwest. The spreadsheet is even in alphabetical order."

"Here, let me have that paper. I'll read the victims' names and you tell me if there was coverage and how much."

As Jack read the names, J.D. scrolled down the spreadsheet. After thirty minutes they had completed the list. All nineteen had polices on their lives from two hundred to five hundred thousand dollars, with double indemnity in the event of accidental death.

"You made that list before Rob was killed. Was he covered?"

J.D. took a minute to get to the right place on the spreadsheet. "There he is. Five hundred thousand dollars in coverage, in effect for fifteen years, beneficiary Allison Southwest."

"Now there's one more," Jack said. "See if Colby is on that sheet."

J.D. clicked his mouse a few times. His eyes grew big as he drew in a breath. "Oh my God, Dad. There's a policy on Colby for two and a half million dollars. Why would Allison have put the biggest coverage on her?"

Jack poured another cup of coffee as he thought. "I suspect she was a rising star back when she worked there. If she'd stayed, she probably would have run the finance operations for all of the dealerships. On top of that she was young and female. The premiums had to be dirt cheap."

"Wow, Dad, we've got him. We've got Allison."

"No, we don't, son, not yet. We've got information. I can't offer one bit of this in evidence. Not to say that I can't use it to make Allison sweat and hopefully lay a trap so we can force him to provide this same information during trial. That's my job as a trial lawyer. I'll figure out a way."

"Why don't you turn all of this over to Joe Sherrod and let him run with it?"

Jack shook his head. "Two reasons. We might lose the element of surprise in our trial, which is just a week away. As to the charges against Colby, all this would do is give the Fort Worth cops a motive for Allison. They think they've made their airtight case against Colby. They don't have any other evidence, and they're not likely to bust their butts to look for proof that Allison had Rob killed. This won't change their minds. Joe can wait. As I said, one way or the other, I'll use this information. There's got to be a way to tie Allison to Willie's death and all these other deaths. I just need to think on it for the next week, and then we'll see how the trial plays out."

75

Jack awoke at four o'clock in the morning, tossed and turned for a few minutes, and resigned himself to the inevitable. It was the first day of trial and his body was already pumping with adrenaline. He stopped by the bathroom and then went to the closet to pull on his cutoffs, T-shirt, and running shoes. He walked to the kitchen and saw that the coffee was not set to come on for another hour and a half. After he pushed the start button, he went to the back door and hollered to Killer, who was asleep in one of the patio lounges. Killer bounded to the door.

"Come on, let's you and me go for a walk." He hooked a leash to Killer's collar, and they went out the front door and across the street to the country club. Killer's leash was twenty-five feet long on a spool that gave him enough leeway to sniff out new smells or the scents of dogs who passed by the day before.

Jack thought about the days to come. He remembered the early days of his career as a trial lawyer when he wanted to be in the courtroom but still dreaded setting foot in the court's threshold. He smiled as he remembered his first trial when not only did his voice crack on voir dire but throughout the trial his hand shook so badly that he couldn't take notes. Then there were the years that he couldn't sleep more than four or five hours a night and by the fourth trial day he was functioning on adrenaline and coffee. All of that had now changed, except for this morning, the first day of trial. Now he knew what to expect and knew he could handle anything thrown at him by the judge or opposing counsel. He fully expected to be in command when he set foot in the courtroom. It was his stage and he expected all eyes, particularly those in the jury box, to be on him.

By the time he and Killer turned after going twenty minutes away from the house, he had thought through his preparation once again and was satisfied that everything had been done. In the past week he had met with June Davis and explained what she should expect. He paid for Jerry Buchanan to drive up from Palestine to make sure there were no gaps in his testimony. David Gamboa, his local insurance broker, was prepared to testify that dead peasant policies were illegal in Texas. Then he smiled. His legal assistant, seated right next to him at counsel table, was J.D. If J.D. did decide to go to law school in a few years, that would be the one thing that would bring him out of retirement. The law firm of Bryant & Bryant had a nice ring to it. Last, but, of course, not least, Colby would be in the audience, acting as another pair of eyes and ears, a thirteenth juror, so to speak. Her job would be to listen to the evidence and offer her lay opinion of witnesses and constantly keep her eyes on the jury to see how they were receiving the evidence. Now her role took on new meaning after the criminal charge against her. And it would be good for her to have something to focus on other than her own problems.

When he and Killer walked back to the house, he found the *Star Telegram* on his driveway. Hopefully, Hampton had done his job. Jack wanted a human interest story on June Davis and her fight with Allison Southwest. It didn't need to be big, but Jack wanted it to remind Judge McDowell that others were watching him and his rulings. Jack stopped on the front porch under the light to glance at the paper. It wasn't on the front page, but it was the second story in the local news section. That would do for now.

After pouring coffee and making sure Killer had food and water, he sat at the kitchen table to read the story and glanced at the rest of the headlines. Nothing good going on in the world with the exception of TCU football. The first game of the season was the following weekend. The coach was quoted as saying that J.D. might be activated by the second game. Jack was getting his second cup of coffee when J.D.

walked into the kitchen, rubbing his eyes and yawning. "Damn, Dad, I thought I was the one getting up early."

"I beat you by about an hour. Your coach says he may activate you for the second game. You think you'll be ready?"

"Heck, I was ready before preseason started. I'll just have to convince him I'm okay to start that game. Will we be through with the trial in two weeks?"

Jack nodded. "Shouldn't be a problem. This is not a long one. We might even finish before the week is out."

J.D. poured his double helping of Cheerios, heavy on the sugar. "Which of those three new suits you bought me last week should I wear?"

"Your call. They're all conservative. Don't carry a cane, though. One Bryant with a cane is enough. Let's plan to leave here at seven thirty. I always like to get to the courtroom early. Besides, on the first day, I want to grab the counsel table closest to the jury."

J.D. looked up from his cereal. "Any particular reason?"

"Not really. It's just another one of those quirks of trial lawyers. We'd be in the middle of the jury box if we could. I'm going to wake Colby. Lucille leaves in an hour and a half."

76

Jack's team parked in the courthouse parking lot about ten minutes before eight. J.D. put three boxes on a dolly, and Jack carried his briefcase and his Bat Masterson cane.

At the light Jack remembered his encounter with the guy who threatened his life. *Too bad that son of a bitch isn't around now. I'd let him go one on one with J.D.,* he thought. They mounted the steps. The only problem with being in the old courthouse was that J.D. had to haul each box to the top, one at a time, and then retrieve the dolly. When they entered the building, only one deputy was on the metal detector. Jack started to empty his pockets until the guard stopped him.

"Hell, Jack. That won't be necessary. I know you and no one else is around to complain. This your son?"

"Yep, that's J.D."

"Why's he all dressed up in a monkey suit like you. We need him out on the field."

"I pulled a hamstring a couple of weeks ago," J.D. replied. "I'm out until week after next. Meantime, I'm helping my dad in a trial."

"And if this lovely lady is with you, she can just walk around the metal detector, too."

"I'm Colby Stripling. I'm part of the trial team." Colby said.

They took the elevator to the second floor. When it opened, they saw June sitting alone on one of the benches outside the courtroom, wearing the same black dress that she had worn to bury her Willie. She rose as they approached. Colby and Jack hugged her. Jack introduced J.D. The decision to have her attend the trial alone was another strategic one. He considered having Willie, Jr., or her daughters join her and then thought better of it. He wanted the lone widow to be up against a big corporation. Jack believed there were multiple ways to send a message, and he used them all.

They entered the courtroom and found a new bailiff seated at the desk inside the rail to the right side of the bench. While J.D. unloaded boxes and placed them along the inside rail, Jack went to the bailiff to introduce himself. The bailiff was medium height, wore glasses, and had a full head of gray hair. Jack guessed he had been on the street for twenty or so years and had enough seniority to take this job to fill out his thirty years until retirement.

"Morning, Bailiff, I'm Jack Bryant."

The bailiff rose and extended his hand. "Gregg Waddill. Pleased to meet you. The regular bailiff is on vacation this week. I'll be taking his place. This your associate?"

Jack turned to J.D. "Step over here. Actually, this is my son, J.D. He goes to TCU but is taking a short leave of absence to act as my paralegal this week. J.D., this is Deputy Gregg Waddill."

"Pleased to meet you, sir."

"Deputy, unless the judge dictates a preference, we'll take the counsel table closest to the jury box."

"It's first come, first served in here. That one is yours. I see you have another assistant in the audience. It'll be a while, but when we get the jury in here, I'll ask that she join you at counsel table for jury selection."

That prompted Colby to come through the gate and shake the bailiff's hand. Fifteen minutes later Ace Leyton entered the courtroom, trailed by Dwayne Allison and what appeared to be a young associate. Leyton was in that small group of lawyers that thought that he had entered a war zone when he stepped through the courtroom door for trial. He refused to look at Jack or his team or even acknowledge their presence. He would address Jack only if specifically instructed by the judge. Early in his career some older lawyer must have instilled in him the idea that such tactics would intimidate the other side. All it brought from Jack was a smile.

Dwayne Allison was not quite sure what to do with himself. He watched his lawyer unloading his briefcase, then glanced around the courtroom, finally settling on Colby. Getting no instruction from Leyton, he walked up to the rail and stuck out his hand. "How are you, Colby? Sorry about your house and all of your current problems. I want only the best for you."

"I'm fine, Mr. Allison. The road's been a little bumpy lately, but it'll be okay."

She turned to take a seat at Jack's counsel table as the judge entered from his chambers.

"Good morning, gentlemen and ladies. We're here to try the case of *June Davis v. Allison Southwest*. Announcements, please."

"Jack Bryant here for the plaintiff. We're ready."

"Phillip Leyton here for the defendant. We're ready too, Judge."

"Now, would you be so kind as to introduce your clients and any members of your staff who will be present during trial."

Jack rose. "Judge, this is June Davis."

"Pleased to meet you, Mrs. Davis."

"Also, Judge, my son, J. D. Bryant, is a paralegal in my office and will be with me at counsel table. This is Colby Stripling. Other than voir dire, she'll be in the audience."

"Mr. Leyton?"

"Judge, this is Dwayne Allison. I believe you and he have been on some rodeo committees together."

"That we have. Welcome, Dwayne. From this point forward, I'll be calling you Mr. Allison."

"Understood, Judge," Allison replied.

"Judge, this is my associate, Ryan Fairchild. This will be his first trial."

"Listen and observe well, Mr. Fairchild. These are two excellent lawyers."

McDowell certainly got up on the right side of the bed this morning, Jack thought. *Maybe Hampton's stories did some good.*

Leyton had just taken his seat when something occurred to him. "Judge, there's one matter that I'm not sure how to handle and seek the court's advice. Mr. Bryant's son is his *so-called* paralegal. I know he's on the Horned Frog football team and is being touted for all-American. Looks to me like his son ought to be out practicing with the team for the opening game this weekend. It appears that Mr. Bryant is trying to gain an unfair advantage, having his son sit beside him through the trial."

McDowell pondered for a moment, then turned to Jack, obviously buying into the spin Leyton was putting on the issue. J.D. squirmed in his seat, not sure what all of this meant.

"How about it, Mr. Bryant. Why's your son here?"

Jack pushed to his feet with his usual courtroom demeanor—total, calm control. In fact, the only reason that a judge or jury would ever see Jack blow his stack was if he saw some tactical advantage in doing so. "Not an issue, Judge. J.D. spent the summer working with me as a para-legal. As you may have seen in the paper, he pulled a hamstring and is out until at least the second game of the season. Unlike Mr. Leyton's national firm, I'm a one-man shop. J.D. is thinking about going to law school and since he can't practice for a while, I need him here with me."

McDowell reluctantly nodded his understanding.

"Then that brings up another issue, Judge," Leyton said. "What do we tell the jury about J.D.? We can say nothing, but some of them are going to recognize him and wonder what he's doing here. Or we can have you or Mr. Bryant say something about why he is here. Frankly, I don't like either solution."

"Judge, I don't really care. J.D. is going to be here. We'll accept whatever the court decides."

McDowell drummed the fingers of his right hand on his bench as he thought. "Okay, this is not a big deal. I'll introduce him to the jury myself and make it brief, then move on. Okay with everyone?"

Both lawyers nodded their approval.

The judge looked around the courtroom and turned to the bailiff. "We don't have a reporter. Would you buzz her, please? We need to be on the record."

Two minutes later a large, fiftyish woman with purple hair marched into the courtroom like it was a grave inconvenience and took a seat at her machine. "Can I have a card from any lawyer who will be speaking in this trial?"

Jack and Leyton complied with her request.

"Now, my rules are that everybody keep their voices up so I can hear them, and no one will be talking over anyone else. If that occurs, I'm just going to throw up my hands like this." She lifted her hands like she was a referee signaling a touchdown. "That means I'm not getting a good record and nobody wants that. Right, Judge?"

McDowell shook his head at his court reporter. "She's right. This is Ms. Cartwright. She's been in this courthouse for thirty years. What she says, goes. Now, what pretrial matters do we have?"

"None from me, Judge," Jack said. "I know the rules and expect to follow them."

"Mr. Leyton?"

"Judge, just a couple. I don't want the life insurance in this case being called a dead peasant policy. That's pejorative and prejudicial to my client."

"Agreed, Mr. Leyton. Mr. Bryant, you will refer to the life insurance policy as the policy or the life policy, nothing more."

Jack nodded his understanding.

While they were talking, Hartley Hampton had slipped in the hallway door and took a seat in the back row. He was already taking notes.

"Then, Judge, you've already ruled that any evidence of other life insurance on other employees was not discoverable. We want to extend that to any mention of them in the trial of this case."

"That will also be sustained, Mr. Leyton." McDowell looked to the back of the courtroom at Hampton. "I see that a member of the media is already here. I don't want either of you or your clients talking to the media during the trial of this case. There's already been an article written by Mr. Hampton about the start of this trial. I want this case tried in the courtroom, not in the media. Understood?"

Jack jumped to his feet. "No sir. It's not understood. I expect to abide by the disciplinary rules when it comes to talking to the media, but unless you're going to enter a gag order, I don't agree with you. My client and I are entitled to talk to the media and respond to their questions. What you are suggesting is infringing on our First Amendment rights."

Part of the speech was to make his point with the judge and part was to give something to Hampton to put in the paper if the judge maintained his position.

Leyton rose to his feet. "I agree with you, Judge, and have no reason to be talking to the press."

The judge looked at each lawyer and out to where Hampton sat before speaking. "If both counsel don't agree, then I'll withdraw my previous comments. But listen good, Mr. Bryant, you stray beyond what the disciplinary rules permit and I'll personally report you to the grievance committee after the trial. Understood?"

Jack shrugged his shoulders and sat down.

McDowell glared at him for not responding. "Okay, I've ordered a panel of forty-eight." He looked at his watch. "They should be here in about an hour." McDowell pushed out of his chair as the bailiff said, "All rise."

77

Thirty minutes before the jury arrived, the clerk handed copies of the jury cards to each side. The jury cards provided some basic information: name, age, address, occupation, race, sex, marital status, religion, number of children, length of residence in Tarrant County, prior jury service, and involvement in other lawsuits.

Jack made sure that J.D. and Colby had a highlighter and directed them to mark anything they considered pertinent about a prospective juror. When the jury panel filed in, Jack studied each of them intently as they walked down the middle aisle. He was looking at how they dressed, whether they carried the morning paper or a book to read, whether they had any physical deformity, anything that might give him one additional clue as to what was going on in their minds. He was pleased to see that there were several African Americans in the panel. Of course he wanted them on the jury. Once they were seated, the bailiff advised the judge.

"Good morning, ladies and gentlemen," McDowell said. "Thank you for being here this morning. Our judicial system wouldn't work without public-spirited folks like yourselves. This is the case of *June Davis v. Allison Southwest*. It's a case about the proceeds from an insurance policy. Mr. Bryant, you may proceed."

Jack started to get up, but was interrupted by the judge. "I almost forgot. Mr. Jack Bryant represents Mrs. Davis. His son, J. D. Bryant, is his paralegal. Some of you may recognize Mr. J. D. Bryant because he plays football for TCU."

Most of the men and several of the women looked at J.D. and nodded their heads.

"He's got a minor hamstring injury and will miss this week's game, but he should be back for the second game of the season. That's all you need to know about him. Proceed, Mr. Bryant."

Jack got to his feet, cane in hand, and stood before the jury. "Ladies and gentlemen, I represent June Davis. She's a widow. Her husband died in an accident while he was out fishing near his house up in Denton. After Mrs. Davis buried her husband, she received a letter from the post office, enclosing a check made out to Allison Southwest for four hundred thousand dollars. We intend to prove that money rightfully should have been hers and have filed this lawsuit to recover that amount along with treble damages, punitive damages, and attorneys' fees. There's more, but I'm only allowed to give you a short summary at this time.

"The judge has already introduced J.D. Now let me ask who knows or has heard of Dwayne Allison, the owner of Allison Southwest?"

Thirty hands were raised.

"Among you folks who raised your hands, how many of you feel that your knowledge of Mr. Allison will cause you to start off this case leaning toward his side of the case or putting more weight on what he has to say?"

Several hands were raised.

Jack looked at his jury list. "Juror 34, Mr. Brown, you have those kinds of feelings?"

"Yes, sir. I'm a Shriner, and Mr. Allison was potentate of our temple a few years back. He's a fine man."

Allison beamed and Leyton noted the comment. Jack planned to challenge him for cause.

"Now, is there anyone here whose employer has taken out a life insurance policy on your life without your knowledge?"

Juror 4 in the front row replied, "How would we know if our employer didn't tell us?"

Jack grinned a little sheepishly, knowing he had made his point. "Actually, you wouldn't unless, maybe after you left the employment, your employer offered you the opportunity to continue the policy, or maybe the information leaked out by mistake."

The jurors looked confused and wondered where this was all leading. Jack knew that he could go no further, but wanted to plant just a small seed in their minds about the issue to come.

Jack inquired about jurors who had worked for car dealers, those who had been parties to lawsuits, those who had purchased a car from an Allison dealership, those who had life insurance, and a new category of questions that came with the recession: those who were out of work. After an hour and a half the judge told him his time was up. He thanked the jury panel for their time and sat down.

Leyton rose to take his place. He explained that Allison Southwest had taken out a life insurance policy on Mr. Davis early in his employment and had paid all the premiums on it. Before he could get beyond that, Juror 16, a black man, asked, "What did Mr. Davis do?"

When Leyton replied he was a porter and tried to move on to his next question, the juror interrupted. "Don't make any sense for him to take out a life insurance policy on a porter. Did he take out these policies on his other employees too?"

Leyton looked at Judge McDowell, who addressed the jury. "Ladies and gentlemen, we're here to decide issues on this one insurance policy, not others. Please move on, Mr. Leyton."

Several of the jurors shook their heads as though they disagreed with the judge. Jack suppressed a grin and noted their numbers.

Leyton elicited favorable comments about Dwayne Allison from many of the jurors. He accomplished his goal of letting the jury panel know that Allison was a public-minded citizen and a civic benefactor. His last question dealt with prospective jurors who had a problem with a car dealer. About half the jury panel raised their hands. He had to take the time to discuss each of their problems to decide whether to attempt to strike them or to take a calculated risk to leave them on the jury. Then his time was up.

The judge excused the jury, and each lawyer made challenges for cause. The judge's rulings reduced the panel to thirty-one, and he excused the lawyers to make their remaining six strikes. Jack asked to use the jury room and led his team and June to it. They had twenty minutes. Jack had tried to get all of the jurors who had a high opinion of Allison off the jury with challenges for cause, but he had not succeeded.

"We're going to have to use most of our preemptory strikes to get rid of the rest of them. I hadn't counted on the number of people in this town who knew Allison."

"I think I told you to expect that some time back," Colby said. "His public persona is a lot different from the Dwayne Allison we have come to know."

Jack eliminated six more jurors and surveyed the rest of the list, concluding that the remaining jurors would be okay, maybe not great, but okay. When they returned to the courtroom, Jack was surprised to find that Leyton had already made his strikes, handed his list to the clerk and was seated at the counsel table, quietly talking to Allison and his associate. It only took another five minutes for Jack to find out the reason why. When the jury panel was called back in, the clerk called out the names and numbers of the final jurors.

As they took their seats in the jury box, Jack did a slow burn. *That son of a bitch,* he said to himself. *He used five of his six strikes to eliminate African Americans. Who the hell does he think he's dealing with?*

McDowell turned to the remainder of the panel. "Ladies and gentlemen, thank you for your service."

The judge was hurrying to excuse the remaining members of the jury panel when Jack got to his feet. "Your Honor, we need to approach the bench."

McDowell knew what Jack was about to do. He had seen the same thing and was trying to get rid of the panel before Jack could make an objection, knowing that by then it would be too late. *Obviously,* Jack thought, *I still don't have a level playing field.*

"Very well, Mr. Bryant. Approach, Counsel."

At the bench and out of the hearing of the jury, Jack said, "Your Honor, the *Batson* case, decided by the United States Supreme Court, makes it quite clear that when one party is a minority, the other side cannot strike jurors of the same race without a showing of some other basis besides race as a reason. Mr. Leyton has struck five African Americans. I've checked their jury cards and my notes, and there's no basis other than race. We formally challenge."

Leyton was now obligated to give some reason other than race for his challenges. The problem was that while Leyton was a seasoned trial lawyer, he had gotten to that stage of his career where he took very few notes and just winged it in court. He figured that his reputation and powers of persuasion could carry the day. This time he was in trouble. He really had struck those five jurors because he thought they would lean toward June Davis as a member of their own race. He fumbled through his copy of the jury cards.

"Your Honor, I struck Juror 2 because he worked as a truck driver and William Davis sometimes drove a truck to pick up and deliver parts. I struck Juror 19 because her daughter works as a maid and Mrs. Davis did that at one time. I struck Juror 12 because . . ."

McDowell looked to the back of the courtroom and saw Hampton making notes. He had no choice in this ruling. He interrupted Leyton. "Look, Mr. Leyton, so far your explanations do not overcome a *Batson* challenge. Unless you've got better reasons for the other three, I'm going to do something I've rarely had to do. I could declare a mistrial and start all over, but that will waste all of our time. I'm going to excuse the jury to the hall and give you another opportunity to make your challenges. I strongly suggest that race not be used as a factor. Frankly, Mr. Leyton, I'm disappointed in you. A lawyer of your stature should know it's going to raise red flags when you have an African American plaintiff and you strike five of her race. You have twenty minutes. I'll be in my chambers. Bailiff, let me know when we're ready to proceed again."

After the jury panel was excused for the second time, Jack explained to his team what he had done and why they were delaying.

June beamed her approval. "Thank you, Mr. Bryant. I was worried when I only saw one black face in that box. I grew up in the days of separate black schools, separate water fountains, riding on the back of the bus. Some of those racist feelings die hard."

When Jack saw Hampton motioning to him from the rail, he walked over.

"Jack, you don't have to tell me what happened. Let me guess. I saw that Leyton struck five African Americans. You called his hand on it, didn't you?"

"Yeah, I did. Surprisingly enough the judge went along with me. Leyton has twenty minutes to rethink his strikes."

Hampton let out a low whistle that drew a shake of the head from the bailiff.

The judge decided not to explain what had happened to the jury. There would be no way to do so without impugning the character of either Dwayne Allison or Ace Leyton. Only this time when the final panel was called to the jury box there were four African Americans, two Hispanics, and six Anglos, a much better representation of the ethnic mix in Tarrant County. Jack nodded his satisfaction as the jurors took their place.

78

Jack rose from his table and took a position in front of the jury. He leaned slightly on his cane. "My client, June Davis, was married to Willie for fifty-three years. They were wealthy people, not in terms of dollars, because they had little. Their wealth came from their love, their three children, eight grandchildren, and their relationship with God through the Greater Mount Zion Baptist Church."

Leyton rose to object that this should be saved for closing argument, thought better of it, and sat down.

"June worked off and on, cleaning houses. Willie spent the last twenty years of his work life as a porter for Allison Cadillac. He made twenty thousand dollars in his last year before his retirement. That was fifteen years ago. He was killed in a tragic accident while he was fishing near his home. June and the kids buried him and went on with their lives."

Jack heard quiet sobbing and looked over to see June reaching in her purse for a handkerchief.

"A few months later June got a letter from the post office, enclosing a check for four hundred thousand dollars in life insurance proceeds. The check was made payable to Allison Southwest. She never knew that Allison had put a large life insurance policy on her husband or that Allison kept paying premiums for fifteen years after he retired. It was a dead peasant policy."

Leyton leaped to his feet. "Objection, Your Honor," he almost yelled. "He's intentionally violating the court's prior ruling."

McDowell glared at Jack. "Approach."

When both lawyers were at the bench, McDowell kept his voice low but chewed out Jack. "You have intentionally violated my ruling. You will not do that again or there will be sanctions. Understood?"

"Sorry, Your Honor. It just slipped out."

"Return to your places." McDowell turned to the jury. "That last comment will be stricken from the record and you will be instructed to disregard it. Proceed, Mr. Bryant."

Jack returned to face the jury, thinking of something an old lawyer had told him years ago. *Once the cow's peed in the milk, you can't strain it out. No way the jury's going to forget about dead peasants.*

In the back of the room, Hampton smiled. Now that the term had been used, he had the lead for tomorrow morning's story.

Jack decided to cut his opening short. He had made his point. "Ladies and gentlemen, I'm going to give you back some of the twenty minutes I was allocated for opening. Suffice it to say that when June learned about the life insurance policy, she asked Mr. Allison to pay the proceeds of the policy to her as his widow. He refused. We're here because Dwayne Allison and Allison Southwest intentionally profited from the death of Willie Davis, and we expect them to pay for it." Jack thanked the jury for their time and sat down.

Leyton rose and paced up and down in front of the jury twice, his hands in his pants pockets. "William Davis signed an employment agreement over thirty years ago. In that agreement he authorized

Allison Southwest to take out insurance on his life. My client did so and paid the premiums on it for all those years. It was not an issue until he died. Now this lawyer is telling you that his client should be unjustly enriched by the proceeds from a policy that she never paid one red cent for."

Leyton was very careful to lay the blame on the lawyer he wanted to paint as greedy, not the widow, particularly since there were now four African Americans on the jury.

"On top of that, he wants to treble the four hundred thousand and punish my client when he did nothing wrong. The evidence will show that Dwayne Allison and his company kept their agreement with William Davis and are entitled to the proceeds from the policy. Thank you."

Judge McDowell looked at the clock on the back wall. "I apologize, ladies and gentlemen. I've worked you through your lunch hour, but I wanted to get you in the box and get opening statements done so we could keep this case moving. Let's take an hour for lunch. Bailiff, please escort the jury to their room."

Once the jury was gone, Colby pulled ham sandwiches from a bag in one of the boxes. "Here, I made these this morning. Can I get sodas?"

"Water's fine," Jack said. "Thanks for the sandwiches. How are we doing?"

"Everything looks good to me. Why did Leyton try to strike so many African Americans?"

"My guess is that it wasn't his idea but Allison's. Looks like Leyton's letting Allison call some of the shots. Bad mistake, particularly for an experienced lawyer. There can only be one lead dog in a trial, and it can't be the client. Leyton must be getting a lot of heat from Allison about something." Jack turned to June, who was quietly eating half of her sandwich. "June, you'll be the first witness this afternoon. We have to go through all of those documents. You'll be on the stand for the rest of the day. You okay with that?"

"I'll be fine, Mr. Bryant. I'd just like a bottle of water up there with me. I've handled Mr. Leyton once. No reason I can't do it again."

79

After being sworn in by the court reporter, June took the stand and smiled at the jury. "Good afternoon, ladies and gentlemen," she said without prompting.

"Good afternoon, Ms. Davis," twelve voices replied.

Damn, thought Jack, *she's going to be good.*

"Tell the jury a little about yourself, June."

June turned to look at the jury. "I'm seventy-five years young. I grew up in a rural part of north Denton County. Willie and I went through the fourth grade together before he had to drop out to help support his family. I made it to the eighth grade and would have liked to have gone to high school, but the Negro high school was fifteen miles away and I had no way to get there. Willie and I got married and had three children. We saved our money and bought a little two-bedroom house with five acres. That's where Willie planted his garden. Willie had a variety of odd jobs before getting on with Allison Cadillac, where he stayed for about twenty years. Once my kids got a little older, I cleaned houses when I could. We managed to get by. Didn't have much, but didn't need much."

Jack rose and stood behind his chair, leaning on his cane. "Judge, I just need to stretch my knee out a bit." The judge nodded. In reality,

Jack just wanted to keep the jury's attention after lunch when he knew there was a risk of one or two members dozing off.

"When did Willie retire from the Cadillac dealership?"

June looked out the window as she thought. "Must have been about fifteen years ago."

"Did Willie get any pension?"

"No, sir. Got nothing but a key chain with his retirement date on it. After that he did get a little Social Security check every month, and we got by okay."

"Now, June, I don't want to upset you, but how did Willie die?"

Colby saw several of the jurors shift uncomfortably in their seats. One woman looked away, turning her head to the back of the room.

"He left early to go fishing at a creek near our house, same creek he'd been fishing in since he was a boy. He didn't come home, and I sent Willie, Jr., looking for him. Willie, Jr., found him lying in a shallow part of the creek with his head bashed in. They said it was an accident, but I know my Willie and I know it wasn't."

"How did you learn about that life insurance policy that Allison took out on Willie?"

"First I knew of it was when I received a letter from the United States Post Office. It was an official letter."

"June, let me interrupt. I'm handing you the original of that letter and putting a copy on the overhead. Can you read this paragraph here that I'm pointing out to the jury?"

"It says they're sorry that a letter was mangled in their processing machine. My name was the only one legible on it. They located me and forwarded the letter, the mangled envelope, and a check payable to Allison Southwest for four hundred thousand dollars. I called the person who signed the letter. He said they checked the Social Security Web site and found that my Willie had died recently. That's how they tracked down our address and sent the letter and check to me. The check says it's in full payment of death benefits on the life of William Davis."

Jack walked over to stand beside the jury and leaned against the rail. "What did you do with the check?"

"I took it to you, Mr. Bryant, and you said you would deliver it to Mr. Allison. I presume that you did."

"Did Mr. Allison offer to pay you one penny out of that four hundred thousand?"

"No, sir. Not to this very day."

"June, I want to put up on the overhead an employment agreement. I'll also hand you a copy. Have you seen that before?"

June studied her copy and turned each page carefully, then looked up.

"Yes, sir. I saw it in your office for the first time two, three months ago."

"It's four pages, single-spaced. On the fourth page is a signature on a line that has 'William Davis' typed underneath it. Can you identify that as Willie's signature?"

June shook her head. "No, sir. Can I explain?'

Jack nodded.

"My Willie only went to the fourth grade. He wasn't much for reading and writing. I told Mr. Leyton here that he may have signed a few things in his life, but I doubt if he knew what he was signing. I did all the bill paying. So the answer to your question is that I can't identify that as Willie's signature."

Jack zoomed the camera into one paragraph on the last page. "You see this paragraph where it says that Allison Southwest can take out life insurance on Willie and keep it in force until he dies, whether or not he's still employed?"

Several of the jurors squinted to read the fine print.

"Was your Willie capable of reading and understanding that paragraph?"

"Objection, Your Honor," Leyton said as he stood. "Calls for an opinion she's not qualified to make."

"Judge," Jack said. "She lived with him for fifty years. Certainly, there's no one better qualified."

McDowell again glanced at Hampton in the back of the courtroom. "Overruled, Mr. Leyton. Proceed."

June looked at the jury. "No way he could understand all that legal talk."

"And this section that says that you were to receive ten thousand dollars on his death, did Mr. Allison ever send you a check in that amount?"

June looked at Allison. "You certainly did not, Mr. Allison, and you know it. Ten thousand dollars would have helped me bury my Willie. Instead, we had to take up a collection at the church to buy him a casket."

Allison leaned over to Leyton and whispered, "Can I write her a check right now?"

Leyton shook his head.

Jack looked at the jury and found some of them to be visibly upset.

"One last series of questions, June. We provided Allison's lawyer with a bunch of checks and income tax returns and so forth that you had stored in your garage. We know that a few of those for sure had Willie's signature on them. Did you look at those?"

"Yes, sir, I certainly did," June said, now with defiance in her voice.

"Did his signature on any of those documents look anything like the one on that so-called employment agreement of thirty or so years ago?"

"They did not, Mr. Bryant."

Jack looked at the jury and checked his notes. "Pass the witness, Your Honor."

"Mrs. Davis," Leyton began. "I want you to know how much Mr. Allison and I sympathize with you for the loss of your husband."

Leyton was doing his best to come across as warm and caring.

"Thank you, Mr. Leyton."

"Ma'am, I won't be very long. First, did I understand that you never received a check for ten thousand dollars from Allison Southwest after your husband passed?"

June straightened her back and looked at the jury. "No, I certainly did not."

"Mr. Allison assures me that he'll correct that oversight immediately," Leyton said, syrup almost dripping from his mouth.

"Now, I want to put a couple of documents on the overhead. And I'm going to ask Mr. Fairchild to provide you with copies also. One is a tax return from back when Willie was working and you had to file them."

Leyton put up one tax return and then blew up Willie's signature. "You can see that all right, Mrs. Davis?"

"I can, thank you," she said as she put on her distance glasses.

"Bear with me, Mrs. Davis. I'm using a little technology here, and I may mess it up." Leyton fiddled with the overhead until he had the signature from the tax return blown up with the signature from the employment agreement below it. "You see some similarities, Mrs. Davis?"

June shrugged her shoulders. "Maybe one or two."

"For example, you see the big *W* in 'William' looks almost exactly the same, and the looping *D* looks like it was made by the same hand."

June put her glasses down on the rail in front of her and looked at Leyton. "Sir, I'm not a handwriting specialist."

"And one more thing, Mrs. Davis, let me see if I can do this right. I think I can superimpose one signature over the other."

Leyton did so and the signatures were nearly a match. Two of the men in the back row noticed the similarities and nodded to one another. Without waiting for an answer, Leyton thanked June and passed the witness.

Damn fine job, Jack thought. *Now what do I do?* He rose from his chair and walked with his cane in hand to stand beside the witness. "Approach the witness, Your Honor?"

"You may, Counsel."

"June, are you familiar with forgeries?"

June blinked her eyes and didn't know how to answer.

"I mean, do you know that forgery has been around since the days of the ancient Egyptians, and in this age of identity theft it's even more rampant."

June nodded her head, not sure what to say.

Jack turned and pointed his cane at the overhead. "If someone had forged your Willie's signature on that document, say in the past year or two, would you have any way of knowing?"

June shook her head. "I suppose not, Mr. Bryant."

"Nothing further, Judge."

McDowell looked at the clock and said, "It's a little before five, but I think it's time to call it a day. I instruct you not to talk with anyone about these proceedings. Further, you are not to read anything in the paper about this case. If something about it shows up on television, turn the TV off. Understand?"

When the jury was gone, Judge McDowell excused the lawyers and their clients. Jack led his team and June out into the hallway and around the rotunda where they could talk quietly.

As soon as they were alone, June asked, "Did I just lose our case for us, Mr. Bryant?"

Jack patted her on the back. "No such thing. I have that covered. Is Willie, Jr., picking you up?"

"Yes, sir."

"Then J.D. will walk with you down to the street and help you find Willie, Jr. We'll see you in the morning. You did just fine."

Once Jack, Colby, and J.D. were in the truck, Jack had a little different tune. "That hurt us. Buchanan warned me that he could have taken the other side of this case."

"Dad, when are we going to start talking about the other policies? Won't that turn the case in our favor?"

"We've got to bide our time and wait for the right moment. It'll come. It's like a running back, hesitating until you've given him an opening with a block on the linebacker. Once it happens, I'll know it and we'll be running to daylight. Trust me on that."

80

Hampton's story the next morning made it to the front page, below the fold, but still where it would catch the eye of anyone who even glanced at the paper. He described Bryant's objection to Leyton's original jury strikes and quoted an unnamed trial lawyer's opinion that Leyton being ordered to start over with his strikes was almost unheard of. Next, he discussed the judge's ruling about the use of the term "dead peasant policies." That was followed by June Davis's testimony that she never got one penny from the life insurance on her husband. In the last paragraph he described the similarities between the signatures which obviously were going to be a major point in the case.

Jack read the article and mulled over his trial presentation. He had originally intended to call Dwayne Allison as part of his case. Now, he rethought his order of proof. With June's testimony, all he needed was his insurance expert and he had what lawyers called a prima facie case. It almost surely would withstand a motion for directed verdict in favor of the defense, particularly since he figured that Hampton's story would draw more of the media this morning. He would save Buchanan for rebuttal. It was a gamble, but the more he thought about it, the more he liked putting on a short, simple case and cross-examining Leyton's witnesses. Still, he had to watch for his opening to cram the information

J.D. found on the policies down Allison's throat. Jack told J.D. and Colby his plan on the way to the courthouse.

"Dad, you're the trial lawyer, but are you really sure that's a good idea? I mean, couldn't it backfire and leave us out on the street?"

"You're right. That's the nature of any trial. It's like a chess game. You make a move and anticipate what the other side will do. I've got a pretty good feel for Leyton at this point. He's not going to do anything fancy. He thinks he's got the upper hand and is just going to play it out. I like him thinking that way. I'm just a little more of a gambler, that's all."

Colby heard all of the discussion and merely gazed out the window, praying that Jack was right. Her life might depend on it.

When they got to the courtroom, everything had changed. The audience was half full of reporters, print and other media. Hampton was holding court since this had originally been his story. Jack and J.D. were unpacking briefcases when Deputy Waddill raised his voice.

"Ladies and gentlemen." The talk among the reporters continued. More loudly he said, "Ladies and gentlemen." Hampton motioned them to be quiet. "Judge McDowell is pleased that you are in his court. However, there are a couple of rules. First, no cameras or recording devices are permitted. If you have them, turn them off. If I find you have violated this rule, I'll confiscate your equipment and you can pick it up at the conclusion of the trial." Several reporters moaned their protests. "Those are the rules, so just follow them. Also, no talking while court is in session, not even whispering. If I hear your voice, I'll escort you out at the next break. Any questions?"

81

"Your Honor, plaintiff calls David Gamboa."

McDowell nodded toward the bailiff who went to the hallway and escorted Gamboa to the clerk, where he was sworn in. As he took his seat, the jury saw a rather small Hispanic male, about five feet seven inches, wearing an expensive, well-tailored brown suit and a tan, striped tie. His mustache and black hair were speckled with gray. There was an air of quiet confidence about him as he laid his file on the rail, poured a cup of water, and turned his attention to Jack.

"You're David Gamboa?"

"I am, Mr. Bryant."

"Please tell the jury a little about yourself and your professional career."

Gamboa looked at the jury. "I was born and raised in Fort Worth, not far from where Mr. Bryant has his pro bono clinic."

Leyton didn't like the mention of Jack's free legal services, but said nothing.

"After I graduated from North Side High School, I commuted to Arlington State. I was there about the same time as Mr. Bryant, but it was a commuter college, and I didn't know him. Most of us just went to classes and then went to afternoon jobs. Mine was at the old Leonard's department store, where I sold appliances."

Several of the older jurors nodded at the mention of Leonard's, Fort Worth's predecessor to Walmart.

"I graduated with a BBA with emphasis on insurance. Next, I spent four years in the air force where I learned to fly fighters. I never saw combat, but I stayed in the reserves and am now a colonel."

"Do you still get to fly?" Jack asked.

"Unfortunately, mine is now primarily a desk job, but I manage to sneak one of our fighters out once a month or so and fly with the young guns."

Jack looked over at the jury and saw they liked his witness.

"Anyway, I left the air force and started my own life insurance and financial planning business. Between growing up on the North Side and attending Arlington, I knew quite a few people. So I just started knocking on doors and my business grew slowly at first and then developed quite nicely."

"Do you have any advanced degrees or certifications, Mr. Gamboa?"

Gamboa nodded. "Once I started my business, I went to TCU nights and weekends and completed an MBA. I'm a chartered life underwriter and chartered financial consultant. I also just completed my term as president of our state association."

Jack rose at his table. "Your Honor, we tender Mr. Gamboa as an expert witness in the area of life insurance."

"No objection," Leyton said with a wave of his hand as if to say, "get on with it."

"Mr. Gamboa, I've asked you to study certain issues in this case and offer your opinions, have I not?"

"Yes, sir."

"And, I'm paying you three hundred dollars an hour for your time away from the office."

"Correct, sir."

"Approach, Your Honor?"

McDowell grunted.

Jack walked to the witness and handed him the application for insurance on William Davis, the Euro Life insurance policy, the employment agreement, and a copy of the check for the proceeds made payable to Allison Southwest. "Mr. Gamboa, for purposes of my questioning, I want you to assume that Mr. Davis went to work for Allison Cadillac in the seventies as a porter. He never made more than twenty thousand dollars in one year and retired about fifteen years ago, not knowing that Allison Southwest had taken out life insurance on him and paid premiums on the policy until his death. Assuming those facts, do you have an opinion as to whether such a practice is acceptable and ethical in Texas?"

"Objection. This witness cannot offer opinions as to legality."

"Your Honor, I carefully avoided asking about legality, at least at this point."

"Overruled," McDowell said.

"This is what is known as a dead peasant policy . . ."

Before he could get any further, Leyton leaped to his feet. "Objection. The court's already ruled on that term as being prejudicial."

Before Jack could say anything, Gamboa turned to the judge. "Your Honor, there's nothing wrong with that term. That's what every life insurance agent in the country calls these policies."

McDowell looked over his bench at the witness. "That will be enough, Mr. Gamboa. Bailiff, please escort the jury out of the courtroom."

Once the jury was out of the room, the judge said, "Mr. Gamboa, you are to answer only questions from counsel and not volunteer any information. Do you understand?"

"Yes, sir. I apologize."

"Your Honor, defendant moves for a mistrial. That's twice this term has come up, once from Mr. Bryant and once from his witness who he should have instructed not to mention it."

"Mr. Bryant, your response?"

"Judge, as part of my response, I request permission to ask this witness some follow-up questions."

McDowell nodded. "Make it fast."

"Mr. Gamboa, is the use of the term 'dead peasant' intended to be derogatory to anyone?"

"Absolutely not, Mr. Bryant. It's just jargon used by people in my industry. I even sold dead peasant policies back when they were legal in Texas, but not in the past twenty years. And, by the way, I can testify as to their legality. I'm fully familiar with that issue. You're called a plaintiff lawyer, Mr. Bryant. Some people would connote that with being an ambulance chaser. Maybe they do, but you don't ask people to call you something different. Mr. Allison here is a car salesman, maybe he was a used car salesman. Some people would react negatively to those terms. That doesn't mean we don't use them."

Allison tried to keep a poker face but he knew Gamboa was right.

"Mortgage lenders, Wall Street bankers, even congressmen may conjure up negative feelings in a lot of people. We can't all be politically correct all of the time. Again, 'dead peasant' is what we call these policies. That's a lot simpler than saying, 'It's a life insurance policy taken out by an employer on the life of an employee without his knowledge and the premiums are continued after he leaves his employment and the beneficiary is the employer.'"

The judge rubbed his cheeks and then scratched his belly as he thought. He gazed out at the reporters. "Okay. I withdraw my previous ruling. The fact of the matter is that the jury is going to understand all that Mr. Gamboa said before we're through with this trial, anyway."

"Judge, can I have a running objection?" Leyton asked.

"You may, Mr. Leyton. You can even refer to Mr. Bryant as a plaintiff lawyer if you choose. Let's take our morning break."

After the judge had retired to his chambers, Jack walked over to his table, where Colby joined them. "Well, the wind just shifted a little in our direction. Not sure how long it will last."

"Personally, I thought it was a whole lot of uproar about nothing," Colby said.

"I couldn't agree more, but Leyton raised the issue, and now it's put to bed."

When the jury was back in the box, Jack asked, "Please explain to the jury what you meant by a dead peasant policy."

Leyton remained at his seat, strangely subdued.

"These are life insurance products. A lot of companies wrote them on employees, even low-level ones, thirty years ago. I even wrote some for business clients early in my career. They usually flew under the radar because the employers never told the employee and just quietly collected the proceeds of the policies when the employee or, often, the former employee died."

Jack looked at the jury and saw he had their attention, but he needed to move along. "Are these policies legal in Texas on former employees?"

"Not anymore. The Texas Department of Insurance determined that once an employee left, there was no more insurable interest by the employer. To comply with the insurance code, the employer has to cancel such a policy when an employee terminates. There are a few states where employers can still buy such policies, and they still fly under the radar. I hear that some employers even go offshore. If an insurance company will sell the policies, the employer and his family will never know."

Jack got up, approached the witness, and picked up the policy. "Then, if Allison Southwest had no insurable interest, who should have gotten the proceeds?"

Gamboa flipped through the policy to a paragraph near the last. "This paragraph says that if the primary beneficiary cannot collect the proceeds, they go to the nearest relative. In this case, that would be Mrs. June Davis."

"Pass the witness, Your Honor."

"Mr. Gamboa, you're familiar with the agreement that Mr. Davis signed, are you not?" Leyton asked.

"I'm familiar with the agreement that has a signature that purports to be that of Mr. Davis. I understand there is a dispute as to whether he signed it or not."

Allison shook his head at Gamboa, clearly trying to convey to the jury that there was no real dispute, merely one manufactured by Bryant.

"If that is his signature, you would not dispute that he approved and, in fact, agreed to Allison Southwest taking out coverage on his life that may continue beyond his employment, correct, Mr. Gamboa?"

Gamboa thought carefully about his answer. The silence was long enough that the judge said, "Mr. Gamboa, answer the question, please."

"I suppose that's correct, Mr. Leyton. I have a problem with Mr. Davis knowingly authorizing a dead peasant policy to continue after his employment, but I suppose that two adults can enter into such a contract. I've just never seen it. It's conceivably putting a target on the back of the former employee."

"Objection, Your Honor, to the last comment and move to strike."

"Sustained. The jury is instructed to disregard."

Leyton conferred with Allison and rose. "Nothing further, Judge."

Jack stared at his table for a moment, then got to his feet. "Your Honor, plaintiff rests."

Leyton was caught by surprise. He turned to look at Jack as if he clearly didn't know what he was doing. The judge ordered a lunch break, and the reporters left the courtroom like a covey of quail, followed by Leyton and Allison who went to the floor above to find a quiet place to talk.

Leyton set Allison down on an empty bench on the third floor and discussed the points they had already been over a half dozen times before. In the middle of the conversation, Allison's cell vibrated. He took it out of his pocket, glanced at the caller ID and said, "I'll call you back."

When they were finished, Leyton said he was going to stretch his legs and maybe grab a barbecue sandwich at the joint a block down the street. Allison declined to join him. When Leyton was gone, Allison went into the men's room and, after checking each stall to determine that he was alone, walked to the window for better reception and returned the call.

"Beau, why the hell are you calling me? You know I'm in this goddamn trial."

"Just checking to see how it's going," Quillen said in a modulated tone. "You know we both have a lot riding on the outcome of this case. If you lose, you may have a precedent on your hands that will make all of those other dead peasant policies worthless. That would be a serious blow to both our companies."

"Look, Quillen. I've got my hands full. Stay out of my hair until this son of a bitch is over. Then we'll talk." Allison clicked off the phone and jammed it back in his pocket. When he washed his hands and rubbed water on his face, he realized he was beet red. *Dammit,* he thought. *I can't let my temper show on the witness stand. Calm down. Calm down.*

82

"Defense calls Dwayne Allison, Judge."

Allison rose from the table and smiled at the jury as he walked to the witness stand. This time it was Judge McDowell who swore him in. Jack noted the subtle difference in how McDowell handled Allison and figured it was not lost on some of the jurors.

Leyton chose to lead Allison through segments of his life. He started by taking him from a college dropout to car salesman to his purchase of his first dealership with money borrowed from what later became Quillen Bank and Trust. He followed with the purchases of dealerships of all shapes and and sizes, in big cities and small towns, until he got to one hundred and twenty-five. Leyton knew he couldn't and shouldn't hide the fact that Allison Southwest had struggled in the past few years.

"Yes, Mr. Leyton, these last several years have been tough. I'm down to half of my dealerships. Worse than that is that I've had to lay off thousands of employees. Just last month I knew I had to close three more. It's almost like deciding which ones of your children are going to live or die." Allison choked up. "I apologize, ladies and gentlemen. I hope that I've closed the last of my dealerships."

"How's your company doing now?"

Allison smiled. "Things are picking up as the economy improves. I now have sufficient net income to pay employees, vendors and loans with Quillen Bank and Trust. I still owe my bankers quite a bit of money, but we're stronger financially than we've been in years. Sometimes you have to prune a tree, Mr. Leyton, to make it grow."

Two of the jurors were small businessmen themselves and understood the struggle just to keep the doors open. Jack remembered the conversation with his Beaumont banker when the banker said Allison Southwest was on the brink of bankruptcy and made a mental note to explore the issue further.

"Do you have a family, Mr. Allison?"

"I certainly do. Both my boys, well they're adults now, are in the family business. They're running stores of their own." He turned to the jury. "That's what we call dealerships in the family. I'm sorry to say that I lost my wife to cancer a few years back. That left a void in my life that will never be filled."

Leyton had Allison describe all of the various civic services he had performed in Fort Worth, including being the current president of the livestock show and rodeo. Satisfied that he had shown Allison in the best possible light, he turned to the matter at hand.

"Let's talk about William Davis. Do you remember him?"

Allison tried to conjure up a memory or a face but failed. "I'm sorry, I don't. We had a lot of employees, and it's been fifteen years since he worked for my company. I'm sorry, Mrs. Davis, and sorry for your loss."

June squared her jaw and stared at him. She knew he was just putting on an act.

Leyton wanted to move things along. He could tell the jury was inclined to like Allison and believe what he said. The jury had seen the exhibits. No sense in displaying them again. "Let's talk about that agreement and the policy you had on William Davis's life. Is there any doubt in your mind that he signed that agreement?"

"Absolutely not, ladies and gentlemen. I even made sure that my personnel staff explained the terms of the agreement. If Mr. Davis couldn't read it, I know he had to have understood it. I thought I was doing my employees a favor, and it also benefited my company too. They got a free life insurance policy. Ten thousand dollars was quite a bit of money thirty years ago. I might add someone like Mr. Davis also got free health insurance. I tried to take care of my employees."

Leyton wanted to be careful how he asked the next question. He had to face up to the fact that some jurors would eventually conclude that Willie's life was not the only one insured with one of these policies. So, he carefully phrased the question, intending to follow up with a few more carefully prepared questions and answers on the subject. Leyton knew this series of questions would be critical to a successful defense. "Mr. Allison, was Willie the only employee whose life you insured?"

"No, sir," came the reply, just as they rehearsed. Then Allison forgot the most basic instruction every lawyer gives his client: answer the question, shut up and let your lawyer take you through the minefield. Every trial lawyer has seen it happen. A lawyer has done everything he can to prepare his client, and the client still can blow the case with one wrong answer. Leyton would never know whether Allison had a lapse in memory or was so certain the jury was going his way that the salesman in him thought he could embellish the truth. Whatever the reason, Allison continued, "We were experimenting at the Cadillac store and a few others. We placed coverage on the employees in a handful of stores, for, I think, about a year, maybe two before we dropped the idea."

Dammit, Leyton thought. *Now we've got a problem. My client has flat out lied, and he had to know it. Somehow the son of a bitch thought he could get away with it. He was supposed to be vague, claiming that it was too many years ago and saying that any more details would have to come from his insurance department.*

At the other counsel table, Jack whispered to J.D., "We just got our opening."

Leyton tried to clean up the mess his client had created. "Are you sure about that? Shouldn't your insurance department be the source to discuss other life policies?"

Before Allison could respond, Jack was on his feet. "Objection, Your Honor. He's now trying to impeach his own client, and he's leading him to boot."

The judge had also recognized the problem and wanted to help Leyton out, but reluctantly said, "Objection sustained."

Leyton realized that he had played his last card for now and decided to rely on the goodwill that his client had created. So far, anyway, the jury didn't know that Allison had lied. He had successfully fought Bryant's attempt to get the other life insurance policies or even know how many there were. Without that information, he figured that Bryant was still in the dark about them and had nothing with which to impeach Allison. Leyton decided it was better just to just leave well enough alone. "I'll pass the witness, Your Honor."

The judge ordered a midafternoon break.

Jack called J.D., Colby and June over to a corner of the courtroom away from the court personnel and reporters. "What's your take, Colby?"

"He did well and the jury likes him. We know he's lying, but they don't. Did he give you that opening you were talking about?"

"Yeah." Jack smiled. "He did. Now, I've just got to see if I can make it big enough to drive a bulldozer through. If the judge just gives me a little latitude, I can do it."

83

"Mr. Allison," Jack began. "You said this policy was a benefit to William Davis—a free benefit was, I believe, the phrase you used."

Warned to be on his guard by Leyton at the break, Allison replied, "Yes, sir."

"Yet even as we sit here today, months after Willie's death, you've never paid that ten thousand dollars to June Davis, have you?"

Allison squirmed in his chair and folded and unfolded his arms. Small beads of sweat popped out on his forehead. He kept intending to write a check for the ten thousand, but at the end of every month he postponed it to pay other more pressing bills. "I'm sorry, Mr. Bryant, Mrs. Davis. That was an oversight in our accounting department. Here, let me write a check this very minute."

Allison reached into his coat pocket and extracted a checkbook. He hurriedly scratched off a check to June Davis for ten thousand dollars and signed it with a flourish. Then he wasn't sure what to do. "Judge, can I hand this to Mrs. Davis?"

"Just give it to the bailiff and he can give it to Mr. Bryant. I must say, Mr. Leyton, this is most unusual."

Leyton nodded.

"Let me see if I've got this straight," Jack said. "It's been all these months since Willie's death. I delivered your check for four hundred thousand dollars to you right after I received it. But you required June to file a lawsuit and get you on the witness stand before she finally got what was coming to her." Jack shook his head in disgust.

"Objection, Your Honor," Leyton said halfheartedly.

"Sustained. Jury will disregard."

Jack nodded and moved on, knowing he had made his point.

Allison was losing the credibility he and Leyton had so carefully crafted. Two of the African American jurors were looking at Allison with disgust. Jack was now standing at his table. "Now, let's talk about that Cadillac store where Willie worked, one of those where you experimented with dead peasant policies for a year or two."

"I, I may have been off a little on that, Mr. Bryant. It could have been more stores and several years," Allison said, remembering the counseling Leyton had given him at the break. Actually, it was more than counseling. Leyton chewed his ass up one side and down the other when they went up to their bench on the third floor. Given the chance, Leyton told him to inject more stores and more years into the testimony in an effort to clean up the problem his prior testimony had created.

Jack ignored the answer and continued. "You still have seven thousand dead peasant policies in place this very day, don't you, Mr. Allison, about half of them on former employees?"

Several jurors looked back and forth between Jack and Allison, wondering where that number came from and, more importantly, its significance.

"Objection! Objection, Your Honor."

"Your Honor," Jack replied. "Mr. Allison has testified that he had dead peasant policies on a few employees at the Cadillac store and a couple of others. Now, he's wavering. I'm entitled to explore his credibility on this issue."

The judge leaned back in his chair, his hands behind his head as he stared up at the ceiling. "Overruled. Mr. Bryant, I'll let you have a little latitude here, but hear me good. Don't push it too far."

Jack nodded his understanding. "Mr. Allison, you actually have seven thousand, three hundred and fourteen of these dead peasant policies still in force, even to this day, even after cutting the number of dealerships you own in half?"

"Since the issue came up, I, uh, checked during the break with my insurance department. I'd be curious to know how you got your information since it seems you know more about those life policies than I do, but you're exactly correct." Allison turned to the jury. "I apologize, ladies and gentlemen. It's been a lot of years and I just lost track."

Leyton looked up from his notes with a quizzical look, likewise wondering where Jack got such precise information and now having to figure out how the hell to downplay Allison's earlier lie. Maybe Allison had handled it the best he could. Then another thought entered Leyton's mind: *Was there a mole in Allison's insurance department?*

"Mr. Allison, let me see if I can just cut to the bottom line. Isn't it true that nineteen of your employees have suffered violent deaths in the last six months, and you've collected benefits on every one of them?"

Leyton rose to object, but before he could open his mouth, Allison had interrupted. He jumped to his feet and banged both of his hands on the rail before him. "Dammit, Mr. Bryant. Okay, I did collect on those policies, but you're suggesting that I had people killed. There's no way I'd do anything like that." He turned to the jury. "I'm sorry. I can't explain those deaths."

McDowell had enough of the disruption in his courtroom. "Mr. Allison, please take your seat and lower your voice. Otherwise, I'll have the bailiff escort you from the courtroom."

Allison took his seat. "I'm sorry, Judge. I got carried away. Besides, Mr. Bryant, as I told you, my company has turned the corner and is in very good financial shape. I didn't need the life insurance proceeds on

Mr. Davis or any of those other employees to keep going."

McDowell looked around the courtroom and saw that several of the jurors were shaken, either by the testimony or the witness's demeanor. "That's enough for the day. We'll recess until nine in the morning. Counsel please remain in the courtroom."

When the jury was gone, Judge McDowell looked at both lawyers in turn. "So, what do you propose we do at this point? This trial is now overflowing with evidence of dead peasant policies that I intended to keep out, and on top of that Mr. Bryant has injected that Allison has not only collected on the William Davis policy but a bunch of others. Mr. Leyton, do you have a motion?"

Leyton rose to address the court. "Again, I am reluctant to do it, but I move for mistrial. I think we better start over on another day."

"Not necessary, Your Honor." Jack was on his feet. This was a critical motion that he had to win. "My insurance expert has testified that even if an employer took out these policies when they were legal in Texas, once the legislature banned them, the employer was in violation of the Texas Insurance Code if he continued to carry coverage on a terminated employee. If he violated the insurance code, I can ask the jury to award treble damages as punishment. That's one point two million on top of the four hundred thousand in insurance proceeds." Jack thought for a moment and added one more argument. "Evidence of the other policies and Allison's admission that he collected on nineteen of them shows a pattern and practice under the Deceptive Trade Practices Act. It's also relevant to impeach Mr. Allison on the financial status of his company and goes directly to his credibility as a witness. We expect to show that his company is still under water."

McDowell stared at the clock on the back wall as the second hand made a full circle before he spoke. "Mr. Leyton, I'm going to deny your motion at this time. I invite you to raise it again at the close of evidence if you choose."

84

Jack, Colby, and J.D. sat out by the pool, rehashing the day's events.

"Okay, Dad, I got one question. How did you know you were going to be able to do that after the judge ruled for the third time that the dead peasant policies were out?"

Jack sipped his bourbon. "Twenty-five years as a trial lawyer and the instincts that come with it. I just needed a little crack, and once I got my foot in the door, I knew I could kick it open. Allison did us a favor by lying. I know damn well that Leyton didn't want him to do it, but it was too late. And the bonus is that he admitted to everything we learned about the policies. Your work paid off, J.D., and I suspect my law license is safe. Leyton and Allison are wondering about how we learned the specifics about the policies, but all they have is suspicions."

"Were you worried about Leyton's motion?" Colby asked.

"Yeah, just a little," Jack conceded. "I was really pushing the envelope on that testimony. Sometimes you just have to skate where the ice is thin. I think we'll be okay. Besides, this has really become Colby's case at this point. I've talked to June and she's in agreement. She wants me to do whatever it takes to get those charges dropped. I still intend to get her a good payday, but if I don't, she understands."

"What's next, Dad?"

"We've still got Allison on the stand, but I've done about as much damage as I can with him unless he says something else dumb. If the jury believes Gamboa, they already have the impression that Allison is an employer just preying on his employees and waiting for them to die to collect on the dead peasant policies."

85

Jack woke at five. This time he didn't even try to drift off to sleep. He had six hours of rest and that would get him through the day. He put on his cutoffs, T-shirt, and running shoes and was out the front door with Killer on his leash. A good walk with Killer would clear his mind and help him concentrate on what was to come. Jack's mind was at the courthouse as Killer trotted along in front of him. There was a rustle in some bushes, and a man stepped into their path. Jack couldn't see him well, but it looked like the same man that had confronted him two weeks before at the courthouse. He had a gun.

"You just wouldn't listen, would you, Mr. Bryant?"

Before he could say anything more, Jack said in a low voice, "Go, Killer."

Killer's training immediately kicked in. He saw the man with the gun and let out a deep growl. With two leaps, he was on the man, his mouth on the assailant's gun hand. Killer crunched his jaws until something snapped in the man's wrist. The man screamed and fell to the ground as he jerked his hand out of Killer's mouth. He was big enough that he threw Killer to the side and then was up and turning to run.

"Heel," Jack called, worried that the man might have a second gun. Killer stood and let the man disappear. Jack picked up the man's gun and patted Killer. "Good dog. You get a full bowl of treats this morning."

Jack returned to the house to find both Colby and J.D. up early and having breakfast. J.D. was reading the *Star Telegram*.

"Dad, Hampton laid out yesterday's events very well. He's not painting a very pretty picture of Allison."

Colby looked at Jack. "You look a little pale. Are you feeling all right?"

Jack poured his coffee and sat down. "I'm okay now, other than the fact that someone just tried to kill me."

"Oh my God, Jack. What happened?"

Jack described the event and how Killer came to his rescue. Killer perked up his ears as he heard his name several times in the conversation.

"Jack, I think it's time you called Joe Sherrod."

"I agree. It's still a little early, though. I'll call him about seven, after I'm dressed."

Jack was ready to go to court when he picked up his cell.

"Damn early to be calling the Tarrant County district attorney. This better be important," Joe growled.

"Joe, someone just tried to kill me."

Joe sat upright in his bed. "Shit, Jack. What happened?"

Jack described the event.

"I'll send a squad car right over."

"Sorry, Joe. I don't have time to give a statement right now. I'm on the way to the courthouse." Jack looked at his watch. "If they can be here in fifteen minutes, I can show them the location and give them the gun. The guy was wearing latex gloves. So the only prints on the gun are mine. Maybe you can trace the ownership. He may also have left some footprints that may be useful."

Ten minutes later a police car stopped in front of Jack's house. He talked briefly to the officers and handed them the gun. Then he got in the backseat and directed them to the location. One officer called CSI and waited at the scene. The other returned Jack to his house with the understanding that they would meet in Joe's office at the close of the trial that afternoon. When Jack went back into the house, he told Colby and J.D. that he would need to meet with Joe later. Not knowing how long it would take, he suggested that J.D. drive the Hummer. Colby would ride with Jack.

Trial lawyers must constantly change strategy as the evidence un-
folds. Jack had several more pages of typed notes with questions for
Allison. As they drove to the courthouse, he mentally tossed them in a
waste can. He had made the points he needed.

Colby interrupted his thoughts. "Are you sure you're going to be
okay today, Jack? How can you possibly concentrate on the trial after
what happened to you this morning?"

Jack turned to Colby while they were stopped at a light. "I've learned
to compartmentalize. Trust me. That attack will be out of my mind until
we visit Joe's office this afternoon. By the way, I want to thank you for
all your help in the trial. I know how much you have to struggle just to
keep your sanity."

"I'm hanging in there. Striplings come from strong stock. Call it
woman's intuition or whatever, but I now believe that we're all going
to be okay in a few days. Are you going to tell the judge about the
attack?"

"No reason to, but I want you to watch Allison when he sees me for
the first time and knows I'm still alive."

"You think he set it up?" Colby asked.

"Right now I'd say he's at the top of the list, and the list doesn't go
beyond his name. That reminds me. Tell J.D. to go to the clerk's office
and get a subpoena issued for Beauregard Quillen to appear at one
o'clock this afternoon. Let's just see how truthful Allison was when
he said that Allison Southwest is doing well financially."

86

***

Jack had unpacked his briefcase and was talking to the bailiff about TCU's opening game on Saturday, acting as if he had a refreshing night's sleep and an uneventful morning. J.D. joined in the conversation as they discussed their prospects away from home with Rice.

They stopped talking when the hallway door creaked as it opened. Leyton entered, followed by Allison. Allison gave no sign of surprise when he saw Jack, but merely nodded his head in their direction as he pushed through the gate. *Damn,* Jack thought. *He's a great actor, or maybe someone else tried to kill me. No. That doesn't compute. It has to be Allison.*

When the jury was in the box, Jack rose and said, "Pass the witness, Judge."

Leyton did his best to rehabilitate Allison. He established that he had thousands of employees and former employees. Then he elected to change course and face the dead peasant policy issue head on.

"Mr. Allison, being a businessman, does it strike you as unusual that with all of those employees and about seven thousand insurance policies that after all of these years you would start having a few former employees die?"

Allison shook his head. "Not at all, Mr. Leyton. As any group of people advance in age, more of them are going to die." He looked at the jury. "Just common sense, ladies and gentlemen."

"And one more thing, when we were talking about your activities in Fort Worth, is there a current one we failed to mention?"

Allison turned to the jury. "You remember that I told you my wife died of cancer. When that happened, I became very involved with cancer charities. This year I'm president of the local chapter of the American Cancer Society."

Leyton figured he had done what he could to rehabilitate his client. "Pass the witness, Your Honor."

Jack rose at his table and leaned with his hands on his cane. "Just one question, Mr. Allison. If it turned out that all of those dead employees met violent, unexplained deaths, would your answer to Mr. Leyton's question be the same?"

Leyton was hunched forward in his chair, his arms on his knees and hands folded. The judge looked at him, expecting an objection; only Leyton just stared at the floor.

Allison sighed, wanting this whole experience to be over. "I don't know, Mr. Bryant. I do know I had nothing to do with their deaths."

Leyton recognized that his client had taken some body blows on cross-examination. The kindly civic benefactor had been replaced by an employer who preyed on the deaths of his employees. Leyton knew he had to shift the emphasis back to the policy on Willie Davis and the agreement behind it. He had two witnesses left, his forensic document examiner and an insurance expert. Terri Christopher was a woman in her midfifties who had been studying documents and handwriting for thirty years. She was short, trim, nicely dressed and carried an aura of confidence that whatever she said would be believed by a jury. After establishing her qualifications, Leyton put the same signatures on the overhead. Christopher used a laser pointer to highlight the similarities in the signatures. The jury watched with interest as she explained the loop in the *D* and the way the *s* in Davis was almost exactly the same. Her opinion was that there could be no conclusion other than the two signatures were made by the same person.

Next came Erwin Steinman, a former director of the Texas Department of Insurance. He completely refuted Gamboa's testimony and added that if an employee agreed, a life insurance policy could continue to be in force after the employee left, particularly if the employee was to receive benefit from the continuation of the policy, like ten thousand dollars going to his family at the time of his death. After his two experts testified, Leyton rested his case.

The expert testimony was typical of almost every trial in the country. There were experts with opinions for hire on any subject, any time. It was like Jerry Buchanan said to Jack. If Leyton had hired him, he could make an equally compelling argument that the signatures were the same. Jack made a few minor points with each of the experts and then quit. His gut told him that the case was no longer going to be decided by opinions from experts. In fact, he had decided not to call Buchanan.

87

Allison was shocked when he returned from lunch to find Quillen sitting on a hallway bench outside the courtroom, a frown on his face. He didn't even get up when Allison approached.

"Beau, what the hell are you doing here?"

"That goddamn Jack Bryant subpoenaed me this morning."

"Shit. What does he want with you?"

"Damned if I know. The subpoena just said to be here. I know that I can't ignore it. I wish your lawyer had let me know it was coming. I could have gotten out of town."

"Sorry, Beau. We didn't know."

When the court was assembled for the afternoon, Jack announced, "Your Honor, we call Beauregard Quillen in rebuttal. He's under subpoena and is waiting in the hall."

McDowell nodded to Waddill who went out the door and returned momentarily with Quillen in tow. Quillen was dressed in his banker's three-piece, pin-striped suit with his customary red tie. He took the witness stand with an air of confidence. While not quite as well known in Fort Worth as Allison, most jurors recognized either him or his name. They had all seen commercials for Quillen Bank and Trust.

Before Jack could ask his first question, Leyton asked to approach the bench. "Judge, we don't understand what evidence Mr. Quillen can bring to this jury. We object."

"Your Honor, Mr. Allison has testified that Allison Southwest is in the best financial condition it's seen for the past several years. I have information to the contrary and believe that Mr. Allison's banker would be the the person to enlighten the jury on that condition. It goes to the credibility of Mr. Allison as a witness, Your Honor."

"Your Honor," Leyton said, taking a shot at Jack. "I'm beginning to question the legality of how Mr. Bryant is obtaining this information on my client."

"Mr. Leyton, this is not the time or place for that. Take it up with the grievance committee or the DA after the trial. Objection overruled. You can begin your questions, Mr. Bryant. If I believe you are going too far afield, understand I'll rein you in."

Jack noticed a subtle shift in the judge's attitude almost as if the evidence was impacting on his opinion of Allison. Jack forged ahead, quickly establishing the long relationship between Allison and Quillen, going back to that first loan. "Allison and his dealerships are your biggest customers, are they not, Mr. Quillen?"

Quillen looked at Allison for several seconds and concluded that he was under oath. The last thing he needed in his life right now was a charge of perjury. He elected to answer the questions, including the good, the bad and the ugly.

"Allison and his company were certainly my biggest clients for a number of years. They are still a major client, but the economy has gotten to Allison just like it has to a number of my other customers."

"Mr. Allison has described his company as being financially very strong. Is that an apt description?"

Quillen folded his hands on the rail in front of his seat. "Look, Mr. Bryant, Dwayne has half the dealerships he had five years ago. That ought to give you a pretty good clue."

Jack got up from his table and walked over to stand in front of the witness, leaning on his cane. "Sorry, Mr. Quillen, but clues aren't good enough. Is he current on his notes to you, floor plans, that kind of thing?"

Quillen hesitated and looked at Allison again. "No, sir. He hasn't made a principal payment on any of his notes in three years. Currently, he's behind on interest to the tune of fifteen to twenty million dollars."

"Has Allison Southwest made any payments at all on loans from your banks in the past three years?"

Quillen saw the opportunity to help Allison out. "Of course, Mr. Bryant. He's begun to pay down the interest. Maybe his business is improving. I'm just happy to see the debt coming down."

The wheels were spinning in Jack's head. "Are these regular, monthly payments, Mr. Quillen?"

Quillen saw where Jack was going and didn't want to go there. "Sometimes, counselor."

Jack walked toward the witness until he was about five feet away. "In fact, most of the payments have been in the last six months and are large sums that show up randomly. Isn't that true, Mr. Quillen?"

Quillen shifted in the witness chair, took a sip of water and thought about his answer. "I suppose that's at least partially true."

Jack had just confirmed what he suspected all along. The proceeds from the dead peasant policies were being used to pay on Allison's loans. "Those payments are usually round figures, from two hundred to six hundred thousand dollars, right, Mr. Quillen?"

"I couldn't say for sure without looking at the books."

Jack asked a throwaway question. "How are these loans secured, sir?"

"I have a lien on everything Mr. Allison owns. That includes his real estate, buildings, cars, trucks, horses, his house, even life insurance policies on his employees."

"Shit," Leyton said softly to Allison. "Why the hell did he have to say that?"

"Do you have records on the employee life insurance policies?"

Quillen didn't want to answer, but he was in too deep to back out now. "I do. Mr. Allison is required by our loan agreements to update those records monthly."

"And the reason for that is because he's required to turn over the proceeds of any of those policies to you upon their receipt, and that would explain the lump sum payments for the past six months, wouldn't it, Mr. Quillen?"

Quillen looked at Allison with an apology etched on his face before he answered.

"Probably true, Counselor."

Jack walked to stand in front of the witness. "So, the fact of the matter is that Allison is not making payments from net income from his business because he doesn't have such income. Those payments are coming from proceeds on life insurance on the lives of his former employees, correct, Mr. Quillen?"

Quillen looked for a way to avoid answering the question and could think of none. "You're correct, Mr. Bryant. His payments have coincided with proceeds from those policies."

Jack looked at Leyton and let a small smile cross his face. At last he had a way to *legally* get his hands on the entire list of dead peasant policies. "Your Honor, at this time we are advising the court that we will be issuing a subpoena for production of documentation of Allison Southwest dead peasant policies in Mr. Quillen's possession as well as payments from Allison Southwest to Quillen Bank and Trust for the past six months, to include, of course, Your Honor, dates of any such payments.

If Mr. Leyton chooses to object, I direct the court's attention to my statements as to relevance yesterday afternoon after the jury was gone and Mr. Allison's testimony that his payments to Quillen Bank and Trust came from net income from his business. We will serve it on Mr. Quillen as soon as he leaves the courtroom today."

J.D. took his cue and quietly left the courtroom to get the document from the district clerk's office.

Leyton rose and made a halfhearted objection about relevance, which the judge overruled.

Quillen turned to the judge. "Judge McDowell, this will be a grave inconvenience to me and my staff. I have an important meeting tomorrow that I can't get out of."

"Mr. Quillen, I'm quite certain that you've got someone in your office who can pull that information from a computer. It's your choice as to whether to be there or not. We're adjourned for the day."

88

Once the judge and jury were gone, Jack had his team remain in the deserted courtroom to discuss the day's events. With the evidence he expected to get from Quillen, he thought he now would have all the pieces to the puzzle. When he started the trial, he thought he was going to establish a pattern and practice of defrauding employees out of their benefits under the policies. Now it appeared that pattern and practice may have included murder to collect on the policies. Jack turned to J.D. "Did you get Quillen served with the subpoena?"

"Yes, sir. Out in the hallway like you said. He was not a happy camper."

"Okay," Jack said. "You walk June to where Willie, Jr., is waiting and meet Colby back at the Hummer. I'm going to go over to Joe's office and give my statement."

"Jack," Colby said. "Don't you think it's about time to tell him what we've uncovered about these policies?"

Jack pondered the question. "You're right. I'll tell him what we've put together with the understanding that we need to finish this trial before he starts investigating Allison. We ought to wrap this up tomorrow anyway."

Allison was washing his hands in the men's room when Quillen entered.

"Dwayne, I'm glad I caught you in here. I don't like the way this case is going. I think you're going to lose your ass, and there goes our chance to recover on seven thousand dead peasant policies." Quillen raised his voice. "You need to settle this damn case. Pay the widow her four hundred thousand and shut this son of a bitch down. You hear me!"

Allison dried his hands and turned to face Quillen. "Dammit, Beau, maybe you haven't looked at my financial statements lately. All of that money from those policies went to your bank, including the four hundred thousand dollars on Willie Davis's life. I'm broke."

Quillen's anger boiled over and he shoved Allison up against the wall. "You bastard, you're not the only one in financial trouble. You're the cause of my banks being close to failure. The main topic I have with regulators currently is Allison Southwest. Goddamn it! I've waited long enough. Understand me. If you fuck this up, we'll both be in bankruptcy court. Those dead peasant policies are keeping both of us afloat. If you don't do as I say, you won't like the consequences. You get what I'm telling you?"

"Shit," Dwayne yelled, "I've paid you about five million in the past six months. The feds ought to see that I'm doing what I can. Tell those fuckers to go regulate the damn Wall Street bankers." Allison pushed back away from Quillen. "Wait just a goddamn minute. Bryant has pounded me in the courtroom, accusing me of murdering my employees to collect on those policies. *I didn't do it.* You're the only person besides my brother who knew exactly which of my employees had life insurance coverage and how much. You son of a bitch!"

Allison shoved Quillen aside and stormed out the door. When Allison was gone, Quillen pulled his cell from his pocket.

Allison was walking down the courthouse steps when he saw Colby about to reach the Hummer in the now almost deserted parking lot across the street. He waved his hand. "Colby, hold up."

Colby felt uncomfortable with having Allison confront her but stopped. Allison ran across the street. When he reached her, he paused to catch his breath. "I think I know who killed my employees and tried to kill you."

Before he could say anything else, a white panel truck wheeled around the corner, and a shot rang out. Allison crumpled to the ground as the panel truck sped away. Colby had the presence of mind to get a partial license plate number before she bent over Allison and called 911. Next she called Jack, telling him what happened and assuring him that she was unharmed.

The ambulance was there in five minutes. The wound was in the right side of the chest. The lead EMT said Allison had a collapsed lung. Working rapidly, he stemmed the blood flow and inserted a breathing tube before loading him on a gurney. Ten minutes later Allison was on the way to the hospital. By then Jack and Joe had arrived.

"I'm okay, Jack. Allison was shot. The EMT says he's got a collapsed lung, but he'll live."

Joe sized up the situation and said, "You're both coming back to my office. I want some answers."

When they were settled in Joe's office with the door closed, Joe said, "Tell me why you guys are in the middle of a crime wave."

Jack told Joe everything they had learned, including that they had subpoenaed policy information from Quillen Bank and Trust. When he got through, Joe said, "Holy shit! Dwayne Allison. Never in a hundred years would I have pegged him to be doing something like this."

"But, Joe," Colby said. "Maybe it's not him. He's the one shot and in the hospital."

Joe shook his head. "Colby, that shot may have been intended for you."

Colby's face went white and her hand came to her mouth as she gasped at the thought.

"Look, I'm putting one of my investigators on this first thing in the morning. I'll be calling Judge McDowell in just a minute. He'll most likely postpone the trial for a while, depending on Allison's condition. That means my investigator will need copies of those records of policies and the former employees who have died. I'll also post a car and two officers outside your house. They'll follow discreetly when you go anywhere, including the courthouse. I'll also have a second bailiff assigned to help Deputy Waddill. Oh, and I'll put someone on tracking down that partial license number. You're going to be okay, Colby, and it sounds like with one more day of evidence I may be able to dismiss the murder charge."

That night Jack received a call from Judge McDowell's clerk, advising that he wanted a conference call with the two lawyers in thirty minutes.

"Gentlemen, I've talked to Joe Sherrod. Ace, let's start with you. How's Dwayne doing?"

"He's doing okay, Judge. He's stable. The bullet went through his lung and came out the other side. They had to do laparoscopic surgery and then reinflate the lung. He should be out of the hospital in a few days."

"That's good to hear. Jack, are you going to oppose a mistrial?"

"Judge, you know I don't want that. I figure we just have a few hours of evidence left. I don't have any reason to recall Allison. I want to keep going, but it's really Ace's call."

"Judge, this may surprise you. Allison is intubated but alert. He wrote me a note, and said he doesn't want the case continued. He wants to testify again. He'll write out notes on the witness stand if necessary. We just need a two-day continuance."

"You sure about that, Ace?" the judge asked, concern in his voice.

"Judge, that's our best estimate for now. If it changes, I'll let you and Jack know."

Jack received a call early the next morning from Joe Sherrod. "Jack, here's what I've got on the partial license number. This is not certain, but the most likely owner is Federal Bank Security, a company that provides security services for banks in Texas and several other states. I'll be putting someone on it, but I figure you've become Sherlock Holmes. You may beat me to the punch. Just keep me in the loop."

When the call ended, Colby appeared in the kitchen, her eyes red from lack of sleep. "Jack, would you mind not leaving me today? I got really spooked when Joe said that the shooter might have been after me. I hardly slept at all last night. Can you do some trial preparation or something and maybe by tomorrow, I'll be okay."

Jack hugged her. "Sure, Colby. We don't go back until day after tomorrow. I can prepare my closing argument."

Colby alternated between sleeping and sitting next to Jack at the dining room table while he worked on his closing argument. He gave himself a small pat on the back for not wasting time on closing when he did his trial preparation. The case had turned into one he never saw coming when it began. Now, he intended to take advantage of it.

The next morning Jack woke Colby and had a long talk with her. When he was satisfied that she was back in control of her emotions, he decided that he and J.D. could be gone for a few hours. After setting the alarms and convincing the two officers parked in the front of the house they should stay and watch over Colby, Jack and J.D. drove downtown. Jack wanted to arrive at Quillen's office at eight o'clock, the minute the doors opened. As they rode the elevator to the thirtieth floor, J.D. asked, "You think he'll give us everything he has?"

"He will." Jack nodded. "Our trial and Allison's shooting are the lead stories in the *Star Telegram,* even this morning. Quillen isn't about to do anything that would piss off the judge and put the spotlight on him. We'll get everything."

The door opened. Across the hall were two large paneled doors. Jack opened one and they entered an opulent office, suitable for the CEO of a financial conglomerate. A young receptionist sat at the desk.

"Good morning, gentlemen. How can I help you?"

"Is Mr. Quillen in?"

She shook her head. "He's out at a meeting at one of our banks."

J.D. handed the subpoena to her. She studied it for a minute before she spoke. "Mr. Quillen was expecting you yesterday. I suppose I can get what this says. You want the entire list of employee policies where we have liens on the proceeds?"

"That's correct.

"Please excuse me, and I'll get the information. Will a thumb drive be okay?"

"That'll be fine," J.D. replied.

Thirty minutes later they were back on the elevator and headed out the front door of the building.

"J.D., plug Federal Bank Security in the GPS and let's drop by there before we head back to the house."

The GPS directed them to the main office on a side street off of Seventh Avenue, a few blocks from downtown. The building was unmarked without even an address. Six-inch posts circled the building, rising four feet in the air and placed about three feet apart. From the look of the posts, a tank could not have gotten past them. Finding the front door locked, Jack pushed a doorbell and waited. A voice from an intercom said, "Yes."

"I'm Deputy Jack Bryant. We're investigating a shooting that took place two nights ago. It appears that the shooter was driving one of your panel trucks."

"Just a minute."

"The door opened and a gargantuan man invited them into a small reception area with another door, leading back to the main work areas. The man who opened the door asked for some identification. Jack flashed his badge quickly enough that he did not notice that Jack was a reserve deputy. When he handed the man a piece of paper with the license number on it, the man picked up a reception phone and called to the back.

"That license is one of ours. That's all the information I can provide you without a subpoena."

When they returned to the house, J.D. said he would check the information on the thumb drive.

Jack shook his head. "J.D., you're a better computer sleuth. See what you can find out about FBS. I'll check out the rest."

J.D. spent the rest of the afternoon tracking information. Colby supplied them with sandwiches and sodas. As the sun was dropping below the horizon, J.D. came bounding down the stairs. "I've got it, Dad. I had to trace back through several dummy corporations, including some offshore, but I'm certain I'm right. Quillen owns Federal Bank Security."

Jack got up from his computer and stretched his fingers. "And I think I can top that. The sweet little receptionist gave us a lot more than we asked for. We got the Allison Southwest dead peasant policies on a spreadsheet. I've confirmed that what J.D. found was correct. Every one of the violent deaths was an Allison employee with a dead peasant policy. Colby, that includes Rob."

J.D. drove his fist into the air. "Yes!" he exclaimed. Colby breathed a sigh of relief.

"Wait, it gets better. Once I got past the Allison Southwest employees, and, by the way, there was a red *X* beside the ones who had died, I found more. Quillen has fifteen other bank clients who have dead peasant policies on their employees. None of them individually are as big as Allison Southwest, but I found twenty-three names with the same red *X* beside them. They're scattered all over ten states. Then I went to the Social Security Web site and those twenty-three are all dead. It doesn't say how they died, but does anyone want to place a small wager that they were unexplained violent deaths?"

"Shit, Dad, what are you saying?"

"I think we've been barking up the wrong tree. Allison's business ethics are damn marginal with all those dead peasant policies, but I don't think he's the killer. Quillen Bank and Trust is in deep shit. Quillen picked up the idea of dead peasant policies from Allison years ago. Then it looks like it became standard operating procedure for his bank. If you want a loan, you take out these policies. When Quillen started getting in trouble because of Allison's nonpayment, and he started getting squeezed by the mortgage lawsuits that Jacob and I filed, he needed money and he needed it fast."

Colby's eyes glistened. "That means it wasn't Allison. I knew he couldn't have tried to kill me. I knew it."

"Tomorrow ought to be a most interesting day. I'm going back to work. I need to outline questions for Allison and Quillen. Now, I think I know why Allison is insisting on testifying, even if he has to get out of a hospital bed to do it."

Later that evening J.D. burst through the doorway between the man cave and the dining room. "Dad, the feds just closed one of Quillen's banks. The newscaster says it may be the first of many. Quillen was not available for comment."

"Well, isn't that an interesting turn of events."

"What are we going to do, Dad? What if Quillen doesn't show up tomorrow?"

Jack walked over to the back door to his collection of canes. He sorted through them until he found the one he wanted. "I think you and I better take a little drive over to Shady Oaks. Grab a couple of bottles of water. We're going to watch Quillen's place for a while."

Jack parked Lucille a half block down the street, in the darkness between two streetlights, and waited. J.D. spent the hours texting Tanya and then his teammates, encouraging them to run up a big score. After all, they were going for a national championship. Jack was content to drink his water and watch the street for any signs of activity. It was getting close to midnight when Jack saw a truck approaching in the rearview mirror. "Put down that phone, son. There's a white panel truck coming up from our rear."

When it passed, Jack began to follow and said, "Your young eyes are better than mine. See if you can make out the plate." J.D. squinted until the truck came under the next light. "Can't make it out, Dad, but it's the same kind of truck the shooter was driving."

The truck turned into Quillen's driveway and stopped at a mounted keypad. The driver punched in several numbers, and the gate opened and shut slowly behind him once he was through.

"Now what, Dad?"

"Now we wait and let our instincts direct us."

Hawk pulled he truck around to the back of the house where two men stood with Quillen. "Hawk, you've been well paid. There'll be another hundred grand in your account tomorrow. I'm leaving the country for a while. These wrapped frames contain my most valuable artwork: two Picassos, a Remington, two Russells and several lesser-known but expensive artists. The rest of this is jewelry and some cash. I trust you to take all of this out to my private jet at Meacham Field. I've got some other matters to wind up and will be there in a few hours. Any questions?"

"You still want me to try for that big score?"

Quillen shook his head. "No, it's too late for that now. Leave her alone."

"Then, Boss, it's been a pleasure to work with you and profitable at that. Hope your plan works."

Fifteen minutes later the truck was loaded, and Hawk eased out the front gate. A steady drizzle caused him to turn on his wipers. He never noticed the truck parked to his right when he turned to his left and headed for Camp Bowie.

"We'll give him a block and then get in behind him. Hopefully, he won't notice us in the neighborhood. Once we're on Camp Bowie, even at this time of night, there should be plenty of other traffic to hide us."

Hawk turned left on Camp Bowie and glanced in his rearview mirror. Even though he was a block away, he noticed a red pickup stopped at the same place where he turned. It also made a left. The speed limit was thirty-five. Hawk sped up to fifty and the truck maintained a two-block distance. He slowed to twenty-five and the truck was still behind him.

"I think we've been made," Jack said. "Only we can't afford to lose him. I don't know what he picked up from Quillen's house, but I doubt if it was a bunch of old clothes for Goodwill. Watch him to see if he turns off."

When Camp Bowie ended at Seventh, Hawk took Seventh. At the old Montgomery Ward, he suddenly turned right into the park. Jack forgot about keeping a distance and sped up, making the same turn with screeching tires. The white truck was a block ahead. The drive through the park was winding, intended for families to have a leisurely drive at about twenty-five miles an hour.

Hawk sped up to fifty, ignoring the wet street, as he followed the road that weaved among the trees. He passed the duck pond where this project had started months before.

At fifty miles an hour, Jack was staying up with Hawk by doing everything he could to keep the truck on the slick pavement.

Jack felt like he was weaving through a tunnel of trees with no margin for error. "That son of a bitch can't keep this up on wet pavement. He's driving a goddamn panel truck, not a Ferrari."

As if hearing Jack's words, Hawk pushed it to seventy and began to pull away. When he glanced in his mirror to estimate the distance he had put between himself and the red pickup, he took his eyes off the road at just the wrong time. The road curved to the left. Hawk hit his brakes, but it was too late. He careened into the forest where his truck thudded into a large oak. Steam erupted from the radiator as Hawk freed himself from his seat belt and forced open the door.

Jack saw what had happened and followed the white van, stopping behind it as Hawk stumbled out. J.D. leaped from the passenger side and bull-rushed Hawk. Hawk tried to raise his pistol, but J.D. hit him full speed like a linebacker flattening a tight end. He wrapped his arms around Hawk and drove him into the ground. Hawk was no lightweight and was not going to go down without a fight. He and J.D. wrestled for the gun until Jack walked up with his cane.

He stuck the cane into Hawk's neck. "Now, that'll be enough. This cane fires a gas-propelled bullet. It's only accurate to about twenty-five feet. But with the cane pushing into your neck, the bullet will blow clean through it, rupturing arteries in the process. So, you have two choices. You can continue to wrestle around with my son. He'd kick your ass anyway. But if you do, I pull the trigger. Otherwise, drop your hands and J.D. is going to sit on top of you while we have a little discussion."

Hawk relaxed and remained on the ground with J.D. straddling him. Jack kicked Hawk's gun a safe distance. "Now, there are a couple of more parts to this little deal. You threatened me at the courthouse and tried to kill me. You also tried to kill Colby. The next conclusion I draw is that Quillen paid you to kill a bunch of other people in several states."

Hawk knew he had no bargaining position and nodded his head.

"Very good. Final choice. You'll either be going to the death chamber, or, if you're willing to confess and dime out Quillen—I think that's the term you thugs use—anyway, you turn state's evidence, I know the district attorney, and I suspect he'll let you cop for life with no parole. So what'll it be, death chamber or life with no parole?"

Hawk twisted just a little and Jack shoved the cane farther into his throat, making it even more difficult for him to talk. "It was all Quillen's idea," Hawk said in a hoarse whisper.

Before J.D. could call for help, two police cars drove up, lights flashing and sirens wailing. Officers leaped from the cars with guns extended.

"About time you guys got here. We've been needing some backup. Look in my back pocket. I'm a Tarrant County reserve deputy."

One of the officers pulled Jack's wallet from his pocket and confirmed what he had said. "Who's this guy?"

"Serial killer. We've got evidence of about forty deaths in several states. If you'll permit me, I'll call Joe Sherrod. This guy wants a plea bargain."

Jack called Joe and explained what had just come down.

"Damn it, Jack. You could have got yourself killed. I'll do the deal. Let me talk to one of the officers. They can bring him to my house. We'll take a recorded statement and have him sign a short confession."

Joe was standing on his front porch, already dressed in a suit and tie. The officers dragged Hawk up the steps and pushed him into a chair on the porch. Joe turned on a pocket recorder and explained that if Hawk told everything he knew about the killings and Quillen's involvement, he would get life from Tarrant County. Joe explained further that he could not control what other district attorneys did, but thought they would follow his lead. Hawk nodded his understanding. With Jack's help, Joe recorded all of the murders Hawk could remember and confirmed that all had been ordered by Quillen. There would be wire transfers, documenting his payment a few weeks after the murders. The last one he covered was the suffocation of Robert Jones. Hawk confessed to that one too. Joe looked at Jack and nodded. When Joe was approaching the end of the confession, Hawk said he had picked up some valuables from Quillen that night and was supposed to deliver them to Meacham Field.

Joe looked at Jack. "Looks like we better hightail it over to Beau's house. We don't have a search warrant, so we'll have to wait for him to leave. First, let me call another couple of squad cars to take care of Hawk."

89

Joe positioned his car, Jack's truck and the two police cars in the street in front of Quillen's house and instructed them on what he wanted done when Quillen tried to make a run for it. Around four thirty, a limousine drove slowly around the house. As it approached, the gate opened. When the nose of the limo passed beyond the gate, Joe gave the signal on the radio. Suddenly, the driver was blinded by four sets of headlights on bright. Joe approached the rear door and knocked on the window. Quillen slowly lowered it.

"Morning, Beau," Joe said. "What brings you out this early in the morning?"

"Nice to see you, Joe," Quillen lied. "I have to be in court this morning and thought I would get a head start to beat the press and the crowds."

Joe looked at his watch and shook his head. "Tell you what, just to make sure you're there in plenty of time, we'll escort you to the courthouse." Joe tapped on the driver's window until the chauffeur lowered it. "We're going to have a little procession to the courthouse. A police car will lead you with one directly behind. I'll be next. I suggest you don't try anything stupid."

Joe turned to Jack. "You guys have had a long night and may have a long day coming. Go home and get a shower, and I'll see you at the courthouse in about three hours. Don't worry. I'll take good care of your friends."

At the courthouse Joe escorted Quillen to a conference room and stationed two cops at the door. Quillen demanded to call his lawyer, and Joe had no choice but to agree. When the lawyer arrived, he talked privately with Quillen and told Quillen to take the Fifth Amendment to every question. Quillen nodded his understanding.

Before the jury was seated, Quillen was led into the courtroom, now overflowing with reporters, and instructed to take the witness stand. The two cops stood at the door, on high alert for any outbreak. Quillen was followed by Jack and his entourage. This time Jack chose not to unpack anything. He figured that he didn't need notes for what he was about to do.

When the judge exited his chambers, he was followed by Joe Sherrod, who had been briefing the judge on the events of the night. Joe went to the back of the courtroom and stood between the police officers. The reporters and jurors noted the strange goings-on. All of the reporters knew the district attorney and whispered among themselves about what was about to occur. The judge nodded at Jack.

Before he could begin, the door squeaked, and Hawk was escorted into the courtroom by two more cops.

"Mr. Quillen, you're the one who arranged for the murder of William Davis, aren't you?"

The jurors all looked at one another in shocked disbelief. The reporters began talking until Deputy Waddill finally had to call for order. The one person who didn't say anything was Ace Leyton. The case was clearly out of his hands. In fact, he stared at the flag over the judge's left shoulder with a slight smile on his face.

Quillen looked at his lawyer who nodded. "I respectfully exercise my right to refuse self-incrimination under the Fifth Amendment and decline to answer."

"In fact, there are eighteen other Allison Southwest employees who were murdered, including one Robert Jones, all under your orders in an effort to save your bank."

This time Quillen was short in his answer. "I take the Fifth."

"And you also arranged for the murders of at least twenty other people who worked for your bank clients. They paid you the insurance proceeds under dead peasant policies you required them to place on their employees."

"Fifth, sir."

By now the audience and jury had fallen silent as they watched a drama they had never anticipated.

"Last, you attempted to murder both Colby Stripling, this lady sitting here on the first row, and even me when you saw how this trial was going."

"Fifth."

"And every single one of these murders and attempted murders was done by the man seated in the back, one Mike Hawkins, all under your direct order."

"Fifth."

Again the back door opened. This time Dwayne Allison was wheeled into the courtroom by his brother, Don. A nurse followed close behind. He had an oxygen tank attached to the back of his wheelchair and a nasal cannula feeding the oxygen into his lungs.

"Your Honor," Jack said, "Mr. Allison is in the courtroom. As you can see, he's been severely injured, but wants to testify. May we excuse this witness briefly while I recall Mr. Allison?"

"You may, Mr. Bryant."

Don wheeled his brother to the front of the witness stand while Quillen took a seat beside his lawyer.

"Your Honor, Mr. Allison cannot speak at this time. I request permission for his answers to be written out and marked as exhibits for the record."

"Granted, Mr. Bryant."

"Mr. Allison, even though you cannot talk, can you understand my questions?"

"Yes," he wrote.

"What happened to you?"

"I was shot outside the courthouse after trial two days ago. The bullet punctured my lung. I should be okay in a week or two."

"Who did this to you?"

"I've read the confession of that man in the back of the courtroom, Mr. Hawkins. He admits to doing it under the orders of Beauregard Quillen." As he wrote, he pointed a trembling finger at Quillen.

"Had Mr. Quillen previously threatened you?"

"We had an angry confrontation in the men's room on this floor. Ten minutes later I was shot."

"That's enough," the judge interrupted. "Mr. Leyton and Mr. Bryant, come with me to my chambers. Mr. Allison, you're welcome to leave if you need to."

The judge shut the door to his chambers and took off his robe. "Have a seat."

"Look, Joe Sherrod just explained what has occurred. I've also read a transcript of Hawkins's confession that Joe had completed just before we convened this morning. This case has become small potatoes in the overall scheme of things. It needs to be settled. Ace, what would your client be willing to pay?"

Leyton responded. "I've talked to Mr. Allison. He'll pay the four hundred thousand dollars that he got from the insurance company."

"Not enough, Judge. I'd rather take a verdict. The jury is going to give me at least three times that much, likely a lot more."

The judge rose from his chair and walked around to sit on his desk in front of Jack. "Look, Mr. Bryant, you and I have had our disagreements, but you've done a helluva job for your client. Along the way you solved crimes in three states."

Jack nodded his head at the compliment, but his arms remained folded.

"Here's the bottom line," Judge McDowell continued. "You might get a bigger verdict, but I'm not going to let anything more than treble damages stand. I'm telling you that now, and, by the way, if I reduce it to treble damages, the appellate court will uphold my decision in a New York minute. Dammit, Jack, Allison didn't kill Willie Davis. Your client is being compensated beyond her wildest dreams."

Jack thought about what the judge said and concluded he was right. "I want four hundred thousand in actual damages and then treble it. That'll make one point six million. I'll wave my attorney's fees."

"Jack, be reasonable. It's a compromise," the judge almost pleaded.

"Sorry, Judge, it's nonnegotiable."

McDowell turned to Leyton. "What do you say, Ace?"

Leyton walked to the window and stared out. When he turned, he said, "Allison will need a payout. Four hundred thousand up front and then a hundred thousand a month thereafter. I'm pretty sure he can do that."

McDowell beamed as Jack said, "Deal," and stuck out his hand to Leyton.

The door to the chambers opened and the lawyers came out, followed by the judge. The entire courtroom rose.

"Keep your seats. This won't take long." He turned to the jury. "Ladies and gentlemen, this case has been settled. You are excused. You may or may not choose to talk to the lawyers and reporters. That is your prerogative." McDowell turned to Quillen. "Mr. Quillen, District Attorney Joe Sherrod is walking up behind you. You are remanded to his custody. I suspect charges will be filed against you within twenty-four hours. Court is adjourned."

Joe had the officers handcuff Quillen and lead him away. After the jury was gone, he said, "Judge, I'm obviously not a part of this case, but I'd like to put something on the record."

McDowell nodded his agreement.

"The State of Texas hereby dismisses all criminal charges against Colby Stripling, and I personally apologize to her for what she's been through."

Standing beside Jack, Colby smiled as tears rolled down her cheeks.

When Jack and his team were the only ones left in the courtroom, June asked, "Mr. Bryant, I'm not sure I understand what all has just happened."

"Mrs. Davis, Mr. Allison has agreed to pay one million six hundred thousand dollars in settlement. It's all yours. I'm not taking a fee."

"Oh my Lord," June said as she slumped into a chair. "Thank you, Mr. Bryant. And my kids and grandkids thank you."

"Well, I will require one small fee. I want a lifetime supply of vegetables from your garden."

90

There was a quiet knock on the hospital door.

"Come in," Allison said in a raspy voice.

Uncertain what she should do, Colby stopped at the foot of the bed. "I, I just came by to see how you were doing, Mr. Allison."

Allison coughed. "Sorry. They just got that tube out last night, and I'm still pretty hoarse. Do me a favor and push that button on the bed control. I want to sit up a little."

Colby hesitated and then did as he requested.

When he was sitting upright, Allison held out his hand and Colby took it. "I'm sorry, Colby. I started all of this in motion, and it almost caused your death."

"It's okay, now, Mr. Allison. I always told Jack that I didn't believe you were trying to kill me or anyone else."

"Still, I've got to take some responsibility. I thought I was being a really sharp businessman when I took out all those policies. Who would ever have thought it would lead to this? But then I thought I knew Beau Quillen. Turned out I knew the facade, not the real man. Are you going to be okay?"

Colby sat on the side of his bed. "I'm going to be fine now."

Allison turned to face her. "Hey, how about this. I've been thinking a lot in the past couple of days. I've decided I'm not going to run for mayor. I need to focus all my time on rebuilding Allison Southwest. My first step is to cancel all of those policies. I could use a really good finance manager. I'm talking about over the whole company."

Colby smiled. "I'm flattered, Mr. Allison. I really am. Only, I have a sense that the real estate market is coming back, and I like being my own boss." She bent over and kissed him on the forehead and left the room.

Joe Sherrod knocked on the RV door and entered without an invitation.

Jack was at his desk in the back. "Joe, come on in. You need a little free legal advice?"

Joe took a seat in one of the client chairs across from Jack. "Not today. However, if you ever want a job as one of my detectives, just say the word."

Jack shook his head. "My detective days are behind me. I'm content to be a pro bono lawyer. Turns out I like helping folks who can't help themselves."

"Speaking of your pro bono clients, how's June doing?"

Jack smiled at the thought. "She's taken a chunk of that first payment from Allison and has donated it to her church. They're building a new sanctuary, named in honor of Willie. What's happened to Hawk and Quillen?"

"Quillen's trial is in three months. If Hawk testifies like his confession, he'll get life. I'm prosecuting Quillen, and I expect him to fry. By the way, it's about time you, Colby, and J.D. join my family for dinner. My son still wants to meet J.D."

Jack and Colby had just returned from the sixth game of the season. J.D. had won his starting place and scored three touchdowns. Although there was coolness in the autumn air, they were seated on the patio, watching the sun set. As day turned to evening, Jack turned to Colby and asked, "Is it okay if we start dating now?"